Copyright © 2014 by Robert Lawrence Brown

All rights reserved.
Printed in the United States of America
First Edition

Library of Congress Number: 2014918609

ISBN 978-0-692-22258-4 (Paperback)

If you would like to use material from the book (other than for review purposes), prior written permission must be obtained by contacting the publisher.

MiddleRun Press
New York, NY
info@middlerunpress.com

STARS CAME TUMBLING

by Robert Brown

MiddleRun Press
New York

This is a work of fiction. All incidents and dialog are products of the author's imagination. Some characters were, in fact, historical figures, but have been placed at the author's discretion within the fictional context of the narrative. Otherwise, any resemblance to persons or animals living or dead is entirely coincidental.

For Nancy

1
Bill Arrives

Sometimes Babe awoke in the middle of the night, not so much with a scream as with a cry of shock and pain, so I gave her the benefit of the doubt when it came to her eccentricities. In my imagination, Babe was a princess without portfolio, exiled to the strange, high domain where we lived surrounded by the unconquerable West Texas landscape. And although I was not of her blood, she had chosen me as an heir and would tell me why when the time was right.

That was what I liked to imagine.

Most of the time, I worried that I was expendable. And I worried that the other children might be right when they peppered me with insults they overheard from their parents, the citizens of Wendellton who called Babe a whore. 'Whoreboy' was the battle cry the Fowler brothers used. Sometimes they called me 'Commie Whoreboy.' They beat the crap out of me after school if they caught me before I could reach Lonechap Hill. Darryl, the elder, pushed me while Cameron, who was my age, ducked behind me so I would trip over him if I tried to scramble away. In the mayhem, I took ten blows for every one I gave. As a result, I became a skilled liar, learning first of all to deny that it hurt and secondly never to reveal to Babe that she was the cause, although she knew without asking.

Babe turned her substantial reserve of energy into gardening. That was how she built her fortress, buried her secrets, and remembered a man she could not acknowledge, not even to me. Suffice it to say that she was for many reasons adamant in refusing to abandon even the most hostile environment. Through the unfriendly cycles of nature and opinion where we now found ourselves, Babe's gardens were in a real sense an exercise in sustaining life and beauty—and ownership.

In the summer, she rose early because by mid-morning it was too hot to do much outdoor work. She returned to her flowers in the evening after dinner, sometimes as late as 8:30. "The casual gardener doesn't survive in these parts," she said if I complained about the hours she worked. "Especially not on this hill."

We lived at the top of Lonechap Hill in a ranch-style house with red cedar board-and-batten siding and a front porch made of sturdy oak planks. Buddy built it after the original house, near the bottom of the lower southeast slope, burned down, leaving only its stone shell. "This is the place, yes, sir," he often said emphatically. "The chimney draws so much better up high." Babe was Buddy's widow. They had adopted me.

Our front porch faced the sunsets. Babe's gardens surrounded the house on all sides, taking advantage of the water that ran off the roof each time it rained. Her memories were aroused, especially, by the roses she grew at the front of the house and by the four o'clocks, multi-colored plants with oboe-shaped blooms and the sweet smell of citrus, a scent she once enjoyed in Shanghai. The four o'clocks helped measure the summer days by living up to their name, unfurling in late afternoon and remaining open well past nightfall.

Even things as small as the varieties of basil she grew in pots that hung over our front porch seemed to soothe and reassure Babe. Her favorite was known as 'Tulsi,' or 'Holy Basil.' She bowed toward the plant, lifted the leaves with her forefinger, brushed them with her thumb, and inhaled their spicy, sweet smell. Her mood always seemed to improve, and she made me go through the same routine. "These plants want to be spoken to, and they want to be spoken to with your hand," she said. "This is something precious and ancient that you're holding." If I made a face, as I sometimes could not help doing, she whacked me on the back of my head and threatened that gods I had never heard of would know my name and be offended.

I suspect they were merely amused.

I am growing old now and trying to think again like the 12-year-old I was, atop my sanctuary on Lonechap Hill. It's strange how, as adults, the thoughts and impressions we attempt to recall from childhood seem remarkably lucid and rational, as if they were filtered by the judgement we now possess. But it is impossible to reconstitute a body of reason in the context of another, long-past age. I know that much.

And so I also know that some of the memories that seem real and vivid to me cannot have happened—which things, I must leave for you to determine—because memory is pliable, it revises itself, it mends wounds, it reinforces prejudices, it enhances pleasures, it allows disappointments to nag incessantly through sleepless nights, it fixates on insults, it conjures and conjures and conjures again to catalog and re-route the pathways of experience. It is an independent agent—but not a subjective one—that defines your life, both a taskmaster and an enabler. Oddly enough, it was the fall of the twin towers, a few months before I began writing this, that made me think of the hill and want to reassemble as many details as I could recall from my twelfth year. It's not as if the September tragedy and the fate of the hill are similar. It simply reminded me that lofty places, real or ideal, are always at risk of siege—assaults by the greedy, the fanatical, the discomfited, the envious, the paranoid, wanting to conquer or prove themselves or merely to destroy, all believing they have absolute if not divine rights either to occupy the height or reduce it to their own dismal level.

And despite what she hoped, the siege against Babe and me and the stars that watched over us had not ended.

In August of 1960, the day before my twelfth birthday, a thunderstorm passed over the hill just after breakfast. It released a brief cloudburst, barely more than a tantrum, before it hustled away. In response, on the north end of our house, the honeysuckle vines that had stopped blooming at mid-summer opened a few timid blossoms.

Babe weeded a tomato garden in back of the house until the Coppertone on her face was streaked with dirt. Next, she deadheaded some shriveled rose blooms and marigolds in the garden bed north of our front walk, where she also grew irises. The irises were named for Eleanor Roosevelt. Only their green foliage stood up to the August heat, but Babe hoped they might present her in a few weeks with an Indian Summer bloom, when their long, slim petals—some folding, some outstretched—looked, said Babe, like socialites costumed for a Beaux Arts ball after the first chill of autumn.

That was the garden bed where she had buried a pocket watch.

Babe moved on to the south bed where dahlias grew around the borders and canna lilies in the center. She constantly re-adjusted the wooden stakes that kept the dahlias upright in the fitful wind. Their petals fanned out like the tips of short, thickset feathers to form blossoms the size of softballs dyed pastel orange or muted purple or bright yellow or bold pink. Altogether, as if they had assembled expectantly, posture well-corrected, they were an attentive audience for whatever was on Babe's mind on any given day.

Curved purple streaks traveled through the dense, emerald-green leaves of the canna lilies. Like Shanghai, and like the life Babe had been forced to accept as her own, the cannas were luridly schizophrenic, with vibrant reds and speckled yellows clashing on the same bloom.

Babe enjoyed their insolence in the summer heat.

That was the bed where she had buried the jewels collected by her late mother, a groundbreaking movie star whose history I did not then know because she had been forced to conceal it.

On her knees, jabbing and twisting with a trowel, Babe continued to weed and water past 10 a.m. She filled most of a garbage pail with debris. All the while, she cursed the bermuda grass that ran amok into the flowerbeds. The grass surrounded our house like an island before it gave way to the disheveled and brushy, unmanicured slopes of the hill.

The barn was about twenty yards from the house, to the northwest. That's where the rain had driven me. I sat next to Buddy's industrial-sized turntable, lifted the heavy tone arm out of its rest and set the needle down on the scarred acetate disk, which reflected, on its bare inner circle where the grooves ended, the light bulb that dangled above it from a rafter. Buddy's voice came through the tall, black, dusty speaker next to the turntable, a voice that was mellow, with no edge to it—mellow and tender and stutter-free but anxious, I think, to find a way of preparing me for the world through his stories, even after his death.

Buddy had been gone since early in 1956, a few months before I turned eight. One of his projects in the last sentient days of his life, before he could only nod and smile, had been to record a collection of story disks for me on a machine with a cutting lathe like the ones radio stations used then to make electrical transcriptions of programs and commercials. On each of my four birthdays since his death, Babe had given me a new set of disks from Buddy—disks that continued the stories he was telling, adding information and insights. He had planned it that way. The next day, on my twelfth birthday, the fifth since his death, I was to receive the remainder of the set. I suppose that Buddy had considered twelve a kind of cut-off point, before I became a teenager and was distracted and lured by other interests.

Buddy had inserted the finished disks into brown sleeves, which he labeled sequentially in his careful, trembling script. I packed them into latched boxes that he had left for that purpose, with my name etched onto the plastic handles. I listened to them in a corner of the barn where Babe had let me set up my own private space. On that damp August morning, now that I was soon to be twelve years old, I had decided to transcribe Buddy's stories and make a book of them. I would have the rest of them within a day, and could compile a complete account. It would be a difficult, demanding task that required listening to each disk over and over, because it was impossible to freeze the momentum of a turntable while writing down as many words as my memory could hold. So I would have to lift the tone arm, transcribe what I had heard, and try to set the needle down again without damaging the disk where I had left off.

Some of the stories were entertaining self-contained legends, jovially told, like "Why the Buffalo's Head Hangs Low," "The Barber and the Saloon-Keeper," and "Conrad Camel Joins the Cavalry." But within the growing sequence of disks, Buddy was also telling a darker, episodic story, like the serials that were about to disappear from the radio in 1960. Those serialized stories—in hindsight—were almost always about the dual nature of his characters, people who were displaced and seeking to find some continuity in their lives. There was his hero, a man known as the Phantom Padre, Jesuit-educated, expert in astronomy, but also a gambler and gunslinger who, according to Buddy, roamed our part of Texas seeking a treasure. There was a boy comrade named Young Eagle, kidnapped by Indians from a farm settlement, torn away from his natural family but adopted so thoroughly into the tribe that he considered himself one of them. He existed in a kind of identity limbo that I could identify with. And there was the girl, Selenia—loved by the Phantom Padre, protected by Young Eagle, harassed by a callous and powerful businessman. Well, that had to be Babe. And I did get into vicious fights defending her honor.

What made the stories extraordinary was that the Padre and the people he loved and hurt and saved were more than allegorical figures. They had lived, although none of them, the Padre especially, would qualify for our schoolbook histories that eschew uncomfortable complications in people and events. And unfortunately, the Padre's Boswell, an artist and adventurer named Charles St. George Stanley, rendered him in tabloid accounts that were sometimes pure invention, and in any case far more fiction than fact.

It's obvious to me now that Buddy was hoping I wouldn't feel so isolated and displaced myself if I identified with those stories, knew what other outsiders had faced, and learned from them. I was of uncertain ethnicity, although most certainly part Chinese, and Buddy knew that life off of Lonechap Hill would be hard for me because it had been hard—no, impossible—for him. He had come from one of the most prominent families in Texas, but his relatives treated him with contempt, like an idiot, and had nothing to do with him after he married Babe, not even when he was dying. As for me—I was just another undeserving, alien part of an outrageous scandal that revolved around the possession of Lonechap Hill after Buddy's death.

So there I was, in the barn, in the company of my soon-to-be-completed collection of disks, listening to Buddy, having set the needle down on disk number one.

BUDDY WATKINS [DISK #1]: *Hello, son. I've always gazed at stars and marveled at the stories they tell, those points of light, the fires of the past, still burning to enlighten us. We look at their brightness, their arrangements, how they're aligned, and we connect them into figures that represent our visions of life, our strengths and failures, our objects of worship, even the tools we use to condemn or reward ourselves. They are where the best stories begin because, long ago, they are where we looked first to ask questions about who we are and where we came from.*

One of my greatest joys has been sitting with you on our bench, looking at stars from the top of our hill, the doorstep to the universe. You have an ability to see things that others don't. And your questions have always made me proud to witness the wonder you express, and the enthusiasm for making sense of things and seeing beauty in them. One of my greatest sorrows, something I've just learned, is that I won't be here when you are older to share my favorite stories with you, stories about this strange part of the world that we inhabit and the trials we face and the benefits we can look forward to. That's why I'm sitting at my record-making machine on this night, because I want to leave those stories behind for when you may enjoy them or learn from them, or even need to hear them. I'd like to say they'll all have happy endings, but if they did then they might not make us think about how we face our own hopes and fears, how we learn to decide between the many selves we inherit from the stars.

I'm going to begin by telling you a true story about a man who also loved to stargaze. He was known later in his life as the Phantom Padre—a gunslinger in a priest's outfit who was looking for a lost treasure. He packed a Remington Army revolver within his custom-tailored black duster cassock, and he knew how to use it. I like to think that he visited this very hill back in the day. Now, how did he learn about the stars...?

Ready to start the process of immortalizing Buddy's stories on paper, I licked the tip of my thick blue pencil, tasting the graphite and newly shaved wood, imbuing the pencil with something of myself, my anguish, my hopes. The pages of my tablet rustled intermittently in the breeze of a rotating fan. Whereas I could only swallow my anger, the Phantom Padre had done something about his.

Then I heard Babe fire her revolver. She wore a holstered .22 caliber sidearm whenever she was outside on the hill—protection against varmints of all types, she said. But she rarely fired it, and on such occasions it was usually pointed toward our spook. That's what we called the rider who often sat on his horse for hours on the other side of our western fence line—sometimes in the morning, sometimes as darkness fell—clearly an attempt by the Fowlers to haunt and unnerve Babe and, I suppose, to spy on our mundane comings and goings, whatever that was worth. It was the first time in my life that I realized the extent to which people would go for no reason other than to disturb or intimidate. The spook was always well out of range of Babe's revolver. She was just making a point. But he hadn't shown up that morning, so the gunfire might have been directed at some real threat.

I put down my pencil and tablet, lifted the tone arm but left the turntable spinning, and ran out of the barn to see what the trouble was. Babe had crossed the bermuda grass lawn and was walking west through stiff yellow weeds, heading toward the tire tracks that served as our driveway, a dirt scar that ran the length of the hill down to the front gate. Her right arm was rigid. The gun in her hand was pointed toward the sky. With her left arm, she pushed back her wide-brimmed bonnet and wiped the perspiration from her forehead. Below us at the gated entrance, parked on a shoulder of the county road, was a gray pickup truck with a large trailer hitched to it. The bed of the pickup was covered by canvas. A man wearing a red leather vest, a white linen shirt, a loosely-knotted cloth bandana, and jeans sat on our gate with his hands in the air, smiling.

I stayed a few yards behind Babe, dodging back and forth through the higher grass because I didn't want her to notice me and tell me to get back into the barn. Halfway down the hill, well within pistol range, she stopped, stared at the stranger, and slowly lowered the gun toward him. He took off his battered straw hat and waved it in the air.

"You don't need that gun, lady," he shouted.

"Nobody comes here without calling first," Babe replied. Her accent was an eclectic blend of a dialect that sounded British—you could hear it in the way she pronounced the word 'first'—and a Texas twang she picked up in her adolescent years. "You were just gonna drive that truck and trailer on up this hill?" She also was fluent in Mandarin, courtesy of her mother, who privately disdained the Guangdong dialect spoken in the San Antonio Chinese community where Babe grew up. But it didn't really matter whether you clearly understood what Babe said. Her meaning and intent were always unmistakable. "This hill is private property."

"I was just driving by. I wanted to ask your permission to do some work."

"We don't need any hired help."

"That's fine, because I do sketches and watercolors—wildlife and landscapes."

Babe cupped her palm over her brow and squinted down at him, less intent on dismissing him out of hand than she had been the second before. She had studied art history in college and worked at the Fowler Plains Museum in Wendellton before she met Buddy and made eternal enemies of the Fowlers. "What's your name?"

"Pony Antone."

"Never heard of you."

"You're in good company."

"Where do you sell?"

"Bars. Restaurants. Gun shows. Festivals. I just sold a watercolor of the Monahans sand dunes to a motel there. You've got a nice view from the hill, I imagine."

"Yeah. We've got a view of grass, far as you can see. Artists come here all the time, you know. They want to move on from painting sand to watching the grass grow."

Pony laughed, unhooked his thumbs from the pockets of his faded red vest, and tipped his hat toward Babe with a shrug. "I've got a case full of rigger brushes, if that's what it takes. But I've got my subject with me in the trailer." He looked to be in his early 30's, about Babe's age. His nose was too prominent, his brow too high, and his face too thin and weatherbeaten. But he was one of those people with features so unusually and incompatibly arranged that you come to accept them as handsome—maybe appealing is a better word, or even magnetic—after you get used to them. Plus he had that slightly cocked head, the quizzical look that made you wish you could read his mind. "Look, I'll tell you what. I'll walk to the other side of the road." Without waiting for a response from Babe, Pony scissored his legs together, dropped nimbly off the gate and began to walk backwards across the two-lane county road, still with both hands slightly raised. "You and the boy come down and meet Bill. He's who I want to paint up there. If you want to see some of my work, there's a sketch book on the front seat of the truck."

Babe holstered her gun and looked back at me. "You can come on if you want to. Just stay behind me till I've sorted this out. And keep your mouth shut."

Cautiously, we walked to the bottom of the hill. Babe opened the door of the truck and inspected the Moleskine sketchbook, lowering it in her hands so I could look, too. She knew and appreciated good art when she saw it. In a larger sense, she felt that art—and she included her hilltop gardens in that appraisal—legitimized people more than any other pursuit. She flipped through the Moleskine, nodding with each turn of the page. The sketches included finely detailed and shaded pencil sketches of virtually every aspect of Bill's anatomy.

Pony leaned against the sign post for County Road 207 with his arms folded across his chest and one tan boot crossed behind the other. He retrieved a silver piece from his jeans pocket and flipped it into the air several times, catching it without looking. I could see that he was studying Babe. She was extraordinarily beautiful, thanks to her exotic mix of features, with an oval face, skin that remained flawless under a punishing sun, and a delicately-turned chin. Even with her ebony hair pulled under her bonnet, Babe could exert a power that was frightening. I was seven when Buddy died, but I remembered the worship in his eyes as he looked at her. It didn't matter that he could barely raise his head to speak. His eyes said everything.

Babe returned the sketchbook to the truck cabin, and we walked behind the pickup to peer through the vaulted iron bars of the trailer. Bill barely seemed to notice us. "He looks like he should smell a lot worse than he does," Babe sniffed. Then she called to Pony. "What the hell are you doing toting around a buffalo?"

Although Buddy had taken me to watch the buffalo herds in a refuge near Toomis Canyon, I had never seen a buffalo up close, and neither had Babe. Bill was still growing, but already stood more than five-and-a-half feet tall from his front hoofs to the top of his hump. And because bison can't raise their heads above their shoulders, it looked as if some faulty measurement had resulted in Bill's enormous noggin being situated too low on his body without taking his hump into account. It was just like one of the stories that Buddy had recorded—"Why the Buffalo's Head Hangs Low." A jet black mane spread over Bill's shoulders and sprouted in the broad space between his horns, dangling haphazardly down his forehead. He was breathing steadily, with a barely audible one-note hum.

"You know how birds imprint? Buffalos do, too. I found him a year ago March. He was a newborn standing alone with his head in the grass along the fence line of the Toomis Canyon refuge. They must have moved the herd, mother and all, without noticing the little guy." An unlikely event, but neither Babe nor I knew. "What's your name, boy?"

"John."

Babe rolled her eyes, shot an irritated look at me, and shook her head, resigned to my disobedience.

"Well, John, he had a nice red coat then, and he stood stock still with his eyes shut when I went up to him—like, if he couldn't see me, then he must've figured I couldn't see him."

"Did you rescue him?"

"Sounds more like he stole him," Babe said. "I told you to hold your tongue."

"He would've died if I'd left him there. They might never have found his mother if I'd turned him in. So I covered his eyes, blew into his nose, put him in the truck, and off we went. Fed him on powdered milk out of gallon jugs."

"Blew into his nose, did you?"

"George Catlin said it's what he did, out on the plains after a buffalo hunt. Catlin the artist, you know?"

"I know."

"He learned it from the Indians. Have you ever seen his buffalo sketches? There's a couple in the plains museum back there in Wendellton."

"I've seen them." Babe's lack of enthusiasm had more to do with her past at the museum than the Catlin sketches.

"I always liked the expressions he drew on them, like he could imagine what they were thinking. You know what I mean? Kind of surprised and panicked at the same time." Babe didn't reply but Pony was loquacious enough not to let any gap of silence last too long. "Well, those little calves he picked up, they'd follow him for miles back to his camp after he breathed on them."

"And this one still follows you?"

"He does."

"He's not a calf anymore."

"That's why I'm on this expedition with him. There's a new frontier coming. I want to paint him out here where his ancestors used to roam on the old frontier, and I want to borrow some of his wisdom. Then I'll take him back to his kind when the summer's gone, before he gets too old."

"So you're showing him the world in the meantime."

"He gets along well with the world. He's not tame like a dog, but he won't cause you or the boy any trouble. You'll see."

I tugged on Babe's hand, raised my eyes to her, and mouthed the word "Please," hoping she wouldn't turn Bill away. I didn't care about Pony. To indicate I would follow whatever rules she set starting then, I zipped my fingers across my mouth.

She gestured for Pony to come back across the road, and they made a bargain. Pony and Bill could come onto the hill as guests. Pony would do a portrait of the two of us after he finished his studies of Bill. We also could look through watercolors he had done and pick anything we liked. It was clear that Babe thought Pony had exceptional talent—enough to cause her to let her guard down.

Finally, she formally introduced me to Pony and I was free to speak again. We shook hands. Pony's grip was strong but the pressure he applied was even, unlike the handshakes of a lot of adults who squeezed my knuckles with viselike holds as if to expedite my torturous initiation into manhood. "You suppose there's any puddles left up there from the morning rain?"

"Likely not," I said. "If there is, it'll be near the barn."

"Well, whatever's left in it, if you could get a garden hose and add some more water, you'd do Bill a favor. It'll help him fight this heat."

"Yes, sir," I nodded eagerly.

"I bet you help your dad a lot."

"Well..."

"I'm a widow," Babe said.

"Ah. I'm really sorry. I didn't mean to speak out of turn." Pony apologized with a solemn smile. "This boy acts more like a man than most his age. I figured he must have a good example to follow." He raised his eyes toward the hill. "Has your hill got a name?"

"Lonechap Hill," Babe said. "For as long as anyone can remember."

"Lone...chap? Like a hermit or something?"

"It's a long story."

"Nothing like it for miles, pretty much in all directions, is there?"

"Nope."

"Doesn't really look like it should be here."

"Nope."

"Kind of a natural wonder, if you ask me."

Pony was right. Lonechap Hill always must have been a notable feature in the landscape, called by many names through many eras. But any being approaching it across the great sea of grass could be forgiven for ignoring the hill's finer points and viewing it as a wonder, both for its size and for the opportunity it offered to climb out of the all-engulfing landscape. As it undulated from its base to its peak, the hill sloped gently upward out of the plains as if some giant god-child, unattended while his Mother wrestled with the business of Creation, had set out to create a perfect mound, tamping and caressing and creasing its sides, plumping them here and stamping them there, working into it the vigor of sunshine and the grace of moonlight, so that we mortals could ascend easily to survey the past and future from its generous, wind-blown crown.

From a southern approach, through our front gate, the hill seemed to spread two welcoming arms that gave it a luxuriant width. Between the arms were long ridges that hid gentle depressions, perfect for lazing privately. And, just as it had cycles of sleeping and waking, just as it could be barren and jaundiced in the winter or drunken and giddy with Babe's flowers in the spring, it had a heartbeat, I am certain. I was hypnotized by it. And no matter how depressing things got at school, I never failed to be exhilarated by my treks home to the top of the hill, as I climbed farther and farther from the vexing world that shrank beneath me. The hill lifted me above my enemies and troubles and allowed me to see without being seen.

To the north, the hill overlooked a vista so imposing and yet so empty that only by consulting the arc of the sun or the rotation of stars could you tell where you had come from. "Forced to consult the sky," I once heard Dwight say, "you are forced to confront the essence of the plains." Even a trained eye found no object to rest upon, except what a military scout once described as the shadows of broken flying clouds "coursing rapidly over the plain and seeming to put the whole in motion." The surface, he said, "will certainly bear comparison to the waves of an agitated sea."

Babe and I climbed into the cab of Pony's truck, and up we went, up to what Buddy called the doorstep to the universe. Sometimes life leads you to the place where you are meant to be and loans it to you, but only for a while, and for me, Lonechap Hill was one of those places.

2
Origin Story: The Phantom Padre

BUDDY WATKINS [DISK #3]: *The treasure that the Phantom Padre looked for was a star—not like the ones he knew so well in the heavens, but an earthly star, long-lost and priceless. It had belonged to the Perazas, the Phantom Padre's noble Spanish family. The star was made in the 1400's at the beginning of the Spanish Inquisition. An inquisition is a thing that people have created to prove that their god is bigger and better than anyone else's—and to torture and rid the world of others who don't believe as they do...*

A few years later—out of the army and knowing by then how Pony was connected to the Phantom Padre—I found my tattered handwritten transcripts of Buddy's disks and used them as source material to research a community college paper for a history class. I never had ceased being fascinated by one of Pony's comments—that no story truly ends; that it is somehow connected to another and another and another, sown by tumbling stars, fertile in the harshest climates, evolving in the least likely ways; that you cannot segregate yourself even from the most remote and alien stories in this absurdly polarized world, because it will prove to be part of yours.

Antonio Peraza, also known as the Phantom Padre—the phantom whose story Pony set out to reconcile with his own—was the dissolute son of a noble and haughty family.

His forebears in Seville, Spain, made soap.

They earned their title and established a commercial trading franchise after helping drive the Moslem rulers from Andalusia and declaring their loyalty to Ferdinand III of Castile in 1248.

They increased their prominence during the Spanish Inquisition.

For the Inquisition's first auto-da-fé, held in Seville in 1481, the family commissioned an ornate star, made by the finest goldsmith in Seville. The star was set with emeralds at each of its ten points, and with a blood-red ruby at the center. Although it was large, it could be hung by a thick cord around the neck of the wearer, and it would rest, big and brilliant, on his breast. The family's patriarch, Rafael

Peraza, wore the exquisite golden symbol around his neck while he and his sons attended the auto-da-fé prior to the execution of six men and women. Afterwards, Rafael predicted to all who would listen that auto-da-fés would become as popular as bullfights. He was right. The Perazas encouraged rumors that the very sight of the Star inspired non-believers to convert to the faith.

The prosperity of the Peraza family grew in conjunction with the Inquisition and the discovery of the New World. The *piloto mayor* of Seville from 1508 to 1512, Amerigo Vespucci, was a loyal friend. The family suffered a period of decline that began in the 17th century and continued through the rule of the Bourbons. As a result, some of the Peraza land was mortgaged for cash. The youngest sons of each generation—now born to a family with fewer holdings to manage—typically went into the church.

In the mid-18th century, one especially passionate young Peraza, Manuel, joined the Franciscan order, believing that God had called him to the New World—specifically to the College of Santa Cruz de Querétaro, founded by Franciscans as the first institution in America to train missionaries. At the request of the family, he sent a letter to the King of Spain, proclaiming his passion and his desire to dedicate his heart and soul to God, King, and Country. The family hoped to gain new attention with Manuel's declaration but didn't count on the young man's rash suggestion—that he carry with him to the New World the jeweled star the family had commissioned nearly 300 years before. The King agreed that Manuel should go on his holy mission with the finest symbol of his faith that Spain could provide. And—wouldn't you know?—the Perazas had boasted too often and too publicly about how many people over the centuries had been set on the path of righteousness by their Star.

"There is no better place [than the New World] for this Star to become the instrument of the Holy Mother Church and His Royal Catholic Majesty," Manuel promised. "This Star of Andalusia and the Peraza family will achieve heaven's glory through our mission. And I pledge to have the Star returned to Seville by one of the heathens who has been saved by it."

Prodded by the King, the family had no choice but to agree to Manuel's request.

The Star of Andalusia, as Manuel now called it, was worth an estimated 200,000 ducats, but it was hardly a liquid asset. It would have destroyed the family's reputation to sell the Star, as it would have been considered a sign of ruin. Sending it with Manuel would undoubtedly bring the ambitious Peraza family to the renewed attention not only of His Royal Catholic Majesty, but also of those in power in the vast new lands. Consequently, when Manuel left Seville, the family made a public show of entrusting its prized possession to God and King in an elaborate ceremony to enhance the Peraza reputation and, of course, to sell more soap.

As Manuel boarded his ship, his father patted him on the back and beseeched him to remain aware of contacts in the New World that could benefit the family.

After training at the College of Santa Cruz de Querétaro, Manuel's first impressions were of failure. Missions founded in the San Xavier area of New Spain were abandoned because of conflicts between Indians, priests, and soldiers at the nearby presidio. As a fallback, the Nuesta Señora de Guadalupe mission was established near San Antonio. Manuel arrived at the mission in the summer of 1756. In his last letter to his family, he expressed excitement about a visit he planned early in 1758 to another new mission to the northwest. The mission was called Santa Cruz de San Sabá and was protected by the Presidio San Luís de las Amarillas. The San Sabá mission, small and built of logs, Manuel wrote, was

> ...for the miserable heathen Indians of the Apache Nation and was sponsored by Pedro Romero de Terreros, a native of Cortegana near our own homeland and now one of the wealthiest men in New Spain. He has given 150,000 pesos to establish this holy enterprise. In charge is his cousin, Reverend Father fray Alonso Giraldo de Terreros of the Apostolic College of Santa Cruz de Querétaro. I met him there and shared stories of our homeland. I am told that the Commandant of the Presidio, Colonel Don Diego Ortiz Parrilla, is concerned that the state of the Indians is [acutely] different from what he expected. He doubts that these Gentiles can be pacified. He worries that others of the barbarians may be incited by [French] political agents. I believe that they will welcome the chance to congregate there and intend to pay a visit with our Star of Andalusia to help inspire them and my friend Fr. Terreros. I offer a special prayer each night over our Star of Andalusia and remember each of you to Our Lord.

Despite the failure of the San Xavier missions, Manuel was naive about the deep hostilities and resentments that were boiling where the Spanish had intruded. To some extent, missionaries and soldiers were being used as pawns. Comanches who had appeared on the plains only a half century before had driven the Apaches south in a methodical campaign to annihilate them. In turn, the Apaches hoped to draw Spain into their war against the Comanches. Apache raiding parties planted Spanish clothing at the sites of skirmishes to further implicate those at the mission. The Lipan Apaches, for whom the San Sabá mission was established, had made the mission a target of their wrathful enemies.

On March 16, 1758—the day Manuel Peraza intended to arrive at San Sabá—an estimated two thousand Comanches, Tayovayas, and warriors from allied tribes attacked and burned the mission in a murderous rampage. Father Terreros was shot; another priest was decapitated. Among those who escaped was Father Miguel Molina, who told soldiers at the presidio, "I saw nothing but Indians on every hand...arrayed in the most horrible attire." Father Manuel Peraza, who must have wandered into the horrors of the attack as he approached the mission to visit, simply disappeared along with the Star of Andalusia.

For nearly a century, the family sought to learn the fate of Manuel and the Star from those who traveled to Spanish settlements. The Perazas' quest became legendary. No body was recovered; the Star never had been seen again. In 1804, there was a glimmer of hope that a vigorous search of the area might be conducted by a member of the family in service to the Spanish crown. Frontier commanders in New Spain issued urgent requests for a plan to resist American aggression following the sale of Louisiana to the United States. In the summer of 1804, nineteen-year-old Bernardo Peraza enlisted in a mounted light artillery company from Seville. The company was designated to join thousands of immigrants in settlements intended to reinforce and develop those vulnerable regions of Texas for Spain. It was Bernardo's hope to look for the Star and his great-uncle's remains with a contingent of the military party. Instead, British warships blocked the bay of Cadiz and captured four Spanish frigates that were assigned to escort the would-be immigrants. The settlers, soldiers, and officials—possibly as many as five thousand people, well supplied with arms and provisions—never sailed from Cadiz.

Spain, in North America, was effectively finished.

After his discharge from the military, Bernardo fathered three sons, four daughters, and, finally, a son named Antonio, born to

Bernardo's second wife in 1830. Of course, Antonio was destined for the church. His mother, resentful that Bernardo's other sons would claim his inheritance, wanted to make the best of her only son's fortunes. She saw to it that he was given Jesuit schooling, despite the controversies that surrounded the order following its expulsion from Europe and the New World, an exile that lasted nearly fifty years. The order was again thriving after having been restored to Spain in 1814. Moreover, the Jesuits were not bound by the medieval traditions that governed orders like the Franciscans. The reputation of the Jesuits was that they were rich and powerful, and that they ran into trouble because they were feared even by kings.

Antonio excelled in school. At heart a star-gazer, he was inspired by the extraordinary achievements of Jesuit astronomers. Through their colleges, before the expulsion, the Jesuits had overseen as many as thirty observatories, the most sophisticated in the world. Francesco Grimaldi had mapped the moon itself, and named craters for other Jesuits. In very real ways, they had written their names in the heavens. Antonio learned all he could—and indeed, he was a brilliant student—hoping he might discover something that would let him emblazon his own name among the stars some day, to prove to his family how valuable he was, and to raise his mother in their estimation. When a Latin instructor gave him a copy of Festus Avienus' translations of *The Phenomena* and *Diosemeia* by Aratus, Antonio's obsession with the stars was complete—not necessarily to his advantage. He memorized passages describing how the stars told us when to plant, when to harvest, when to explore the farthest horizons. He timed how the stars crossed the sky each night, in each season of the year. And he came to realize that the stars told the story of mankind if you studied them closely enough. It shook his faith in a God.

At the age of 16, barely acknowledged by other members of his family, Antonio was sent for his novitiate training to the new Republic of Mexico. There, his path began to diverge from his Jesuit instructors. He remained bitter at not being considered a "true" Peraza worthy of the family legacy. Shipped away from Spain—expelled, as he viewed it—he was consumed by that bitterness. He became more and more argumentative and mindful of the conflicts between science and the teachings of the church, which still had not formally accepted that the sun, not the earth, was at the center of the planetary system. To add to his dissatisfaction, Jesuits in Mexico were not as sophisticated as the ones who had taught him in Spain. "Christianity and science are not compatible," Antonio's Superior told him. "One must yield to the other. You must make your choice."

Antonio was dismissed from his novitiate not long after the end of the war between the United States and Mexico.

Shorn of his ties to the church and his family and with no means of supporting himself, Antonio became a gambler, womanizer, and thief. Just as he had learned the secrets of the stars, he was equally clever at learning the tricks of criminals in the Mexico City underworld, who viewed his intelligence and sophistication as an asset.

In 1857, when the military took control of Mexico City, Antonio left for New Orleans to work the riverboats of the southern United States, where he perfected the art of cheating—dealing "seconds;" palming aces; using table mirrors and confederates to con unsuspecting players; bribing bartenders to supply him with decks that had been marked and resealed with forged stamps. At first, he teamed with confederates who attracted other players to the table by casting him in the role of a Mexican who would be easy to swindle. He never was. With his winnings, he bought beautiful clothes and practiced English with the other gamblers until he spoke it like a gentleman. His life was threatened three times. The third time, Antonio had posed as an ignorant Mexican while he and a confederate fleeced four other players in a poker game. Later, on a starry night, one of the players found Antonio on the deck of the steamboat, explaining the constellations in flowery English to a beautiful woman. The player shot Antonio through the shoulder, pistol-whipped him, took his money, and dumped him into the river. He would have drowned had he not been fished out by a runaway slave.

Just as other gamblers had left the riverboats when they became too well known, Antonio returned to Mexico City. Accounts of the civil war in the United States persuaded him to remain in Mexico. He again wandered the criminal underworld, where he reconnected with old friends and sought easier if less profitable ways of acquiring money. Rumor had it that he occasionally impersonated a priest to gain access to the houses of the wealthy and steal from them, especially during the years when Maximilian ruled Mexico from Chapultepec Castle. Remembering the riverboat humiliation that almost cost him his life, Antonio practiced daily with pistols. He developed into a deadly shot who was said to have given, blasphemously, the last rites to each of the three men he killed.

His first victim was a monarchist spy, whom he confronted on the Paseo de la Emperatriz after a night of gambling. The spy had played cards often to gather information from the table conversations. Antonio, who had been disguised in priest's garb, had pickpocketed the spy's coat as he left the game; discovered notes on himself and a number of his friends; then pursued the man on his way to the palace. He waved the notes in the spy's face. The spy reached for a pistol but was dropped by a bullet to his heart from the revolver within Antonio's cassock. Despite the prominence of the location, when bystanders were asked what they had witnessed they claimed to have seen only a priest administering the last rites to a man whose deadly assailant had disappeared like a phantom.

He also shot the pimp of his favorite whore and a French colonel who, thinking Antonio was a priest, followed him into an alley to insult the custom-made duster that Antonio wore as a cassock. The colonel asked in fractured Spanish whether all priests in Mexico were as filthy, drunken, and unworthy of the protection that French armies provided the church. "Protect yourself, sir," a drunken Antonio had replied. "My breath is perfumed by honest drink. Your breath has the stench of a coward." The colonel had slapped him and was dead before the slap could echo into the street.

Antonio's love of pulque—a cheap drink made by fermenting the *agua miel* from agave plants—was renowned in the underworld. Once, on a dare, Antonio donned his cassock and went with friends to an agave plantation where the workers customarily recited *Ave Marias* while the pulque fermented. He tested the drink for its "mystical properties" until, while offering his full blessing to the labors of the workers, he fell into a barrel of it. Friends in the underworld called him "Bishop"—a term with double-meaning, since it also was a slang word for "prick," an appendage which he used freely and intemperately.

It was the family's objective to forget he existed. But in 1873, one hundred fifteen years after the tragedy that had befallen Manuel Peraza, the family in Seville received a letter from a priest in Ramosa, Mexico, that exists fully preserved in the family history.

"A miracle has occurred here in tiny Ramosa," the priest's letter began.

> ...Riding out to visit my one of my flock who was ill, I met an Irishman who hunted Indian [Apache and Comanche] scalps for the bounty that is placed on them here. The Irishman, named Le Hane [sic], has flowing blonde hair, a scar on his cheek and a bulging eye. He rides like the Indians and knows much about them and their history. He was thirsty, and I offered him water and asked if he had concern for his soul. I invited him to make a confession. Instead, the Irishman laughed. After determining that we were alone, he pulled from his saddle bag a gold star and said it had protected him and those who held it before him and he thought it would also see to his soul. From the stories I have heard of it, and of the great mission intended for it, I am certain it was your holy Star of Andalusia, which our faithful have sought for more than a century. You may be assured that I will reveal this miracle to no one else until I have heard from you or a representative of your noble family or a messenger from our Holy Mother Church...

Suddenly, it seemed as if Antonio might become useful.

An emissary of the Peraza family found him dazed and reeking in a neighborhood pulquería near Mexico City's Alameda park. He sat in a corner beneath a mural of a naked woman with her legs spread in both directions at the intersection of the walls. On either side of the mural were framed French cartoons of gambling priests fanning decks of cards. He had just finished a bad run of luck and had paid for his pulque by winning a coin-tossing game. "Welcome to my academy," he said when the disgusted emissary sat next to him. Antonio was no less disgusted with himself, although he wouldn't have put it that way. He would have been a handsome man, with a Roman nose and a full head of hair, had his face not grown sallow and his eyes, baggy. He remained clean-shaven only because it was easier to disguise himself with false facial hair when he needed to do so.

He went to sleep every night knowing that he was a man who had been robbed of a noble birthright. He admired the famed French criminal Vautrin for the cold-blooded, ruthless amorality with which he engaged in schemes and frauds requiring eloquent, ruinous persuasiveness. While he still dreamed of somehow claiming his noble privileges, he understood that he had made himself a prisoner of the underworld who relied, like Vautrin, on disguise, impersonation and thieving. He was the most desperate type of failure—a gifted one, whose gifts were either paralyzed or perverted because of his obsession with his bloodline and his hatred of its bias against the order of his birth.

And so it was that the emissary delivered a message that Antonio could hardly refuse. The family would pay all his debts, return him to Spain if he wished, and supply him with an allowance, house and servants if he used his perverse talents and connections to find the outlaw who carried the Star of Andalusia—missing for more than a century since Fr. Manuel Peraza, who carried the Star, disappeared on the day of the attack on the San Sabá mission northwest of San Antonio.

Antonio knew well that the offer would not only be to his advantage. It would benefit the family to receive such attention if he succeeded. He was prepared to handle dangerous situations, spoke impeccable English and could move freely as an imposter priest. The emissary nevertheless made clear the risks that Antonio would be taking if he tried to take advantage of the Peraza family's trust. "I warn you," he said, "this is about your family's honor, pride, and position. I don't have to tell you what it would mean to their name to return the Star to Spain and remind all of the suffering and sacrifice the family has made throughout its glorious history."

Antonio suppressed a laugh, folded his arms across his chest, cleared his throat, and said he would dedicate his life from that moment to seeking the Star. He was forty-two years old, and knew he was facing his last chance to claim his heritage.

The emissary gave Antonio a copy of the Ramosa priest's letter.

In addition to the letter, Antonio was given a scale pencil drawing of the Star, copied from a family manuscript; a horse; and a generous sum of money—the equivalent of $2,500 in Mexican gold coins, in case he needed cash for bribes or to hire help during his search. With the gold came a letter of credit, allowing him to draw on more resources should he acquire and submit proof that he was close to locating the Star. For weapons, he owned a derringer and a .46 caliber rimfire Remington Army revolver. When sober, he was, of course, an expert at using both.

Antonio purchased a second specially-tailored outfit in which he could pose as a Jesuit. The black cassock, with short lapels, was cut slightly longer and looser, so he could conceal the revolver that was holstered on his right side and the gold belt he wore beneath his shirt. The canvas belt was ringed with pouches to hold his valuables and the gold he was given. Rawhide strings that wrapped over metal buttons held the flaps of the pouches in place.

Finally, he purchased a new pocketwatch for his journey. He still loved to track the stars at night—timing the heavens, as he had learned to do when he once had intended to follow the examples set by the great Jesuit astronomers.

Because many Jesuits had been driven from Mexico, he did not lack a purpose for wandering in the disguise he chose. Should he be questioned, Antonio decided, he would claim to have been recruited by the Bishop of Galveston to travel the enormous Texas diocese, seeking Catholics who had been separated from the church by distance, isolation, or prejudice.

A week after the emissary's visit, Antonio set out for Ramosa riding an old seal brown horse and garbed in his priest's cassock. He had rehearsed his story well, but had little need of it. It was an uneventful journey. Although some spat at him, most bowed slightly when he passed on the road.

He was accosted only once, while he timed the stars. As the man snuck up behind him, past the ashes of a dying fire, Antonio rolled onto his back, pulled his revolver, and killed the accoster with an upside-down shot. He found the man's horse—a fast, grullo stallion, sun-bleached to a smooth, silvery color, with a smoky black mane and fetlocks, stolen, no doubt. He took it for himself and left his old brown horse behind to graze in the scrub.

He rode the wagon road that led to Ramosa, a town that was established to support nearby mining operations and the cattle ranches to the west. The town's church had a lovely carved stone facade, completed up to the cornice level of the walls. The niches on either side of the doorway contained sculptures of saints, chipped, worn and sorrowful. A second stage above the cornice never had been completed, nor had construction begun on the two towers intended to flank the facade. All further work was abandoned during the war with the United States.

Antonio walked into the church and knelt at the wooden altar. Above and behind it were risers and ledges holding sculptures of saints and, at the center, a crucified Christ. A heavy fabric canopy served as a backdrop. To the priest, he presented himself as Father Lopez, a Jesuit on his way to serve the Bishop of Galveston. As the two discussed the trials of the Jesuits, Antonio, with clever questioning—professing that he still sought to collect evidence of miracles on his way—led the priest into volunteering the story of his encounter with the outlaw Lehane. "I am amazed," Antonio exclaimed, "for like others before me, I carry an image of the Star and pray that it may be restored to its place." He showed the priest the drawing he carried. "As God is my witness, that is it," said the priest, gasping. "I have written to the Peraza family but they have not yet replied, and I have said nothing to others. I did not want the story to spread to those who would seek the Star to enrich themselves. But you, brother, you are the messenger I have expected."

"Then perhaps," said Antonio, "I will have the good fortune to encounter this man on my journey. Do you know of anyone who might tell me more about him?—without revealing our secret, of course."

That evening, in the relative coolness of the church, the priest arranged a meeting with José Espinosa, who had paid thousands of dollars worth of bounties to Lehane and his men for the Indian scalps they delivered. Espinosa was a member of the payment committee that authenticated the scalps as Indian, as the bounty law required. Lehane had remained murderously active despite the fact that scalp-hunting against the Apache and Yaqui Indians had declined significantly over the previous twenty years (although 150 Yaquis had been burned to death inside a church only six years before, an operation possibly under Lehane's control). More recently, bribes and kickbacks had become common. Sometimes, the scalps of murdered Mexicans and children were deemed to have been those of Indian warriors.

"And why might you seek this man?" Espinosa inquired.

"Believe it or not," Antonio lied, "we believe he may have protected a holy object for the church, and I wish to thank him and present him with a Bible from the Bishop of Galveston himself."

"A holy object?" Espinosa snorted. "Of what sort?"

"A Christian symbol of little material value," Antonio said, "except to those who are moved to express their faith by its presence."

Espinosa shook his head and suppressed a chuckle. "Well, Padre, he always rides with a few other men. And he always seems to show up with his scalps after a new outbreak of Indian attacks. Now, we don't see near as many Indians around here as we used to.

Not as much killing, not as much livestock lost. Some say Pigeye Lehane and his men are the ones who made the attacks to keep the bounties active. I don't say that, but some do. You look at a scalp, you never know whether it came from a peaceable brave or not. Besides, Pigeye liked to roast his scalps after he took 'em, said he liked to see the fat ooze out of 'em over a fire. Nice and preserved, those scalps, but hard to tell how long ago they'd been taken. And this is the man, you're telling me, who is protecting some holy cross? A cross, is it? Someone may have been joking with you, unless..." Espinosa thumped his heart with a fist.

"Yes?"

"Well, I did hear he was in love, God help the poor woman, but that he'd lost the poker game he'd played to win her. Some barmaid, I think...at a fort where the buffalo hunters trade up in Texas. Wherever he's going, he won't be a hard man to follow. Everybody knows when he's been there, and he makes no secrets about where he's going. If there is a woman he wants, he will do what he has to. He's a fearless man."

"I'm hoping he will at least fear his God." *And,* thought Antonio, *I would like to meet this woman.*

* * *

BUDDY WATKINS [FROM DISK #4]: *...The barmaid would play a big part in the Phantom Padre's plans, but so would a boy from a Plains Indian tribe and a Chinese laundress—and her immortal cat. So stay tuned for the next disk, son. We're just getting started.*

3
The Dust in the Stars

Pony parked the truck in front of the barn. Bill, impressively dexterous for such an ill-designed behemoth, backed quickly out of the trailer, leaving behind a large, dirty, crumpled red blanket. Withered blades of grass were stuck into it and scattered over it. "I lay it out on the ground at night," Pony said. "He likes to sleep on it."

"Then lay it in there," Babe said, pointing to the barn. "When do you plan to work?"

"Late afternoon and evening." Pony turned away from Babe and looked toward the west, standing tip-toed as if he wished to see beyond the horizon. "There's not much of a sky to paint before then. I'd like to study everything this evening, get some ideas, and paint tomorrow evening." He rested on his heels again. "Is that okay? I can sleep in the bed of my truck."

"On what?"

"I've got a sleeping bag. If it rains, I can take it to the barn."

"Fine. There's a hose to wash with and an outhouse behind the barn." Babe patted her holster, a sign that she would not brook even the slightest violation of her trust.

Pony lifted a hand in a half-salute. "I understand. Thank you."

Babe went into the house to wash and make sandwiches. I got the garden hose.

The rain puddle had all but dried up, a mottled scab on the earth garnished by a few weeds. I unwound the hose as far west as it would go and muddied the ground again. Bill stood for a few seconds, his tail twitching as if he were waiting impatiently for an acceptable consistency of dirt and water. Then he lumbered over to the puddle and dropped onto one knee. "Just keep the water flowing there," Pony said. "You'll see something."

Bill thrust a horn into the softened earth, shoved with his head, and created an enormous divot which quickly filled with water. He stood again, paused, and hit the ground like a hairy, lopsided boulder. I kept a steady stream on him while he thrashed around in a circle. He wallowed, grunting and churning and shaking the dumbfounded earth, until a comfortable bed of mud spread beneath him and covered his coat.

"Does he do that a lot?"

"All the time. Buffalos wallow to keep the flies and pests off their hide—and because they like it. Back in the day, herds of buffalo would use the same wallow again and again. Once the bison moved on, those old wallows would fill up with soil and fresh grass." Pony pointed north. "And out on the plains, there would appear these strange rings that some people thought had been made by fairies. They hadn't invented flying saucers back then. Today they might blame it on UFO's."

"I like to look for UFO's. I see a lot of shooting stars."

"Who knows what you'll see up there, right?"

"Yes, sir."

Bill got up slowly, ambled to the corner of the barn and rubbed against it. The barn responded with a low, complaining groan. Pony and I sat at a picnic table near the swing set Buddy had put up for me when I was two or three. The table was bolted to a concrete foundation that kept it steady, although the wood was splintering with age and Babe kept hinting that I was old enough to repair it.

"You don't smoke yet, right?"

"No, sir." I laughed weakly.

"Mind if I do?"

"No, sir."

From his shirt pocket, Pony removed a slim, crooked cigar and a matchbox decorated with a drawing of a Christmas wreath and the name 'Wachyerback Saloon.' He lit the cigar, shook the match until it was extinguished, wet his fingers, clamped them over the blackened head, and put the matchstick in his vest pocket. Then he took the cigar out of his mouth and studied it, turning it in his hand as he spoke matter-of-factly. "Has your mom got boyfriends that would get mad at me being here?"

"Just me."

"But you'd tell me if you were mad, right?"

"Yes, sir."

"And you're not?"

"No."

"That's good."

"She doesn't like me to call her mom. I'm adopted."

"What do you call her?"

"Her name. Babe."

"Is that like a nickname?"

"Kind of. Her full name was Elizabeth Bei Wong before she married Buddy. People took her middle name for Babe and that's what they called her." I would have loved to call her mom, but she wouldn't stand for it, and I wasn't about to tell Pony how I felt. I had long since accepted that she just wanted to be who she was.

"Mmm-hmm." Pony smoked for a moment. He exhaled, through puckered lips, a contrail instead of a cloud. "Not from around these parts, either one of you, right?"

I began the lie that fortified my existence. "Babe won't tell you this, but she was a kind of Chinese princess. She was born here, then she and her mom went back to China to visit her people. Then they had to escape the Japs and come back."

"That's some story."

"I'm part Chinese. That's why Babe picked me to adopt when she and Buddy wanted a son." That, I feared, might be another lie. She might have had other reasons.

"Buddy was her husband."

"Yes, sir."

"So he became your dad, too."

"Yes, sir. He died of the cancer."

"I'm sorry about that." I looked away and Pony patted me on the back. "What did you like best about him?"

"Everything, I guess. I liked that he never got mad. I like his Phantom Padre stories. He left a bunch of them behind for me."

I expected Pony to laugh at the name 'Phantom Padre.' It did sound silly, like some dime novel fabrication, but to me it had a comforting ring to it.

Pony didn't laugh. He coughed before he could exhale a toke on his cigar. "The Phantom Padre? No kidding. I know some Phantom Padre stories." He inclined his head slowly downwards and looked at me as if he didn't quite believe what I'd said. "So you've heard about the Phantom Padre. That's what you're telling me?"

"Yes, sir."

"That's some coincidence."

"Maybe there were two...two Padres."

"I don't think so. Don't see how there could have been."

It would be an understatement to say I was astounded. But no more so than Pony.

"Well, what do you know about him...the Padre?" he asked, clearing his throat.

I wasn't sure how to react to his question. Suddenly, his personality seemed to alter from that of a kind of cocky, good-buddy, quasi-interested interrogator into the demeanor of someone less easygoing, whose eyes narrowed and face tightened. I was a little happy, a little frightened.

I managed a smile and began the story of how Antonio Peraza came to be exiled from his family. Quickly, Pony waved his hand to interrupt me, as if he was satisfied that the story was the same one he knew. "That's...pretty...well, what can I say? Sounds like you've memorized a lot of it. Buddy told you all this?"

"Yes, sir."

"And who told him?"

"I guess I never asked. Before he...before the cancer got him, he made me some record albums with stories on them. I haven't heard them all yet."

"And you know how the Padre wound up in this part of the world?"

"Yes, sir."

Pony shook his head. "That beats all."

"You mean..."

"I mean it sounds like Buddy was some kind of historian. You won't find those stories in books."

"I'm writing them down. Starting today."

"Are you, now?"

"You know there was a treasure he was after, too."

Pony rubbed his chin with a balled fist, and swallowed hard. "Must be a gnat flew into my mouth. A treasure, yeah, you know what it was called?"

"It was a star made of gold and jewels—the Star of Andalusia. Babe says the Fowlers looked through all kinds of records once, trying to see if there was a map or a clue..."

"I heard of it. But it was lost forever, or...something. You know treasure stories. There's usually nothing to them."

"Yes, sir. There's no map or nothing."

"That's amazing, all right. Well, I'd like to hear some of Buddy's stories, too, when we have the time. If you wouldn't mind playing them for me."

"No, sir, I wouldn't mind. I'm just about to get to the end."

Pony paused as if he were grasping for a way to change the subject. He pointed toward Bill with his cigar. "What do you think Buddy would have thought of Bill over there?"

Buddy loved bison. He loved what they once had represented, and he grieved for how they had suffered. I know he wished he could have seen one of the herds that stretched in infinite numbers across the plains. And I could still picture how he had said, in a rare display of melancholy, that we could read our own future in what had become of them—driven nearly to extinction, then bred anew but protected only as long as they stayed within the boundaries of a refuge. He smiled—ruefully, I remembered, because he was usually unfailingly positive—and said, "It's in there that I see what happens to people. They're fine as long as they don't cross the fence line. God help them if they do."

After a moment's thought, I answered Pony's question. "Buddy would be talking to Bill right now if he was here, asking him all kinds of things. I mean, he wouldn't expect Bill to answer out loud, if that don't sound too funny..."

"Not at all. It sounds natural, to see if you can look into the soul of a creature like Bill. And Buddy wouldn't be doing any more than I've done, or you could do."

"What could...I could do what?"

Pony looked into my eyes and his personality shifted again, into an expression of caring, of confidential understanding, of concern. Before, it had seemed as if he was merely trying to get to know me. Now, it seemed as if he already did. When I saw that look, I twitched and lowered my eyes. Then he said, "You'd like somebody to talk to, wouldn't you?"

"Yes, sir."

"Well, then...there's me, while I'm here. I'm happy to hear whatever you've got to say, man to man. But you might think about Bill, too. Like you say Buddy would have done. I know that...that need. I've gotten a lot off my own chest talking to Bill. People would say it's crazy, but he...he seems to understand. And I think I understand him better than I understand people. You know what I mean?"

"I don't understand people that well."

"It's better than understanding them too well. With Bill, he is what he is."

"Is that why he follows you like he does?"

"Maybe that's part of it. Plus I raised him from a calf. I know those little grunts he makes sometimes when I'm out of sight are his way of telling me where he is, that we're connected. We like each other's company."

"You think he might take to me?"

"I have no doubt he would. Animals have a way of knowing, don't you think?"

"Yes sir, I do."

"So tell him what's on your mind. I'll leave the two of you alone sometime and you can say anything you want to him. You might be surprised what an easy conversation it is. It's like magic, what happens, how you see things afterwards. At least it is for me."

"I'll look forward to that."

I had a lot of things to say that I had never told anyone.

Babe called us in for sandwiches.

Afterwards, we spent time exploring the hill. Babe insisted on giving Pony a tour of her gardens—I think she was happy to have an audience who would appreciate what she had accomplished—and Pony seemed not only impressed, but knowledgeable about the plants and flowers. I had never seen Babe flirt before, but I got the feeling that flirting was what she was doing. Just before evening, when the sun dropped toward the brim of the western horizon, Pony excused himself and walked around the top of the hill to study the light and the landscape. He made crude pencil sketches in a small book. As darkness fell, Babe went back into the house to warm up a stew. I stayed with Pony. He took a metal box from the cab of his truck—he didn't say why, and I didn't ask—then we strolled to a level area beneath a slope south of the house, in a tongue-shaped depression where Buddy had placed a bench and a birdbath. Bill lowered himself to the ground, resting.

"I guess Bill likes it here," I said. I hoped I was right.

"He does, indeed." The stars were brightening and Pony sat on the bench, placed the metal box on the ground, and leaned back slowly until he was gazing straight upwards. "That can make you dizzy."

"Yes. sir."

"So you and Buddy stargazed...like the Phantom Padre did, watching the heavens roll around."

"Yes, sir. And the shooting stars. Once we were walking down the hill—I was real young—and there was a meteor shower, like it was following us. At least I thought so. I started laughing and calling 'Come on, stars.' I asked Buddy, what if I leave the hill? Will the stars come along with me? And he made up a Jack-and-Jill rhyme for me while we watched the sky."

Shooting stars
Played tag with Mars
So they could hear John's laughter.
John took a spill
Straight down the hill
And stars came tumbling after.

"So," I continued, "I kind of thought—I still do—that maybe the stars are staying up there, I don't know, as long as I'm..."

I didn't finish my sentence. "As long as you're up here, too, sure," Pony finally said. "Well, you can't see half this many stars from most other places on earth. Stars and constellations. You know the constellations, too?"

"My grandfather Dwight showed me constellations from a star chart."

"There's lots of ways to look at them. You know that, don't you?"

"Yes, sir. Buddy said the Indians made their own charts of the sky, maybe from this very hill."

"That's why I thought you might be interested in this." Pony set the box on the bench and opened it slowly, as if he were about to reveal a treasure. He pulled out a thin, soft, light-brown strip of buckskin, about 19 by 14 inches and oval in shape. Around the edges of the buckskin were tiny, evenly-spaced holes, as if it once had been trimmed with lacing. The buckskin was marked with symbols that looked like four-pointed stars, all black, of four or five different sizes. Clusters of tiny dots were strewn down the center of the oval. "This is a star chart, too. These colors set you to looking at it the right way. Sunset..." Pony tapped the left side, which was colored with a yellowish pigment. "And sunrise." The right side was a faded combination of red and yellow. "West and east. This chart could have been made from a hill like this a hundred or more years ago."

"Who made it?"

"It's an Indian chart. The Indians, they had their own names for what's in the sky. You know any of them?"

"Not exactly."

"Like the Milky Way, for instance. The Greeks said it was the milk spilled by Hercules' mother while she fed him. That's the legend the Phantom Padre learned from the Jesuits. But out there on the plains, there was an Indian tribe that believed it's the dust left behind in the sky by a buffalo when he raced a horse. What a hell of a contest that must have been. Can you see it that way?"

I could. I glanced at Bill, picturing some ancestor of his thundering through the universe, and felt a surge of pride that he was with us on the hill. Before, I had admired the Milky Way as some great stream of stars that spilled and spread across the sky. Now, it looked even more alive to me—the billowy dust of a heavenly race between two magnificent beasts. Bill rose from his resting place, as if he was posing beneath the evidence. Buddy would have loved the story. "Who won the race?"

"The horse did, naturally."

Disappointed as I was to learn the outcome, I allowed to myself that Bill definitely did not seem built for racing. Demolition derbies, maybe, but not racing. "I wish the buffalo had."

"Don't feel sorry for him." Pony pointed upwards. "He gave it his best."

"Where did you learn about that?"

Pony hesitated. "Oh, from some old fellow who didn't want the legends on this buckskin to die." He began to point out other features from Indian lore, and the sky I thought I knew so well was transformed that night, as if some previously invisible writing had slowly revealed a long-hidden message, a new code. I can close my eyes and still picture the sky that night, tingling with stars—

yawning and stretching and looming over the plains like a cat arching its back to wreathe the wayward moon that hung to the northwest of us, low in the sky. I remember the sounds that accompanied Pony as he spoke, symphonies that seemed to reach to the stars from our faraway posts in the universe—distant cars passing, nightowls hooting, crickets chirping, calling and calling again, measuring the darkness and their own desire. And Pony's low, musical voice, the voice of a storyteller repeating tales rooted deeply in his heart and making a sally into mine. "Where the Greeks saw Scorpio, those plains astronomers envisioned a snake. Look in Delphinus, and you can see the outline of a bow. Scattered up there...there's a great meeting of tribal chiefs. And there in the southwest, a bison, in profile, with a large, bright eye. The stars—look around there, now—those are their campfires. Do you ever get up before sunrise?"

"Yes, sir, all the time."

"Then you know there's a streak of white in the sky, just before dawn. That's because one of the gods told us to add some dried grass to the embers of our campfires when we got cold at night. Well, when we do that, first of all there's smoke that curls up from the grass. That's what makes the streak of white. Then what happens?"

"What happens when?"

"When the dawn starts."

"It gets red..."

"That's right, and here's why. The red dawn, that's when the grass catches fire and blazes up." Pony folded the buckskin and returned it to its box.

"So, mister..."

"Just Pony."

"How long can you and Bill stay?"

"Well, it's kind of up to your mom. As for me, if things go the way I hope, I'll have an appointment to keep, but it's not for a couple of weeks yet."

"What kind of appointment?"

"Family business, stuff I have to take care of."

"Maybe Bill could wait here."

"Maybe he could."

To the west, our spook, who had appeared late that afternoon, turned and rode away. At least we'd given him something to see—Bill grazing near us, a great, dark silhouette, suspended in a web of stars. I explained the lone rider to Pony, who had a good laugh. "I wonder how he makes out his time sheet," he said. It helped to know that he viewed the spook as absurd and not at all menacing.

After dinner, Babe sent me straight to bed. "Big day tomorrow," she said. "You don't want to sleep late on your birthday."

Pony shook his head. "He didn't say a word about it. Most kids wouldn't have been talking about anything else." He gave me a soft jab, barely more than a push, on my shoulder. "I figure you'll be twelve or so, right?"

"Yes, sir. Exactly right."

"Well, then, I think I know a special way to celebrate if I can work it out with your mom."

I nodded vigorously toward Babe. "Please, Babe?"

"Maybe so," she said. "We'll talk about it tomorrow morning."

I didn't mind going to bed. I wanted to be alone, to think about the stars and the Phantom Padre and what I would say in a conversation with Bill. A rotating fan, the twin of the fan in the barn, blew lengthwise across my bed. I felt perfectly relaxed and detached. The fan's motor purred hypnotically, pushing streams of air over me, back and forth, head to foot, steady and reassuring, droning a one-note lullaby as it scanned the darkness. The breeze from the fan set every centimeter of my skin to the same cool, even temperature. To my right was a four-paned window that faced east. I could see the stars through it, and began to count them. They were bright and bare, despite a distant flash of lightning. A few raindrops drummed tattoos on my window, calling me to my dreams. A few more drops, hurled by a gust of wind, spattered the glass impulsively, recklessly. Clouds with transparent edges floated by as if inspecting the stars. I was obsessed by the thought of the race and the dust and the cosmic pandemonium it must have caused. But I could not have imagined on that night in August of 1960, even as I fell to dreaming, that the next day I would be betting in desperation on a race just like it. Nor could I have imagined how a treasure deemed lost would exert its pull on my life.

* * *

BUDDY WATKINS [FROM DISK #5]: *...and that treasure—the Star set with emeralds and a blood-red ruby—looking for that treasure would change Antonio forever. He never thought about the difference between the stars he loved, the night's flawless, untouchable gems, and the one he was chasing.*

4
The Stakes for Selenia

BUDDY WATKINS [FROM DISK #6]: *...What Zebulon did after he took Selenia under his power—he said he'd give her to any man who came to Big Fort and could beat him in poker. Lots of men tried, because she was the most desirable girl anyone had seen—ever—in these parts. Zebulon was too crafty to spoil her himself. He used Selenia to lure folks into games they were sure to lose...*

Once I had learned about her from Buddy's disks, Selenia Garza also became a regular occupant of my dreams, far more often even than the thought of lost treasure. She was the kind of ideal that Babe, as my adoptive mother, never could have been. She was vulnerable and in need of rescue, which sealed my illusive infatuation with her. And of course, she was from the distant past and therefore unattainable, so I could mold my daydreams around the what-ifs that are the wellspring of imagination. What if I had lived then, what if she had been under my care, what if the world and its troubles could be made to disappear and leave us stranded and safe on a hilltop? Nothing seemed too unlikely because there was, after all, a boy in her life who was also a tortured soul, and who protected her faithfully and indefatigably before the Phantom Padre arrived.

Selenia Garza's family—New Mexico sheep herders—had been murdered in a Comanche raid while she had been visiting a friend. She thanked God that she had taken with her the drawings she had made of her parents and siblings. She had natural artistic talent, and the drawings gave her something to remember them by. Her closest relative was an uncle Luis, who, ironically, was a Comanchero who traded with the Indians. He was also a drunk who had lost his wagon and mules in a poker game. He reluctantly accepted Selenia as a ward, got two mules on credit from other Comancheros, and took her east along the Comanchero wagon road to the trading post known as Big Fort, where he had obtained weapons for Comanches in the past. During their journey, Comanches of all bands were being called and assembled for a Sun Dance that would lead to an attack on the trading post at Adobe Walls. Big Fort, no less unsavory or rough than the few other trading posts that sprang up as bison and their hunters migrated into the Panhandle, was nevertheless protected by the high walls and bastions of its main building. From there, wagons carried cargo both north to Dodge City and east to Fort Worth. Comanches had come to trade there, but had never attacked it or raided its protected stables and adjacent corrals. It was built as the first business venture of Zebulon Fowler, who had founded the fortune that was being used to hound Babe and me.

In his teens, the year the Civil War ended, Zebulon had worked his way west from Virginia as a mule-skinner and trapper. When he reached the Great Plains, he took up buffalo hide-hunting. Buffalo still roamed the plains in countless numbers, and from those beasts, Zebulon—wielding a .44 Sharps rifle and stinking of the bear oil with which he saturated his long hair—earned the money that helped stake his ambitions in the 1870's. He built the adobe trading post known as Big Fort in 1873 to compete with traders at Fort Griffin on the Texas frontier. Fowler had been prescient enough to hire two trains of wagons to build the outpost—one with the lumber and other building supplies, and the other, fifty wagons in all, to bring in merchandise to stock the stores and warehouses, not to mention ample amounts of red liquor and cigars for the saloon. He built his own quarters just inside the front gate, including a private room for high-stakes poker games that insulated players from the violence that could break out in public games. He multiplied his fortune with extraordinary cunning, transforming himself from a greasy, smoke-stained, ill-kept hunter into a trader with a neatly-trimmed beard who dressed in tailored clothes. But he was not so fancy as to alienate himself from the traders who supplied him and the men who bought from him. To all comers at Big Fort, Zebulon sold guns, ammunition, groceries, and prostitutes. He accumulated hides and other goods from Indians and Comancheros by illegally dispensing whiskey to them.

He sold railroad contractors buffalo meat for their crews, and many of his freightloads of buffalo hides were transported all the way to the east coast, where they provided buyers with fur and leather used in fashionable robes, carriage tops, cushions, military gear, padded chairs for affluent bankers, and belting for the pulleys that churned the industrial revolution. He augmented his income with cards. He was a shrewd poker player, a risk-taker who enjoyed gambling for high stakes and delighted in the ruin of his opponents.

Selenia and Luis arrived at Big Fort late one morning in May of 1874. The trading post was crowded and stifling in the heat. Bales of buffalo hides were stacked everywhere. The air stank with them—Selenia could smell little else—and bugs flew in such dense swarms around them that it was difficult to see what lay beyond. Tents were pitched outside and around the fort, where hunters and traders and cowboys and soldiers camped. The thick adobe walls promised protection from Indian attacks, and another, smaller square in the rear of the fort contained stables where Luis left their mules, a jail, a laundry, and a morgue that doubled as a makeshift chapel. Inside the main post, buildings were crammed together around a kind of patio—stores and a saloon, warehouses and offices. Luis pulled Selenia by her arm through the winged doors of the saloon. Only a smattering of customers had begun drinking. Luis presented Selenia to the bartender, Frank Peppert, a man he knew well.

"Watch her for me, just a while," Luis said. "I want to see the boss about her. She can work while she waits."

Peppert, a large man with a square, mottled face and a drooping mustache, slowly looked her over. "She can clean up, but I ain't paying nothing. She'll do better as a whore if she wants money. But they'll mark her. She's too pretty."

"Just a favor. I make it worth your time."

Peppert shrugged. "Ain't nothing to me."

Luis went to the headquarters building, where he insisted on seeing Zebulon Fowler, the owner of the post. He was told to wait.

Peppert tossed a stained apron and a broom to Selenia. "Look around. Use the broom. Watch the other wait girl. She'll say if she needs help."

Selenia tied on her apron and tried to get her bearings among the chairs and tables crammed together along the walls and in the center of the long, windowless room. Inside the front doors of the saloon, immediately to the right, was a full-sized buffalo, preserved by a part-time taxidermist at the post and bearing his name on its side. To the left of the doors, where Peppert stood, was a gleaming walnut bar fifty feet long, hand-crafted in Chicago. Nothing like it had been seen at any other outpost so close to that edge of civilization, including Fort Griffin. Towels were spaced around the edges of the bar, and a brass rail ran around it. In the shadows at the end of the bar, two cockeyed customers finished another round of drinks and began to strip off their clothes and dance, singing as they leaped around.

*Rainin' and a-pourin' and the creek's runnin' muddy
And I'm so drunk, Lord, I can't stand studdy.*

Near the wall opposite the bar, regarding a mural he was painting, was a man dressed like a dandy in a gray silk vest and gray trousers, a man who apparently was practiced in ignoring the drunks and vagrants who populated the saloon. He was gazing over a raised thumb and whistling "God Save the Queen." The mural was life-sized—a nude woman stretched seductively over the wall. He touched up an ample breast and paused to inspect Selenia. She was staring fixedly at his work. "Oh, my dear," he said. "I never saw anyone like you in Denver and certainly not in this hellhole." He turned to his painting. "Does this offend you?"

Selenia hung her head. "I like to draw," she whispered.

"Is that it? Then no need to be shy. My name is Charles St. George Stanley. I'm a Bohemian and an artist. My interest in you is purely—well, should you ever wish to earn a few extra pence modeling for me in this wasteland, I would be delighted. And if you wish to draw, I can spare a pencil and paper for you. Perhaps both are possibilities?"

The bartender, Frank Peppert, scowled. "It'll be busy before long, your highness. There's plenty of working girls, if that's what you want."

St. George Stanley ignored Peppert and addressed Selenia. "I'll spare a few moments for lessons if you want them. You'll find me here of a morning before the bloody riffraff come." He cocked his head at the sound of a ruckus just outside the saloon. Several gunshots were fired. The dancing men lost their balance and disappeared behind the bar. "Sounds as if they're already here."

"You wanted to work, here's some work." Peppert gestured to Selenia. "Go out and see what it is. If it's a fight, offer 'em drinks. The boss don't like trouble if it don't have to happen."

"Brave man," St. George Stanley muttered. "Send the bloody girl."

Selenia looked over the top of the saloon doors. Two horses were tethered at a water trough. A buffalo runner named Carl Janssen fired one more shot just past the head of a young Indian boy who was lashed to one of the horses. The other shots apparently had been fired in a similar manner, as there were no bodies on the ground and none of the few spectators were running. Janssen loudly cursed the boy, whose hands were tied behind his back. "Don't speak unless you're spoken to. You ain't gettin' water till you learn not to ask for it." Janssen undid the lash, jerked the boy off the horse, threw him to the ground, kicked him, and splashed water onto him from the trough. Then he looked up at the other men who had paused to watch. "I killed his daddy and let him bury the heathen savage. Not likely I ever done something like that before. And yet he ain't grateful. I ain't sure what I'm going to do with him," he said. "He's a worthless piece of shit. Whoever taught him to speak our language should of taught him to shut up."

"So what's he doin' here?" asked a bystander. "And how is it you let him bury his heathen pa?"

"That's for me to know," was all Janssen said. "Something he said before I could blow his worthless brains out. I aim to find out what he meant or make him pay for the kindliness I showed." He kicked the boy again, pushing him beneath the horses, and walked into the saloon. While Peppert served Janssen, St. George Stanley retrieved a large tin cup of water from near his painting materials and handed it to Selenia. "For God's sake," he said, "give some of this to the boy while that bloody lout's not paying attention." He gave her a bar towel. "And wipe the blood off of him. I'll keep an eye out."

Selenia took the cup and returned outside. She held the cup to the boy's lips and poured water over wounds on his face, wiping his forehead with the towel. He was shirtless, but wore buckskin leggings and a breech clout ornamented with two shells. It had been less than a month since Indians had killed her family. By all rights, she should want nothing to do with him; and yet she knew why she agreed to tend the boy, whoever he was. He had been forced to bury his murdered father, just as she had buried hers. And he was now completely at the mercy of men who scorned him as less than human. He did not smile, but he met her with his eyes. The few men who had been observing the scene drew back, then turned to walk away quickly, as if avoiding a fight. Selenia pulled a piece of bread from her pocket and was about to offer the boy a bite when she heard St. George Stanley say, "Let me buy you the next one, old boy." She looked up to see Carl Janssen shove the painter out of his path.

"By God, under the law I could kill you for that!" Janssen screamed, grabbing Selenia by the shoulders and hurling her against a post. Her head slammed into the wood and she reeled forward, dizzy and gasping. "Nobody feeds or waters my red slave except me. See?" Janssen pulled a piece of jerky from his shirt pocket and waved it under the boy's nose. "Are you hungry, Taco?" he teased, circling the Indian. "You'd get this waiter bitch killed for a bite of bread, would you? How about this jerky? Ain't this better? Have a bite of this."

Janssen swiped the dried buffalo meat across the boy's face, then guffawed and stuffed the jerky into his own mouth. He swallowed it whole, and within seconds he was choking. His croaks grew louder and louder, echoing in the dusty trading square. St. George Stanley stood and watched. He brushed his neatly-creased gray pants with his hands. No one else made a move. When Janssen stopped choking, his face was beet red and he was dead. He lay in the dirt with a hand still poised over his throat. Selenia shook her head to clear it, withdrew a knife from Janssen's belt and cut the Indian boy's hands loose. The boy quickly reached for a feathered pouch that hung from Janssen's belt. Selenia let him take it before anyone noticed. He hid the pouch under a flap in his breechclout. Then she led him into the saloon behind St. George Stanley.

Peppert, the bartender, angrily threw them out again, cursing and threatening her.

Among other things, it was against the law to serve Indians.

A small crowd gathered near Janssen's body. One man peered into the saddlebag on Janssen's horse, but apparently found nothing worth stealing and walked away.

A short, well-dressed, bearded young man in a black slouch hat, a gray silk vest, and Wellington boots stared at Selenia and grinned. Selenia's uncle Luis stood next to the man, Zebulon Fowler. Fowler turned to two men who positioned themselves behind him with revolvers in their hands. "No trouble here," he said. "Carry the body to the Methodist morgue. If nobody claims him in two days, take him out and bury him."

Peppert pointed to Selenia. "That girl is the one who caused this, Mr. Fowler."

St. George Stanley intervened. "As a gentleman, I confess it was I who gave her the water and started this," he said. "Perfectly fine, what she did. The bloody lout caused his own death. She didn't know better about the redskin."

To Fowler, the fright on the girl's face enhanced her extraordinary beauty. His mind began to churn with possibilities, but he kept a poker face to conceal his interest. He turned to Luis. "This is the girl you want to bargain with?"

"For a wagon and oxen," he said. "She's yours. I take the wagon and work for you, for hire."

"Leave us be," Fowler shouted to the others. The crowd dispersed. Fowler beckoned to Selenia and walked back toward his office with Luis.

"Her family is dead," Luis continued. "But everybody know her. People went to pray with her family on Sundays just to look at her. You see? And she would draw their children when they asked. Pretty pictures."

"And you brought her here to my fort?" Fowler asked. "You see any children?"

"You're smart. You do lots of business. She can whore for you. She's worth what I ask. I know you have eyes."

"Whores ain't worth much around here, or didn't you notice? Some are so cheap they work in the hide yard with the flies." Fowler rested his thumbs along the edges of his vest. "You understand what we say, *señorita*?"

Selenia, whose mother had taught her English, looked straight into Fowler's eyes. "Yes, *señor*."

"You ever had a man, missy?"

"I don't know."

"Yes, you do. Has a man ever done this to you?" Fowler gestured with his hands, shoving two fingers into the circle made by his thumb and forefinger.

"No."

"This man is your uncle?"

"Yes, *señor*."

"No other family?"

Tears rolled down her cheeks. "No, *señor*."

"I own the saloon in here. Can you work in the saloon?"

"*Sí*. Yes."

"Your uncle says people used to go pray just to look at you. That so?"

"I..."

"You can see for yourself, *señor*," Luis interrupted. "You'd have to go very far from here to see a woman like her."

"She ain't a woman yet. So much the better. That artist fellow who's cheating me to paint naked girls in my saloon, he could do worse than paint her. Ain't been had yet?"

"I swear on her mother's grave. My sister's grave."

"Take a team and two wagons and load up at the hide yard. There's wagons leaving tomorrow for Fort Worth. Tell the yard boss I sent you. Now here's what you need to know. This girl ain't related to you no longer. Savvy? That's how you stay alive."

"Yes, of course."

"You see her here, it's like you never knew her."

"I forget her."

"You never knew her. I asked if you savvy. Savvy that?"

"*Sí.* Yes, of course."

"That means stay away from her. I don't want to see you in my saloon when you're back here. Bring your own pulque and drink it in your wagon. This agreement is final, and I'll give you my hand on it." Fowler extended his hand and Luis shook it. "Now get out."

Luis left without a backward glance at his niece. Fowler smiled. "You're a waiter girl now. You know what a whore is? Savvy *puta?*"

"*Sí.* Yes"

His face turned hard. "You stay away from whores. There's whores gonna hate you. You stay away from 'em no matter what they say they can get for you." Then he put a hand on her shoulder and smiled again. "Me—I protect you like your uncle should of. Here." Fowler rolled a silver dollar through his fingers and handed it to Selenia. "Don't take these from no one but me, savvy? My job—I'll find you a husband, but he's gotta pass my test, just like in them schoolbook legends. You—no men friends. You stay with my Chinee laundress, around back there. That's where you sleep, savvy?" As Fowler pointed beyond the saloon, Selenia saw the Indian boy slip away through the front gate. "The Chinee laundry woman, she'll watch you."

Fowler walked Selenia back into the saloon. "She works for you," he said to Peppert. He pointed toward the customers. "They look. They want. They don't touch unless I say. She ain't a whore. She's better money. They'll come to me with dicks so hard you could nail a poker deck to 'em. Tell 'em that's her face his royal highness is painting on the wall. Show her how to get to Ping's laundry when she's done." He grinned at Selenia. "You're lucky I got an eye to the future. I always see a brighter future in a hand of poker."

By the early afternoon of Selenia's first day, thick cigar smoke engulfed the saloon. Kerosene lamps with glass chimneys hung from the ceiling, their reflections dancing in the mirror behind the bar. The mirror was flanked by shelves stacked with glasses and liquor. Beyond the far end of the bar where the drunks had danced, an arched, open portal led to another room for gambling.

The din of voices was as loud and disquieting as anything Selenia had ever heard. She learned to repeat the drink orders as best she could, but sometimes had to make her way through the crowded barroom twice. She was groped and insulted as long as she was on the floor, protected both by men who were as excessively polite as others were rude, and by Peppert, who occasionally called a groper over to the bar, gave him a free drink, and explained Fowler's rules. Fowler was not a man to cross.

Selenia worked for ten hours in the smoke and noise until Peppert told her she could leave. "That's enough for today," he said. "You don't go where the whores go. Out through the back, where the stables are, there's a laundry shack. You'll know it by the overhang. That's where you stay. Chinee laundress. You can find her yourself. Understand?" Selenia nodded. "Chinee laundress," Peppert repeated, then waved her away. "Be back here tomorrow morning at eleven."

Selenia was too exhausted to notice that a man snuck behind her and followed her out the back entrance, which opened onto the service square. At the sound of the door closing, she heard a silky, drunken voice. "The stench is overwhelming back here," St. George Stanley said, "but we must look beyond this drab place to the stars above us. We must make the best of our wishes upon them." He placed his hands on her shoulders and turned her around. "Please understand I mean no harm," St. George Stanley said. "I'm drunk, the stars are watching, you are irresistible, and I am a graduate of the Royal Academy of Art. I will give you free lessons." He leaned to kiss her with an open mouth, but before his lips could touch hers he dropped to the ground, unconscious. A rawhide ball rolled in the dirt not far from the dandy. The Indian boy stood a few feet away holding the strap he used as a sling. Selenia quickly picked up the ball and returned it to the boy.

"Go! Go!" she said, waving her hands toward the west. "*Vaya con Dios!* Go!" She leaned over St. George Stanley, who was still breathing and smiling.

The boy shook his head. "You save me," he said. "You are my sister." He spoke strange English, but without an accent.

"No!"

"I wait wherever you are, sister."

"Go! Someone will kill you. I'm not your sister. Please."

The boy smiled. "Please to you, my sister."

Selenia sighed. She did not think the boy knew what he was saying, or, worse, that he was trying to needle her for some reason. "Do you have a name?"

"I am called Young Eagle."

"You go, Young Eagle. Please."

"No."

"I cannot help you. Adios."

Selenia walked away from the boy and across the service square, looking for the laundry. The stench turned her stomach. She passed a small building that served as a jail and headed toward the only light she saw, filtering through the boards of a shack. The shack had a crude veranda shaded by an overhang built as an extension of its front wall. She looked back. St. George Stanley was still lying in the dirt, but the boy had disappeared.

A cat raced out of the darkness and stopped in front of her, startling her. Neither she nor the cat moved for a few seconds. She stared at the animal as if she expected it to speak. It meowed. Gently, she picked it up, stroked it, and began to cry. Within seconds, a woman burst out of the door, saw Selenia, and stopped abruptly. "Sorry for cat," the woman said. "Bad Ah Toy." She held out her hands and the cat wriggled away from Selenia and leaped into her arms. The woman leaned toward Selenia as if to study her. "My name Ping. You no whoa," she said simply. "Boss say you stay with me." She held up the cat. "Her name Ah Toy.

Ah Toy and me, we wait for you all night. You no whoa. I know." Ping's English may have been fractured—in fact, she knew it was to her advantage not to sound intelligent—but her mind was quick and she had learned to read people instantly. It was how she survived.

Ping wore a patch over her left eye. A scar descended from the patch and reached nearly to the corner of her mouth. The skin on her face was so tight it seemed glued to her skull. Her gaunt body was covered by a loose gray, cotton tunic that reached nearly to her knees. Her trousers were of the same cloth and color. She wore thick-soled sandals. Her black hair was thin and looked like a helmet, combed back over her head and ears. She appeared to be much older than she was—barely 22. Ping smiled crookedly, showing a mouth with several teeth missing, then turned and held open the door. "Come for tea, No-Whoa."

Ping kept a newspaper clipping with an illustration of Chinese railroad workers and a cartoon of a pigtailed Chinese man standing in front of a washtub and holding a pair of lacy women's undergarments. The caption read, "Lucky Washee Man." Ping pointed to the words and pictures, and then to herself before she served tea to Selenia.

Selenia had never met someone who seemed, at once, so gracious and accepting. In fact, Ping had been lost to herself for so long that she could not dream of lives other than the one she led, nor could she remember much about the one she had left behind. She recalled that, in China, her mother often told her that her life would be one of hard labor—that her feet always would be ugly, never bound. When she was eleven, her father sold her into prostitution for $100. With dozens of other girls, Ping was crowded onto a steamer to San Francisco. She was taken from the boat directly to a whorehouse in Church Alley, where the madam threatened her wards with a hot branding iron if they failed to satisfy dozens of customers each day. The prettiest things Ping knew were the artificial flowers she was told to wear in her hair. She spent nearly seven years as a prostitute, occasionally traded among madams seeking to refresh their stock. She was pregnant once, and the child grew within her despite the concoctions she was given. When she started to show, she worked as a laundress and chambermaid for the other prostitutes until she gave birth. The baby, a girl, died before she was a day old.

After one of the prostitutes told Ping that men were superstitious about lying with whores who were deformed, she heated a metal rod and blinded herself in her left eye, claiming a customer had done it. She was only nineteen years old, but she had made herself worthless as a prostitute. Ping's madam slashed her beneath her eye as additional punishment, opening her cheek to the corner of her mouth. She then sold Ping for $250 to a trader who was stocking up for a trip east and had no objection to the eyepatch. Ping knew deep within herself the distress that Selenia felt. She understood it when she first looked into Selenia's large eyes.

In a way, Ping believed her own fortune had turned for the better. After she was sold to the powerful boss of Big Fort by the trader who had brought her from San Francisco, her job was to wash and iron only the laundry that Zebulon Fowler sent to her—his clothes and sheets, and, once or twice a week, the clothes of women or friends. Her laundry kettle, ironing table and wash boards were crammed within the shack where she lived. She went to a nearby creek to gather kettle water and haul it in a three-sided wooden cart back to her laundry. She heated her irons on a small stove. A clothes wringer was mounted on the canvas-covered wall near the kettle. She emptied the kettle and hung the laundry on poles in a small, open area formed where a corner of her shack met a corner of the stables. The area was protected on the other two sides by the adobe walls. She slept beneath her ironing table on a mattress stuffed with buffalo forelocks and made of Fowler's discarded clothing, including dresses that never had been reclaimed.

The old clothes were the reward she got when she served the private poker games that Fowler held. She was under strict orders never to talk and never to show the inside of her mouth by smiling. Fowler enjoyed showing her off. "As you can see, gentlemen," he would say, "the only other person allowed in this room until our game is over is this ignorant one-eyed Chinee woman who'll bring us drinks and cigars, and five of the only ten words she knows in our language are 'wine' and 'whiskey' and 'light me up,' so she'll carry no tales out of here. I bought her personal from a trader to do my laundry. He bought her from a whorehouse in San Francisco and you can see why they sold her. What'll it be, gentlemen? Whiskey for everyone?"

The other players believed Fowler's claims that Ping was sub-human because she was Chinese. They never suspected that while she served drinks, she sent Zebulon signals that told him what was in the other players' hands.

Ping had only one friend and steadfast companion—Ah Toy. Eight years before, the cat found its way into one of the crib houses where Ping labored as a prostitute in California. The trader allowed Ping to bring Ah Toy with her when their caravan left San Francisco. She did not know why. It was the only kindness he showed her, although if he was displeased he would threaten Ah Toy with the bola that Ping herself had fashioned to kill rabbits and other small game for meals. Ping's favorite possession was a white porcelain bowl for Ah Toy's water. The cat, however, preferred to jump onto Ping's table and drink from the tin bowl that Ping used to sprinkle water on the clothes she ironed. Ping was flattered by the attention and teased her companion in Chinese. "Hurry up, hurry up, that's what they all say and now you, too, Ah Toy. Have your drink and let me work. We can't play till I'm done. Then I shall have tea with you."

Ping looked at Selenia and knew the girl would find no kindness at Big Fort—that it was only a matter of time, perhaps hours, perhaps a week, before her youth would be savaged, whatever plans the boss had for her.

"What you do here?" she asked. "You no whoa."

Selenia gestured toward the saloon. "I serve whiskey."

"I see in your eyes. You no like."

"I want to escape. Go away."

"No, no, no, no, no. Worst thing. Not now. You learn what to do first."

"Why?"

"They do worse than kill you. You wait your time."

Selenia began to sob. Ping patted a pile of old clothing. "You sleep here with Ping and Ah Toy, no money, no problem. Fuck the rest." Selenia nodded and lay exhausted on the bundle of dresses. "Ah Toy glad to have sister," Ping said.

Ping lit a long, thin pipe and leaned against her clothes wringer, stretching her back against the rollers. Ah Toy came over to her, as she often did while Ping enjoyed a smoke. Suddenly, the cat bolted upright and faced the door that led to the small open area where Ping hung her laundry. Without making a sound, Ping stood, opened a box with one hand and, with the other, picked up her coiled, braided-leather bola. At the ends of its three cords, the weapon was weighted by small bags filled with stones. Ping shot through the canvas flap that hung over the door and flung the bola toward the movement she saw. Young Eagle stumbled against the wall of the tiny yard. Ping was on him with a knife at his throat before he could try to disentangle his legs from the bola.

"Speak fast," Ping hissed.

"Wait." Selenia stood behind Ping.

"What?"

"I know him. I gave him water. A man beat him as a slave." She explained as quickly as she could the incident with Young Eagle and Janssen, then the episode with St. George Stanley, who was still lying outside the saloon, snoring. The boy said nothing. "I told him—go to his people," Selenia said. "He won't go. He said I saved his life. He said he will protect me. He calls me sister and looks at me like a brother."

Ping lowered her knife and said something in Chinese. The boy was facing the wall. Ping turned him around by the shoulders and stood face to face with him. He was precisely her height. She tapped her eye patch, looked him up and down, and laughed. She pulled on his greasy hair as if to uncover something. "Lookee here, sister."

Beneath the dirt and grease, the boy's hair was full of lice, but that was not what Ping had noticed. Young Eagle's hair was not black, but a lighter shade of brown. His face had been tanned and roughened by the sun, and dressed as he was, he looked, for all intents and purposes, like an Indian. On close examination, however, his true hair color and features revealed something else. "No Indian, here," said Ping. "White boy. Right?"

"I am Chenowah," said Young Eagle. "Indian."

"You not Indian. Not fool Ping." He continued to stare straight ahead, saying nothing. Ping patted him on the shoulder. "No matter white, Indian. You slave. Me slave. She slave. All slaves except Ah Toy. You sleep out here when you want." She stamped her foot on the ground to indicate where he could stay.

Selenia tried to protest, but Ping interrupted her. "You lucky girl, don't you know? You no find other man here to protect you and want nothing else."

Ping gave the boy a gray cotton tunic like the one she wore and insisted that he put it on. The tunic fell over his leggings. Young

Eagle smiled for the first time, then took off the tunic and rolled it into a pillow. Ping shook her head, and she and Selenia left him in the tiny clothes yard, where he lay with his head against the western wall, so he would awake to the sunrise in the east.

While Selenia and the boy slept, Ping opened the door of her laundry. Ah Toy scampered out to scavenge among the garbage. The cat went directly to the crumpled body near the back of the saloon and climbed on top of it, turning her head back and forth as if she were inspecting it. In the shadows, Ping smoked and watched with a grin while Charles St. George Stanley, rubbing his head, rose and lifted the Ah Toy gingerly from his body. "Perhaps someday you will tell me how I got here," he said. He staggered across the square and out the broad, open gate.

Every morning, Ping sent Selenia off to work with bread and a slice of apple. She massaged her feet when Selenia returned from the saloon. She washed the stink out of her clothes. The boy, Young Eagle, moved like a ghost, and seemed always to be present and watching when Selenia was exposed and vulnerable to anyone waiting outside the saloon. Sometimes he slept in the laundry yard. Sometimes not. But he refused to leave and return to his people, whoever they were. By that point in his life, he was as much Indian as white, as were many other children who had been kidnapped during Indian raids. His white family had been massacred on their farm. He was grabbed by an Apache warrior as he fled through the fields. The warrior carried him on horseback across the plains, on a hard ride that lasted for days. The Apaches sold him at a Chenowah camp where they had been offered hospitality. At first, he was assigned to carry water and do other chores for the women of the camp, who often pushed and beat him. He was called, simply, "White Boy." When one of the children didn't come back to his teepee after dark, the young white captive was told to join the search for him. He was warned that if the child was not found, or was dead, he would be blamed for bringing bad luck, and would be killed.

The searchers feared the child had been killed by wolves outside of camp. Young Eagle stayed out all night, despite the dangers. He was not allowed to carry weapons to defend himself against animals. But he was afraid to go back, and he roamed in a broad circle around the camp.

That night, a shaman of the tribe had a dream. He dreamed of an eagle that flew down from the heavens and became a boy when he landed on earth. A party of warriors captured the boy. The warriors had been separated from their tribe in battle and were lost. The boy asked them to take pity on him. When he spoke, sparks seemed to glow around him. "I have been in the sky," he said, "and I will guide you to your people if you do not harm me." The warriors let him live, and he took them back to their people as he promised. They asked him to stay with them. He agreed. Whenever the tribe was hungry, he became an eagle again and told them where the buffalo were. When war parties were formed, he told them where their enemies were. He grew old, but did not die. He flew back into the sky again and became a star in the bow that gave hunters and warriors their strength.

The morning after the shaman's dream, Young Eagle returned to the camp carrying the lost child with him. The child had stumbled into an arroyo and had broken his leg, which was stuck in the cracked earth. But he was alive, and he recovered from his injury.

That evening, the shaman, who was married but childless, adopted the white boy and gave him the name Young Eagle. He vowed to teach Young Eagle all the signs and pathways in the sky, so that Young Eagle could do as the eagle had done in the shaman's dream. "And when you die," said the shaman, "you will watch our people from the sky."

Young Eagle never imagined being rescued or returning to a white community. He had spent enough time as an Indian to believe he wasn't meant to be anything else. But Selenia had added an extra debt of allegiance to his life. She not only had defended him and saved him from enslavement and death, but when he saw her for the first time, he was reminded in a sudden shock of the sister he had failed to protect, the sister he had lost when his family was massacred. He felt an immediate duty to look out for her, one that he never questioned, one that forever after took precedence over his own well-being.

It didn't take Zebulon Fowler long to learn about Young Eagle—the Indian boy, he called him—and although a less canny man might have had the boy killed, he didn't. He realized that the boy also safeguarded his investment, Selenia, when she was away from the scrutiny of his own men. He ordered Peppert leave garbage scraps for Young Eagle, as long as the boy kept out of sight. Which he did.

Fowler showed up at the saloon to inspect Selenia nearly every day. When a man came to him with designs on her, Fowler always professed that as her guardian, he had to know the man's worth. That inevitably led to a high-stakes poker game in Fowler's private quarters. Fowler never lost. Selenia was not unlike a princess, desired by many who competed for her hand but who routinely failed to pass the compulsory test and in the process left their money on Fowler's table. The only man who had become troubling because of his loss was the outlaw and scalp hunter Pigeye Lehane, who stopped short of calling Fowler a cheater, but nevertheless vowed to collect a new stake for the poker game and return to win and claim his bride. He vowed to kill any man who beat Fowler before he could amass the means for his second chance.

* * *

BUDDY WATKINS [END OF DISK #7]: *...Well, good night, son. I always say good night when I'm done, because that's when I'm making these recordings, while you're asleep. Next, it'll be time for Antonio to ride into Texas, on the trail of the Star of Andalusia. That's also when he met the man who would christen him as the Phantom Padre. Of course, you and I know he wasn't really a Padre, but no one else did, and the name was too strange and offbeat not to stick...*

5
A Birthday at Harvey's

Young Eagle's history had haunted me ever since I learned of it through Buddy's disks because of my own doubts about my unorthodox origins—mixed, to say the least. What about myself could I focus on, count on? What would give me definition, my life clarity? Young Eagle, Selenia's protector, was not in fact who he appeared to be at first—like me, I supposed. He had wound up out of time and place, gravely misunderstood, accepting of whatever gave his life structure.

Buddy himself had said, at the end of one of his disks, "These may sound like some sad and scary stories I'm telling you. But if you've read fairy tales, you've learned stories that were just as scary. This is kind of a fairy tale from our part of the world. And that's what they're about—where you came from, why life has brought you where you are, and whether you should fight it or change it or just get on with it. It'll be up to you to decide how it ends."

I had spent an inordinate amount of time wondering how I compared to Young Eagle—what the fate of my birth family might have been, whether I had somehow been removed from my true origins and shaped by an alien heritage, what my role in Babe's life was or should be in some future plan when I would be older and better able to shield her from her tireless antagonists. So I was more than ready to forego the tension in my life and await a welcome resolution. And because of that, I was willing to believe that the arrival of Pony and Bill might help reveal a design to life, a destiny that I had not identified before, and I was anxious to awake and pursue it.

Babe and Pony already were drinking coffee at the breakfast table when I got up on my birthday. Through the kitchen window, I could see Bill grazing on the west side of the hill beyond the barn. Babe, freshly scrubbed and beautiful, was looking at some of Pony's watercolors. "Sit down, John," she said. "Pony says you can pick one of these for your birthday to hang in your room."

The paintings were of playa lakes—shallow, ephemeral bodies of water, formed during the rainy season on the high plains. One of the watercolors showed Bill standing in a playa, drinking. He was directly in the center of the picture, a focal point between the red, cloud-streaked sky behind him and its reflection in the water. In the distance, toward the horizon, were other, smaller playas dotting the landscape, also reflecting the sky, all destined to shrink or disappear after a brief life under a scorching sun. Pony had written a short poem at the bottom of the painting.

The playas dance before your eyes
Like lanterns when the daylight dies
And if you heed the forward view
You'll see the past ahead of you.

Pony uncovered a second water color. "This is the one I want you to see," Babe said. It showed a boy who closely resembled me, standing in a lake just beyond the tall grass around the edge of the water. The boy was naked, but shielded by some cattails. He had waded ankle-deep into the playa and was watching an eagle soar into the distance. In the margin of that painting, Pony had written,

You cannot hide yourself in here
Some day it's bound to disappear
And you'll be grown before the rain
Can bring it back to life again.

In a third water color, the same boy lay beside a glassy playa at night, his arms crossed behind his head, looking up at a bright star.

Though others have tried to tell my story
My history is in my heart when I lie down at night
And when I rise in the morning it is still there.

"Who's the boy?" I asked.

"Ah, that's a secret," Pony said.

Babe smiled. "It looks just like you, John, doesn't it? Like Pony knew you before he came here."

I was mesmerized by the likenesses. I was still young enough to believe there was no one like me. I was maybe a quarter or half Chinese and the rest Caucasian according to Dwight, who had arranged my adoption. Some people thought I had Indian blood, or they saw the unusual configuration of my eyes, more western than eastern, and wondered what was different. It's possible that Pony simply could have given the boy features that resembled mine by coincidence. Nevertheless, there, on that watercolor, was that improbable boy who could have been my twin.

"Can I pick later?" I asked.

"Sure," Pony said.

"I like them all," I added hastily. I needed to think about what they might mean while I attacked the corn flakes Babe set before me.

"So, listen," Pony set his coffee cup on the table. "Your mom—Babe and I had our talk, and I was wondering, how'd you like to take a short trip with Bill for your birthday, have a special lunch and all, up toward the canyon?"

"If we do, you won't get your cake or Buddy's present till after," Babe said. "But here's a starter from me." Babe gave me a card with a ten dollar bill in it—a record-setting bonanza—and a gift-wrapped box with a three-bladed jackknife from Gamble's. With ten dollars, a new jackknife in my pocket, and the prospect of choosing one of Pony's watercolors, I didn't care about the cake. And I could certainly wait to hear the rest of Buddy's stories.

Pony's plan was to show us the town of Wachyerback, where he and Bill had stayed for a few days before they came to Lonechap Hill. "I've got an old friend there named Harvey, makes the best chicken fry in Texas," Pony said. "You won't believe his saloon, either. He never takes down his holiday decorations. Too lazy to do it, he says. It's a perfect spot for a celebration. And you can ride with Bill, if Babe doesn't mind."

That settled it for me. A chance to have a private conversation with Bill.

When we were ready to leave I got into Bill's trailer and sat on an inverted metal tub in a small, open compartment, separated by bars from where Bill stood. I waved at the spook as we drove down the hill. "You can take the day off," Babe called. Once we were on the two-lane highway north, I could hear Babe and Pony talking, but I couldn't make out what they were saying over the whine of the tires on the asphalt road. They laughed a lot and seldom grew quiet. I stared at Bill, concentrating on the eye that was angled toward me. Bill stared back. The iris of his eye was as black as night, and sat partially sunken beneath the lower part of his eyelid. Above the iris, the vast, white expanse of his eyeball reminded me, strangely enough, of the arc of a fortune-teller's globe, set in his massive head.

I began to talk without thinking. I don't know how else to describe the impulse, but I spewed words as if some dam of neurons had burst in my brain. I said things to Bill that I had never said, nor had I realized that I thought them quite so vividly. I come from nowhere. I have nowhere to go. I am beaten by other children who know I must fight when they call Babe a whore, a thief, a bitch, and when they say that she adopted me only so she could steal the hill from the lamebrain to whom the Fowlers had entrusted it. Some said she murdered the lamebrain, the man I remembered as my adoptive father—that he did not die wasted from cancer but from poison. Worst of all, I did not know where the truth lay. I sensed, rightly or wrongly, that something about me was a burden to Babe, and that it might have to do with a burden of guilt. Because of my own Chinese blood, she said, she had picked me to adopt when she and Buddy wanted a son. That, I feared, might not be completely true. She might have had other reasons. What if she had used me to claim and hold the land, the hill that was as out of place as I was on the implacable plains and coveted by the people who were her enemies? What would happen if she had no more use for me? The most agonizing realization was that I loved her so much that I could not condemn anything she might do. I stubbornly fantasized that she was a Chinese princess. She told me that when she was a little girl, she and her mother once had traveled to visit their relatives in China, but they had to escape back to San Antonio because of the Japanese invasion before World War II. She wouldn't say more. "I'll tell you some day when you'll understand," she said. I wanted to reply that by the time someday came and I understood everything, what difference would it make? Or maybe people thought I'd forget. I didn't forget. And then I had to wonder. Did they really mean it, or was it just a way of putting me off? Is it better to hear a well-intentioned lie or a brutal truth?

I chose to live on the edge between the two, not knowing which was which. To me, Babe could do no wrong, and yet I believed against the deepest yearnings in my soul that it was possible there was some truth in what the other children said about her.

For my birthday, my wish was not to be frightened of those things and never to believe the other children. And to understand why she often seemed to withhold herself from me. She was tough, I knew, and that was part of it. And maybe she didn't want me to get too close to whatever burdens she shouldered. But was there something about me that made her so reluctant to be called mom?

I was perspiring heavily by the time I finished talking, but I was calm. So was Bill. He tolerated the trailer ride well, with the asphalt-heated summer air whipping through his tousled mane as he listened to me. Suddenly, my mind seemed clearer than it ever had been. Then I began to ponder the germ of an idea that surprised and elated me, and I told myself that it could be the meaning behind Bill's arrival. Maybe, even, Bill had communicated it to me in a subtle way. How else would it have occurred to me to wonder whether there was a scintilla of a chance that Pony could be my father? He knew things about me without being told. He had shown up the day before my birthday and knew my age. He acted surprised, but what if that were merely a ploy so he could study the situation before revealing himself? He knew about the Phantom Padre. And that little crick in his personality, the one that had unsettled me when he was questioning me about Buddy's stories—maybe he had become more sober because he had missed so much of my life, and knew that I felt hopelessly adrift sometimes, just as the Padre did. Then he said he had an appointment—family business, he said. Maybe it had something to do with me. Most telling of all, the boy in his paintings looked just like me.

How anxious we are to reach blindly and believe that whatever we find will be exactly what was missing.

In less than an hour, we turned onto a one-lane stretch of gravel. That's where the ride got rough. I heard and felt the ping of rocks on the undercarriage of the trailer as we bounced along the ill-kept road. "Hold on," Pony called out the window, "we're almost there."

Wachyerback was situated on the south side of the road, a few miles below the northwest bend of Toomis Canyon and just past a stand of tall, haggard emory oaks that sagged over a barbed wire fence where some brown curve-billed thrashers sat, still and imperious and orange-eyed. Beyond, where we had come from, stretched the haycolored plains to the ends of the earth. The town was no more than a collection of buildings—a small feed and convenience store, a gas station, a corral, the Wachyerback Saloon, and some crackerbox houses that looked as if they'd been tilted on their foundations by the overbearing plains wind.

The few people who lived there did well enough serving the Fowler ranch and other nearby spreads. They also did business with seasonal deer hunters who were headed to the canyon and anyone who got lost and happened to pass through by accident. We passed a rusty, steel-pipe corral just west of the saloon. A large, lone bull paced within it. I heard Pony whistle. "That's usually where Bill stays," he called, "in that big corral, where he can lie down in the sun. Now he'll have to stay in Harvey's hog pen."

Bill didn't seem to notice. Several horses were tethered to a post in front of the saloon and a couple of pickups were parked not far from the animals.

The saloon was a rectangular wooden building with a beige brick front that came to a peak above the roof line. Two gas pumps stood in front of it, and a pay phone was mounted on a metal post near a corner of the building. If the words Wachyerback Saloon weren't painted on the brick in white letters with red trim— "Wachyerback" in a straight line, and "Saloon" in much larger letters that curved over a faded rattlesnake curled inside a Christmas wreath, also painted onto the brick—you'd never have guessed what it was. Some cowboys mingled at the front of the saloon, finishing cans of beer.

We pulled into a dirt lot behind the building. There was a wooden hog pen on the other side of the lot—much smaller than the corral, but empty. When Babe got out, she cursed beneath her breath. "I hope that doesn't mean what I think it means," she said.

"What?" Pony asked.

"If those are Wyatt Fowler's ranch hands, you might have to fight 'em all to get me out of here again."

"How come?"

"Later."

"Should we turn around?"

"Not on your life. Not after they saw us."

Pony unloaded Bill from the trailer and walked him into the hog pen. The bull in the nearby corral stood stock still, staring across at Bill, frozen as if he were a hair's breadth away from launching into a furious bellow. "Harvey, where the hell are you?" Pony yelled. "Hey, Harvey."

A moment later, Harvey Olsen, wearing an apron streaked with brown stains, came out of the back screen door of the saloon and ambled past a row of metal garbage cans, extending his hand. He was rawboned, with black stubble that somehow looked almost as smooth as the skin on his face, curly salt-and-pepper hair, and a permanent grin that raised his cheeks and set his eyes into a jokester's squint. "Pony, you old sod." He looked from me to Babe. "Didn't know you was traveling with women and children, now. How's young Bill takin' it?"

"Bill's just fine with it. He's in your hog pen, if you don't mind. The corral..."

"It's got a no vacancy sign, that's right. The hog pen's fine, if it's okay with Bill. Ain't been a hog in it since Davidson died six month ago. Couldn't bear to eat him, you know, so he's buried there, too. To what do I owe the pleasure?"

"For starters, it's this boy's birthday..."

"Well, Merry Christmas and happy birthday, son..."

"...and we all came for some chicken fry."

Pony introduced us, and I could tell by the look on Harvey's face when he heard Babe's name that he knew all too well who she was, even though they never had met before. Still grinning, he shook my hand and slapped Pony on the shoulder. "I'll be happy to do it, now that this young man's reached drinkin' and smokin' age. But you might want to know..." He paused as if wondering how to put his next thought. "You might want to know that they's some boys from the Fowler ranch, about eight of 'em, came up this way chasing that outlaw bull that made a getaway from his pasture somehow. You know they love to look for trouble. Ain't the first time it's happened, neither. I think they might let him loose on purpose so they can board him in the corral for an hour or so and gin themselves up. They damn sure don't need eight men to chase one damn bull. You know any of them cowboys, Pony?"

"Not really."

"Well, they's fine men but they's rough and ready and don't always talk like you'd want a boy to hear. So if you all want to wait till they clear out again, then we'll turn over the whole saloon to this boy and have us a ball. And I'd keep Bill away from that corral till that bull's gone, too. You know they call him Killer?"

"We don't mind waiting," Pony said. "And you know Bill. He's a lover, not a fighter."

But it was already too late to avoid trouble. Two of the cowboys had carried their beers to the side of the saloon to check us out. I saw one of them point at Bill and laugh. Another stared at Babe, elbowed his companion, and drawled, "If it ain't the Lonechap whore. Who's minding the hill?"

"Must be the lice she left behind."

Harvey's Cheshire smile slid away like shit on Vaseline.

The other ranch hands wandered slowly around the saloon, looked back and forth at each other, and traded foolish, smirking grins as if they couldn't believe that Babe and her boy stood not ten yards from them. Unlike cowboys I've known since, Fowler's hands were a surly bunch—at least the ones who stayed for more than a year or two and were paid twenty or thirty percent more than what typical cowboys earned. For that price, they also shared their boss's grudges, and their boss had an almighty grudge against Babe and, by extension, me. They spoke among themselves, anxious not to let such a ripe opportunity for insults pass, but they were loud enough for anyone in the vicinity to hear.

"Brought a friend to the hog pen," said one.

"That ain't all," said another. "I think she done escaped from my sorry old grandpa's hog ranch."

That thinly-disguised reference to a bottom-of-the-barrel whorehouse drew the biggest guffaws of all and brought angry tears to my eyes. I had heard the same thing from kids in school. Babe didn't flinch.

Harvey did his best to defuse the situation. "Boys," he said, walking toward them, "how about a last beer on me before you take old Killer back to his rightful place in this cruel world of ours?"

"I guess because we ain't ready yet, Harvey," said a man with a handlebar mustache. "We're kind of hungry, too. You don't suppose you could cook us some buffalo burgers, could you?"

"You mean like from that one over yonder in my hog pen?"

"You see another one?"

"Well, that's my friend Bill," Harvey said. "We're kind of like saving him for Old Lady Baker to stuff someday." That drew a laugh. "Hell, don't laugh boys, you never know when she might come for you. That woman is merciless. I know for a fact that everything they say about her is true, and she's nigh on 200 year old to boot." Old Lady Baker was a plains legend who supposedly lived alone in an ancient, isolated trailer near a barn where she pursued her hobby of taxidermy on virtually every species available, including—so the stories went—her late husband and other human beings. Especially children. Harvey paused to shade his eyes and look toward a rider who was approaching at full gallop from the southwest. "Looka there, looka there..."

"Besides, Bill's too damn fast to catch," Pony interrupted. "He's even faster than that horse Harvey's looking at. I never saw a horse he couldn't beat."

Harvey continued to watch the horse, which flew like the wind across the grass. Pony was lying, I presumed, to divert attention from Babe. The lie worked.

"And who might this man be, Harvey?" The question came from the largest of the bunch, whose black, dust-stained hat was pulled nearly over the bridge of his nose. He was stocky and in his late forties, with the hint of a belly above his beltline.

"This might be Pony Antone, a friend from way back. He's done some cowboy work, too. Pony, that's Mr. D.B. Bulland, the foreman of this bunch."

"Nice to meet you, D.B."

Bulland spat into the dirt. "*He* don't seem to know where he belongs." He gestured toward Bill. "Like the company he brought with him. Or maybe he does know. That's a hog pen, ain't it?"

The cowboys snickered. Babe's fingers dug into my shoulder. I prayed that the approaching horseman was by some miracle coming to our rescue, like a righteous, all-seeing, lightning-draw Phantom Padre, appearing out of nowhere. The rider was on a large, sorrel stallion and clearly at ease in the saddle. I had never seen the man in person before but Babe certainly had, and I knew my prayer was worthless when I heard his name. Bulland stepped forward and raised a hand in greeting. "Howdy, Mr. Fowler. We got the bull."

Wyatt Fowler, owner of the largest ranch in Texas, head of a business empire, enemy of Babe, demon of my nightmares, boss of the devil's cowboys, symbol of our troubles, leaned casually on the neck of his horse. He glanced, somewhat bemused, at Bill. "Afternoon, boys. Afternoon, Harvey."

"And to what do we owe this pleasure, sir?" Harvey bowed.

"I was out for a ride and heard the boys were chasing Killer again. I see the fun's over." He turned to Babe. "Hello, Babe. You're a long way from home."

"You, too, Wyatt." Babe's voice was firm, as if she felt nothing. One of the cowboys grunted at her insolence.

"Not really. As long as I'm somewhere on the plains, I'm close to home."

The bastard was smiling. His voice was relaxed and polite. He was 36 years old, tanned, and handsome—not ruggedly so, but like the well-groomed executive he was most of the time. If only by the back of his neatly-trimmed neck, you could tell he didn't belong with anyone else who was standing around in Wachyerback on that ninety-five degree fly-infested day. By all accounts, Fowler was an exceptional man, which made him even more detestable in my eyes. Those who admired him were positive he would run for some important office someday, although he constantly denied the rumors and now I understand why. You don't have to run for things you already own.

He was unquestionably an expert horseman. People in Wendellton who drove on one of the north-south county roads often mentioned that they'd seen him riding on some section of the ranch that reached, at its longest span, from Wendellton to Wachyerback—seventy-five miles. He had inherited and expanded his family's oil, ranching and manufacturing businesses. He was a philanthropist and a patron of Western art. The museum he supported in Wendellton, the one where Babe had worked, was among the finest of its kind, with a collection comparable to Gilcrease's, albeit much smaller. Scholars drove a hundred miles out of their way to visit the museum, which was built around and within a replica of an old adobe fort. The modern wings of the museum contained art and sculpture. The fort itself—simply called "Big Fort"—held a collection of regional artifacts that was constantly refreshed by teams of anthropologists from Canyon State University, also funded by Fowler. The original Big Fort had been built as the defensive center of an outpost where the fortunes of the family were founded on the buffalo trade. Knowing that and knowing Bill made me hate Wyatt Fowler even more. The only consolation was that Babe, with Granddad Dwight as her attorney, had beaten him in court when the Fowlers challenged Buddy's amended will that left Lonechap Hill to us instead of returning it to the Fowler family.

Fowler raised the brim of his white Stetson, wiped his brow with his arm, and turned to Harvey. "What's the meeting all about?"

"Well, sir, I believe when you rode up we was all a-dither about whether that buffalo in the pen yonder was fast enough to win a horse race."

"And who even thought so?" Fowler settled his hat on his head again.

The approving mumbles and chuckles of the cowboys punctuated virtually every sentence of Fowler's.

"That was me." Pony raised his hand.

"That's your buffalo?"

"He is. And he can outrun a horse, even one as fine as yours."

Fowler rolled his eyes condescendingly. "What're you doing with him?"

"He rides in that trailer. We travel around. I'm a wildlife painter, so he's been kind of modeling for me the last few weeks..."

"Really? What's your name?"

"Pony Antone."

"Never heard of you."

Pony shrugged and jerked his head toward Babe. "That's what she said, too."

Fowler glanced at Bill. "Antonio, is it? Well, Mr. Antonio, it's not too smart to let a buffalo run wild around here, even a Speedy Gonzales like that one."

"It's *Antone*. He's Bill. And Bill never goes where he's not wanted."

"And you're kind of a braggart, too, aren't you?"

"I don't know what you mean, Mr. Fowler. How so?"

Fowler ignored Pony and turned to Babe. "That your boy, Babe?"

I didn't wait for Babe to answer. "I'm her boy, yes, sir." I spoke as emphatically as I could, through the bile that was washing into my throat. I wondered if he knew that his sons tortured me at every opportunity.

"That's enough, god damn it," Babe whispered to me. "He only talks to people like us to humiliate them."

Fowler saw her scold me but didn't hear what she said. "Let him answer for himself without waiting for you to tell him what to say, Babe. Good for him."

I refused to accept even a backhanded compliment. "I guess that buffalo could outrun your horse if he wanted to." I pinched my palm when I spoke, especially since I knew in my heart that it wasn't true. It was the closest thing to an insult that I could manage.

"You guess? Well, let's think about that, son. My horse Tony here weighs about 12 hundred pounds. That buffalo is a ton or so, am I right?" Bill grabbed a mouthful of grass from the edge of the pen with a sideways swing of his neckless head. "That's an 800-pound handicap for Speedy Gonzales."

"Pony told you. His name is Bill."

"Well, what would you be willing to bet on that race, boy? I wouldn't bet the used beans in my latrine."

Babe raised her hand from my shoulder to the back of my neck and I kept my mouth shut.

Pony didn't. "Right here and now, I'll put up a case of beer and a hundred dollars on Bill. We'll make it an even start, no handicaps. Harvey holds the stakes. He and D.B. and I will stand at the finish line to call the winner."

As if on cue, Bill keeled over with a thud and rolled onto his back. He writhed and flopped in the dust and stirred up a new burst of derision from the cowboys.

"An even start?" Fowler laughed. "You've got a deal—what's your name? I don't need your money. Just split it among the boys when we're done. And Babe, I hope your boy learns a lesson from this, about the price you pay when you let your mouth run off with your brains in tow." Fowler never lost his genial manner, but he paused just long enough for me to understand that he was referring to more than a preposterous challenge over a buffalo. "Sooner or later, son, somebody's going to call your bluff and make you a liar and a loser. You should learn to go for the gold instead." He turned to Pony. "How do you want to do this?"

6
Bill's Dust

"Let's make it quick and easy," Pony said. "Give me a moment." He led Bill out of the hog pen to a papershell pinyon tree near where Fowler sat on his horse. "Start where Bill is now. Finish at the next tree." Pony pointed toward a bushy, 12-foot-high one-seed juniper that was about a quarter of a mile east of the pinyon.

"Then hand the money over to Harvey and let's do it. What's the signal to start?"

"What if I just whistle? Is that good enough for you?"

"You mean that buffalo comes like a dog? Whistle away."

Fowler never had to reach for his wallet to cover the bet. His ranch hands quickly collected the money among themselves. Pony pulled out five twenty-dollar bills, then turned his wallet upside down to show it was all he had—exactly one hundred dollars.

The ruckus also drew some spectators—a couple of clerks who wandered out of the convenience store, and an elderly lady who stood in the back yard of a tiny home, watching with her hands on her hips.

Harvey winked at me. "This is a birthday you won't forget, son. We about to have one hellofa race."

"Can I bet, too?" I reached for the ten dollar bill in my pocket.

"John, god damn it," Babe snapped. "That's your birthday money."

"Aw, come on, momma," Harvey grinned. "It's his birthday. This is a done deal. It got us out of kind of a unpleasant situation. I never seen hostilities turn to festivities so fast. Let's all have some fun with it. Be a good sport like Bill."

"Babe?" I looked up at her imploringly. "You taught me never to back down from anything. I'm twelve years old."

"You're such an old man," Babe sighed. "Go ahead."

"That's the spirit." Harvey clapped me on the back. "What do you want to bet, my boy?"

"I have ten dollars."

"Ten full dollars. You want some advice on how to lay it?"

"I guess."

"Don't put none of your money on Bill, son, no matter what you think. That buffalo's way too fat and lazy to outrun a pregnant gnat. So lay your money on that young horse and let Pony owe you."

"Pony's my friend. So's Bill."

"Then here's my birthday present to you, son. Always keep your friends and investments separate unless you mean to lose both."

"I want to bet on Bill, anyway."

I handed Harvey the ten dollar bill. "Well, I guess we better put this to work," he said, waving the bill in the air. "Attention, folks. Who wants to cover this boy's ten dollar ride on the buffalo? We done run this pot up to one-ten. That's a record for a race like this, no doubt."

"I'll do the honors on this one," said Fowler. He folded a ten dollar bill and tossed it down from his horse.

"Babe, you don't mind if I borrow John for a moment, do you?" Pony asked. "Bill needs a second for this duel."

Babe shook her head at Pony's cockiness, then did the last thing I expected. She smiled in resignation. "Like everybody's been telling me, it's his birthday. As long as he remembers that tomorrow isn't."

If Bill was aware of the tensions around him, he didn't show it. "Come over here," said Pony as if I were suddenly part of a great conspiracy. "I want you to stand next to Bill till the race starts."

"You didn't need to bet all that money."

"The fact is, I did. What would Bill think if I didn't have faith in him?"

"Aw, come on. The buffalo lost that race that was in the, in the..."

"The Milky Way. That's right. It's written in the stars. But when all's said and done, that's the point. Do you see what I mean?"

"I guess."

"I don't think you do."

"Well, it's my birthday so you might as well tell me. Everyone else has. I wish to goddam hell I was still eleven."

"You're twelve whether you like it or not," Pony laughed, "so here's the deal. That horse left nothing behind, he just kept running till he turned into a shooting star and disappeared. But think of all the dust the buffalo kicked up, big and clumsy as he was. You can look up and see it every night—the dust in the stars, the remainders of a great race—and it makes your jaw drop at the thought of it, and what a hellofa buffalo that must have been. Nobody ever wins in life, son. Someday, we all reach the end of our fortunes. It's a race we're destined to lose, whether we're fast or slow. So the best you can do is leave behind all the damn dust you can kick up. Let people know you were in the race, and that you left your story behind for all to see. That's worth a hundred dollars to me, and it's worth your ten dollars, too. And you know what?" Pony winked. "Sometimes you find out your opponent isn't as smart as he thinks he is. Now you stand here next to Bill and give him a pep talk while Harvey and I walk to the juniper tree with that hired hand, Bulland, and we'll see what happens. If Bill seems to get restless, scratch him under the eye. He likes that."

"Laydeez and gentlemans," Harvey cried, holding up the small bag in which he had deposited the money. "First of all, I declare this another official Wachyerback holiday, and we can decide what to call it later. Give us a few minutes to walk to yonder juniper, and when you hear the whistle, it's on. I also got me a camera." With his other hand, Harvey held up a Brownie Hawkeye. "Just in case there's a photo finish, then you'll have to wait for Mr. Kodak to make the final decision."

"What happens to our money while we wait?" a cowboy yelled.

"Scotty, if you think there's a chance of a photo finish, why'd you risk your beer money?"

Bill was already facing east. I stood about five feet from him, and all I could think of to say was, "Just stay calm, Bill." In the light of that merciless, sweltering August day, he seemed dramatically different from the creature who had loomed so majestically on Lonechap Hill only the night before. The unsightly mane between his horns made him look hung over. His black beard was matted and filthy as were the hairy clusters on his forelegs. At the other end, his rump, encircled by a languid squadron of flies, was pathetically skinny. His disproportionately small hind legs, I worried, were barely capable of propelling his one-ton bulk, even if he were equipped with wheels. And with a head that looked as if it had been jackhammered onto his body, he had no neck to stretch across an imaginary line in the unlikely event of a close finish.

To my mind, leaving a cloud of dust was no consolation.

Fowler maneuvered his horse to a position about ten yards south of Bill. "So how old are you, boy?"

"Twelve."

"You're kind of small for twelve, aren't you?"

"I guess."

"You're not worried that buffalo could turn on you?"

"Nope." My teeth chattered. I hoped Fowler couldn't tell how nervous I was, so I breathed deeply and cleared my throat.

"Let's hope you're right. I've got two boys about your age, named Darryl and Cameron," Fowler said, sounding as if we were best friends. "You know them?"

"Yep."

"Are you friends?"

"Not exactly." Not unless two brothers who live to beat the crap out of you can be called friends. During the school year, most of my spare energy was spent agonizing over encountering the Fowler brothers and planning how to avoid them.

"No reason you can't be friends." Fowler was especially frightening in his congeniality. "You know, I've really got nothing against your mom. She thinks I do, but I don't." I felt as if I were being lectured by the snake in the Garden of Eden. "Whatever happens about Lonechap Hill, son, none of it's personal." I wanted to say that I wasn't his son and he shouldn't call me that, but I kept my mouth shut. Bill snorted. Tony jerked his head. "Whoa, boy," Fowler snapped, pulling his reins. "Stand still."

I didn't know what to say to Bill. I had lost enough fights to the Fowler brothers to identify with his hopeless but inescapable task—entering a contest you were destined to lose in order to settle someone else's affairs. Why did he need to settle something he didn't start, just to be left alone? "All you have to do is run to that tree, Bill," I mumbled. "It don't matter if you lose, as long as you kick up lots of dust and make that sonofabitch eat it." Slowly, Bill turned his head toward me and seemed to fix me with a stare from his left eye, the stunning, white orb I had looked into on the ride to

Wachyerback. At that moment, it occurred to me how still the fevered day was, and how that silence had enveloped us all as the moment approached.

Pony strode the last few yards to the tree that would mark the end of the race. I studied him carefully—the way he walked, thumbs hooked into the back pockets of his worn jeans, drumming on his hips with restless fingers. He held his head slightly askew as if contemplating everything he saw with amusement bordering on disbelief. How could he do this to Bill? The outcome already was foretold by the dust in the stars, the residue of a race lost long ago. My birthday money would go to the man I hated most in the universe, who would probably pass it along to his sadistic sons as an allowance bonus.

Then—there they were, standing at the one-seed juniper tree, Harvey with his arm in the air, D.B. Bulland slouching grumpily, and Pony with two fingers in his mouth. The arm dropped. Pony's whistle followed, ear-splitting even at that distance.

In response, Bill gamely launched his ponderous, one-ton, non-aerodynamic body toward the juniper. Tony, all muscle and grace, took off like the powerful and beautifully-made creature he was. His hooves hammered the ground loud enough to make the gods hold their ears. Fowler leaned expertly over Tony's bulging neck, shouting encouragement. His Stetson blew off before they had covered thirty yards.

As for Bill—what I remember seeing most vividly was his undersized rump bouncing wildly across the clusters of grass and shrubs. If you've ever seen a buffalo run, then you know it looks as if two different motors are driving the same body. There's the turbo-charged front end, barreling along like a runaway semi. And there's the two-stroke ass, with back legs pumping like pogo sticks.

After the first hundred yards—about a quarter of the distance to the juniper—Bill seemed to be holding his own. His head was low, and his beard nearly touched the ground. On the other end, his tail—strangely, it seemed—was erect. I bit my lip and held my breath when I realized that he was still close to Tony. How close, I couldn't tell through the gathering veil of dust that Bill left behind. I clapped until my palms were stinging, and started to yell despite myself. "Bill—go, Bill—Run." I could hear the cries of the others—not words, just whoops of amusement and excitement and drunkenness as the ranch hands, accompanied by the citizens who had turned out, crowded together into the area where I stood. In the distance, Pony stood calmly with his hands in his pockets. D.B. Bulland had decided to pay attention. Harvey raised the Brownie Hawkeye, squinted, and held it at arm's length in front of him.

It didn't take long for the two animals to run a quarter mile—a little more than thirty seconds. It seemed like five minutes to me because the prospect of defeat had been so crushing, and the path to it so inescapable. We all knew the race was over when we saw Harvey's camera flash. The cowboys stopped yelling. Bulland turned his back and spat in contempt. Tony slowed immediately but Bill continued running until Pony whistled again. Bill returned to Pony and did a stiff-legged hop that looked to me like a when-do-we-start-for-real dance. I would get to know that hop and love it.

Harvey didn't need to rely on a photo. The outcome of the race was undisputed. I raised my eyes to the sky in case there was some kind of sign that a miracle had occurred. Then I looked back at Babe, who had remained in the parking lot, just in time to see her mutter the words "I'll be god damned"—in awe, not anger. Because Bill had beaten Tony by a buffalo length.

Pony jumped back several paces to avoid the spatter while Bill peed like a racehorse.

Babe was smiling when she came over to me, balled her fist, and gave me a punch in the shoulder. "Just don't overdo your smiles around these folk," she whispered.

Fowler rode Tony back toward the saloon. D.B. Bulland jogged behind Fowler. If any of Fowler's men had planned to rib him, they were quickly silenced by his stony expression and Bulland's scowl. The townspeople scattered, laughing.

"Can I?" I asked Babe.

"Go ahead."

I ran across the field to Bill, Pony, and Harvey. Harvey pointed at me and clapped his hands. "You held your own, son," he said. "Called it straight. Doubled your money. Twenty U.S. dollars. Hey, hey."

"Did you fix it somehow?" I called to Pony. I would have been just as happy if he had.

"How could I have done that?"

"Did you know he was going to win?"

"I knew he could," Pony grinned.

"Well, what's his secret weapon?" Harvey asked.

By then, the four of us were walking back to the road together. I never had felt prouder.

"It's the way he's made—the ligaments and tendons in these legs." Pony pointed toward the lower joints on Bill's hind legs. "You might think those are his knees...but they're more like raised heels. It's like he's always on his toes. He's got a lot of spring for a short sprint. That, and he eats his carrots. But if that juniper had been a hundred yards farther away, the horse would've had him."

"Like you thought, son. Pony fixed it." Harvey tossed the camera to me. "Here's for your birthday. And Merry Christmas, too. We'll put it on Pony's tab."

"Don't you want the picture?" I asked.

"Hell, the flash was just for show, there's no film in there. I figured there was no need, the horse had it won. If it *had* been close, I would've owned up to a mistake and called it even and saved you ten dollars and Pony his hundred."

"That would have proved Bill won."

"Son, this is a land of legends and bullshitters. The last thing we want is proof of anything. Kills a good argument dead as buzzard bait. Let's take care of bidness here and then you'll get your chicken fry."

With Harvey's help, Pony retrieved a tub from the kitchen of the saloon and set it down near Bill. We lingered in the parking lot, avoiding glances, while Harvey went back for a case of Shiner Beer.

Fowler never dismounted, but he reached down to shake hands briefly with Pony, barely offering his fingers. His irritation was palpable. "Damn horse got spooked as soon as the buffalo took off," he grumbled loudly. "Skittered instead of running." He looked at Pony and tried to grin. It was a feeble attempt. "I guess you've done this before, eh? Something in the whistle, right? Gets on a horse's nerves."

"The horse didn't look spooked to me," Pony shrugged. "Wasn't his fault he lost. Bill was faster to the tree."

"If the horse doesn't beat the buffalo," Fowler said, "the West turns out a lot different."

"The problem wasn't so much that buffalos couldn't run," said Pony. "The problem was, they couldn't hide."

Harvey arrived with the case of Shiner. Pony opened all twelve of the beers and poured them into the metal tub. Bill watched patiently. When Pony was done, he made a gesture toward the tub and Bill dipped his head into the suds and sucked up the beers like a frat boy till his beard was soaked and dripping. He stood unmoving for a few seconds, then broke the silence with a long, rasping blast that was the mother of all farts.

Before Fowler looked away, I could see that his face was screwed into an expression of disgust and anger. "Tell those boys it's time to get the bull back where he belongs," he told Bulland. Without a goodbye, he rode off at a gallop.

Pony led Bill to the trailer. "No more hog pen," he said. "You rest here, champ, while those cowboys go about their business." Without protest, Bill turned into the trailer and Pony shut the door behind him.

The front door of Harvey's saloon was made of metal, and the two square four-paned windows on either side of the door were hung with closed curtains. Inside, it was another world. Harvey had mounted Christmas tree lights, the multi-colored kind with bubbles, around the upper portions of the walls. He also had activated an electric train that glided on an oval track above the bar, disappearing into a tunnel-shaped hole-in-the-wall at one end of the bar and emerging again from a hole at the other end. The square tables, about a dozen of them, had red-and-white checked vinyl covers with deep, chili-colored stains. A Gottlieb Grand Slam pinball machine, with a batter poised in front of a target above the pinball field occupied a front corner of the saloon, just beyond and to the left of the door. To the right of the door was a full-sized cardboard dummy of a longhorn steer with a real pair of horns mounted on its head and a Fourth-of-July rocket attached to its ass.

"Take a good look, son." Harvey patted the dummy's rump. "A gen-you-wine Bevo. You go ahead and look around while I get the chicken fry ready."

A Louisville Slugger bat was mounted in a case above the longhorn with a sign that read "In case of fight, break glass." Next to that case was another. "In case of rattlesnake bite, ask Harvey to open the freezer." That case contained a first aid kit, a syringe wrapped in cellophane, and an empty bottle of antivenom. The walls were cluttered with pictures, all of them drawings and illustrations in keeping with Harvey's prejudice against photographs. One of the drawings, of a grizzled man wearing a bandolier and a sombrero, had the words "Sincerely, Pancho Villa" written in script across it. Another, framed under glass, was from an ancient cover of Frank Leslie's *Illustrated Newspaper*, showing two preachers, a gentleman and a ruffian sitting at a poker table. The preachers had amassed all of the chips. The illustration was captioned, "The Phantom Padre and the Religion of Poker."

"Look," I said to Pony and Babe.

Pony laughed. "That's an old magazine from the 1870's. Does it say who wrote the article?"

It did. And I knew the name, because Buddy had mentioned the author in his story disks—the author who had dubbed Antonio Peraza the Phantom Padre. "Somebody named Charles St. George Stanley."

"Fancy name."

Two window-mounted air conditioners, one on either side of the darkened room, gasped and shuddered pathetically. The best relief from the heat was afforded by a large fan situated at one end of the massive, two-piece cherry wood bar and blowing lengthwise across it. The bar gleamed with a ribbon of light that shone from above the electric train track. "It's the one thing Harvey's always kept up nice," said Pony as we took our places on the stools. I sat on one side of him. Babe sat on the other.

Behind the bar was an original painting of Harvey feeding a large hog, no doubt the recently departed Davidson. "That painting—one of yours, am I right?" Babe asked.

"It's worth a couple of chicken fry's, don't you think?" Pony said.

A five-foot, 165-pound waitress named Thelma, in her fifties, wearing heavy blue eye shadow and Barbie-pink lipstick, took our drink orders. Thelma had pale skin, as if she only went out at night. "Merry Christmas, y'all," she called. She seemed to know Pony and like him. "When're you gonna paint my picture like Harvey's? Don't you think I'm a lot prettier than him?"

"Hell, I had to work to make him look prettier than the hog," Pony said.

Babe's eyes followed the electric train that scooted along the track above us. "What's all this business with Christmas in August?"

"It's year round, honey," Thelma grinned. "I heard it was the only day Harvey didn't get whupped in reform school. Or some such like that. You want chicken fry or chicken fry?"

Babe leaned toward Pony when Thelma retreated to the kitchen. "That's all there is to the story?"

"Far as I know. The decorations never come down. The great thing about Harvey is, he doesn't need a reason for everything he does. Not like the rest of the world. He just does what makes him happy and that's the way it is."

Babe ruffled my hair. "Like someone else I know. You probably just made my life a lot harder, birthday boy, but I can't say it wasn't worth it. I'm gonna hang Harvey's Brownie photo in the kitchen."

I set the camera on the counter. "There isn't a photo. There wasn't any film."

"Aw, honey..." Babe started out on a note of sympathy, then broke into laughter. "No film. That old silver-tongued sonofabitch."

"I don't think it's funny," I said. "That picture could've been valuable."

"I'm really sorry, honey...Bill would have been just a blur, don't you think?"

"This was the best day of my life, besides."

"I'll tell you what," Pony said. "I'll throw one more painting in on our bargain. I'll paint that race, dust and all, and I'll go one better than that Brownie would have done. I'll put you in it like you deserve to be."

"How will you do that?"

"I'll think of a way. You know, that race'll get better and better as you remember it. A snapshot's just a snapshot. The right kind of painting is what makes a legend. And here's Harvey with our chicken fry."

Just as Harvey carried our plates to the bar, we heard a terrible, almost supernatural bellow and a loud thump. Pony bolted from his stool and ran around the bar, through the kitchen, and out the back door. Harvey dropped the plates and followed Pony. Babe and I were close behind.

In the parking lot behind the saloon, D.B. Bulland stood alone with a knife in his hand. The cowboys, already mounted on their horses in a semicircle around Bill's trailer, were egging him on. Bulland's black hat was on the ground. His lips were wet with spittle. His face, beneath a heavy, bulging brow, wore an expression that alternated between anger and uncertainty, for Bill stood in the semicircle with his head lowered, surveying the taunters who had hemmed him in. Blood from Bill's hind quarters had left a spotted trail in the dirt. It looked as if Bulland had tried to castrate Bill, but Bill had managed to back out of the trailer before he succeeded.

Pony charged Bulland like a madman. One of the cowboys leaped from his horse and bulldogged Pony to the ground. Quickly, expertly, he shoved Pony's face into the dust and pinned his arms behind his back. Another cowboy looked at Babe and me from his horse. "Best not to get involved in this," he said. "It's just a little game." Then he spoke to Pony, who was writhing beneath his attacker. "And you and the buffalo started it, grifter."

Babe pulled on my arm as if to plant me into the ground where I stood. "You are not to move no matter what I do," she said. She turned and ran to the front of the saloon.

"We didn't put up beer for no animal to drink." Bulland picked up his hat, brushed the dust off of it, and shook it toward Pony. "We don't take insults like that."

Pony continued to struggle, but the cowboy remained on top of him with a knee planted in the small of his back. The cowboys on horseback moved closer to Bill. I have had nightmares in which I see them, again and again, in a kind of slow motion, driving Bill toward the corral where Killer, thickset and agitated, a prized menace, paced restlessly. I desperately wanted Bill to fight the horses that jostled him, but he didn't. The cowboys moved him closer and closer to the corral gate.

From inside the saloon, I heard the sound of breaking glass.

As soon as a cowboy swung open the gate, Bill trotted, unresisting, into the corral where he once had stayed peacefully and stopped about twenty yards from where Killer waited at the far end. Bill stood for a moment, seemingly oblivious to the danger that confronted him. Then—again, with alarming insouciance—he lay down in a warm circle of light as if he wanted nothing more than a nap. The gate slammed shut with an ominous clang that traveled in ripples through the pipes of the corral.

Killer appeared to be assessing the situation, for he made no move at first. Finally he took two or three cautious steps backward, pawed, and bellowed. "Somebody get a stick and give old Killer a poke in the ass to start him up," yelled a cowboy.

Before another move was made, an ear-splitting voice, fierce and feral, screaming in Chinese, came from around the corner of the saloon, followed by Babe herself, who had smashed the glass case that held Harvey's white ash Louisville Slugger and who now ran, clenching the bat so tightly that her knuckles bulged like marbles, toward the cowboy on top of Pony. I had never heard Babe speak Chinese in public—only with her mother and Dwight. She clearly was fluent in ways I couldn't have imagined, as if her soul had been possessed by an avenging demon. Switching no less demonically to English, she shouted, "You chickenshit low-lifes," and brought the bat down behind the shoulders of the cowboy. The cowboy yelped and fell to the side. Pony rolled free, leaped to his feet, and ran toward the corral. Babe ran with him, still wielding the bat.

Harvey was nowhere to be seen. He had strolled with no particular urgency back toward the saloon, against the flow of townspeople who were gathering for the second major event of the day.

Killer began to display his aggression without prodding. The physical contrast between him and Bill was dramatic. Killer was smaller, but everything about him seemed suited for combat. He weighed 1600 pounds. His head was high, not plugged somewhere between his shoulders like Bill's. His horns were lethal bayonets. I had never seen a bull fight, but I could tell he was about to attack. His neck was bowed and bulging, and his eyes gleamed. His body stiffened as if he were fixing his muscles into one singular, devastating engine of ruination.

Pony vaulted over a rail and ran to the center of the corral, where he stood between Bill and Killer. "Go get 'em, grifter," shouted a cowboy.

Bill finally took notice in his own, nonchalant way. That is, he rose and kicked the dirt. Otherwise, he didn't move and didn't appear to know or care that he was in mortal danger. Instead, he stood with his side exposed to the path of the deadly bull, presenting a target ready to be disemboweled.

Pony took off his red vest and waved it, then ran a few steps toward Killer and veered to the right, drawing the bull out of Bill's path. Bill didn't budge. Killer did. He headed straight for Pony. Pony stepped to the side, turning his back, but feinted too little and too late. Killer knocked him to the ground and wheeled to avoid the corral fence. Pony lay on his stomach, gasping for breath, lucky not to have been gored, his fingers kneading the dust, while the cowboys whooped with delight. "Don't worry, grifter," one yelled. "We won't let him kill ye all the way dead."

Killer circled back to the rear of the corral, snorting, having disposed of a petty irritation, and turned his attention back to Bill.

I was on the verge of disobeying Babe and running into the corral myself when I saw Harvey walking slowly from the back of the saloon, carrying a shotgun. "Why don't you use that goddam thing, Harvey," Babe shouted.

"If I have to, I will," he replied. "But it ain't quite happy hour yet."

Killer ran forward a few paces and stopped, staring at Bill like a boxer intent on intimidating his opponent. Again, Bill struck the dirt with a hoof. Otherwise, he couldn't have seemed less concerned and didn't bother to change his position. His unprotected broadside remained exposed. He may have been trained to race, but he clearly wasn't trained to fight. He was going to die in front of our eyes.

That was enough for me. I ducked under the corral rail and ran toward Bill.

"Get back here." Babe screamed. "Get my boy out of there."

Waving the bat, Babe lunged toward the corral gate. The cowboys broke their horses out of her path and spread around the sides of the corral, more amused than afraid. Babe opened the gate and ran in. She pivoted with her bat raised to make sure no one had followed her. "Go on, get the goddam hell out of here," she yelled at me.

My intention had been to protect Bill by getting him to run, to follow me, if possible. But when I got near him, I was dumbstruck with what I only can describe as a kind of stage fright—that is, I was simultaneously aware of a hostile audience, an angry mother, agitated co-stars, and my own lack of performance skills given the circumstances. My eyes widened, my legs were rubbery, and I could do nothing but stare as if I had forgotten the one line I was given to speak.

Pony—back on his feet—glanced between me and Killer. "When I run, John," he shouted with what breath he had left, "you go the other way."

He circled in front of his murderous adversary, waving his vest like a towel, then slapped the bull on the snout, tossed the vest at him, and turned to run. I did as I was told. I took off for the other end of the corral. Killer shook off the vest and made a beeline for Pony, who was heading for the open corral gate. "He's got you dead on," Babe yelled.

Pony cut to his right and for the second time avoided Killer's horns but was struck by a body blow, tumbling forward into a headlong slide as if he were stealing second base, and smashing sideways into one of the corral poles. Killer continued toward the open gate and shot through it.

"Son of a bitch," yelled a cowboy.

Killer paused briefly outside the corral. As soon as he saw one of the horses surge toward him, he juked and ran toward the vast table land to the south. The cowboys took off after him. They didn't have much trouble catching up with him, but they didn't come back. They disappeared whooping into the plains and no doubt returned Killer to whatever pasture he had forsaken.

Babe closed the corral gate to keep Bill inside while she waited for Pony to get up again. She looked at me with fire in her eyes. "Come over here," she commanded. I did as I was told and stood next to her. Harvey and the townspeople peered through the rails at Pony, who hadn't budged. "Well, won't somebody do something?" Babe asked.

Pony moaned and spat. "It's okay, I think I'm in one piece." He was, but he stood very slowly, slapping off dust. "I'll get Bill and me out of here."

Harvey raised his shotgun and fired it into the air.

"What the hell was that?" Babe snapped.

Harvey ejected the shells and blew on the gun barrels. "Happy Hour."

I turned to Babe as we walked out of the corral. "What's a grifter?" I asked.

She ignored the question. "I'll deal with you later."

Her attention was focused on Pony, who hopped to Bill's trailer on his left leg. Bill dutifully followed him. Harvey bent over and looked at Bill's rump.

"That cut near his balls ain't deep, but Bill might be sore for a while," Harvey said. "Can't lick his *cojones* like a dog. Ever since

Eve stole that apple, God's tried to put the best things out of reach. Don't know what the dog must have done to win His holy favor."

After we had our chicken fry, Babe drove back so Pony could nurse his leg. I rode in the cab with them. I was still a bit unnerved by how I had poured out my heart to Bill and then watched him court death heedlessly, it seemed. And I had questions.

"Would that bull have killed him?" I asked Pony.

"He could have."

"He could have killed you, too," Babe said. She shoved in the cylindrical, accordion-like clutch pedal and shifted the pickup into third gear as if she wanted to stomp through the floor and rip off the gearshift. She was mad. Over the field where Bill had won his victory, clusters of tiny insects swarmed in a thin cloud of dust, darting in the filtered sunlight through the haze of the past. Bill had left plenty behind.

"So why wouldn't Bill fight him? He just stood there."

Pony grinned. "Maybe he'd had a little too much beer."

"No, really—why did he just stand there?"

"Who knows all the reasons? Bill needs some lessons that I can't teach him. By rights, I should have snuck him back into a herd already. I guess I will when summer's over."

"You mean this summer?"

Pony laughed. "Not till after I keep my appointments. He came from that refuge on the west edge of Toomis Canyon. He deserves to go back there and live his own life."

"But he won't be free."

"None of us are."

"Won't you miss him?"

"Sure, I'll miss him."

"He thinks you're his dad."

"He's nigh on a teenager, and you know how teenagers get about their parents. They're ready to leave home. You will be, too, someday."

"No, I won't. I'll stay and take care of Babe."

"That won't get you out of trouble," she said.

But I think it did. She didn't punish me then because it was my birthday. And only on one or two occasions afterwards did she say, as a mild threat, "I still owe you one for the bullfight."

I sat quietly the rest of the way back, wondering whether the plans I had just begun to form were slipping out of reach.

When we drove up Lonechap Hill again in the grizzled, retiring light of a summer afternoon, the trailer rattled and swayed all the way to the top. Pony limped out of the truck to open the trailer gate. Bill stepped down the ramp and back onto the hill. Suddenly, Pony leaned down to inspect the hitch that connected Bill's trailer to his truck. "I thought this looked low," he muttered. "Lucky I had safety chains. The flange is damn near broken off. One of the nuts was loose. Bill's not riding anywhere else till I get this fixed."

"Did one of those bastards sabotage it?" Babe asked.

Pony shook his head. "I don't know." He stood again in obvious pain. "God damn it."

"I wouldn't put it past them. Well, now you know what it's like when you piss off the Fowlers."

Despite his injury, Pony was anxious to paint. Babe ran to the barn to get a wheelchair that was stored there. Pony protested, but she made him sit in it while she and I got his supplies. Then she wheeled him to the location he had chosen, facing west toward a blooming sunset, and they set up his easel and watercolors.

He placed a small bowl inside a larger one and asked me to fill both with water from the hose. The rim of water between the two bowls was for cleaning his brushes. The small bowl was reserved for mixing his colors. His palette was rectangular, with pans of dampened colors set into it and trays that unfolded from the sides. Pony took off his red vest, tossed it into the grass, and stretched his arms.

He already had made pencil sketches of Bill and selected one that showed Bill's full profile. After taping the sketch to a thin board, he set the board on his easel and dampened the paper with a sponge. With his brushes, he began to wash the paper with color, mixing in various yellows, then more red, filling in the deepening reddish-orange of the sky above, lifting portions of the color with a clean brush to expose the white paper where the distant clouds hung. He worked quickly, shaking his head as if he were never satisfied with the combinations he chose.

Babe watched calmly. I was both excited and nervous, witnessing an act of creation that seemed to fashion a parallel world, to transform the place where we stood, a new vision of it that would mark the time and place and augment whatever memories had preceded it. I waited anxiously for Bill to appear there, where he would stay forever.

Pony spread a yellow wash where he had sketched Bill's silhouette, then applied a darker color, a burnt sienna, beneath the figure. He carefully scrubbed a dry brush filled with a darker color over the sienna patch to give it a grassy texture. Then he flicked tiny splatters of pigments into the grass, suggesting small rocks and irregular patches of earth. He looked up again, paused for a few seconds, and began to darken the yellow wash around the space where Bill was soon to materialize. Before Pony was done, the paper was infused with the tones of the setting sun, the drifting clouds, the bands of sky, the nearby grass and faraway plains.

Finally, he worked on Bill's figure, backlit by the dying sun, dark and brooding, with strong, sharp highlights around Bill's profile emphasizing his dense black mane and coarse beard. In the lower foreground, Pony also had placed objects that weren't there—three fenceposts, set askew in the tall grass on either side of Bill's profile, with a broken strand of barbed wire between them and a silver piece like the one he carried visible in the grass next to the right fencepost.

In less than an hour, he was done, and the last loose ribbon of orange drifted beneath the horizon, snuffed out in a faraway sea.

He gave the painting to me. My hands trembled as I took it.

"It's a first try," he said. "Why don't you keep it? Along with whatever of those watercolors you pick."

One other moment had defined my day. "And the painting of the race?"

"And the painting of the race. You bet. I'll get around to it."

I had forgotten that I was due a birthday cake until Babe marched out with it. It was a round, two-layer cake with white icing and my name on top. The flames of all twelve candles quivered in the evening breeze but stayed lit. Their glow danced across the three of us until I blew out the flames with one breath, and Babe and Pony sang "Happy Birthday" again. After the song, everyone fell quiet for a while. Best of all, there was no discussion about how much longer Pony and Bill might stay. For the time being, at least, Babe considered them welcome guests and Pony had painting to do. I could get Buddy's last disks whenever I wanted them.

I wished Buddy could have been with us. He of all people enjoyed the comfort of silence—no footsteps approaching, no voices calling, no fears to express, no thunder to heed. The wheelchair had belonged to Buddy. Babe hadn't touched it since the day he died in it, sitting in his favorite spot, looking toward the vacant north, turned away from the blemish of civilization while a wind corkscrewed wildly up the hill and he hallucinated an endless herd of bison crossing the deserted plain, and his industrial turntable, attached by a train of extension cords to an outlet in the barn, played Bob Wills' *Stay a Little Longer*.

I thought it was fine that Pony could make use of the chair. Maybe it would help extend his stay. The spell of the hill was exerting itself as if to grant my wishes. Near Babe's gardens, the summer air had a special fragrance. After nightfall, the hill was like the floating island of the Laputians—the universe above, the lights of Wendellton below, a constant breeze that left the impression you were moving if you closed your eyes, and the supple, scented darkness in between. Every shade in the sky seemed to be flowing against gravity toward the deep black above us, undamming the heavens so stars could flood the night in a cosmos newly arranged and spangled with dust from a magnificent race.

* * *

BUDDY WATKINS [FROM DISK #8]: *Tonight, son, I'm going to tell you how the Phantom Padre got his name, a name that would follow him to the end of his life. We'll catch up with our man Antonio, now, as he rides from Mexico into Texas, dressed like a priest so if anyone is curious, he can say he's on a church mission...*

7
How the Phantom Padre Got His Name
(And Ah Toy Became Immortal)

BUDDY WATKINS [FROM DISK #8]: *...As he rode the cracked earth in the summer heat, even when he was alone, he kept his cassock on. He was comfortable in his disguise, confident in the education he'd received from the Jesuits before he quit their way of life to become a gambler and con man and gunslinger...*

After crossing into Texas, stopping to rest in the shade of a limestone bluff, Antonio came upon a collection of Indian pictographs—images and symbols the color of red clay that depicted a massacre at a Spanish mission. Had he still been a man of faith, he might have interpreted them as a sign. The pictographs included a crude representation of a mission afire as well as figures of priests, one of them headless. Antonio picked up a smooth red rock, scraped it, spat on it, wet his finger in the fulvous liquid and swiped the outline of a prick onto the bluff. What he did not realize at the time was that one one of the figures near the mission was drawn in a horizontal position, a sign that whomever the figure represented had been taken captive or kidnapped—but not killed.

A day later, he came upon a team of eight buffalo hunters who were packing their hides for a journey to Big Fort, Antonio's destination. The hunters, teamsters and skinners were breaking camp after a month of successful hunting. They had taken down the smokehouse they used to cure the buffalo meat for sale, and they were folding and stacking bales of hides onto their wagons for the trip north. Eight of the wagons were drawn by teams of oxen, and two by mules.

The first man he encountered couldn't possibly have been a hunter, he was certain. The man was lean, sunburned, sporting a tailored vest and pants and a large, flat-brimmed hat, walking slowly around the camp and making sketches of the scene. "A mirage," the man exclaimed, looking up from his sketchbook as Antonio rode toward him. "A priest of old, riding out of nowhere, no doubt seeking to save our heathen souls." He introduced himself as Charles St. George Stanley, a graduate of London's Royal Academy. He was a striking man with dark, curly hair and a long face, unshaven for at least a week. He flashed a ready smile beneath bright blue eyes and a prominent nose.

He introduced Antonio to Robroy Wallace, the rifleman in charge of the team of hunters. Wallace asked Antonio whether he had seen signs of Indians. He had not. The hunters had gone to a great deal of trouble to avoid Indian hostilities, stopping for a while at Fort Sill in hopes of a military escort to Fort Griffin. When no escort was provided, they detoured to Denison and proceeded to Fort Griffin from there. After finally reaching the outpost, they broke up into groups that hunted in different sections of territory.

Fort Griffin was also where the hunters had met Charles St. George Stanley, who had just finished painting recumbent nudes on a saloon wall at Big Fort. He asked to accompany them so he could make sketches for "A Buffalo Hunter's Life," an article he was writing for Frank Leslie's *Illustrated Newspaper*.

Wallace was the one who did most of the killing for his group. The others worked as teamsters, skinners and cooks, and cured the meat they sacked for sale.

"Unfortunately," said St. George Stanley over coffee, "They've had a bloody boring time of it here. Mr. Leslie's publication likes battle stories with lots of stalwart heroes in them. Forgive me, Padre, but you have made this even more resemble Sunday school. What's worse, you speak the King's English like a native, not like the fire-and-brimstone preachers who'd have us think we're already sent to hell. Which we may have been. Myself, at the very least." The artist was garrulous and charming but always entertaining, as no doubt he needed to be among the men he followed and sketched, rough or civilized. Antonio thought of friends he had known in the Mexico City underworld—talented, charismatic, observant, ingratiating, able to travel in virtually any circle and wait for whatever opportunities presented themselves. That was Charles St. George Stanley.

Wallace laughed. "And even where preachers dare to go, we don't see your kind, a left-footer like ye." Wallace was round-cheeked and prematurely gray, a solid man with hard and piercing eyes. "Ye sure you're a padre, man?"

"I am a Jesuit."

"Ah, the rich and dangerous kind, that the Pope himself fears, so I've heard. And not welcome down south, either, among your own. Ye're not preachin' out of your own pulpit in these parts, for certain. Ye fixin' to join the army, perhaps?"

"I go where I am needed. The Bishop of Galveston has asked me to find Catholics wherever they may be in this unsettled area, to offer them the comfort of our faith. So many have been separated from it."

"Well, I heard there's a call for left-footers to salve the spirits of their fighting Catholic brethren in these territories. Some say it's bad for discipline, divides the soldiers, I'm sure you know, do ye? Ah, I see it in your face. Perhaps ye do, and ye'd just as well keep it to yourself. Well, I care not about it, Padre. Nothing wrong about a chaplain to join the soldiers and bless the killing. If that's what ye're about, I'll bless you myself. I'd spit on the bastard refused us an escort, but nothing against the fighting man."

"Seen any miracles on your way?" St. George Stanley asked. "I need something to illustrate other than carcasses and hides."

"Only the miracles of each new day," Antonio replied.

"Enough said, Padre," Wallace said. "Ye're welcome to ride with us up to Big Fort if ye wish. There's Indian trouble up and down the range. The reservation agents have told them now's the time to declare for peace or war, and the ones that take the warpath will find Uncle Sam comin' for them. It's only these rifles we carry that keeps 'em at a safe distance. Nothing beats the range of a Sharps. But we can always use the divine help, if ye're a padre."

"I am with you." Antonio grinned. His pistol was still hidden in the folds of his cassock, holstered beneath the belt in which he carried the gold from the Perazas. "And if the fight is bad, I can take your confession quickly."

St. George Stanley already was working in his sketchbook on a portrait of Antonio. "I hate to tell you, Padre, but for eliciting confession there is nothing like the buffalo himself, from what I'm told. I've heard there are tribes in the north that choose a brave to keep a buffalo skull in his teepee so they can go there and confess all their sins and shortfalls to the skull. Even if they buggered the skull-keeper's wife, they still confess. Not because they want to brag, mind you. They think that buffalo skull has the power to curse them and cause them an almighty calamity if they lie. And won't that be why anybody ever confesses, Padre? Because they believe if they don't, something even worse will happen. The buffalo is God to the Indian folk in lots of ways, and that's why they take to war against these men whose hospitality we are enjoying around this campfire."

"Then their god's going to disappoint them by disappearing from these lands," Wallace said.

St. George Stanley closed his sketchbook, offered a cigar to Wallace, who accepted, and lit one for himself. "I should warn you, Padre, you will not find men to be any more civilized than those skull-worshipers if you go with us to Big Fort. I spent time there myself, just before joining this journey, and I would wager there are no souls there worth saving—well, maybe one—and certainly no signs that your God has yet discovered that outpost. Am I to presume you know no one there?"

Antonio smiled as he saw his opening. "You are correct. I know only of a man who may or may not be there, someone a fellow priest met once, a man named Lehane."

St. George Stanley's blue eyes widened as his mouth twisted into an expression of dismay. "Lehane? Did you hear that, Wallace?"

"I heard. Pigeye Lehane, I'm guessing, although you'd best call him Patrick if you want to live."

"A giant of a man, so I'm told," said Antonio. "With long, blond hair and a bulging eye."

"Do you know much about this Lehane? Do you count him as a friend?" St. George Stanley asked.

"No, nothing like that. It's simply that the priest referred me to him as a man of our faith, journeying in the direction I was going. I am carrying a Bible that my fellow priest asked me to give to him in exchange for...well, an object of the church that he protected. And if he is of the faith, it is men like that who I seek to help me."

"Well, the man may profess the faith, but he'd be bloody laughable if he weren't also a cold-blooded killer. He's the type who finds the only thorn in a field of flowers so that he might prick himself and take offense from the multitudes—and then proceed with his revenge. And I doubt he reads the Bible, Padre. Although Pigeye puts the fear of God into those who don't believe, so I suppose he's a better preacher than you. He was a bloody scalp hunter, among other things. Got in early, before your Civil War. Famous for blowing up one Indian village with cannon fire, then scalping all the dead. Fought for the Southern states and, they say, he got a head wound that swelled up around some shrapnel and caused one of his eyes to bulge. When the war was over, he went back to what he knew best, robbing and even more scalp hunting, though its time seems to have passed. Hard to tell a man he's been made obsolete when he's had so much enjoyment from his work."

Antonio appeared shocked and shook his head. "That is valuable to know. Thank you."

St. George Stanley blew smoke rings, perfect, feathery circles that dissolved into the night past the edge of the firelight. His face changed expressions constantly and he spoke with bursts of speed, as if his thoughts were racing too far ahead of him and he needed to catch up to them. "I do know the strangest story about him—about what the weaker sex can do, actually. Happened at Big Fort, too. Damned if he didn't fall in love, if that's what you'd call it in a man like him. A beautiful girl. Almost a goddess. Works in the saloon as a wait-girl, but not as a whore. I knew her somewhat myself, as I studied her face to paint a likeness of it on the saloon wall. I also gave her drawing lessons. She's quite talented. A natural. Draws children and animals, mostly, and very realistically. I gladly left one of my sketchbooks with her, poor girl.

"Well, your Mr. Lehane declared he would marry her and return to Missouri to buy a farm, make himself an honest man and father little pig-eyed brats. The problem was, her guardian—my patron, the trader who runs Big Fort—seems to understand her power over men, and uses it to fleece any and all prospective suitors. He has made poker his virtual religion, and insists that any man worthy of the girl must be tested in the game against Fowler himself—that's the guardian's name, Fowler, Zebulon. So far, rumor has it that he has cleaned out a few rash men, and if you wonder that he hasn't been killed for it, well, he supplies the losers with their choice of a whore for the night, no hard feelings. And most men have come to regard the contest as the kind of entertainment sadly lacking in these territories and a reason to tease the girl when she serves them. They've actually become somewhat protective of her. The curious have made a special pilgrimage just to look at her, which adds to Fowler's saloon profits. All in all, I'd wager she's better business than a whore. And now there is this...this suspense over the great game. Can anyone win her? Fowler himself is well-protected, and he is popular." St. George Stanley's gesture swept across the camp. "He pays well for what these buffalo runners bring him. And then there is your Mister Lehane. He played for the hand of our beautiful barmaid, but like the others he lost his entire stake to Fowler, refused the whore, and left town in a huff, vowing to return with a new stake and not be beaten the next time. He didn't need to kill Fowler. He simply threatened to kill any man who tried to win the girl before he came back. Love-struck in the extreme, and no one who knew him could have guessed he'd make a fool of himself that way."

"What does the girl say to all this?" Antonio asked.

"If she confides in anyone, they manage to keep her secrets well. She does her job, smiles rarely, tolerates her fame, and lives away from the whores with a Chinese laundress who works for Fowler. She is kind, I know. I saw her care for an injured Indian boy once. And she prays, I'm told, probably to the God of your faith, Padre, but who knows? In a corner by the stables behind the saloon, there's a little room with a cross and some benches in it. The altar is a wooden table used to lay out corpses for burial. Some good Methodist preacher saw to it. She goes there of a morning, I'm told, stinking corpse or no stinking corpse." He tossed the stub of his cigar into the fire. "I have a few sketches of her in my case. Would you like to see them?"

St. George Stanley was a more than decent artist. His sketches of the barmaid Selenia Garza captured even her melancholy shyness when it would have been more to his advantage to make his subject openly alluring. Antonio thought the sketches were breath-taking. "That is the most beautiful woman I ever saw," he said.

"Careful, Padre. I take that as a compliment on my abilities, not your libido."

"And she is real?"

"Even more bloody beautiful, if you can imagine that. All she lacks is a knight in shining armor who can pass that perverted test for her hand."

Antonio took the sketches in his own hands and, by the firelight, studied each portrait.

"The rest of those boys prefer some of my other sketches." St. George Stanley picked up another book and flipped through the pages, which were full of nudes, most recumbent but some standing with arms behind their heads, staring toward the artist. "I do sell these, for a pittance, to support my Bohemian life. Would you care to see?"

89

Antonio shook his head. "No, thank you."

"Of course not. Virginal innocence for you. But then you might be interested in one of my most popular items, an object of faith, indeed, you might call it." St. George Stanley withdrew a small, rectangular framed picture from a knapsack. It was a portrait of a nun. "I've sold these to a few of the devout to keep in their homes or businesses, even those not of your persuasion. It appears to be of some historic value, but..." St. George Stanley flipped a lock on the back of the frame, removed the portrait, turned it over, and slid it back into the housing. On the other side was a portrait of a voluptuous nude. "In the privacy of their rooms, family men find this a pleasant diversion which they can hide in plain sight. A profitable sacrilege, it is."

Antonio wanted to laugh, but he turned his head away. "No offense meant," said St. George Stanley. "Saint or sinner, we are all treading the same death-dealing expanse as a reward for our exertions." The artist yawned and excused himself to go sleep.

The teamsters and skinners alternated picket duty during the night. One man patrolled the outskirts of the camp while the others slept. Antonio laid out his saddle and bedroll. He remained in his cassock. Each night, before sleeping, he wound his pocketwatch and noted the positions of the stars. He enjoyed picturing himself living the life of a grandee in Spain. He had never rested as well. But on that night, his mind was roiling with schemes based on Pigeye Lehane and his weakness for the barmaid Selenia. He rose after an hour of sleeplessness and walked to a mesquite thicket near a draw west of the camp, where he could keep an eye on the camp while he formed a plan. He sat, leaned against a mesquite tree, and watched the camp's picket approach from the south.

Suddenly, Antonio heard a light twang and—less than twenty yards from where he sat—he saw the picket drop forward onto his face with an arrow in his back. He jumped to his feet and skirted the back of the thicket. Then he saw the man who had shot the arrow rise out of the tall grass and approach the dead picket. Two other men joined the bowman. Antonio looked quickly around but saw no other men, only the silhouettes of horses—he counted three—in the distance to the west. The other two men were equipped with rifles, and they were pointing left and right. They were so close that he could understand their whispers. They had scouted the hunting party, and their intent was to separate and enter the camp from three directions. Each man would choose three sleeping bodies to kill.

Antonio reached through the pocket he had tailored into the fold of his cassock, pulled out his Remington revolver, and stepped into the open, walking briskly toward the men. He had decided not to act until he was spotted, so he could move as close to them as possible.

The man who first heard Antonio's footsteps grunted and peered into the darkness. He raised his rifle and turned toward Antonio, who immediately cut him down with a blast from the Remington. Those who were in camp were awakened immediately by the first shot, then heard two more in quick succession.

All three men lay dead in the grass.

Once the camp was roused, Wallace was the first to arrive. Speechless at first, Wallace looked at Antonio, saw that the camp had been saved—"Ooh, yah cun'," he said finally—then broke out laughing. "I never knew ye was armed, Padre," he cried. "But that's not the half of it. By God, ye drilled three armed men like they was sacks of flour. Is that what they teach ye in the seminaries, now?"

"I was steadied by the hand of God, I suppose," Antonio said. He was sweating, but his voice was even. "Of course I carry protection from rattlesnakes and the like."

"God must love his Jesuits. Even I am proud to stand with you tonight, Padre. And if the good Father won't mind, we'll bury our own and leave the other three to rot. See, the cowards used an Indian arrow to start their mayhem without wakin' us."

By that time, St. George Stanley had joined the group. "I'm a bugger," was all he said. "Are there more, do you think?"

"Not likely," said Wallace. He kicked the bodies and sent a man to retrieve the horses of the intruders. "There's no way they could have done business with our hides. All they wanted was to kill us and rob us for what they could get—valuables and horses and livestock and such. Probably knew exactly how many of us there were. Just some damn stupid hungry outlaws..." He grinned. "But they didn't count on the Holy Ghost stealing up on them like the phantom he is."

"Well, by God, I have my action, now," St. George Stanley exclaimed. "Frank Leslie's never read an adventure like this one. Saved by the Padre—the Phantom Padre, he'll be. You'll be a famous man, Padre. I love it. The Phantom Padre saves the day. Some bloody hack will re-do my sketches for the cover, that's the sad truth of it, but I'll make them so bold even he can't ruin them."

"It's fine ye're excited because there'll be no more sleep tonight," said Wallace. "I doubt they had friends, but we'll take no chances. We'll finish loading and start early for Big Fort."

"And there's a nice, grand ball of a moon to add into my sketch of this scene," said St. George Stanley. "Moonrise upon the prairie when one is confident of security and peace presents a beautiful picture, but when the zest of danger is added, the scene then is one of indescribable peculiarity, don't you agree? Things are exactly the same, and yet they're not. How to capture that in a painting, eh?"

* * *

BUDDY WATKINS [FROM DISK #9]: *...Far from the excitement of the camp, in the small square behind Big Fort, another strange and horrible incident was unfolding, and it would also have its effect on the newly-dubbed Phantom Padre...*

Selenia was asleep. Ping sat beneath the overhang of her laundry shack, watching Ah Toy explore. The cat always made Ping smile. Ah Toy was spirited and entertaining—witty, even, in her own way—and most certainly a gift from the southern gate of heaven, a sign that Ping was noticed and worthy. That much, Ping allowed herself to believe despite the fact that her view of the world from the laundry shack revealed the filthy, stinking, garbage-strewn square and stables behind the saloon.

Ah Toy went into the square on her scavenger hunts during the quietest hours at Big Fort. Then, when Ping's pipe smoke wafted from the porch in front of the laundry, Ah Toy sensed that it was a signal to come in. On that dark, early morning in August, the cat climbed over a drum of garbage and paused at the top to look toward where her mistress sat smiling and puffing. Ah Toy jumped down and began to skirt the walls of the stables, heading home. A man, large and burly, leaned against a post in front of the stables. Ah Toy continued to walk briskly toward the laundry, then stopped to clean her coat.

The man's arm swept forward. Within seconds, he had grabbed the cat and bashed her head against the post. The beginning of Ah Toy's scream sounded like a curse from the depths of hell. The end was a wail of excruciating pain as the man heaved her into the service square. He yawned and wiped his hands on his pants and walked out of the square. The side of his face was visible in the early light. Ping was too afraid to move or cry out. As soon as the man was gone, she rushed into the square to pick up Ah Toy and carry her back into the laundry.

Selenia was shocked out of her sleep by the cry. She jumped from her mattress so Ping could set Ah Toy gingerly onto the stack of old clothes. Then she went to get Ah Toy's porcelain bowl, but Ping waved her off. Instead, Ping rose and retrieved the tin bowl of water from her ironing table. She shook as if she was buffeted by some unseen force. "Fucking bastard,' she said. "I remember his fucking face. I kill him." She placed the tin bowl near Ah Toy's nose. Selenia stood behind Ping and steadied her while the laundress lowered herself to sit cross-legged near the cat. Ah Toy's head was bleeding and her back was broken. She hunched her front shoulders, dipped her head toward the water and lapped up a few drops. Gradually, she extended her front paws and dragged herself slowly off the mattress of discarded clothing and towards Ping. Finally, Ah Toy came to rest in front of her mistress and companion. Ping bent forward with her good eye fixed on Ah Toy. The cat tilted her head briefly toward Ping, returning the gaze. Then she died. Ping picked up Ah Toy and placed her gently in the lap of her trousers and vowed again that she would kill the man who had hurt her.

* * *

At sunrise, before Antonio and the buffalo hunters set out, a lone buffalo bull crossed the distant northern horizon. Antonio pointed toward the animal. "Will there be a herd of them to follow?"

"There's plenty out there, but they won't be following that old one," said Wallace. "He's on his last legs, and he knows the end is near. He's no longer the source of fortunes, just part of the scrapheap."

"He is worth nothing to you?"

"Look at them stacks of hides on our wagons. Why shouldn't I leave him be? When I became a runner, somebody told me there was twenty million buffalo running loose and each one was worth three dollars, maybe more, mainly for the hides. It's nothing to kill a hundred in a day. The wagons cost me two thousand. Took six days shooting to pay for them, and four more for the mules. I already had me good saddle horses. After that, costs me 25 cents for a cartridge to shoot one with. That's a pretty return the world over, three dollars, even three-fifty, for one bit. 'Course, the man you spoke of, that Pigeye, he'll kill ye for naught. And the least I can do is to tell ye to keep away from him."

Charles St. George Stanley rode beside Antonio as they left camp. "I owe you my life, Padre, and perhaps even a small percent of my fortune. And on my honor as an Englishman, if there is ever anything I can do to repay you, I stand ready."

"I may wish to call on you then," said Antonio.

"Feel free."

Antonio was more anxious than ever to get to Big Fort because of the sketches he had seen of Selenia. He had known more than his share of women, whores and virgins and aristocratic beauties alike, but something about the sketches had affected him in a strange, almost mystical way. *I must already be in love with her*, he laughed to himself. And he was determined to bed her after he used her to swindle the Star of Andalusia from Pigeye Lehane.

He was delighted that he had found a confederate of sorts in St. George Stanley. Antonio felt comfortable telling him, in confidence, that he not only was on a mission from the Bishop of Galveston, but that the real reason he sought Lehane was that the object the outlaw protected was not just an artifact of value only to the church. It was a priceless jeweled gold star that had disappeared, along with the missionary who carried it, more than a century before. St. George Stanley whistled when he heard the history of the Star of Andalusia. "So this will require much more than just finding the man and clapping a Bible into his hands," he said. "You must somehow discover where and how he keeps it, and convince him—or use other persuasions—to take leave of the possession he values most. That requires a plan, Padre."

"It does, I'm afraid."

"You may trust my discretion. Although when this is over, I may make a Penny Dreadful out of it. The Phantom Padre and the Star of Gold. I'll help in any way I can."

The Englishman was immediately of service, since he knew both the barmaid Lehane desired and the owner of Big Fort. When they arrived at the outpost, St. George Stanley guided Antonio straight into the office of Zebulon Fowler and supplied a glowing introduction. "Meet the next great legend of the West," he said, "the

Phantom Padre here in your very establishment." He waited outside while Antonio placed his gold and his letter of credit in Zebulon's safe. Zebulon was impressed and curious to know more. He laughed when Antonio opened his cassock to strap the gold belt back around his waist. "You're eight or nine pounds lighter now, eh, Padre? But you like the feel of the belt, I'll wager, even when it's empty. Your gold'll be safer here than in a Mexican bank, I guarantee. This is one of the few iron safes within a thousand miles." Then he asked the question Antonio had been waiting for. "And why might you be carrying such a fortune, Padre, if you don't mind my asking?"

Within the next five minutes, the two men decided they had mutual interests. Lehane's threats had been costing Zebulon Fowler money.

Zebulon sent a man to arrange a hotel room for Antonio, and advised him to leave whatever he could in his saddlebag. Antonio carried another cassock, two Bibles, some eating utensils, and even a host box so he could conduct a mass if someone insisted. "Better to leave them with the horse," Zebulon said, "instead of a hotel room where they can disappear before you reach the bottom of the stairs on the way out."

Antonio nodded and grinned at the comments he received as he walked in his cassock past hidemen, traders, and teamsters. It was appropriate, he thought, to first visit the shabby chapel made of cheap wooden slats between the saloon garbage dump and the stables. The chapel—otherwise the morgue—was small, barely ten by twelve feet. A table on a platform was used both as an altar and as a slab for bodies. On the wall above it, two lengths of wood, nailed together and hung by a wire, served as a cross. There were no windows. The table was partially covered by a bloodstained sheet which, in turn, covered the stinking corpse of a Fort Griffin corporal who had been knifed to death two nights before, still waiting to be claimed by the military. The corporal's hat sat on top of the sheet.

That is where Antonio saw her for the first time. In the light that crept into the room from its half-open door, Selenia Garza was kneeling and praying, with her hands clasped together and resting on the bench in front of her. She looked back when she heard Antonio enter. Then, without a word, she rose and walked to him, touching him on the arm as if she barely could believe he existed. A tear ran down her cheek. "My prayer has been answered," she said.

In the second it took him to catch his breath, Antonio understood how much truth there was in the tales he heard of her from St. George Stanley. Even the sketches he had fallen in love with failed to do her justice. Selenia was stunningly beautiful. She was nineteen years old, with a delicately turned nose, full lips—wider than most—and eyes so dark and magnetic that Antonio wished he had nowhere else to look. The expression on her face was perfectly composed, even when streaked with tears. She wore a sleeveless, beltless, white cotton chemise over a perfect figure. When a shaft of light struck her shining black hair, Antonio was certain he saw within it streaks of dark colors, purple or red like the iridescent streaks of a bird's feathers. In Mexico City, he would have had her in bed that night, no matter what it took or what he had to promise.

But as lost as he was, drinking in the sight of her, he knew she also must be a pawn, his pawn, in his quest for the Star of Andalusia. And he had a role to play. He took her hand gently. "I am Father Antonio Peraza," he said. "Please, tell me what it is that you have prayed for."

"That God might come to this place, Padre." After she spoke, her eyes darted to the door. Antonio glanced back and saw what appeared to be the figure of a young Indian boy in a white shirt holding a sling of some sort. The boy shifted back and forth on his bare feet. Selenia held up her hand as if to calm him. "He is just a boy," she said. "He means no harm to you. He only wishes to protect me. His name is Young Eagle." She smiled and nodded toward him, and he bowed and disappeared without a word. "I am Selenia Garza."

"And how can God answer your prayers, Selenia?"

"I am sad for myself, Padre, but sadder for a friend who is in mourning. I was praying for her."

"And who is she mourning?"

"Her cat."

"Her cat?"

"Her cat. She had a name. Ah Toy. She was killed by a bad man, and my friend will never forget his face."

Selenia went on to describe Ping, who had no one but her cat to speak to openly and honestly. The Chinese laundress had been kind to both Selenia and the boy, Young Eagle. "So before we speak of my other prayers," Selenia said, "will you help her?"

"I will speak to her of God, but I have heard the Chinese are a heathen race."

"She is not of our faith, of course." Selenia's voice was soft, almost hypnotic. "But she suffered and loved as if she were."

"She loved her cat."

"Yes, Padre."

"What are you suggesting?"

"In the saloon there is a buffalo—not alive, but stuffed. It looks alive, though. Could the cat be made to look alive again?"

Antonio could say nothing other than yes, he would try to have it done.

Selenia paid him a compliment. "I think that you have seen more and understand more than most priests, if you will care for such a small thing as the soul of a cat."

"You are good as well." Antonio squeezed her hand. "And you must have many admirers."

"That is what hurts me, Padre. If you stay more than a few hours, you will hear why. But why have you come here? Here there is no Holy Church. Here we have no dignity."

"That is the mission I was sent on—to find those who are like you, separated from our faith." Antonio proceeded with his cover story and also—swearing her to secrecy—with a history and description of the Star of Andalusia which, he said, the church and its agents had been seeking to recover for more than a hundred years. It was his belief, based on what a priest in Mexico had told him, that the Star had been seen in the possession of a man whose destination was Big Fort. He did not mention who the man was.

"It must be a beautiful star," Selenia said.

"It is made of gold, with a ruby at its heart."

"Some people understand only the gold, Padre. Not the sacrifice of Our Lord."

"I know only too well. And you may trust me with your confidence as I now trust you with mine."

"I do, Padre." Selenia reached into the pocket of her dress. "And please accept this for your good works, and for the Holy Mother Church. And for Ping's cat." Selenia handed him the silver dollar that Zebulon Fowler gave her when he bought her from her uncle. The image on it was of a woman seated on a rock, gazing into the distance, her right hand touching a shield. "This woman, could she be a saint?"

"Her shield says, 'Liberty.' *La libertad.* Freedom."

"Oh. Anyway, please take her, even if she is not a saint. She is all I have. I have been so far from the church."

Antonio took the coin and kissed it. "I will hold this for you. But it will always be yours, whenever you wish to claim it."

At the laundry, somewhat reluctantly under Selenia's urging, Ping agreed to give the body of her cat to the priest who could see that it was preserved. Lovingly, Ping folded Ah Toy into one of her old shirts and handed the bundle to Antonio. She turned away as he left the shack. She had forgotten how to cry, but her body was twisted with grief and shaking nevertheless.

Antonio was referred by the clerk at the hotel to a former hideman named Lester Turner, who had preserved the buffalo in Fowler's saloon. Rather than carrying the dead cat with him, he left it under the bed in his hotel room while he roamed Big Fort and looked for Turner. That evening, he finally found the part-time taxidermist behind the counter in a warehouse where he earned his living as a foreman. Turner rummaged beneath the counter and came up with a mahogany piece to serve as a mount. Antonio gave him a twenty dollar gold coin, far more than the job was worth. "If I am away when you're done," Antonio said, "whoever claims the cat will have a piece of paper with my signature on it. It will match the signature I'm about to give you." On the bottom of the mahogany mount, using a pen and ink supplied by Turner, he wrote, "Fr. Peraza."

"Well, Padre," said Turner, holding up the gold piece, "this guarantees I'll do my best, but that means it'll take time to skin the cat, preserve the skull, tan the hide, then make a straw form. I fit the hide to the form. It'll have wires running through it to set the pose. At the end it's filled out with some newspaper stuffing. So count on getting it back in two or three weeks, including time for it to dry properly if you want it to last."

"God created it," said Antonio. "Do your best to imitate Him." He tipped the flat brim of his black hat, adjusted his cassock and walked back into the square, blending into the night.

* * *

BUDDY WATKINS [FROM DISK #10]: *...People think of phantoms, they think of ghosts. And things you don't see. And then you do. And then you don't again. No doubt that's what Charles St. George Stanley had in mind when he invented his Phantom Padre stories and drew his pictures of a man in black camouflaged by the very darkness around him. But there's also a phantom that's part of all of us. Something unfinished. Something about ourselves that haunts us till we come to terms with it. If you're not sure what I mean now, maybe you will be by the time I get to the end of these stories.*

8
Under the Spell of the Hill

The next few days after Bill's race were the best of my life. In the morning, while Babe gardened, I explored the hill with Pony and Bill. Pony had a metal detector in his pickup. We might find old coins, he said, or bullets that were signs of long-ago battles, maybe even a shell from a Remington Army revolver—why not? He seemed most interested in the areas where the hill bulged as it sloped, creating protrusions that, when the sun was not directly overhead, threw bulky shadows broad enough to sit in. Something beneath one of the southeastern outcroppings covered in mesquite shrub set off a strong, persistent tone in the detector, and we agreed that at some point we'd see what we could dig out of it.

He taught me the whistle that called Bill. In each hand, I joined my middle and index fingers, then made a 'v' by placing the tips of my index fingers together. I shoved the fingers into my mouth, pushed back my tongue, and blew. It took a lot of practice, but I eventually perfected the technique. It always brought Bill running to us. Bill's eagerness also had to do with what Pony carried in his vest pockets—the carrots that were Bill's favorite snack food. Bill did a kind of stiff-legged jump-dance when he wanted more. "That's what I saw after the race," I grinned.

"You're catching on," said Pony.

Babe went to the market in Wendellton and bought bundles of carrots so I could feed them to Bill and watch his dance.

We paid no attention to whether the spook had appeared or not.

I loved observing all of Bill's playful moments—bumping and butting a bale of hay that Pony got from the barn, or, most astoundingly, vaulting into the air as if he expected to fly when he reached a dropoff on the hill. Often, he returned to leap again until he tired of it. When Pony scratched him under an eye, Bill turned and licked Pony's face with a gloppy, dripping tongue, a giant sponge of saliva. Pony fell over backwards avoiding a second lick. The side of his face was red and he was laughing, but he warned me to be mindful signs that Bill was about to deliver a kiss. "If you get a couple of licks, you'll know he likes you, and the rest of the world will know, too. They'll see it all over you. That tongue's as rough as an emery board."

Bill also liked to be brushed. First, Pony pulled tufts of hair from his coat, then ran a stiff brush through his mane, over his hump, and along his side. Pony let me try my hand at it, but I was too short to reach the top of Bill's hump. Using Buddy's old riding gear from the barn, Pony fashioned a makeshift bridle that slid over Bill's nose and mouth. The long reins were connected by a strap that fit across Bill's back just behind his hump. Beyond the strap, the end of each rein was looped to serve as a kind of stirrup so I could insert my feet for balance. Pony lifted me onto Bill's back, where I sat just behind the hump and steadied myself in the stirrups while I brushed. Pony stood by to catch me in case Bill decided to take off, but he remained perfectly still until I was done.

"The day I'd like to have seen," Pony said while I brushed, "is the day they let the buffalos back out on the plains after almost driving them to extinction. You know where Bill's ancestors came from?"

"From somewhere around here?"

"A few generations back, no doubt. But his recent ancestors came from the Bronx. New York. They were rescued and protected in the Bronx Zoo when the bison slaughter was ending. Enough people had decided they loved bison as creatures, not just as tanned hides and leather goods. In the Bronx, zoo employees nursed the rescued bison and their offspring as if it were the last call for the buffalo, because it nearly was. And twenty-five years or so after the slaughter was over and the buffalo had all but disappeared, they put fifteen bison onto some horse cars from New York and sent them on an 18 hundred mile journey back to where they had roamed for thousands of years. With all kinds of fanfare, they let them off the railcars in the southwestern Oklahoma prairie. Eight thousand acres. That was the nation's first buffalo refuge.

"I'd love to have been there to paint the hullabaloo—the mobs of people that cheered along the rail sidings, while the buffalo were marched off the cars. The ones who thought that somehow things could be put back to rights, and that it was worth a celebration. I'd have painted the crowds big and colorful and full of motion and faceless, in a roiling, chaotic mass on the right. The ones I'd have put at the left edge of the picture were the ones whose hearts must've broken at the sight, the old warriors who knew that everything was lost because they had lost it, too. And I guarantee you, son, if the day comes again when a buffalo steps out of his refuge and crosses the line to someplace he's not welcome, he'll be shot down just like his ancestors. The difference is, the bodies'll wind up behind chain link fences in garbage dumps instead of rotting out on the plains."

I remembered a poem with which Buddy had ended one of his stories, "Why the Buffalo's Head Hangs Low."

Buffalos were everywhere
When hunters took their measure.
Some say bison made us rich
With carcasses for treasure.
We never tendered gratitude.
We never spoke our sorrows
To those great beasts who made our feasts
And gave us our tomorrows.

Bill walked with us, but at his own pace, sometimes deliberate, sometimes brisk, grunting whenever we were out of sight. Once, he buried his nostrils for several minutes in the patch of shame vines where Babe made me sit when she was mad at me. The vines grew on the northeast side of the hill, running along a broad, rippling arm just above a series of gullies that bubbled with water in a heavy rain. The pink, fragrant flowers looked like puff balls with tiny yellow tips on their filaments. Shame vines are so named because their leaflets recoil against each other when touched, as if to decline companionship. I liked to test them with my fingers while avoiding the curved, prickly extensions on the stems that gave the plant its more common name—catclaw sensitive briar. At first, I enjoyed watching them shy away from my touch. Then I decided that I wanted them to trust me—to stay open and vulnerable and unashamed. But they never did. I was too young to identify them as the Ovidian confessors they were—erring mortals, metamorphosed, doing penance for their vanity by shrinking from all admiring contact. Bill ate them and moved on.

I knew that Bill was not a creature of the elements where others like him were weaned, where behavior was governed by a herd. Nor was I. And the thought, not yet fully formed, that crept into my mind was that neither Bill nor I could stay on the hill forever, that those days, as Buddy had intimated, were loaned to us and that the real future, with all its battles, its triumphs, its disasters, waited elsewhere.

Even one of the things I hated most—a symbol of my ineptitude when confronted by bullies—was transformed under Pony's instruction. He had noticed the punching bag that was hanging in the barn not far from where he slept. It was a sore point with me. Babe had hung the bag and given me boxing gloves a few months before. The clear implication was that I should learn how to fight, rather than continue to come home from school with multiple bruises, lying about how I got them. Without being able to tell her, I felt that any practice with a punching bag would be useless against the diabolically choreographed onslaughts of the Fowler brothers.

When Pony suggested that I give the bag a try, he swore that Babe hadn't said a word to him about it. "You should know something about fighting. You never had a fight at school?"

"No," I lied.

Pony nodded as if he believed me, but his eyes told a different story. "Well, just in case it ever happens, show me what you do know." Pony already had painted a large, flesh-colored nose on the bag. "That'll give you something to aim for."

I put on my gloves while Pony made sure the bag was even with my chin. I had to stand on an overturned crate. Then I threw my own awkward punches, which usually resulted in the bag swinging away before I could hit it a second time. More than once, it rebounded into my face. "Feet apart, shoulder width," Pony said. He demonstrated the stance as if it were second nature to him. "Stand back farther so it won't hit you on the rebound. Use the length of your arms to your advantage. Now—bring your fists up to your chin and raise your elbows till they're parallel to the ground. Fists and elbows together in one smooth motion. Punch the bag, don't flail at it." He showed me how to strike the bag with the side of my fist, then bring the fist back around in a small circle and wait for the third rebound to hit the bag again while it still was tilted away from me. In a few moments, I had a rhythm going, rolling my fists over each other—a one-two-three rat-a-tat that was music to my ears. By lowering my elbows a bit, I could throw a straight punch, then a combination of straight and circle punches. The gloves, I decided, weren't so stupid after all. They gave Pony the opportunity to teach me what a father would teach.

After bedtime, I slept for only a few hours, then got up in the early morning darkness to take carrots to Bill. I put on a shirt and a pair of jeans over my pajamas and slipped barefoot into my boots. Then, quietly, I lifted the sash and climbed out boots first. I also brought my hair brush. Bill was waiting for me, or so I made myself believe. I wandered under the firmament into the high, wet grass south of our house, on the downward slope of the hilltop, trance-like but conscious, aware that Bill stood not far ahead of me. His enormous, humped silhouette, wise and patient and powerful, was perfectly still. His red blanket had been spread out on the grass.

I was familiar with every inch of the hill, every rock, every place to hide in the open. I could feel its pulse quicken if there was danger, as there had been on the day Darryl and Cameron Fowler dared to cross County Road 207 and follow me onto its lower slope to push me into the grass and kick me and call Babe a whore before running back across the road. Now, no one else, no being other than Bill, was nearby in those early hours, I could tell. I drew near Bill and stood for a moment regarding him—he did not return my look—then I lowered myself into the grass and sat there at the edge of his blanket, feeling the dampness seep into the jeans on my crossed legs, looking up at the winking, conspiratorial stars and pretending to have my own agenda of thoughts, as if both Bill and I happened to be in the same spot at the same time by no unusual coincidence. The moon threw just enough light for me to see a slight bulge that glistened and quavered like a tear in Bill's eye. He turned his head. A star shone at the tip of his horn, another at his hump, and another at the end of his hind quarters. I spent a few moments looking for the constellations that Pony had pointed out, and found them easily. I did not know enough then to realize that his novel definitions of the stars were also key to why Pony and Bill were there at that time. I only marveled at those alternate revelations, the way we marvel at discovering new layers of old truths.

Those nights I spent with Bill, I talked non-stop, brushing him occasionally as high as I could reach, until just before dawn. I climbed back through my window and into bed only moments before Babe came to check on me. Usually, she would have awakened me, but those mornings, she left the room silently to let me sleep late. I'm sure it was because she and Pony enjoyed the early mornings together, drinking coffee and looking over his sketches before Babe went out to her gardens. I wondered whether I no longer had to think of myself as her protector, and I wondered whether I liked that.

I was still too young and unseasoned to realize that Babe and Pony had become lovers the night of my birthday, when she went to the barn with a bottle of bourbon to see to his injuries. But I definitely sensed the changes in Babe. I knew something had happened because she quit wearing her gun. She had worn it since the day Buddy died.

Babe had fought fiercely and aggressively for the hill and must have regarded it with notions far less utopian than mine. It seemed strange that now, even Babe was softened by romance.

In hindsight, I can understand why. To Buddy, she had been a caregiver. Buddy adored her unstintingly. Their roles were predictable. Regardless of what phases their marriage ran through, she behaved the same toward me. In other words, she remained in full possession of her emotions and expectations, and her life was never thrown off balance. She knew what to anticipate from it, and I knew what to expect from her. That was the love I had witnessed, although from movies and, yes, comic books I knew even then there were other kinds, good and bad.

Babe did behave differently because of Pony. She admired his talent as if it were an extension of his qualities as a human being, something that in an impersonal relationship she would have known was dangerous. She laughed at his jokes. She doted on Bill, whose finer instincts told him never to trample or consume one of her gardens. She hugged me more than usual. She cleaned herself up after gardening. She seemed to enjoy those vacant hours of the day that normally would have made her restless for a task. She spent some of that time walking the hill with us, and I saw in her a grace and loveliness, an elegance, unaffected but far more commanding than the brusque and unyielding persona she was forced to assume after Buddy's death, all of which augmented her natural beauty to a degree I found astonishing and even disconcerting. As the person closest to her since Buddy had died, seeing the change in her made me question my own ability to make her happy. I no longer took for granted that I was seeing or inspiring or protecting the best in her nature. I was a little jealous, but I would have been much more so had I not been certain before those days had passed that Pony was, without question, my father, and that I should contribute whatever I could to assure that he and Babe stayed together. I didn't even think about who my biological mother might have been. I couldn't think beyond Babe, my princess, my patron. I imagined that her marriage to Pony would be more like a reunion of us all, a fulfillment of what was meant to be. And wasn't it conceivable that, if they married, he would change his mind about Bill—that Bill would stay with our predestined family?

I also saw that something in Babe had been unlocked after years of having been consigned to a guarded and neglected place. Because of my youth, I missed another obvious point—that I, too, had become vulnerable in having identified Pony not only as an entertaining mentor, but as a father. I had no concept of what havoc a father could wreak, or of a common truth of human nature. The less you know about people, the easier it is to believe in them.

Pony did tell us a few things about his family. He was born in 1929 in Borger, Texas. At 31, he was a year younger than Babe. As a teenager, he said, he worked with his father in carbon black plants and oil refineries during World War II. Harvey, a friend of his father's, went from job to job with them. Pony's mother cooked and managed the household. Pony's older brother and sister both died of influenza, and he was the only surviving child. His grandmother on his father's side lived with the family. His grandfather had been an itinerant healer of some type who died before Pony was born. His grandmother made a little money painting delicately shaded watercolors of children and animals, especially cats. She carefully nurtured Pony's talent in an otherwise bleak and lawless environment where men aged quickly and came home looking as if their blank faces were as eroded as the soil. She never talked about herself, and Pony wished he'd had the sense to ask more questions of her before she died when he was eleven. Even Pony's father didn't know quite how old she was, but he estimated she might have been in her mid-80's.

As soon as he graduated from high school, Pony was drafted into the army in 1947 and served for two years as a motor pool driver with the occupation force in Germany. His parents were killed in an auto accident on their way to pick him up at Fort Hood when his service ended. Harvey helped him find work as a ranch hand, a job that suited Pony because it didn't require staying in one place for long. "You can come and go as you please and no one holds it against you," Pony said.

"So for eleven years, you've just...?" Babe left her question unfinished. Pony didn't answer for several seconds.

"Yeah, you could put it that way. I spent a lot of time looking for things that were gone before I was born."

"Such as...?"

"Things, here and there. Bill, for instance. I found Bill because I used to visit that refuge every once in a while just to watch the buffalos run." He lit one of his crooked cigars, twirled it between his thumb and forefinger, reclined, and quietly recited a poem.

Who has seen the bison run
Knows a neverending swarm
Swift as thunderclouds assembling;
Setting all the earth a-trembling;
Darker than a summer storm.

Who has seen the bison run
Knows the end they're headed for
Where the sweeter grasses beckon
Somewhere far beyond, I reckon:—
And I'll see them nevermore.

The next morning, Pony did sketches of Bill running—head down, kicking up dust as he turned as if he were training for the autumn when he would return to the refuge, and for future seasons. As it ascended, the sun, to eliminate any possible source of respite from the savage heat, pushed aside the thin, flimsy clouds that were strung over the hill, so we went inside for iced drinks and Pony proposed that we make a trip to the Big Fort museum. Babe leaned over her tea and shook her head deliberately, slowly, back and forth, like an automaton. "Can't do it."

"I'll bet you know it as well as anyone," said Pony. "I won't let anyone bother you."

"Can't do it. You two go if you want to. It doesn't make sense for me."

Babe never had taken me to Big Fort. The only time I had seen the inside of it was on a school outing, when I stayed in the back of the group, sullen, paying scant attention to the exhibits because the teacher was praising the Fowler brothers for their family's celebrated contribution to the heritage of the West in general and Texas in particular. But Pony's curiosity made me want to take another look.

"What do you say, John?" Pony asked.

"It's okay with me if Babe doesn't mind."

"Go on ahead," Babe said. After waving us away, she suddenly interrupted us as we rose. Her voice was strident and betrayed a streak of the anger that smoldered in her, too deep to extinguish. "Just remember—they've cleaned it up to look like a bastion of civilization, like Frontierland, nice and sanitary and air conditioned, but that's not how it was. It would've made hell smell like Chanel. The stench may be long gone, but there's still enough of it left that it would get to me if I went back."

Pony whistled softly. "We won't stay long."

The museum was located on a large tract south of Wendellton, facing the empty plains with the outskirts of the town behind it. It was an enormous, whitewalled adobe fort, with tall, wooden gates that stood open at the front. Visitors were invited to walk the perimeters of the thick walls where they could inspect reproductions of antique weapons stacked at the corners. The lot where Pony parked his truck was to the west of the building. On the east side was a large, fenced playground. At the front, rising above a neatly-trimmed lawn divided by two paths, was a statue—twice as tall as the subjects would have been in life—of a cowboy, a conquistador, an Indian, and a buffalo standing together.

The entrance to the art and artifact collection—a two-story, modern, air-conditioned structure—was directly through the gates. The footprint of the structure filled only a portion of the vast space within the fort. The adobe walls were lined on either side with boardwalks that led guests past replicas of a small hotel filled with period furniture, a warehouse (now a gift store where you could buy, among other things, a blanket made to look like a buffalo robe), and various small businesses, such as a telegraph office and a candy store, that hadn't existed in the original trading post. If you walked through the art collection, you could exit at the rear into a saloon that served as a restaurant. At the other end of the saloon were swinging doors (replaced by sliding glass doors on bad days) that opened onto a square with stables where children could take pony rides.

Pony and I walked through the art collection first, past cases containing artifacts of Coronado's expedition, a journey illustrated by dimly-lit floor-to-ceiling murals. Filling the walls in a large room to the left were dioramas of western scenes with elegantly carved, painted, and dressed models—Indian villages; cavalry outposts; a cluster of bison about to be shot by a hunter painted onto the background, leveling his Sharps rifle from a hill.

In rooms on the second floor, Pony studied a collection of Catlins, Remingtons, Russells, Coles, and Morans, as well as paintings from the group that became known as the Kiowa six and other examples of native American art. Occasionally he would ask me what I liked, and I would tell him reluctantly, feeling pangs of guilt for appreciating anything in a place where Babe had suffered such disrespect and disappointment after marrying Buddy. Pony seemed to understand. "It's an unholy alliance," he said, "between people who struggle to create, to express something beyond the obvious, and the people who buy it and then put their own names on the whole collection."

In the last room, near the exit to the saloon, was a color illustration by Charles St. George Stanley, a depiction of an Indian warrior, riding through a village of teepees, knees pressed against the flanks of his horse, raising a spear in one hand and a rifle in the other, titled "Crying for Scalps."

"There's St. George Stanley again," Pony said, appearing somewhat bemused.

"Yep. The Phantom Padre's friend," I said. "You know, the Padre saved his life when some outlaws tried to attack a camp of buffalo hunters."

"I do know. The man wrote some very imaginative stories."

"But that one—how the Phantom Padre got his name—that one was true, I bet."

"I bet."

"You think so...?"

"Yep. Makes sense to me."

Pony leaned over a bronze plaque attached to a podium next to the illustration. He read the text aloud to me. It was a brief biography of St. George Stanley. No one knew much about him, it seems, other than that he graduated from London's Royal Academy of Art, painted barroom scenes in various towns, was considered rather dashing, and traveled the West with military expeditions. At the bottom was a quote from one of his articles:

> We must cast our eyes to the stars above us. They are all calmly looking down upon the great world, upon its sleeping millions,

upon the sleepless scoundrels engaged in revelry behind us, upon the soldiers and Indians moving over those gloomy plains engaged in the dread office of war. We cannot help being humbled by what the stars see.

In the saloon, we bought wrapped sandwiches to take with us back to the hill. Finally, carrying our lunch sacks, we took a stroll around the square at the rear of Big Fort. We passed a window promising high-stakes poker games. Through it, we could see a small, poker-themed pinball arcade. "Hard to imagine that in a room like that—what, eighty, ninety years ago?—people played poker for the life of a nineteen-year-old girl," Pony said.

"Like Selenia?" The girl that Zebulon Fowler used to lure suckers into poker games. I wondered how she might have been like Babe.

"That's who I mean. I guess that's where she would have stayed." Pony pointed to the northeast corner of the square near the stables, where a multi-colored sign read, *Ping's Laundry*. "She would have slept in there, with the laundress and her cat."

Inside the laundry shack stood a mannequin of a grinning Chinese woman with a patch over her left eye and a black wig that looked like a threaded turban. The mannequin was covered by a loose gray, cotton tunic that reached to its knees, with trousers of the same cloth and color. The shack contained a small stove with an iron in the heating plate, a clothes wringer mounted on the canvas-covered wall, a laundry kettle, an ironing table, and wash boards. A cardboard cutout looking very much like the Cheshire cat from Disney's *Alice in Wonderland* was perched on the ironing table. You couldn't step past the rope across the doorway, but you could see through the room to an exit into a tiny open yard with clothes hanging from a line. An explanatory sign next to the door read, "All kinds of people came to Big Fort to improve their lives."

Pony chuckled and shook his head. "Even the cat looks happy. What was her name? Ah Toy?"

"She looks funny."

"Probably so. Whatever else the cat was, it was free. And nobody was playing poker for its soul. So...I don't know. I sort of wanted to visit here, see how lives were laid out. I guess I wasn't making much sense. Like Babe said. Nice and sanitary." He pinched my shoulder and rattled his lunch sack. "Back to the hill, okay?"

9
The Poker Game

BUDDY WATKINS [FROM DISK #13]: *...As the Padre waited for Pigeye's return, he and Selenia took long walks in the sunshine, and they felt joy and the peace of just being together, even in the harsh world of Big Fort. The Padre could not help loving her. And who knows what really happens when we fall in love? Some believe it changes you, but I think it just brings things out, things that were hidden or stifled or forgotten, and you may not realize they were part of you until they get all tangled up in other plans you'd made—plans you can't change...*

Antonio spent little time in his cramped and creaking hotel room, furnished only with a tin sink, water pitcher, chamber pot, wooden chair, and one bed with a thin army blanket. The ceiling was so low that he could barely stand without bumping his head. Mosquitoes and fleas had taken up residence in every corner, and they attacked at will. His only luxury was a window that sometimes admitted a weak breeze. Daily, he picked the fleas from his body and left early in the morning to walk with Selenia before her shift. Inevitably, she poured out her heart to him—a story he already knew from Charles St. George Stanley—and confessed that she desperately longed to escape Big Fort but had nowhere to go, no people, no prospects. She wondered whether it was possible for Antonio to take her under his protection. What frightened her most, she said, was the possibility that a fearsome, violent man, a giant named Lehane, might return to compete for her as he had threatened to do. "I am shocked at what you have just told me, and must leave it to God to guide me in how to respond," Antonio replied. "Because the man you have named is the very man who I believe carries the holy Star of Andalusia."

Selenia was speechless for a moment. Then she saw his eyes flicker—a mistake, he knew, an amateur's tell—and she began to sob. "And is that also the truth of why you have come to me?" she asked finally. "Because this man wants me and he has what you are seeking?"

"Of course it is not," Antonio lied. He steadied his eyes and looked into hers, taking her by the shoulders. "We have met by the grace of God, but not by any scheme on my part. I had no idea that our fates were joined in such a way. And since they are, I feel certain that it is a message from God to await the man here, and to see that you are not harmed."

Selenia was quickly comforted. She was vulnerable to deception. Not only did she need someone to believe in, but Antonio was expert at convincing people of any scenario he needed to promote. Calmly, persuasively, he told her not to be afraid. He would be there, and so would Young Eagle. He prayed with her until her trembling stopped.

And so, day after day, as Selenia worked, Antonio sat in the saloon sharing bottles of foul red wine with Charles St. George Stanley. "I've already sent off a packet of three stories about you," St. George Stanley told Antonio before the week was out. "Putting down the outlaws when you saved my life—that's the first one, of course. I wrote them in a single flash of inspiration. Took an hour. The second one has you rescuing a beautiful girl from the clutches of a villain who tries to kidnap her after her family is killed. That's one we can say is likely, eh? And there's one I made up, but you're very good in it. You're captured by Indians and saved by a heathen maiden who sees the Virgin Mary. It's better than it sounds. I'll soon have a dozen more, enough to keep Frank Leslie in Phantom Padre stories for months."

St. George Stanley also sold sketches of nude women to hunters and traders who crowded around the table where he and Antonio sat. His business was brisk. Many wanted him to duplicate the nude he had painted on the saloon's wall, since it was rumored that it represented Selenia. "Sorry, that was exclusively for Mr. Fowler, but here's one to bid on," he offered cheerily one evening. He began to draw. "This young lady—classic figure, very tasteful—I painted to hang over a bar in Denver. Quite a large frame, like this." His hand flew across the paper as he drew an ornate frame around the image. "Behind the frame we ran two hidden inflatable hoses with rubber bulbs at the ends of them. Depending on which bulb the bartender pressed, he could make the beauty's left or right breast heave as if she were shifting and sighing down at the huddled masses. The secret was, of course, to do the trick with sleight of hand, so as not to give away the—what you might call the artistic technique. I personally witnessed more than one sozzled boy get dizzy and fall when he saw it. Now, who'll bid more than a dollar...?"

Often, Antonio and St. George Stanley were recruited into poker games. Antonio's presence in his cassock brought new players to the saloon, lured by the novelty of challenging him—to the delight of Zebulon Fowler. The story of how he had saved the buffalo hunters already had spread, as had St. George Stanley's sobriquet—the Phantom Padre. Antonio laughed with Selenia about it, and told her he had done no more than any man would have. "It can't hurt to have a reputation for aiming straight," he said, "as long as it serves the aims of God." For the same purpose, he said, priests also had been known to gamble at cards, and she should not be shocked to see him at the tables. "But we alone know my true purpose—to wait and be near you."

Before too many days had passed, Antonio realized that his concern for Selenia had become more than a pretense. He was so enchanted by the girl that he would argue angrily with himself before going to sleep among the fleas that frolicked in his bed. What had he become? Was nothing sacred—not even the trust of a helpless girl? *I will do what I have to*, he told himself, *but I will not desert her. I will make it right somehow.* It was a feeling he hadn't known for the better part of his life—that he owed something to someone other than himself, however weakened his own position might be as a result.

He found himself telling her things he had revealed to few people—stories of his childhood in Spain, of the sacrifices made by his mother, of his fascination with the stars. One night, after her saloon shift, he led her beyond the adobe walls and described the lessons he had learned from the stars. Although no clouds were in the sky, he predicted rain the next day, and he was right.

Selenia, in turn, began to feel close, even attracted to him. Most importantly, she revered and trusted Antonio as someone who was encouraging her to believe in a future she might have outside of the walls of Big Fort, as soon as Lehane was dealt with.

The evening their wait ended was a memorable one.

Other players had brought a Methodist preacher to the poker table where Antonio sat, joking that the two men should see which faith God truly favored. "The Papist versus the reformer," St. George Stanley proclaimed. "And I shall deal."

The Reverend Phillip Scott Wolf once had hunted buffalo with Zebulon Fowler and boasted of saving the life of Big Fort's master. "I rescued him from a real stampede once, gentlemen," he said as St. George Stanley shuffled, "when he had broke a leg. I waved a blanket so them beasts turned right by us on both sides. I could smell their breath, stronger than whiskey, and that was the first time I felt a power greater than both of us. And thanks to that power, now I'm still in the life-saving business. When we've cleaned the beasts and redskins off this land, and my friend Zebulon founds a town to be the capital of it, the next thing it'll want is the Christianizing." He glanced at Antonio. "The right kind of Christianizing. That's the future. To find them demons and show they ain't welcome."

"But how do we know 'em when we seen 'em, Reverend?" a spectator asked.

"Ah, that's the question, ain't it?" Wolf nodded wisely. "Skulking is one thing. The way I noticed a cat skulking 'round back there a few nights back. It were looking for souls to pounce on—you could see its evil purpose if you were chose by the Good Lord like me. Gentlemen, I bashed that cat's head so hard it knocked the devil right out of the beast, and if you heard the unholy ruckus it made, you'd know you heard the devil. That's why men like me are among you, to keep your souls from being sucked and clawed away from you. That's what you need to know."

St. George Stanley glanced at Antonio, whose face had grown as dark as his cassock. "Such a fine champion," the Englishman said. "Must be why God invented poker to distribute his just rewards."

With St. George Stanley dealing—adept as he was with his hands—it took less than an hour for the Rev. Wolf to lose his stake to Antonio's full house of threes and queens. Wolf threw down his hand. "Satan's at work," he mumbled, "with the Pope, I expect. But he can't drive me off." He left the saloon without another word. The spectators cleared away, leaving only one man who had been standing at the rear of the group. The man began circling the table slowly. St. George Stanley looked up and smiled. "Hello, Patrick," he said. "Would you care to sit with us?" He turned to Antonio. "Father Antonio Peraza, meet Patrick Lehane."

114

Antonio already knew who the man was. Pigeye Lehane was enormous and powerfully built. His hair was long, matted and filthy, spilling over a round face with puffy, veined cheeks. His left eye seemed to bulge out of its socket. He wore, as was rumored, a scalp shirt fringed with the hair of his victims. He extended a hard slab of a hand toward Antonio. "A few minutes, Padre," he growled. It wasn't a question.

Pigeye took Antonio by the arm and led him toward the far end of the bar. Others edged away from them. Pigeye ordered two whiskies. "You may wonder why I've sought you out, Padre," he began. "Well, I've an acquaintance with the man who runs this stinking hidetown, Fowler by name, and he sent me to you. Says there's a marryin' man right amongst us if I need one, a man of my own faith, and he laughed when he said it, Fowler did, the bastard. He thought it was a joke of sorts because he don't think I can win my bride. Ain't no joke to me."

The drinks arrived quickly. "In the name of the Father and the Holy Roman Church," Antonio said, raising his glass.

"Well, sir, and here's to Father Felix Zoppa de Connobio, one of yours, Padre. You ever knowed him? Chaplain of the Fighting Irish, saved Houston from the Yankees at the Sabine River Pass. And I reckon you share his zeal, Padre, or you'd not be in a hellhole like this." Pigeye pulled out a cigar cutter attached to his watch chain, snipped off the end of a short stogie, lit the cigar with a match from the bar, and leaned forward into a smoky cloud, drawing the fumes back into his nose with one long, rasping sniff. His dirty blonde hair drifted over the scar on his left cheek. He took another drink. Antonio sensed that Pigeye was not only anxious to get the measure of him, but also to impress him. If so, it opened an advantage in gaining the fearsome man's confidence. "And here's to another good Padre," Pigeye continued. "One I served proudly with myself—the man they called the fighting priest, Father John Bannon, First Missouri Confederate Brigade, God bless 'im. I saw Father Bannon at Pea Ridge, in the thick of the action, tending the dying where most of the holy men stayed out of it till the fighting were done and the bodies laid out neat. Took confession even from a hellbound Yankee, Padre. Took my confession once, Father Bannon did, and perhaps you will someday. A fearless man, he was. Enjoyed a game of cards, like you. Never afraid to say what he thought of the Yankees, which is no more'n he thought of the damned Queen of the Brits. Captured at bloody Vicksburg eleven year ago, as we all were. Got out on a free pass, ran a blockade to go back to Ireland and speak agin the Yankees there. Never gave up. What brung you here, Padre, under the roof of a villain like Fowler?"

"A holy mission from the Bishop of Galveston himself." Again, Antonio told the story he had prepared—that he traveled the untamed territory to find good Catholics and see that they didn't suffer neglect, as they had after the Texas Republic was won. "In many places there are still no materials for the celebration of mass—no candles, incense, host boxes, not even a suitable cross to worship. And so I play a hand or two of poker along the way, hoping to raise what the Mother Church cannot afford." Suddenly, Antonio feigned surprise, as if a thought had just occurred to him. "Lehane," he exclaimed, raising his hands to his face. "I knew I recognized the name, sir. I am carrying something for you, something I was given in Mexico some weeks ago. A gift from God."

The outlaw's bad eye seemed to bulge even further. He glared suspiciously at Antonio. "Go on, Padre."

"A priest in Ramosa, another Jesuit I met on my way to Texas. You know Ramosa?"

"I do."

"Well, he gave me a Bible to carry on my mission, to give to the needy. But he happened to say that if I still had the Bible and met a man named Lehane, that I should give it to him—to you, I suppose he meant."

"And why would he think you'd cross my way?" Lehane spat on the floor.

"For the very reason I have found you. Because it is my holy mission and because it is God's plan. And in fact, it was you who presented yourself to me, as God must have intended."

"And why would he think I need a Bible, Padre?"

Antonio had a ready answer. "My brother—the priest in Ramosa—told me only that you had done the church a great service, safeguarding a holy object. He said the object had protected your own life—that it could have made you rich, but you chose to keep it in fealty to the intentions of Our Lord to keep you safe. And he believed you needed to carry with you the Word of God Himself...and he worried that you had not been to confession..."

Pigeye laughed and relaxed. "I know the rest, Padre. I remember the priest. And I'll accept the Good Book gratefully, since you brung it all this way for me. I'll need one for the house I plan to build."

"Then I'm glad I had not yet found a soul to give it to. We both must accept this as an act of providence, as we are taught from the moment we accept there is a God."

"I hear you, Padre. And the object you was told of, I do have such, and it's protected me well."

Loosened and mellowed by drink, Pigeye proceeded to describe the Star of Andalusia, and how he had captured it from a Comanche warrior. "I'd be happy to give you a good look at it, Padre, in exchange for another favor—that is, seeing as how you're the only one of our faith in this cesspit, which is why I come to you. I've had my wars and my heathen scalps and I'm going to Missouri, and I mean to take a pure woman back with me, you understand. And it so happens, she's of the faith, too. I want you to marry us. We'll be ready to wed soon, Padre. I mean to take that lass over there, that pretty waiter-girl." Pigeye's thick, raised forefinger pointed deliberately, ominously, through the crowd toward Selenia. "I already bought a stove for her to cook on, plan to give it to her as a wedding present. Now I'll have a Bible for our family. There's only the one thing I have to do first, and that's to win a poker game for the lass herself, run by that big-bug-bastard Fowler."

As Lehane recounted the conditions required to win Selenia, Antonio pretended to be shocked, when in fact he was surprised only by the ease with which Pigeye seemed to be falling into the scheme that Antonio had worked out. "Ah," he said, "then I can only conclude that you have a noble motive in mind—that you've come to set her free from this place."

"Exactly that. I'm back to win the poker contest and set her free. And since you're comfortable with a deck of cards, Padre, I'd like you to deal the hands to keep 'em honest."

"Deal your game? Hmm." Antonio pretended to be uncertain. "Are you a devout Catholic?"

"As much as a man of war can be, Padre."

"Are you baptized?"

"I am."

"Do you pray each day?"

"I do. And as you know, now, Padre, I pray on a star of gold as shows the beauty of heaven like naught else. A star such as you've never seen. God's gift."

"Then perhaps it belongs in a church where all can share it."

"Wherever it were, I didn't get it in no church. It belonged to a redskin kept it in a medicine bag. I killed him to help rid this world of them heathen devils. Where he got it, he weren't able to say, with my bullet in his savage tongue. What a man wins in war is his. It's the first rule, Padre."

"It's a rule of men."

"And why not of God? God's took his vengeance, too. And He's kept me safe for rescuing it. He's showed me favor, Padre. And He'll show the same to you. And I'll tell you what. You see me through this. You deal my poker game so's Fowler can't cheat me. You marry me to that waiter-girl, and I'll place my star in your hands to hold with the good book for the wedding. You'll be blessed to touch it, I've no doubt."

* * *

BUDDY WATKINS [FROM DISK #15]: *...Selenia was the bait. Even though the Padre thought it would all come out right in the end, it was a risk and a betrayal that would trouble him forever. You can build a fine new house to cover up an old crime, but that crime still lies beneath your mansion, buried in your soul. And then, suddenly, all the doors are locked against you...*

The next morning, Antonio finally was faced with the task he had dreaded—telling Selenia where she fit into his plan. He met her in the gimcrack morgue and chapel and tried to ignore the body that was stretched out on the altar and covered by the same, filthy sheet that had served as a temporary shroud for dozens of drunks, suckers, belligerents, and soldiers on French leave. As was the custom, a hat had been placed over the portion of the sheet that covered the body's head. No doubt the hat would be stolen before the end of the day. Was he inviting the same end for himself? Was he risking too much? Would his own black, dish-brimmed hat wind up perched on top of the sheet?

"We'll pray for this unfortunate, whoever he was," said Antonio, grateful for any excuse to re-think or delay his intentions.

"And we will then pray for our own delivery through our coming trials."

He again considered saying nothing after his prayers. It wasn't necessary for Selenia to understand. But if she didn't know at least part of the plan, she would feel terrified and betrayed beyond all reason—and how would she ever trust him again? He didn't need her trust, of course. But he couldn't stand the thought of losing it. He rose and took her hands. "The time has come. I am going to rid you of Lehane," he said. Her eyes widened and she smiled, but he put his fingers on her lips as if to erase the smile. "What it involves is that you first stand as the bride in a wedding ceremony with him."

She collapsed without another breath, falling to her knees and slumping forward. "To be married to that man before God?" she shivered. "How can you say that, Padre? You know I would sooner die. I would sooner die. How can you ask me?"

"Listen carefully, now. You will not be married before God." Selenia shook her head and wrenched away from his touch. "We will never finish the ceremony. He'll be taken as soon as it begins."

Still, Selenia shook and gasped for air, gagging on the stench in the room. She brought a hand to her throat. Antonio placed an arm around her and lifted her to her feet. "I know...it's difficult to breathe in here," he said. "Let's walk outside. The morning air will be good for you. But you must hide your distress so no one sees it. Can you...so I can tell you the rest? You have nothing to fear. We have trusted each other. You may trust me still. Nothing has changed."

Selenia nodded and exhaled heavily. She moved away from him and squared her shoulders, then wiped her face with her hands and walked out the door. *Exactly as it should be*, Antonio thought. Had she remained inside the morgue-and-chapel, hysterical, she might have absorbed only part of what he had to tell her. Outside, as she composed herself, he would have her full attention. He nodded with a smile at Young Eagle, who leaned against a post outside the stables. Then he took Selenia by the elbow and guided her outside the small service square and onto the path that led to the creek where Ping collected laundry water.

"It is the best way to catch him off guard so he can be captured," Antonio began. "And you cannot be married before God because I am not a true priest." He glanced at Selenia's face. She did not seem to react. "I was schooled and trained by Jesuits, but...I am a man seeking to regain the noble birthright I've told you of truthfully, who could not travel safely except...except for this ruse. And I will protect you from anything that may happen...do you understand what I'm saying?"

"I understand, Padre." Her voice was flat, trance-like.

"It's also the way I can help you escape this, to break the hold that Fowler has on you. Isn't that what you want?"

"It is what I've prayed for."

"Then listen to me."

Selenia's first reaction had been shock. Antonio knew he had only one chance to restore her trust, her faith in him, her willing belief in the future he had sold to her, her acceptance of her role. It took several minutes for him to explain himself and his strategy. Lehane was one of the most dangerous, unpredictable men on earth. Clearly, no man ever had succeeded in besting him, although many had tried through years of violent, deadly conflicts. He was too canny and suspicious to risk even the slightest chance that he might be tricked. Antonio never could have gotten him to reveal his possession of the Star—or promise to produce it—had he not done so in the guise of a priest. Now that step was taken. The next was predicated on the fact that Lehane's only weakness was Selenia. And the one circumstance that would make him vulnerable was his wedding—or what he believed to be a wedding ceremony. The scheme had begun as a means of reclaiming the Star of Andalusia. But it also had evolved, Antonio swore, into an escape plan for Selenia. "And I would not have set it in motion unless..."

"Unless you had a lure. You had nothing he wanted aside from me. That is what I understand."

"Selenia, no, it's much more than that."

"I have thought before how nice it might be...if you weren't a priest. Now—God help me...yes, of course, I will help you because I must..."

"And yourself. You will help yourself." Antonio struggled to speak calmly. He wanted to appear humbled by his task, not anxious or worried or aggressive.

"I know I have no hope unless it is to join you." She shrugged. "So it was your gold Star all along, your position in the world..." She stopped, unable to continue the accusation she had intended.

"When I began, of course, but not after I came to know you. Then I swore to myself, and I swear again this morning, that I would value your safety and freedom—make it sacred to me as well..."

"Sacred? What does sacred mean to you?"

"As much as it would mean if I had taken my vows. I was trained to be a priest. You are the only one who knows I am not one. And that secret, I trust you to keep."

"I will. I have no choice."

"There is nothing I desire more than your forgiveness."

"Even if I don't believe that, I will forgive you if I no longer belong to Fowler when this is over."

"You will not."

"Because..."

"Because I...I will see to it. Please believe me. Please believe...in my love for you."

"I still believe in the love of God—Padre."

The private parlor where Zebulon Fowler held his poker games was fifteen feet square, windowless, with an octagonal table in the center and cushioned chairs with rounded backs arranged around the table. Only one door led in and out. Fowler sat at the end of the table facing the door. Pigeye sat at the opposite end. Antonio was between them, to Fowler's right, with a box of unopened decks of cards beside his chair. A cart with whiskey bottles and glasses had been placed next to Fowler, but Ping was not there to serve drinks. Antonio had insisted that she be absent, so she would have nothing to report to Selenia. On the other side of the closed door, two of Fowler's men stood as guards.

"I always see a brighter future in a hand of poker," Fowler said. He poured a whiskey for each man. "Your deposit's secure in my safe, Lehane, but I expect to keep it when the night's over. Glad you found the two thousand dollars to try again—double the fee for your first try. Honestly gotten, I'm sure."

"And another five hundred in a gold belt 'round my belly, if it comes to a showdown," Pigeye snorted. "But it's the Padre that makes the honest difference. You may be sorry you sent me to him."

"To a priest? Ain't you been a man of action all your life?"

"What of it?"

"Nothing particular. I was a man of action, too. Dropped a few buffalo in my time to get where I am. You hunted other men. For better pay, I reckon."

"What I did was a damn sight riskier than lyin' on a hillside and pickin' off a herd of dumb animals. I killed me Yankees and I killed me Injuns. I took from them the way you took the hide from the buffalo and got my bounty on top. I done well enough, me and the others who come along. No man I ever killed with would of sold a woman in a hand of poker."

"Careful what you say."

"I say the truth. Do you say I lie?"

Zebulon shrugged. "Do you believe in fairy tales, Lehane?"

"That's a rubbish question for a man like me."

"There's lessons in them, even so. To get the girl of his dreams, a man has to prove hisself—fight dragons, climb the walls of a castle. You hear them tales all over the world for a reason, even in this ungodly territory. Do you know what that reason is? Every man must prove his worth, Lehane, even you. Ain't I right? I ask you this. If the girl was your responsibility, Lehane, would you give her to a lesser man?"

"I'd give her to no man but myself." Pigeye's face was getting redder as Fowler needled him. His blush reached its peak in a crimson gloss before it faded again, spent.

"Then think about this," Fowler continued, ignoring the growl in Pigeye's voice. "What a man values most, he is willing to place before other men and challenge them to take it from him. Ain't that what you did in your wars, Lehane? Ain't that what you do when you declares your faith, Padre? Ain't that what we all do when any of us calls ourselves a free man? And what do you get in return when you do so? You get your dignity and your worth, things that no man can rob you of. You must realize that, Lehane. And even the Padre here knows we have a civilized means of proving those values. Being the girl's guardian and such, why would I not demand that a man show me his means and ability? And if that man wins, why, he has a dowry for the girl to boot. What's more fair than that? Would I make the offer if I didn't myself believe it would set my mind at ease to give her to such a man as can hold his own over other men and prove the Good Lord is on his side?"

Pigeye breathed heavily before he replied. "I'll hold my own in any honest contest. That's why the Padre is here. You can deal now, Padre. I won't be talked out of my game."

Both men were first-rate players, Antonio thought, but Fowler, without doubt, was the best he ever had seen. After three hours, Fowler had amassed the bulk of the winnings with impeccable timing and an uncanny sense of what Pigeye held. Fowler folded far more often than he lost. Not one of his bluffs, if he made them, had been exposed. By the time he caught Antonio's eye and nodded, Fowler had proved himself, and the game suddenly changed.

Shortly after midnight, Pigeye put together a streak of wins that gave him his first lead. After a new ante and deal, he had $2,000 to Zebulon's $1,800. Two hundred dollars sat in the pot. Pigeye took three cards and shoved $1,500 to the center of the table. Zebulon winced visibly, as if he expected Pigeye to catch his tell, then took two cards and raised his eyes from his hand. "I think I smell a bluff," he said. "And it's a perfect time for one, Lehane, as I've let you slip ahead of me, but I don't buy it. I'll call and raise you my last three hundred."

Quickly, Pigeye slid his chips into the pot.

"Well, then," Fowler grinned, "take 'em if you can." He spread a full house, jacks over aces, onto the table.

Pigeye laid down four nines and banged the table with his fist. Then he stood, his eye bulging, his brow covered with beads of sweat. He leaned forward over the table and supported himself with his fists. "By God, I'm meant to have her."

Antonio stood and placed a hand on Pigeye's shoulder. "I'll see you in the chapel at nine in the morning. I'll bring the girl with me. And I'll bring the Bible that was sent to you from Mexico. God's will be done."

"I'll bring you your winnings in gold from my safe in the morning, what you put in and what I owe you," Fowler said. "You can have yours back now if you want."

"It'll keep."

"So it will. I'll tell the girl she's been won. And I'll show you I'm a big enough man to serve as witness."

"Will you have your own?" Antonio asked Pigeye.

"My own...?"

"Witnesses."

"Naw, Padre, I got none that needs to see me get soft. None that's worthy of standing in the same room with her. But I'll bring the star for you to pray on, like you wanted. And I have a wagon waiting to take her away after."

Fowler opened the door and signaled to his two men to step back. "There's a fella come up, said he'd wait in the bar for you," one of the guards called to Pigeye. The guard chuckled. "I seen him passed out in there earlier today. Must be on his second wind."

"Hope it's not the law," Fowler chuckled.

"I know who it's bound to be." Pigeye scowled. "Fella wants to talk me out of marryin' no doubt. That's why I ain't got no witnesses I'd have stand for me, Padre."

"The Padre and me will stay here a while to work it out nice for you, Lehane," said Fowler. "You'd best get some sleep, now."

Fowler closed the door, plopped into a chair, and poured himself a drink. Antonio sat next to him. Fowler reached into his pants for a vial. "Here's what you'll need for your wedding wine, Padre. Some laudanum, like you asked for. Slow him down good, I reckon. They teach you that in preacher school?" He handed the vial to Antonio.

"Where'd it come from?"

"Peppert the bartender. He's the supplier. I've kept this whole thing between us and him and the four men who'll be waiting to take Pigeye down for good, just like the ogre in them fairy tales. Now you tell me something, Padre. Where'd you learn to deal? That was the god-damndest deal I ever seen. If I hadn't knowed what you was doing, I might never have guessed. Lehane, he didn't have a clue. When I pulled that full house, jacks and aces just like you said it would be, I knew you'd set up the last hand, but I still couldn't believe it when he laid down his nines. I could make you a rich man in a few months, Padre, but I guess you'll be happy with what you come here for. Take it back to your family, will you? Back to Spain?"

"Where it belongs."

"Sure, sure. And the girl? She's ready?"

"She's ready. I'll bring her there."

"And she'll still be fresh as a daisy when it's done. And don't worry, Padre, I'll keep her safe and sound like always, ready for the next man to lose his money fishing for her cherry."

"She won't have done enough for you?"

"Not till I let some lucky hardcase carry her away."

Absently, Antonio collected the cards that had been spread on the table and ruffled them into a deck. "I wonder who came up here looking for Pigeye."

"One of his hombres, like he said. He's always got one or two to back him up. That's nothing to worry about."

"Why not?"

"Well, he said hisself, Padre, he wouldn't have 'em on an occasion like tomorrow. The wine'll make him groggy. You can handle a gun like a born killer, so the Englishman says. And my own four men will be waiting outside. Now if we was just to try to catch him in the open, that's another story. He's been knowed to take down four or five at a time by hisself. But you, Padre, you'll have him all softened up for his wedding and unsuspecting that a man of the cloth would invite his enemies into a holy ceremony, ain't I right? And what if he does have friends? Where might they be charging in from? I didn't put up walls around that garbage yard for nothing."

"How has he stayed alive this long?"

"Lemme tell you, if there was something left for him to worry about, that's when you should worry. Pigeye's stayed alive because he's always knowed how to deal with men like hisself. Kill or be killed. They think alike. They watch for the same tricks. They're like them Indians out yonder. They got a certain kind of cunning, I'll admit, but it's all about the corners where the fight happens, and the surprise. The fight's ended here in my corner. My corner. I ain't worried because Pigeye thinks he's won what he come here for. He's already taken the bait, don't you see? And you, Padre, he figures you just want to gander at his gold star. So, strange, ain't it, to finally get what you aim for?"

"I want no more than what belongs to my family and the church."

"And none too soon for a man your age. How old? Forty at least, I'd say. And I'm barely twenty-six and making my move. In this country it's not so much what you're born to, but what you take for yourself, gold stars and Spanish jewels be damned." Fowler laughed and clapped Antonio on the shoulder. "Someday I'll pass as a gentleman, too, before I'm thirty, I'll wager, and fuck 'em all. For now, we ain't so different, and we got a few hours to wait. You know what I'd like? Let's play a few more hands till we're too tired—honest deal, no stakes, just to see who's best. I hate to think the night would end with me pissing away a full house. You have to honor me on that one."

"I've had enough. But all right." Antonio shuffled the cards. "I'll play a few more hands if you'll answer one question. It's Ping, isn't it?"

For the first time, Fowler seemed rattled. "Ping what? She's a ignorant Chinee laundry woman. She can't add two plus two. What do you mean?"

"Cut the cards." Antonio slapped down the deck. "You know what I mean. She fixes drinks and lights cigars and no one hides their cards from her. A few simple signals while she works is all you need to win—to keep the girl."

"Think what you will," Fowler grinned. "No one's the wiser here, nor ever has been, Padre."

"That's enough of an answer for me."

The men played two dozen hands, alternating the deal, and won twelve apiece. Fowler won the twenty-fifth deal. He was eager to play on, but Antonio declined, had a last drink, and walked out into the square and through the front gate. He needed to think, to breathe the early morning air. Nothing was wrong with the plan he and Fowler had devised. Five people would be in the chapel and morgue—Antonio, Pigeye, Selenia, Fowler, and St. George Stanley, who would stand as a second witness. As the ceremony began, Antonio would serve Pigeye wine laced with laudanum—a trick he had learned in the Mexico City underworld to handicap a mark's reflexes. Fowler would have four men stationed outside the chapel, ready to rush in when the laudanum began to take effect. Antonio would back them up with the pistol in his cassock. They would take Pigeye away through the stables, and he would disappear forever.

Antonio would have the Star. As for Selenia's fate—despite what he had promised her, he did not know how he would manage to salvage her hopes. The family had given him gold to pursue his quest. But he already had agreed to leave it in Fowler's safe in exchange for the Big Fort proprietor's help. He had not included Selenia in the bargain. He had told himself he would think of a solution when the time came. The time had come.

It was two a.m. He stood motionless in the silence that enveloped the trading post. Tents were strung out to the east of the adobe walls, and there was a small, tangled grove of scrub oak trees to the south. He walked toward the trees, unaware that he was being watched from them. He couldn't sleep, nor could he face the fleas in his foul hotel room. He simply wanted to be alone. As if aware of that, a figure slipped from the trees and retreated into the darkness. Reaching into his pocket, Antonio rubbed the silver dollar that Selenia had given him. A flash of panic, of helplessness, shot through him—not because he was concerned about the outcome of the sham wedding, but because he could not suppress his conscience, as he had learned to do so effectively over the years of his exile. He knew he could not forgive himself if he left Selenia behind. As a distraction, he pulled out his watch and gazed at the stars, noting their positions on that sweltering August night.

He listened to the steady tick of the timepiece and absently watched the second hand revolve. He was startled by a voice close behind him, calling urgently.

"Padre." Young Eagle tugged at Antonio's cassock. "Quick. Ping." The boy wheeled around and ran toward the service square at the rear of the post. At first, Antonio didn't move. Young Eagle stopped, looked back, and waved frantically. Finally, Antonio followed him beneath a crescent moon poised like a sharp, shining sickle above the neck of a starlit horizon.

They found Ping sitting on her chair in the laundry, still dazed. Her body tensed when she saw them, but the expression on her face was fierce. She was bleeding from a cut beneath her chin. She pointed to the small yard where she hung her laundry. Four bodies, stripped naked, with their hands tied behind their backs, had been dumped onto the ground. The heads of all four were grotesquely cocked and lifeless, wrenched back from the deep gashes where their throats have been cut. Thick pools of blood seeped into the dirt. "No time," Ping said. "Selenia gone. Three men take her." She looked accusingly at Antonio. "You know who."

For a moment, Antonio could only stare at the carnage. Ping rose from her chair and grabbed him by the arm. Using words and gestures, she quickly made clear what had happened. Pigeye Lehane and two other men had marched four men at gunpoint into Ping's laundry. While Selenia and Ping watched, the gunmen first removed the men's clothes, then tied their hands. They tied Ping into her chair.

Pigeye offered Selenia a bargain. "I know that you and the Padre have planned something," he said. If she left quietly with him, he promised, everyone would live. Selenia agreed. Pigeye pushed her out the door and she disappeared with him. No one moved or spoke for a while, until they heard the sound of a wagon leaving. After a few more seconds, Pigeye's two gunmen pushed Zebulon's men into Ping's laundry yard and knocked them unconscious. One of the gunmen cut their throats while the other held his knife to Ping's throat. When the murders were finished, they approached Ping and yanked back her head, laughing and threatening to cut it off slowly.

A wail from the laundry yard saved her. The startled men froze. "By God, it's their ghosts," one of them said. Ping twisted in her chair and toppled into the floor. Without waiting to see what had made the unearthly sound, the men ran from the laundry.

The wail had come from Young Eagle as he discovered the bodies while scaling the wall to return to the laundry. He had been resting in the branches of the scrub oaks outside the fort, as he often did in the early morning hours—communing with the stars in his own way. From the tree where he was perched, he had watched Antonio walk out of the gate. Then, Young Eagle had dropped from his branch and returned to the laundry to check on Selenia and Ping, finding instead the bodies of the four murdered men. He saw that Ping was still alive and ran back to where he knew Antonio would be.

Antonio was experienced enough in treachery to wonder who was the likely source. Fowler already had assigned the four men to Pigeye's wedding. Had one of them revealed the plan in the wrong company? Could Fowler himself have engineered a double-cross— but for what reasons? Would he have sent his own men to their deaths? Was it an exercise of his own brutal power, not even for a larger benefit, but for the thrill of manipulating people and circumstance to some unforeseen precipice and watching them stumble and fall?

Antonio knew he couldn't take the time to speculate. First, he needed someone whose judgement he could trust—someone who was not Zebulon Fowler. "Stay here," he barked to Young Eagle. "Selenia will need you soon. You and I will go together." He ran to wake up Charles St. George Stanley in the hotel. Within ten minutes, they had returned to the laundry. St. George Stanley, groggy and lightly dressed, still carrying his pistol belt, convulsed and nearly heaved out the sour contents of his stomach when he saw the dead men in Ping's laundry yard. "My God, how did Lehane know?" he asked.

"How anyone know?" Ping fumed. "Maybe man tells whore. Whore tells Bad-eye. How anyone know? Now fucking go find." She thrust her arm toward the door. "Ping take care of self. Always take care. I die, so what?"

Antonio had begun to form a plan. "First, you do what I say. Then we'll go."

Ping appeared confused for a moment when Antonio announced that he would tie her into her chair again. It would be her own best defense against being taken for an informer, he said. But before her arms were bound, she touched her eye patch and grabbed the cloth of her tunic, then pointed to Young Eagle. "Yes, yes." Antonio understood and agreed immediately. Ping removed the patch from her sightless, mutilated eye, the eye she had sacrificed to end her whorehouse bondage, and gave the patch to Young Eagle. Then she tossed him the cotton tunic that was her only spare garment—the one she gave him the night they met. The tunic was a perfect fit, hiding his buckskin leggings down to the knees. Young Eagle grinned. He pulled the strap of the eyepatch around the crown of his head and raised the patch, leaving it up for the time being. Finally, Ping gave him a coolie hat with a cord that hung around his neck. She sat while Antonio bound her. "We will save Selenia," Antonio said.

Ping lifted her face to him. "No come back with her. Bad place for her. Take her away. I wishing her happiness." Before Antonio tied a gag around her mouth, she offered one last observation. "You no good. I always know."

"Don't forget your cat," Antonio said as he finished the knot on her gag. He turned to St. George Stanley. "Can you be the one who finds Ping in a few hours? She'll need someone to make her story credible. If Fowler wasn't part of this, he'll need to be convinced."

"Of course, man. But I should ride with you."

"I need a last favor,' Antonio continued. "Your gun and your horse. For the boy. To take them by surprise."

St. George Stanley smiled at Young Eagle, dressed to resemble Ping. He nodded and handed his pistol belt to the boy. "Much better for my story. I'll go with you to the stables, Padre. And you, boy—meet us outside. I'll be leading your mount...ride it well with the Phantom Padre."

Antonio awakened a stable hand, then saddled the sun-bleached grullo stallion once ridden by the man he had killed on his way to Texas. St. George Stanley threw a saddle over his dark bay horse, clapped the animal on its shoulder and kissed its muzzle. Antonio checked his saddlebag for the ammunition, coins, clothes, and other objects he had left in it, including Pigeye's Bible. Then he gave a gold coin to the grateful stable hand and swung into the saddle. St. George Stanley led his horse away from the stables. "Look out there," he said, "where the night is still closed around your quarry and you may well define your life and your faith in the moments to come. No doubt, where you will venture—well, it was once covered by vast lakes clothed with luxuriant vegetation, inhabited by great mammals who would dwarf the bison we have seen together. And what will it be after we have passed through and beyond? It makes me wonder, Padre, about the description of creation set forth in the Pentateuch. This state of change is going on forever and ever, till the boundaries that restrain us shall be unrecognizable on the maps of the future. Cities shall grow, flourish, rise to prominence, and then crumble to decay, the sad remainders of fortune, only to be unearthed by people who will not understand us in the slightest. Let us pray they give us more credit than we're due, and that you earn yours today so that I may immortalize you. Now, off with you."

Appearing out of nowhere, Young Eagle, who had tucked Ping's tunic into his leggings, ran forward and leapt onto the horse, calming the animal expertly. Antonio leaned down to offer his hand to St. George Stanley. "The Phantom Padre to the rescue," St. George Stanley whispered, grasping the hand. "Huzzah."

Young Eagle easily found the wagon's fresh tracks. Without another word, he and Antonio followed the tracks east, skirting the dirt wagon road and the tent city outside the trading post. They hadn't much time, Antonio thought, because if Pigeye's confederates were with him, he would almost certainly leave the wagon at some point, find fresh horses, and let his friends drive the wagon on to a place like Fort Worth, posing as hidemen. At that point, the wagon tracks would be useless and misleading. No one but Ping knew what the men looked like. And whatever Pigeye had stashed in the wagon and couldn't carry, he could retrieve later.

As dawn crept behind them, Young Eagle pointed to the sky. Beneath the waning stars, dark clouds loomed with gigantic thunderheads, like wild animals prepared to stampede across the plains. Soon, the rain would wash away the tracks they were following. They kicked their horses into a full gallop.

They spotted the dust from the wagon several miles east of the town of Fort Griffin. The tree-covered land rose into hilly areas north of the road, and Antonio and Young Eagle detoured behind the hills to shield themselves. Young Eagle flipped down Ping's eyepatch and arranged the coolie hat on his head. When he and Antonio rode back over the rise, they had advanced beyond the wagon by a quarter of a mile. They turned their horses, and the wagon slowed to a halt as they trotted toward it. Now the sun was behind them, as Antonio had planned, intending for it to shine into the eyes of Pigeye and the two men who rode beside the wagon. But the sky was beginning to darken. They had barely beaten the storm. Over Pigeye Lehane's laughter, Antonio heard thunder from the high clouds that approached from the west, threatening to blot the sun.

Eyes shielded by one hand, Pigeye sat on the buckboard with Selenia beside him. He had driven the four draft horses hard. Both of the horsemen—one on either side of the wagon—had drawn rifles from their scabbards. Antonio held up his hand as a sign of peace. Young Eagle remained behind him, partially concealed. They stopped within pistol range of the wagon.

"We don't wish you harm," Antonio called.

Pigeye laughed again. "That's good, Padre. I must say, I thought no one would be looking for us for another long while. But good. Come closer. Might as well get it over with now." He jabbed Selenia with his elbow. "Eh, my darlin'?"

Selenia, numb with fright, said nothing. Antonio turned his horse broadside to Pigeye, hoping for an unobstructed shot. The sun flashed out from behind a cloud again, giving him an advantage. "You forgot your Bible, Lehane," Antonio said. "I've brought it for you."

"And I've got my bride. And the holy star you was so anxious to see."

"I don't care about that. Let the girl go."

Pigeye squinted toward Young Eagle. "Is that why you brung her Chinee woman with you? To give her comfort, be her servant? Oughtta be illegal to put a Chink on a good horse."

"She's worried for her. It was her duty to protect her."

"Well, then, Padre, you can tell her I ain't no savage. I got a cookstove for her in this wagon and some fine land for her in Missouri, where only a fool would try to look for us. I got a pick and shovel back there, too, so's I can offer a proper burial to anyone who tries to stop me."

"You killed four men just this morning," Antonio said.

Another cloud stole across the sun and Pigeye lowered his hand to his side. "I done many more than that in my lifetime. And I'll say you deserve to join 'em 'cause of your lies to me, Padre."

"Who says I lied to you?"

"A dead man done told me. At least, somebody you thought was dead. It were that man there." Pigeye pointed to the horseman to his right. "I heard how you met with my girl every morning when she went to pray. Everybody knowed about it. Did you think I wouldn't? And did you think I wouldn't want to know what you was prayin' for? So, this man of mine—he were lyin' beneath the dead man's sheet last morning when you told this girl you wasn't planning on ever finishing our wedding day. Do you say he lies?"

Antonio rested his hand on his cassock over the hidden pistol. His horse fidgeted. He tried to remember how much he had said before he escorted the shaken Selenia out of the chapel and into the fresh air. He was certain only that he hadn't yet revealed that he was not a true priest. "I dealt your game. You won, didn't you? I say whatever he thinks he heard, he took it wrong."

"Well, Padre, my man here wondered about that, so he went to the saloon, bought a few drinks from Mr. Peppert, says 'Ain't that something how ol' Patrick Lehane thinks he'll be married tomorrow when it ain't about to happen and won't he be surprised.' And Peppert says, 'So you're one of 'em, are you? You think four men's enough?' Well, that started him watching and listening and persuading—everybody knows who works for Fowler—and by the time you was dealing my game last night, he'd come to tell me the whole plan. Had to wait till I'd won the last deal. And you even planned that, too, didn't you Padre? That was one holy double-cross."

"What about the money you won? Don't you want me to get it for you?"

"You're right that I had to leave it there. But I got a bag with more in it, and mad as it makes me to leave what I won to that bunko bastard Fowler, he'll know I beat him. He'll know who was played the fool. It was him." He gestured toward Selenia. "I should of took her when I first had a mind to. I could've. But I wanted her to know I'd won her fair and square, so she'd feel good about it. About coming with me to Missouri. Well, there ain't no such thing as fair and square, so here we sit."

Selenia spoke, trembling, for the first time. "Let Father Peraza and Ping go back without hurting them. I will go on with you."

"It ain't that simple, darlin.' What if everybody thought I did nothing when somebody tried to cheat on me? Even a priest."

Antonio knew the conversation wasn't destined to last much longer. "I have a gun," he said. He turned back toward Young Eagle. "So does Ping."

He got exactly the reaction he had hoped for. Pigeye threw back his head and laughed till he loosened a gob of phlegm in his throat and spat it out. The two men with him looked at each other, smirking, their rifles erect. "I heard you was something with a pistol," Pigeye said, wiping his mouth with the back of his hand. "Like a phantom. Bang bang. Like the good Lord just slips a gun in your hand when you need it. But maybe nobody expected you to draw on 'em like I do now. For my money, I only know what I see in front of me—a priest and a Chinee bitch. Okay, Padre, go on and make your move. Both of you. I want to see God toss you a gun."

Tiny specks of rain spattered the dust. Antonio slid his hand through his cassock and felt for the handle of his pistol. Young Eagle didn't move. He held his arm crooked behind his back, reaching toward where he had tucked St. George Stanley's pistol. The rain came down harder, testing Pigeye's patience. He spat again from the buckboard. "I still don't see nothing, Padre, but it ain't right to threaten me noways. Saint or sinner, any man's a fool to make threats agin a man like me. But I'll give you something to remember afore this ends. I'll give you a sight of the holy star you was so anxious to see."

Pigeye reached behind the buckboard into a bundle. From it, he withdrew a perfect, incomparable gold star, decorated with glistening gems—emeralds on the arms and a ruby at the center. He thrust it aloft in his left hand. "Now here's something else to remember. Here's how to use a gun." Selenia screamed. The sun flickered one last time through a rent in a cloud. Several gunshots rang out—short, precise blasts nearly overpowered by a strange, chilling war cry and the thunder of the storm whose bloated clouds burst over the deadly scene.

* * *

BUDDY WATKINS [END OF DISK #19]: *...Back at Big Fort, St. George Stanley had done as he was asked. He protected Ping. And then when people discovered what had happened on that road, well, Mr. Charles St. George Stanley got a story out of it all right. The bodies of Pigeye's men were found lying where they were shot. One man was still barely alive, but when he regained consciousness he could tell nothing about what happened after the shots. All the horses were gone, and so was the wagon. Pigeye was nowhere to be found. Selenia and Young Eagle had disappeared, too. But the Phantom Padre's bloody cassock...it was found hanging on a crude wood cross above where the shooting happened. So the Englishman called his story 'The Death of the Phantom Padre.'*

10
Bidding Goodbye to Buddy

Without knowing it, during those perfect few days after my birthday, I was, in a way, making my peace with Buddy, saying goodbye to him—just as Babe was. Pony and Bill were the catalysts. Buddy had been a role model for the insecure, out-of-place boy I was because he had been the same. Saying goodbye didn't mean forgetting him. In fact, it meant allowing a long overdue homage to the memory of him, uncluttered by sorrow or guilt or anger at the fact that he was gone and we were bereft of a significant presence, a link to the sense of our own self-worth. Even the hill lost part of its soul when Buddy died. It had gained its present name because of him.

Babe told Pony about Buddy one night as we gazed from the hill down at Wendellton. I think she wanted to make clear to him why the hill had become a kind of sacred place to us, and why Buddy's role in our lives made her so adamant about not giving in to the Fowlers, easy and profitable as it would have been. And of course, the Fowlers despised us because of Buddy. Buddy was Zebulon Fowler's grandson and also the only link in the continuity of the Fowler empire that Zebulon failed to control.

Among other things, Babe was convinced that Buddy's father had been murdered by one of the Fowlers. She believed it fit the pattern of every canny and unscrupulous move that Zebulon had made after he had accumulated the basis of his fortune from Big Fort and was ready to take the next step toward the empire the Fowlers now ran—oil, cattle, banking, and investments.

Zebulon's planning for that empire had seemed brilliant and foolproof. By 1876, less than two years after the disappearance of Selenia Garza, he had enough money to abandon Big Fort and make his first bold move—bringing Eastern money West. He sent a thousand-dollar donation to the Women's Centennial Executive Committee of Philadelphia with a letter expressing hopes for an introduction to members of the committee should he have the opportunity to visit. He received a warm invitation in return. "I haven't gone soft on women," he explained to his accountant. "I plan to find me a wife with a rich daddy, and this money will get my boots within treading distance of her skirts." Indeed, when he returned to Texas he brought a bride back with him. His wife, Augusta, was the eldest daughter of a Philadelphia banker, Wendell Watkins, whose three other daughters already had married into society. Watkins was impressed with Zebulon's zeal and grateful that someone was willing to take Augusta off his hands. He also recruited land investors for his son-in-law and, as a major stockholder in railroads, helped route the rails through Wendellton, the town Zebulon founded at the southern end of his vast cattle ranch and named after his father-in-law and benefactor.

Zebulon and Augusta had a son, also named Wendell, and a daughter, Mary Anne, who was destined to be Buddy's mother. When he moved from Big Fort to build a home for Augusta on his expanding cattle ranch, he brought Ping, his Chinese laundress, to take care of household chores and serve as a nanny for Wendell and Mary Anne.

Ping spoke passable if profane English. Mary Anne was fascinated by her eyepatch, but the laundress always pretended not to understand when asked why she covered the eye. Ping's strangest habit was her worship of a yellow-striped cat that had been mounted in a stalking position by a taxidermist. Thankfully, Ping spoke to the cat in the privacy of her small room in the laundry shed. Augusta concluded that it was Ping's way of practicing and improving her English, and in that regard was happy to silently support the aspirations of her laundress. The presence of the preserved feline was also a way for Augusta, delicately, to correct Ping whenever she let loose with a profanity. "Ah, Ping," Augusta would say, wagging her finger, "save that word for the cat." Ping would smile and nod, and if the word ever was heard again it was only through the closed door of the laundry shed.

Ping was partial to Mary Anne, and Augusta even agreed to let her daughter serve as a flower girl when Ping, in a small private ceremony outside the laundry shed, married a Chinese cook called 'Yep,' whom Fowler had spirited away from a labor camp while inspecting the progress of the railroads. "I got me a Chinee whore already taking care of my wife," he told the Irish crew boss he bribed to obtain Yep's services. "This old coolie will give me a matched pair." Yep cooked for the ranch hands.

Unfortunately, Buddy never got to know Ping. She and Yep disappeared before he was born, after the body of an itinerant preacher named Phillip Scott Wolf was found knifed in the gut on the outskirts of Wendellton. For some strange reason, Ping's stuffed cat, upright and in its stalking position, was found near the body. The owner of a dry goods store displayed the cat in his window for a few days, then sold it.

At the age of eighteen, Mary Anne met her future husband—Buddy's father—in a roundabout way. Thanks to Augusta's determination to civilize Wendellton, Mary Anne traveled to Paris with her mother to hire an architect to design the finest courthouse in Texas, with a high tower and rosy granite walls—a monument grand enough to be the symbolic centerpiece of all that brother Wendell would inherit. If Big Fort now represented history, the new courthouse would represent the future.

At a salon, Augusta and Mary Anne were introduced to a young sculptor named Pierrot Longchamps. Ten years Mary Anne's senior, he began a serious flirtation with the vivacious American girl, who at 18 was fully developed ("pneumatic" was a term often used to describe her) and free-spirited. Mary Anne returned Pierrot's interest with the devil-may-care flair that was uniquely hers. Both women agreed that Pierrot would be the perfect choice to decorate the new courthouse with sculptures. Augusta spared no expense to bring him to Wendellton.

As Pierrot struck his first chisel blows in the stone facing on the east side of the courthouse, his flirtation with Mary Anne blossomed into a full-fledged affair. They were often seen riding together toward the broad hill northeast of the town, and disappearing beyond it. By the time Pierrot's chisel had sculpted the stone adornments on the three other walls, he and Mary Anne were engaged. He had carved a face on the west wall that many townspeople thought looked like Mary Anne. Some skeptics claimed that the last of Pierrot's designs, the one on the east corner of the north wall, could not be politely described. Consequently, it was never discussed publicly. Although Pierrot said it was a Texas rose, it was thought to bear a remarkable resemblance to female genitalia.

The courthouse became more famous for that one carving than for its granite walls. The Fowlers never altered the design, because if they had it would have been an admission that (1) it was indeed what people said it was, and (2) Mary Anne was the model.

Augusta remained oblivious of the sniggering, perhaps deliberately, because she was enamored of Pierrot and hoped he could contribute to the cultural atmosphere of Wendellton. Zebulon hated the idea of a foreigner—a Frenchman—having anything to do with his empire. But he could not stop the marriage. "Pierrot and I couldn't care less about running things, I promise," said Mary Anne. "We'll travel. Maybe we'll live in Paris for a few years. We don't want anything or need anything from the family."

Zebulon was inclined to follow Mary Anne's wishes and bid her goodbye with a train ticket, but Augusta, accepting that their daughter would marry regardless of their opposition, wouldn't hear of it. She insisted that the newlyweds should have a place of their own that would be their gift from the family legacy. "After all," Augusta said, "Her brother Wendell will have the ranch. Wendell will have the bank. Wendell will have Wendellton. Wendell's influence will reach from Texas to New York to—who knows?—China, where our blessed Ping came from. What will people say if your own daughter gets nothing?"

Servants who overheard the conversation reported that Zebulon replied, famously, "They'll say I put nothing into the hands of a rascal."

Augusta won the day. She insisted that Mary Anne not be humiliated by the family, whether Mary Anne cared or not. So Zebulon thought over the dilemma, then consulted his law firm before bestowing upon the couple twenty-five thousand acres northeast of Wendellton which included the large and unoccupied hill, suitable for grazing but little else. Moreover, the hill was easy to separate from his main holdings, as he owned nothing east of it. Local legend, passed along from cavalry scouts, had it that the only person who ever had lived on the hill was a drifter who spent the winter of 1874 in a dugout on the southeastern side then left for parts unknown.

Zebulon retained the grazing rights and even agreed to pay the taxes on the land, because he expected to get it back, to keep it out of the hands of any other potential land barons who might begin acquiring property and find Pierrot and Mary Anne willing to sell. His lawyers worked out the details. If Pierrot and Mary Anne ever stopped living on the hill for longer than six months, or if they died without a descendant, everything went back to the Fowler family interests. The agreement took effect as soon as the wedding vows were solemnized in June of 1897. Zebulon's mistake was accepting Mary Anne at her word and presuming that she and Pierrot would take off immediately for Paris.

They didn't. They were strangely captivated by the hill—Pierrot especially. The business of constructing new courthouses and other monumental edifices was booming, and Pierrot traveled from county to county to take advantage of the available work. Mary Anne used the income from his peerless chisel to establish a modest home on the low, protected southern rim of the hill, building a retaining wall and digging drainage trenches around it to divert the summer downpours. Locals began referring to it as "Longchamps Hill."

Both Pierrot and Mary Anne loved music. They used the money that was a wedding gift from Augusta's family to buy a player piano and acquire a collection of piano rolls that included French compositions by Fauré and Debussy, Stephen Foster songs and the latest Gay 90's hits. People from Wendellton rode by on weekends just to hear the music tumbling off the piano and out of the house.

In 1898, Mary Anne nearly died giving birth to a boy. He was named Buckley—Augusta's middle name, after her own mother's maiden name. Doctors told Mary Anne that Buckley was the only child she would have. She and Pierrot called him "Buddy" from the day he was born. He heard his first lullaby on the player piano. On my desk, I still keep a photograph of Buddy at six months old, looking even then a bit forlorn and confused, as if he knew he would be the odd man out in the Fowler family.

One Sunday after Buddy's birth, when Pierrot and Mary Anne were due to bring him to the six-columned Greek Revival executive mansion that Augusta had designed as the new domicile of the Fowler ranch, Zebulon gave vent to his frustrations during a conversation in his library with Wendell. Wendell was visiting during a break in his studies at Harvard.

"Your future is set, me boy," Zebulon said, "with only one goddamned blot."

"I think I can guess," Wendell grinned, drawing a handkerchief from his coat pocket. "You mean...PEE-rott..." He raised the handkerchief to his nose and pretended to sneeze. "Long-CHAMPS."

Zebulon laughed and slapped his knee. "I mean exactly that. If I don't fix it before Beelzebub gives me the run of hell, it'll be up to you. It's my only regret, giving up that land to a goddamned foreigner with naught more than a hammer and chisel to his snot-blowing name."

Neither Zebulon nor Wendell saw that Pierrot and Mary Anne, with Buddy cradled in her arms, had been standing at the door of the library to pay their respects to the patriarch. A few weeks later, Pierrot went to the courthouse which he had decorated so skillfully and changed his name. In fact, his true name had prompted ridicule wherever he worked in Texas, and overhearing Zebulon's insult was the last straw. Pierrot changed his first name to 'Peter,' but could not very well claim the name Fowler. Instead, out of respect, he chose Augusta's maiden name—Watkins. Mary Anne was happy with the decision. She told the Fowlers that the change improved Pierrot's chances of being hired. Augusta was flattered. Zebulon and Wendell made more jokes about it. Buddy became a Watkins, too.

When Wendell returned from Harvard at the turn of the century, the Fowler Land and Cattle Company controlled more than one million acres. They began buying up oil leases after the Spindletop gusher. The first test well they drilled was in the southwestern corner of their own ranch. It came in, the harbinger of what would become one of the largest fields in Texas. Fowler Oil and Gas was born, and eventually exceeded even the profits of the Humble Oil & Refining Company. Unlike the Humble oilmen, Fowler refused to sell a dime's worth of assets to Standard Oil or any other Eastern concern.

One would think that Zebulon and Wendell might have forgotten about the hill. Had they possessed it, it would have represented only a fraction—five per cent—of their land holdings. But when Mary Anne and Peter refused to sell them a lease to drill around its periphery (Zebulon had thought to retain only the grazing rights), it caused Zebulon's level of obsession to rise even higher.

"Maybe Peter should just have an accident," Zebulon mused one afternoon when he and Wendell were playing catch with Lloyd, Wendell's son. "Maybe his chisel could slip."

Buddy had developed a stammer for which his younger cousin Lloyd mocked him mercilessly. Zebulon simply laughed about it. The stammer grew worse. In school, Buddy all but faded into the walls and spoke to no one. Classmates joked that he had been seen with the fearsome Old Lady Baker—that she had come to kidnap and stuff him and add him to her collection of children and animals, but that she turned him down as too scrawny. Indeed, he never had been cut out for adventure or society. Lloyd was three years younger, but already outweighed Buddy by twenty pounds. Aside from his stammer, Buddy suffered from poor eyesight and dubious health throughout his life. Lloyd became a football star at Wendellton High. During the Great War, Buddy's attempts to enlist in the army were rejected because of his physical shortcomings. Lloyd didn't come of age until the year after the war ended, but talked incessantly of what he would have done to the Huns had he been given the opportunity. Buddy envied him even for that.

Painfully shy and ashamed of his deficiencies, Buddy settled into two hobbies, each of them an alternate form of communication. The first was making piano rolls for his parents. He used sheet music as a guide and cut the holes in the paper rolls himself with a knife and a ruler. When he was eighteen and depressed over his failure to join the military, Peter and Mary Anne got him a reproducing piano, the kind that marked a guide on a blank roll as Buddy played, so he knew where to cut the holes. Buddy became so accomplished at making the rolls that he was given commissions by the American Piano Company. He was proud of the income he earned, and insisted on returning every cent of it to Peter and Mary Anne. His one contribution to the war effort was a best-selling piano roll of "Over There," now in the Smithsonian Institution.

His second hobby was the manufacture of fireworks. Where stammered words and actions failed him, he used fireworks to convey his pleasure or excitement over a holiday or some other grand event. He studied books, made his own shells, and blasted them off from the top of the hill, always on the Fourth of July but also on any other day that called for a celebration—the birth of a child in Wendellton, a marriage, the end of the Great War.

People were charmed by the fact that the reclusive young man cared enough about them to celebrate their personal milestones. He simply couldn't overcome his timidity to tell them himself. Those who witnessed Buddy's fireworks extravaganzas never forgot them. They were visible for miles. Rockets zoomed upwards as if to replenish the shooting stars that had detached themselves from the sky. Great, blossomy bursts showered the firmament, bejeweling the profile of the hill, then separating into downy tufts that floated aimlessly but willfully like the heads of dandelions, now multiplicate, now imperceptible, now lost but nevertheless fertile. His generous spirit made him a kind of folk hero in Wendellton, which infuriated Zebulon, Wendell, and now, Lloyd.

At least once a year, the Fowlers offered Peter and Mary Anne increasing amounts of money for the hill and its environs, without success. By then, Zebulon, Wendell, and Lloyd had convinced themselves that the land had been all but stolen from them. Who knew what oil wealth lay beneath it?

Shortly after turning down a renewed offer from the Fowlers, Peter died in 1922 at the age of fifty-five. He was working on an office building in Lubbock when his scaffold collapsed in a strong wind. Lloyd was the one who informed the family. Having just graduated from Harvard, Lloyd happened to be in Lubbock arranging for gas pipelines to be laid from the Fowler fields into panhandle towns and across the border into Oklahoma. A followup investigation into Peter's death found that some of the scaffolding ties apparently had been removed, but no one knew when or why. A newspaper article quoted a police investigator as saying it was probably due to Peter's own carelessness. "He was born a Frenchman and changed his name," said the investigator, as if no other explanation or epitaph was required.

Buddy had just turned 24. He and Mary Anne buried Peter on the sunset side of the hill. Buddy continued to work on his piano rolls and build ever more elaborate fireworks shells, and after Peter's death, he could be seen on horseback every evening, riding up the hill and down again. Even in the midst of a raging thunderstorm, Buddy and his horse patrolled the hill like restless spirits on some eternal quest. Because of Buddy's solitary rides, the name by which the hill was known and the logic behind it gracefully elided from 'Longchamps' into "lone chap," and few people remembered that it ever had been called anything other than Lonechap Hill.

As soon as Lloyd came of age, he married and fathered another heir in the Fowler line—Wyatt, born in 1924.

As the Fowler fortunes grew in the 1920's, Zebulon openly began calling Buddy the family idiot, even to Mary Anne's face. "People who see him don't know what to make of him," he complained to Mary Anne on Buddy's 30th birthday. "You got to send him away to make a man of him before it's too late." He offered to get Buddy a job at a brokerage in New York and promised to make sure that his grandson was looked after.

Mary Anne just smiled and ignored the insult. "Buddy's an old soul," she said. "Give him some time."

"If we only could, m'dear," Zebulon said with a wheeze that had become far too genuine, mustering all the charm and sentimentality he could fake. "This land is as much a part of us as the very hands we work with and the legs we walk on. Don't ever let some accidental fate amputate it from the family tree. It's the only thing left for me to worry about before I go to my own reward."

"Why would you worry about that, Daddy?"

"There's jackals out there—human jackals," Zebulon said ominously. "Buckley would have no idea how to deal with them. You know—and I say this with great affection—that he could never get a w-w-word in edge-w-w-wise. You and Pierrot"— Zebulon pronounced her late husband's true name for the first time in years and did it properly—"the both of you had the love and sense to make sure that if anything happened to you, your beautiful hill and the land around it would never be torn asunder from them that nurtured it. It's in the papers you signed when I gave it to you."

"I've never forgotten, Daddy."

A smile crept over Zebulon's wrinkled face. "Of course not, little doe. But now it's up to young Buckley to carry on that tradition, and see that it's respected. You're my flesh and blood, so I'm trusting this to you, and I know you can make Buckley see how important it is. No offense to him."

Buddy, of course, took no offense. He promptly added to his will the same conditions (which Zebulon called 'protections') that his parents had agreed to. Should he cease to live on the hill or leave no descendants in occupation of it, the hill and surrounding land would go back to the Fowlers, through the entity that oversaw their enterprises.

Mary Anne died of ovarian cancer in 1934, at the age of 57. Buddy buried her next to Peter and went into deep mourning. He survived comfortably on the trust that Mary Anne and Peter had set up, largely in cash—it weathered the stock market crash nicely— and he added a third hobby, building crystal radio sets that gave him other voices to listen to now that he was alone. He donated hundreds of crystal sets to families mired in the Great Depression, helpless, isolated, and choked by the Dust Bowl. "For a f-f-f-few moments p-p-p-pleasure in a hard time," he told them. At night, he donned a set of headphones and listened under the stars to music, comedy, and drama from faraway places. For all intents and purposes, it was as if the sounds came from another planet, and Buddy marveled at them as one would marvel at alien life forms. Using a flat stick of wood with tiny crosshairs inked onto it, he pretended to speak into a microphone, imitating the brilliantly precise announcers he heard each night. When he did, his stammer went away, just as it vanished when he sang. He could say "Phantom Padre packed a powerful pair of popguns" without so much as a hesitation.

He grew excited about his newfound voice, and arranged for a visit to Dallas radio station WFAA, which broadcast his favorite program, the "inimitable breakfast hour broadcast" of Jimmie Jeffries. Buddy was fascinated by the technology—the microphones, the switches, the machines. Afterwards, he bought his own turntable with a cutting lathe that made 15-minute electrical transcriptions on acetate disks. He installed it in his living room, paid an engineer from Dallas to train him, and used the machine to record himself late at night on disk after disk. "This is Buddy Watkins," he announced, "speaking to the stars on the doorstep to the universe." He found an article on tongue-twisters and began reciting them flawlessly into his machine. Within a month, his stammer was conquered forever (Babe told Pony, as she had said many times, that by the time she met him, Buddy was the most articulate man she ever had known).

Occasionally, he heard Wendell's voice, broadcast from conventions of the Southern Committee to Uphold the Constitution whose wealthy sponsors railed against Franklin and Eleanor Roosevelt, labor unions, the NAACP, and the international conspiracy that was destroying free enterprise and lengthening the Depression. He recorded Wendell's speeches, too, and had a duplicate disk made of an especially good recording. He sent the disk to Wendell, but never received thanks for it, possibly because it was recorded at a speed of 33⅓ revolutions per minute (well in advance of the commercial release of LP records), was sixteen inches in diameter, and would have been impossible to listen to on a conventional 78 rpm phonograph.

Augusta Fowler died beneath a shrouded sky on April 14, 1935, during a black blizzard—a massive, hell-sent dust storm. She left a ten million dollar endowment for the Fowler Plains Museum.

Zebulon succumbed to emphysema two years later. Wendell was killed at the age of 61 when he was bucked off a horse during the 1940 Wendellton Christmas parade. Lloyd, then 39 years old, shouldered the patriarchy, which had been rich and diversified enough to withstand the Depression, and which now included responsibility for the museum. He made a number of unusual—some said questionable—acquisitions, including a painting by a little-known Western artist, Charles St. George Stanley. The painting showed a priest, in profile, holding a Remington pistol and standing over the bodies of three men, clearly outlaws, while two other men gaped at the scene. One onlooker is pushing his hat back on his head in awe and confusion. Beyond them is a florid sky. The priest's face is a pasty white. The silhouettes of grazing bison are also seen on the far horizon. It was, of course, St. George Stanley's illustration of the origin of the Phantom Padre. One critic, possibly in the pay of Lloyd Fowler, called it the equivalent of an allegorical Wild West scene by El Greco.

In his quest for art and business deals, Lloyd traveled extensively. He ran the family enterprises with an iron fist and—no doubt influenced by Wendell's paranoid conspiracy theories—never allowed himself to be photographed in connection with business or philanthropic activities. Most of the time, he traveled under an assumed name and even used the alias to acquire new art for the museum. "Our business is our business," he said often, "and nobody else's." He also looked out for his son. Because of the family's importance in meeting a critical demand for oil, Wyatt was exempted from the draft during World War II. He completed his education at Harvard in 1947. Still in his twenties, Wyatt, a business wunderkind, was more than ready for his turn at the family enterprises, and post-war prosperity gave him an extra boost. He soon took on increasing responsibilities when Lloyd suffered a head injury in 1948 after a fall during a business trip to San Antonio. Lloyd's headaches troubled and angered him, but he continued to govern the business unbendingly until he died of a brain hemorrhage in 1951 at the age of 50.

"And now it all belongs to Wyatt," Babe said. "Buddy never cared about it, anyway."

Pony sat up and stretched his arms to the sky, then lit another cigar. "What I'd really like to know is how the hell did Buddy ever meet you?"

"That's how the story ends, I guess. I got an internship at the museum after I graduated from high school and was accepted as an art history major at Trinity College. Buddy used to visit the museum after hours. His family had founded it and still ran it, of course, and he wanted them to do an exhibit about—guess what—the Phantom Padre and a long-lost treasure. Anyway, he and I would talk. The museum sells a biography of Zebulon Fowler in its bookstore. Makes him sound like a saint. All the employees were required to read it. Buddy used to laugh about it. He filled me in on the stuff that was left out or sugar-coated. But he was a much deeper person than that. He knew a lot about music. And he loved looking at the old bones in the natural history collection. I learned pretty much everything you've just heard from him. Anyway, after my internship, they offered me a job at the museum and I took it, and the person I most looked forward to seeing was Buddy. He took me under his wing, asked for nothing in return, and, I don't know, I'd never met a man quite like him. We got engaged over the Christmas holidays and married after the New Year in 1950."

"And what had led you there in the first place—to the museum?"

"Well, my mother wanted me to study art because art meant rich people, the kind you meet in museums. Buddy thought it was funny. I did, too."

"So I guess your mom was right."

Babe laughed. "She wasn't so happy about how it turned out. When Buddy and I were married, the Fowlers made it intolerable for me at the museum. Cold-shouldered me. Embarrassed me if I made a suggestion. Put me behind a desk licking envelopes. And Buddy didn't own a bank or an oil well. Just kept one horse—Tenbelow was his last, born on a day when it was ten below zero, died not long after Buddy. All Buddy had was Lonechap Hill. He built this house and barn when the old house down there was destroyed in a fire after we got engaged. All his precious recorded disks went up in flames. The odor of acetate was overwhelming. I think they could smell it all the way to Wendellton. Buddy mourned that loss as much as anything. Only one disk was saved—a disk that Buddy had kept in a safe in his old barn—but he just shook his head when I asked him to play it for me and said he couldn't bring himself to do it. When he was sick, thanks to John coming to us, our little adopted angel, Buddy got inspired again. He recorded all the best stories he knew on a stack of disks he wanted John to have." She turned to me with sad eyes. "You listen to them all the time, don't you honey?"

"I do. I like Buddy's voice." I felt a bit guilty. I had not yet listened to the disks Buddy left for my twelfth birthday.

Babe smiled, but the look in her eyes didn't change. Then she laughed a little too loudly. "Mother hated this new place, by the way, especially because I wouldn't cash in after...after Buddy left it to us."

"You did the right thing."

"I know. And I like the thought of Zebulon rolling over in his grave." Far below us, to the southwest, at the edge of Wendellton's lights, a white glow indicated where Big Fort and the Fowler Plains Museum stood, illuminated on all sides by floodlights. "So, anyway," Babe sighed, winking at the stars, "it was Buddy who gave the hill its name."

And that was the Buddy I was saying goodbye to, not because I was rejecting him, but because I felt I was moving on to a new phase of life, thanks to Pony and Bill. The phase didn't last very long. The next day saw the beginning of the end.

In the late afternoons, Pony and I ate sandwiches on Buddy's bench, the one near the birdbath on the south slope of the hill, while Babe worked in her gardens. Bill grazed and wallowed. When Babe was working, even Bill knew to leave her alone. It was obvious to anyone, man or beast, that if you wanted to make her mad, you would interrupt her in the middle of her gardening chores. They were time sensitive.

Babe was in the midst of weeding when Sheriff Leo Johnston's car pulled up to our gate. The sheriff honked his horn, then, after waiting a couple of minutes and getting no response, he let loose a few piercing blasts on his siren. Finally, he unchained the fence himself and drove up to the house. He parked next to Bill's trailer. The spook was back, sitting on his horse to the west of the hill, watching. Pony, Bill and I were barely in the sheriff's sightline, so Pony and I walked a little closer to the house, to move within earshot. Babe got up from her flowerbed, went to the front porch, rubbed a basil leaf, inhaled the scent, and didn't raise her eyes to greet the sheriff. "This is going to be good," I whispered to Pony. "She's furious."

"Good evening, Mrs. Watkins," said the sheriff. "You must not of heard me. Don't mean to intrude unannounced." He cleared his throat, dipped his head and stretched his neck as if he were trying to see past his belly to his feet. "Nice flowers."

"Let me guess," Babe snapped. "That spook that sits on our fence line jacking off in the saddle told you I've got a buffalo living here now. Well, he's not going to stay here forever, and I don't need a license for him."

"Well, that's all fine and good, but it's not the first thing I'm here about. I got other business, too." In the imposing manner he was trained to assume, Johnston walked onto the porch and moved his hulking form uncomfortably close to Babe. His brown Dacron uniform shirt was stained with beady islands of sweat. He fumbled with the silver star over his breast pocket, as if to straighten it. Most people would have reacted physically by retreating, swallowing, flinching, or any of those other things we do when faced with an invasion of that pristine space that separates us from the elemental halitosis of the rest of the world. Babe didn't blink—until she heard Johnston's first question.

"Have you recently seen or spoken with a man named Chen Wu Lee?"

The wind rattled a broken drainpipe that ran down the south edge of the porch from the roof. For a moment, Babe said nothing. Then she raised her lethal black eyes until they were locked onto the vacant blue eyes of Sheriff Johnston. "Who are you asking for?"

"Chen Wu Lee is the name."

"No, I mean who sent you to ask?" Babe said coldly. "Because you need to wipe that little foamy dribble of spit off your lower lip or someone might think you've caught rabies from the son of a bitch you came here to represent."

"That ain't true, and it ain't a proper thing to say to a law enforcement officer," Johnston replied.

Pony exhaled as if he had forgotten to breathe while Babe's temper rose. "Move a little closer," he muttered. "I don't want to miss a word."

I nodded, but I was already nervous. It was starting again. Chen Wu Lee was one of the two witnesses to Buddy's signature on the codicil to his will. He had Anglicized his name by placing his family name last and changing the spelling. The other witness was Chen's daughter, Joan. They helped Babe care for Buddy as his prostate cancer worsened and he refused to die anywhere other than on Lonechap Hill. Joan was a registered nurse and also had been a governess to me. She was, as I recalled, the kindest woman I had known, with the saddest eyes when she looked at me, even when she smiled. Dwight arranged for them to come to the hill after the Fowlers shrugged off the question of whether the family wanted to help with Buddy's care. As far as the Fowlers knew at the time, they were still the beneficiaries of his will. "Why are you bothering us with his problems?" Wyatt asked. "He's chosen that girl Babe. Let's see how he likes her taking care of him."

When an attorney challenging the codicil tried to raise suspicions about the witnesses—the Lees—having been hired by Dwight and Babe, Dwight replied simply and effectively. He noted that he had asked the Fowler family if they wanted to join in providing aid and comfort to Buddy, but they declined to be bothered. Dwight had outsmarted the Fowlers in advance.

I hadn't seen the Lees in more than three years, since the will had been upheld in court. I got Christmas and birthday cards from Joan every year, with hearts and x's and o's drawn all over them. It suddenly occurred to me that I had not received anything from her on my twelfth birthday.

"And you're damn well aware I know Chen Wu Lee," said Babe. "So what's this about?"

"Mr. Lee is afraid for his safety and the safety of his daughter Joan. Do you have any idea why?"

"Of course not."

"You know of no one who might have threatened him—yourself included?"

"That's bullshit, sheriff. I haven't seen him or talked to him since just after Buddy's will was upheld."

"No need to get out of control. Did you use that kind of language with Mr. Lee, by chance?"

"No, I only use it with people who have to clean the shit out of their ears when you squeeze their head."

Johnston looked away from Babe but plowed ahead as if he already had rehearsed his interrogation. "So your story is you haven't spoken in years. Not since he testified for you, I believe."

"That's correct."

"Mm-hmm. So you might be surprised to learn that Mr. Lee and his daughter have changed their story about the will?"

"If that's what you heard, you better wipe your ears again, sheriff."

"It came from a very reliable source."

"Your boss Wyatt Fowler?"

"I respect the Fowler family—unlike you, Mrs. Watkins. Or Miss Wong, whichever you prefer. And if an investigator tells me he can prove that Mr. Lee and his daughter did not witness Buddy Watkins sign any codicil to his will, then I'm inclined to believe him. And if those people are saying they participated in a fraud with you, then I'm also inclined to believe that they might be afraid of what could happen when they step forward to do the right thing."

"In case you forgot, I've already won that case."

"And the only thing under Texas law which would allow it to be re-opened is fraud. Torturous fraud, I believe they call it. I bet you know that, don't you? So here I am, conducting my own investigation like I'm sworn to do, and asking for your side."

"Get your ass off my land, sheriff. Or show me a court order. And tell the Fowlers they can't intimidate me with a limp gob of bacon fat like you."

Johnston looked directly toward Pony and me, then shifted his glance toward Bill. "You want that boy to hear you talk like that?"

"He's *my* boy, not *that* boy, and he's heard worse."

"I guess we'll see about that, too. And don't think I ain't heard about that grifter over there and his buffalo. And since you brought it up, do either you or him have a license for that animal?"

"I've got fences. I'll keep Godzilla here if I damn well please. This is my property. And it always will be."

"He ain't exactly livestock," Johnston continued. "That's a dangerous animal, and unrestrained as I see it. He ain't got his own pasture or corral. He could be a serious problem. I might have to give you a summons."

By that time, Pony had walked to the porch. "If you don't mind, sheriff, my name is Pony Antone..."

"I heard about you..."

"...and I'm the owner of that buffalo. I can get the proper papers if you need them. It'd just take a day or two. There's been some talk about him appearing with the governor for a Labor Day rodeo, and a friend in Austin has the paperwork." Pony was lying, but the sheriff narrowed his eyes and backed off.

"My main concern is the safety of that boy," Johnston said. "That buffalo could turn on him in a minute. We'll see how this goes."

Babe was tight-lipped and clearly agitated when the sheriff left. She shook off Pony, went into the house, and called Dwight. West of the hill, the spook turned his horse and rode away.

This time, the Fowlers weren't saying that Babe had seduced Buddy into doing whatever she wanted. They were saying that the papers she had presented to the court were forged, and that she knew it. The lawyers called it "tortious interference with an inheritance." If the Fowlers could prove forgery, then Buddy's estate would revert to the beneficiaries of his previous will, who were, of course, the Fowlers. I didn't believe Babe had forged the will, but I wouldn't have put it past her.

The last thing Babe told Dwight that day was to bring fireworks. Buddy used them in celebration, and Babe continued his tradition, except she also used them in defiance. She and Dwight had lit up the sky for more than a half hour the night after she won her court case against the Fowlers. "We'll give them a show to think about," she said. "That bastard had the gall to call me 'Miss Wong.'" Dwight agreed to leave for the hill early the next morning.

Dark, thin clouds, hinged awkwardly together like broken wings, obscured the western stars that night when I went to take Bill his carrots. I lay down next to him in the grass, one hand clenched, a small and blurry boy of twelve.

11
The Double Feature

The day that Dwight came, I still didn't know the truth about Babe. I didn't learn it for a few more days, when I ran away from Lonechap Hill. So I also didn't know that Dwight could hardly be considered my grandfather, even an adoptive one. I now believe that Buddy saw all of this coming and that his parables were a way of preparing me to understand those frailties and cruel choices and faithless acts and, most of all, the betrayals for love and despite love that mark our lives.

The gist of the truth was that Babe, my princess-in-exile, was not simply on a visit to China with her mother when they escaped the havoc of war. Nor was she Dwight Wong's San Antonio-born daughter. She was Shanghai-born, with a life torn apart in an August thunderstorm 23 years before the August in which I learned her story.

As a child, she lived for the Saturdays when her father, John Bridges, a British-American Tobacco executive, took her strolling through the gardens, shops, and stalls of the foreign concessions in Shanghai. Bridges was handsome and uncomplaining, and he always bought bouquets for Babe at the end of the day, then entrusted her to select a rose for his lapel from one of the flower girls on the streets. He called Babe his secret flower—not because he couldn't be seen with her, but because Bridges and Babe's mother made her understand, even then, that they could not be connected publicly through her. A few people knew, but loyally kept their silence. And Babe thought if the secret was ever revealed, she would lose her father's love.

Babe was the child of a liaison between Bridges and Bei Lian, a groundbreaking Shanghai movie star in a brief, golden era, who made history of sorts by defying convention and boldly displaying her unbound feet in a film that Bridges helped finance in 1926, when their affair began. After Babe's birth in 1928, which was not announced publicly, Lian continued her career as one of the ruling modern girls of Shanghai cinema, a part she played onscreen and off. It would have ruined Lian's image—and her career—to be exposed as the lover of a British businessman. Most of the time, Babe lived in a wing of Bridges' mansion with an amah who, if asked, claimed Babe as her daughter.

When Bei Lian did see Babe on occasion, she disguised herself with scarves and makeup and she sped through the streets of Shanghai on wild car rides that Babe found both terrifying and exhilarating. Babe saw her mother even less after Lian became the mistress of the head of the Guomindang's secret service in the early 1930's. Lian attached herself to her protector following the Japanese invasion of Manchuria and the three-month battle of Shanghai in 1932—a humiliation that resulted in a standoff to protect the foreign concessions. She made only two films in 1936 and 1937—both deploring the vices of materialism, reflecting the more sober topics that filmmakers were compelled to choose. Her fan base dwindled, but she nonetheless spent hours secluded with a secretary, autographing pictures that never again would be in demand and dreaming of starting a cosmetics business of her own.

On a Saturday in August, 1937, for the first and only time in her life, Babe had tea with both her mother and her father. Bridges brought her to Lian's mansion where a group of children had gathered on the pretext of attending a magic show. The show was staged by a Chinese-American named Wang Déwei, who entertained Babe and the other children with card tricks while her parents talked. Wang Déwei was the cousin of Lian's protector, the secret service chief. It was Babe's last happy moment in Shanghai. Afterwards, she was caught in one of those terrible and grotesque accidents of war that haunt their witnesses forever. Only with hindsight did she realize that John Bridges had foreseen disaster and brought her to the tea to explore alternatives for her protection. What Bridges failed to foresee was that the disaster would occur in a matter of hours.

Days before, the city had been placed under a declaration of martial law. Tensions between Chinese and Japanese troops were at a breaking point. After the Saturday tea, despite a growing crowd of refugees who streamed into the International Settlement to escape the Japanese, Bridges insisted on taking Babe on their regular walk along Nanking Road near the Bund. He explained what was happening and promised Babe that nothing would interfere with their walks, or with her weekly task of choosing a rose for his lapel.

Even the weather conspired against them. By afternoon, a storm was rising. Winds gusted fiercely, stinging Babe's eyes, making her rely even more on the guidance of her father's hand among the hectic crowds. At the sound of thunder, Babe and her father ducked into a flower shop. Then another sound frightened her. It was the buzzing of engines overhead. Chinese Northrop bombers appeared in the skies, flying to attack the *Idzumo*, the flagship of a Japanese fleet, at its mooring on the Huangpu River. Bridges squeezed Babe's hand. "Don't worry, my flower," he said. "I'll see to it." He left her in the back corner of the shop, and walked toward the Bund to watch the aircraft.

The *Idzumo* wheeled its anti-aircraft guns toward the oncoming planes.

A pilot panicked and prematurely released a pair of 2,000 pound bombs.

The bombs sailed, disinterested, through the dancing winds over Nanking Road toward the Palace and Cathay hotels. The first bomb entered through the roof of the Palace. Its errant sibling dropped past the pyramid that topped the Art Deco tower of the Cathay and arrived near a group of refugees huddled for shelter from the storm.

One body stuck like a swatted insect where it was blasted onto a wall. A decapitated policeman lay with his arms still extended to direct the automobiles that had exploded around him, lurching and flipping through the air. Most of the dead were strewn in piles at the edges of the buildings. After the explosions, Babe could not make herself remain in the flower shop. She rushed into the street, jolted by the chaos, following the direction John Bridges had taken. Her eyes blinked uncontrollably when she found her father's body with most of its clothing burned away. He lay amid the heap of bodies just outside the entrance to the Palace. His pocket watch was blackened but strangely intact.

She was nine years old. She picked up the watch and cleaned it as best she could.

A week later, she and her mother were on a boat to Hong Kong with a number of prominent Chinese politicians and underworld figures, as well as the ugly magician, Wang Déwei, who escorted them constantly around the boat. Bei Lian's film career was finished. She had no claim to any of John Bridges' assets. But, encouraged by Bridges, she had made one monumental decision to insure what she thought would be her short-term future far from the hostilities that consumed China. She agreed to accompany her Guomindang protector's cousin, Wang Déwei, to the United States, where he had been born and was a full-fledged citizen, 39 years old.

In Hong Kong, Lian was given registration papers and passports identifying her as Wang Déwei's wife and Babe as his daughter. Moreover, the papers listed them as U.S. citizens and Babe's birthplace as San Antonio, Texas—a ruse necessary to skirt the exclusion laws that prevented Chinese wives from joining their American-born husbands. Lian shed her identity as an actress (her films were not known in the U.S.), but she kept its compensations. She carried with her a stash of jewels she had received from her lovers. In fact, on the day they last saw each other, Bridges brought Lian a beautifully-wrapped gift, insisting that Babe hand the package to her mother. It was payment, inasmuch as Bridges could rely on it, for Lian's future conduct toward their daughter—a quadruple-row diamond bracelet worth more than enough to buy Lian's passage back to China and a Shanghai mansion to live in when it was safe again. It never was.

On the voyage from Hong Kong, Lian spoke only English and drilled her daughter on their new background—that Lian was Wang Déwei's wife. Babe must learn to call him 'father.' She would have a new grandmother and grandfather when she arrived in San Antonio. Babe had learned to honor and protect one secret for her beloved John Bridges. She must now learn to keep an even more important secret for her new father, Wang Déwei. Bridges, handsome and charming, soft-skinned and cologne-scented as he was, must be dismissed from Babe's history. And she must forget everything about her Shanghai life and never speak of it again—not to Wang, not to her mother.

Déwei was among the first of the ABC's—American-Born Chinese—ever to receive a law degree and pass the bar in Texas, a feat he achieved at the age of 31. His father had arrived in the United States to help build the western railroads as a laborer and cook. He later founded a store and restaurant in San Antonio and became a successful businessman in the Chinese community. Déwei earned his living managing the food market that his father had established. Déwei's law practice, run from behind a desk at the market, produced little income, as it was unlikely that anyone outside the 400-member Chinese community would hire a Chinese attorney. In 1937, however, he had helped lead a successful campaign against a proposal in the Texas legislature to strip Chinese of their rights to own property. As a result, his status in the community rose even higher.

Déwei visited China because of a legacy his father had created there. After his economic success in the U.S., Déwei's father journeyed to China to help his impoverished family, even to contribute to Sun Yat-sen's revolution. Déwei's relatives—among them, Bei Lian's Guomindang protector—had risen to become prominent officials. Déwei saw the opportunity to make himself useful on both sides of the ocean.

Déwei was careful to educate Babe in what her duties would be at the food market, and to promise her he would be a good, caring father. When he and his new family arrived in San Francisco, they were processed into the country from aboard their ship, even while others were transferred to Angel Island. Wang had submitted proper paperwork before leaving the country and had cabled contacts in San Francisco before leaving Hong Kong. Whatever favors and skills he had used to manage things, the identities of Bei Lian and Babe were not questioned.

His American name was Dwight Wong.

There was a stir when Babe and her mother accompanied Dwight back to San Antonio, but he suppressed it quickly. Dwight told the community that he had married Bei Lian on a trip to San Francisco—by traditional family arrangement—while he was in law school in his late twenties. That was the lie Babe learned as her new life's history on the boat ride to the United States—that Lian was born in the U.S., and that Dwight had sent her to China as soon as she gave birth to Babe, establishing Babe's status as a citizen. Dwight, so the story went, needed first to dedicate himself to passing his bar exams and building a career; Lian could be cared for by relatives; and Babe, in her formative years, could learn to appreciate the civilization of her ancestors. Dwight's father backed the story, which no one in the community was bold enough to contradict despite the fact that Babe already was nine years old when she appeared in San Antonio. The only joke—by those who dared—was that it would have been natural for Bei Lian to take as long as possible before returning to someone as ugly as Dwight. Sympathies for Babe and Bei Lian were increased by the horror of the invasion and by the death of Dwight's father in 1938, less than a year after they arrived. The old man had loved Babe, and showed it.

Among those who might have remained skeptical, it was also well-known that, as a cousin of the head of the Guomindang's secret service, Dwight had influence that could reach extended families across the ocean. Over the next few years, he organized drives for China wartime relief and made frequent trips out of the city, leaving Lian and Babe in charge of the market with his mother. Some speculated that he helped run a spy network that served both the U.S. and China.

Lian struggled with her new role, especially since her insistence on speaking Mandarin, not the Guangdong dialect that most locals spoke, was a source of friction. Until her death in 1944, Dwight's mother constantly criticized Lian for her haughty attitude and for not taking better care of Dwight. The women also clashed over Babe's upbringing. Babe's new grandmother insisted that she ride a Chinese-sponsored float in the annual Battle of Flowers parade to celebrate Texas Independence. "We must do everything we can to be accepted here," she warned. "It is not an easy life like the one you led in Shanghai."

Lian had other plans for Babe that involved using her beauty to seek wealthy patrons outside the community. "What you call acceptance is only a mirage," she said to Dwight's mother. "If you have glamour and money, you are accepted and don't need to kowtow." That was a not-too-subtle swipe at the older woman. The mother-in-law and the movie star despised each other unceasingly. And Bei Lian, the star and mistress to the powerful, had to accept that for all intents and purposes, her career had been an illusion. It was her duty to forget, as well.

Babe already was proficient in English, thanks to John Bridges, the father she no longer could acknowledge. She was educated in a Chinese School located in a Baptist Church until her final year, when she was accepted at an expensive, private girl's finishing school, at Bei Lian's insistence. She pleased her grandmother by marching in China relief parades when World War II began. She pleased her mother by becoming a noted and popular beauty in the community. It seemed clear from her looks—there were Caucasian traces in her features—that she was not Dwight Wong's daughter, but that was a taboo subject in the community. No one wanted to offend Dwight, or even his haughty wife. His affairs were his own business, they said. His political prominence became even greater when the war was followed by renewed fighting between the Nationalists and Communists, a conflict that convinced Lian she could never go home again. It made her more determined than ever that her daughter's beauty would not be wasted as hers had been.

I must say that my own memories of Bei Lian—she died not long after Buddy—were uniformly unpleasant, despite the fact that Dwight worshipped her. When she and Dwight visited, they always arrived at high noon in Dwight's black Cadillac convertible with the monster-sized fins, jet pod taillights and stacked front bug-splattered grilles that resembled a chrome set of George Washington's dentures. The car didn't really reflect Dwight's taste. Bei Lian was the flamboyant one. Invariably, as she climbed out of the car, she launched into a harangue before her red high-heeled shoes hit the earth. She inveighed against our living on the hill in the midst of nowhere, directing all her comments to Babe and ignoring Buddy as if he didn't exist. "When are you going to get rid of this goddam place and move back to San Antonio, Babe? We're going to die on the highway coming to see you or you'll all get murdered out here someday and no one will know it till they see the buzzards picking your bones. How are you, John? Didn't my daughter clean you up for our visit?"

She told Dwight he was ugly at least ten times a day, in both English and Chinese. Dwight just shook his head as if I were too young to know when I asked him what one Mandarin diatribe meant, but Bei Lian had no compunctions about translating for me. "It means he's the ugly son of an evil-eyed witch," she said. I thought it might have been a common insult among the Chinese, but Babe said, no, Dwight's mother bore him with great trouble late in her life—she was 45—then was certain he could do no wrong. Dwight, of course, had learned never to take sides. When Lian lit into him, spurred by her undying grievances against his mother, Dwight always nodded and smiled. That smile amid the tempest of Bei Lian's harangues was simultaneously abashed, amused and forgiving.

I now understand why Dwight accepted such abuse—because Lian's charisma hovered around her like a ghost. Her body remained taut and reed-thin, like the cigarettes she chain-smoked, and she sheathed it in form-fitting clothes. She tied her hair into a bun, possibly for the mesmerizing effect she had on Dwight when, sipping tea on our front porch, she undid the bun on summer nights and let her hair drop like a bolt of silk over her shoulders. It was in Lian's face that you saw her age—not because of wrinkles, but because of a hardness you might expect in someone who had learned to tolerate regret and disillusionment.

For whatever reasons, Dwight never showed any side other than his modest one to me, but I know that those who opposed him—the Fowlers, for instance, when he defended Babe's right to Lonechap Hill—almost always wound up on the losing end. That helped feed my fantasy that Babe was in fact a princess in exile and that Dwight was her unfailing defender.

The morning after Babe's call, Dwight drove non-stop from San Antonio in seven-and-a-half hours. He arrived shortly before noon, dressed in a lemon-colored suit with a faded blue shirt and black tie. In his early sixties, he was still alert and thoughtful, and with age, his broad features suited him better. His eyes were so wide apart that they seemed to work independently of each other. His heavy cheeks dragged down the outer corners of his eyes, but when he smiled it lingered on his countenance for an extra few seconds until his face settled again into its rumpled expression.

Babe wanted to confer with him immediately, but he waved her off and insisted on being introduced to Pony and Bill. "This is a fine, wise animal," he said as he stood before Bill. He took time to browse through the water colors and sketches that Pony had made on the hill, and complimented each of them. Then he turned to me. "I picked this up for you on the way here." Dwight, ever the magician, reached into his pocket and pulled out an ace of hearts. "For an extra happy birthday." He passed one hand over the other, and the card became a ticket to the Wendellton Movie Theater. "It's a double-feature, both movies made here in Texas. Extraordinary. You'll travel through time."

I tried to look delighted, but it was obvious that Dwight and Babe wanted to speak privately, with no chance of a twelve-year-old snooping around. "Maybe Pony can go, too," I said.

"I'd like to, champ," Pony said. He'd been calling me 'champ' since I learned to box. "But I've got a ways to drive to meet someone Dwight set up to do us a favor."

"For what?"

"Well, I need to take care of some paperwork in case that sheriff calls my bluff about Bill."

"Make sure you write him a good pedigree," Babe said.

I couldn't help but feel insulted at being left out of whatever had to be said, because my life was no less involved in Lonechap Hill than Babe's. Pony offered to drive me into town, but I declined brusquely and got my bike from the barn. It was only a fifteen-minute ride to the Wendellton town square, and I made the trip often to go to the movies, get candy, or visit the rotating rack at the drug store to enjoy the unique, antiseptic scent of a freshly-printed comic book.

Sweating from the heat, I walked into the theater's cool, dry darkness with my popcorn sometime after the first few minutes of *The Amazing Transparent Man*. It was about a nutty former army major who wants to take over the world with invisible soldiers. "You trust no one and hate everyone," he tells the man he has freed from jail to help him. "You're the kind of man I need and understand." Exiled from whatever was being decided on Lonechap Hill, I felt I could empathize. The movie climaxed in the invisibility lab with a fight that set off a nuclear blast. A mushroom cloud rose over the Texas plains. Then it was over and the screen filled with concession ads.

Sitting in the half-light between features, contemplating the potential world-altering destructiveness of only a few malicious men, I felt a wave of anxiety creep over me—not because of the mushroom cloud, but because I thought I heard Darryl and Cameron Fowler talking and laughing not far from where I was sitting. I slumped in my seat, waited for the house lights to dim again, and prayed they had not noticed me. I committed myself to staying through the entire second feature, *Beyond the Time Barrier*, hoping they would be gone when I was ready to leave. I would have given anything for either invisibility or the power to travel through time, whatever it took to avoid facing the brothers.

Nuclear catastrophes also figured in *Beyond the Time Barrier*, which was laced with predictions of the eventual extinction of the human race—threatened by bald post-nuclear mutants. The heroine was a deaf mute with enormous tits who happened to be the last fertile woman in what was left of civilization. She was no doubt some director's fantasy of the ideal woman, and I kind of fell in love with her myself. Then she was killed in the last reel. It was depressing, and I grieved for the fantasy that was extinguished before my eyes. I thought I felt a Milk Dud hit me in the back of the head, but didn't turn around. I remained slumped in my seat for a few minutes after the film ended and sat through the trailers for the coming attractions, *Psycho* and *The Alamo*. Nuclear holocaust, mutants, psychotic killers, Santa Anna, and the Fowler brothers.

After what had been my best week ever, suddenly there was a lot to worry about in August of 1960. I couldn't have imagined the half of it.

The inevitable happened when I reached the bike rack at the side of the theater. I had a Western Flyer with a fender headlight, a chrome tank painted red and black, and red grips and pedals. It was streaked with dirt and the colors had faded, but that was the way I liked it. What it lacked were speed gears. It was especially tough to pedal uphill. I backed it out of the rack and squeezed my eyes together—they were still adjusting to the mid-afternoon sunlight outside the theater—choosing not to look to either side, as if to shut out the rest of the world. It didn't work. Darryl's voice was the first one I heard.

"It's the whoreboy," he said. "Say hello, whoreboy."

I ignored him.

"Why won't you say hello to my brother?" Cameron called. "Are you some kind of Commie snob?"

I didn't need to look at them to picture how they stood. Darryl, who had just turned fifteen years old, had both hands on his hips and a loopy smile on his face. The smile was deceptive, in that there seemed to be no malice behind it. He was already 5'8", with an egg-shaped face and brown hair that flopped down the sides of his head to just above his ears. Cameron, who was my age, was pointing at me stiffly, re-cocking and lowering his arm several times for emphasis. His hair was thick and blonde, combed across his forehead. His otherwise slender nose bulged up and out in the middle, where it had been broken. He had no smile, only a sneer on his narrow lips. He was louder and meaner than Darryl, perhaps because he always had been under the protection of his older brother and never had to adopt any of the compromising postures learned by those of us who fight our own way through the world or surrender to it.

Without a word, I climbed onto my bike and aimed it around the front of the theater, onto an eastbound sidewalk that took me along Augusta Street, out of the town square and into a residential neighborhood. After several more blocks, I would reach Lee Street, which led north past the school and to County Road 207, the road to Lonechap Hill. The bike wobbled as I started to pedal, which drew a laugh from the brothers. "Look at the Commie Chink spaz," Cameron snorted. I was determined to pedal slowly so I wouldn't appear to be panicking. Darryl cruised past me, then jumped his bike over the curb to cut in front of me on the sidewalk. He was riding a three-speed, black Schwinn Racer. I couldn't have outrun it no matter how hard I pedaled, so I continued to go slowly. Cameron's bike came up behind me. I could hear it because Cameron had used a wooden clothes pin to clip a playing card over the spokes of his back wheel. The card fluttered madly against the rotating spokes. "Are you going to say hello or not, spaz?" Cameron called.

The three of us continued to pedal slowly east. Augusta Street seemed endless.

Darryl glanced over his shoulder. "Yeah, you must think something's wrong with us, not to say hello."

"Hello," I said weakly. I knew it was a stupid thing to do, but I didn't want to give them an excuse to go further.

"Did you hear that?" Darryl called to Cameron.

"I heard it."

"Who gave you permission to talk to us, whoreboy?" Darryl barked like a drill sergeant.

"He thinks he's better than we are even though he's a Commie Chink." Cameron's bike was so close to my rear fender that I thought he was going to knock me over.

Weeds sprouted from the cracks in the sidewalks that dipped to meet the cross streets then rose again at the beginning of each succeeding block. The homes we passed were small brick structures which had been built on large, mostly treeless lots. They sat looking like square, somewhat misanthropic dwellings, albeit ones whose front walls aligned as if they had been laid out like military barracks. Shirtless fathers worked on the front lawns. Mothers washed dusty front windows. Children circled on their tricycles in driveways. Adolescents shot basketballs toward nets hung above garage doors. Life went on with a certain insensible automation, deaf to the inharmonious racket pounding in my brain. It was as if I glided invisibly past that hermetic neighborhood, the amazing transparent boy, unprotected even within a tableau of middle class tranquility. I wished that the brothers would break off their chase with an insult or two and consider me properly humiliated, but I knew they would not.

I turned left onto Lee. Darryl, to my front, had continued along Augusta, but quickly reversed himself on a shout from Cameron and was soon in front of me again. We approached the school. Was this where they would choose to attack? A Wendellton Police car pulled out of a side street and I waved at the officer behind the wheel. He smiled and waved back politely. He was headed toward the town square. We were now beyond the school and near the county road.

"I think the spaz called the police on us," Darryl shouted. "He's the one they ought to arrest."

County Road 207 was a two-lane blacktop with narrow graded shoulders and weedy bar ditches on both sides. From the turnoff, it was another half mile east to our gate at the bottom of Lonechap Hill. If the brothers were going to do anything, it would be along that stretch of road. There was still a chance they would turn left and return to their mansion at the ranch on the other side of Wendellton, satisfied with the power they had exercised and unwilling to spend more time and effort on an easy target like me. My heart sank when Darryl turned right, because I could guess what his strategy would be. The brothers had used it before. Cameron would approach from behind and Darryl would push me into him, tripping me into the bar ditch from where it was nearly impossible to escape until they were done.

No traffic was in sight. We were traveling on the south side of the road. Before he had gone another fifty yards, Darryl swerved his bicycle sideways and came to a stop, intending to make me pedal in reverse onto my brakes while Cameron blocked my left side. With a stroke of luck, I wheeled abruptly onto the county road and across it before Cameron could make his move. Now that I was on the north side of the road where the gate to Lonechap Hill would be, I started to pedal for all I was worth. It wasn't fast enough. Just short of the gate, Darryl and Cameron caught up to me. Darryl bumped me. He managed to maintain his balance by spreading his legs onto the ground and scraping his heels. Then he stopped. I had no choice but to brake, because Cameron was riding closely beside me and to my right. I jumped off my bike and let it fall. I already had made up my mind to abandon it, because I was so close to the gate and sanctuary. I ran away from Cameron, who was still sitting on his bicycle. He reached out. I felt his fingers slip off my shirt. I was on the verge of climbing over the gate when Darryl grabbed me by my shoulders and pulled me back into the dirt.

"Get up, whoreboy," he said. "Don't you know you made things a lot worse for yourself? We were just having fun till now."

Cameron already had taken his position behind me. Darryl clearly intended to push me back toward the bicycles and into the bar ditch. I stood and faced him, only an arm's length away. Darryl shoved me in the chest with both hands. "I'm reminding you, this is your fault," he said. "You're about as stupid as they come." I had fought the brothers before to no avail because Darryl could easily outhit me and Cameron only struck from behind, kicking my legs, punching my shoulders, or upsetting my balance. I always flailed at them with roundhouses and hardly ever landed one solidly. This time, I raised my fists to my chin and made sure my elbows were parallel to the ground, as Pony had taught me. Because I stood on an upslope, Darryl's height advantage wasn't as great. His eyes widened. His smile looked almost friendly. Then he cringed in mock fear. After all, he was fifteen and I was barely twelve. It was not within the ability of any twelve-year-old, least of all me, to kick a fifteen-year-old's ass. He bent over laughing as if he couldn't contain himself. When he straightened up again—that was the rebound, I told myself—I moved toward him and hit him twice with straight punches to the nose. Before I felt the impact on my fists, Darryl was on the ground with a thick stream of blood on his upper lip. Quickly, I ran to the gate, vaulted over it, and made the mistake of looking back. Darryl was up, wiping the blood from his face with the back of his arm, and Cameron was next to him shouting, "Let's go get him."

The brothers stormed the gate. I turned and ran. Both brothers were faster than I was, and Darryl was screaming "I'm going to kill you when I catch you."

"Get him, Darryl," Cameron shouted.

No one was outside the house to see the chase. Pony's truck hadn't returned, either. I was barely a quarter of the way up Lonechap Hill when I stumbled, rolled over, and looked back to see that Darryl had stopped running when I fell and was approaching me deliberately, circling to my right.

"Kill him, Darryl," said Cameron. "We'll throw him on the highway and they'll think a car hit him."

I stood and scrambled backwards. "I will kill you," Darryl shouted. "Then I'll have you stuffed by Old Lady Baker and use you for a scarecrow." His eyes flashed to the right, then back to me. He laughed. He looked to the right again. This time, his head shook a bit. Otherwise, he didn't budge. At the sound of a roaring, guttural bellow that made my heart leap, he dropped his hands and screamed, "Oh, shit."

When Darryl finally moved his feet, it was to turn and run back toward the gate. Cameron ran with him. Around the eastern side of Lonechap Hill, Bill came charging through the grass. His great bulk heaved against the downward slope of the hill, his mane flopped on his forehead, and his hoofs flung divots of sunbaked earth and brittle grass behind him.

Babe didn't take me to church. It was too full of hypocrites, she said, who would see our Chinese features and consider it their missionary duty never to leave us alone. She did pray to a higher being, for me and for her gardens, but I had only a vague concept of divine promise, no more specific than the fanciful adventures of Phantom Padre, until I saw Bill, like a shaggy, tornadic, redeeming force, heading straight toward the brothers. They made it over the gate and never looked back. I did hear Darryl shout, in a voice that had become much more high-pitched, "I'm going to have that goddam animal shot." He and Cameron climbed on their bicycles. "I'm about to get my learner's permit," he cried. Only Darryl could make that statement sound like a threat. But the concept of him behind the wheel of a car was frightening. "And when I do, I swear I'll catch you and run you down like a goddam armadillo."

With that, he and Cameron pedaled west toward Wendellton in third gear. Bill stopped at the gate, thrashed his horns on a post, and turned to scratch himself. It wasn't the kind of situation that called for a hug. I opened the gate and retrieved my abandoned Western Flyer, which I had expected the brothers to destroy. It was one of the few incidents I wished the spook could have witnessed, but he wasn't there.

Bill walked up the hill with me. I hosed him down and watched him wallow passionately near the barn. Then I gave him a good brushing. I didn't go into the house to announce myself, but leaned against the back side of the barn and noticed how heavily I was breathing. I sat there with my head swimming, serenaded by the buzzing of the flies weaving drunken patterns on the west wind. I couldn't stop thinking about what had happened and whether I should tell anyone.

I heard the front door of the house open and close and could discern, faintly, the voices of Babe and Dwight. "It will be a shock to John," Dwight said. "So think about what you wish to tell him about Joan."

That got my attention. Joan Lee was the nurse who helped care for Buddy in his last days. She also was a governess to me when Babe was occupied with Buddy's medical issues and with the lawsuit over the will to which Joan and her father were witnesses. According to the sheriff, both Joan and her father now had recanted their sworn testimony that they had seen Buddy sign the will, leading to Babe's distressed call to Dwight.

"I'm going to let you talk to Joan," Babe told Dwight. "You're the only one who can set her straight."

"Yes. But you must explain to John."

"He's smart. He may start to unravel things on his own."

"Nevertheless."

"I suppose."

"He must know everything someday."

"This hill is his—what did you call it in the Old Monkey stories you told me?"

"You mean a secret spot of heaven?"

"Yes. It's his secret spot. Buddy called it the doorstep to the universe. I can't lose it for him, whatever I have to do."

"Even...you know...?"

"It's never going to come to that. It makes me nauseous to think of it."

"Your dahlias are lovely."

I waved the maddening flies away from the trickles of sweat on my forehead and tried to comprehend what I had just overheard. Having escaped the Fowler brothers, I now faced the prospect of some other kind of upheaval in my life, one that might be substantially worse. It did not take me long to connect the dots, once I replayed the conversation in my mind. Only one interpretation made sense, and Babe was right—I didn't need to have it spelled out. Joan Lee was my mother. That part of the equation fell into place so logically that it was frightening.

The scenario I constructed was this. When Babe and Buddy were married and wanted to adopt an heir (so I deduced), Dwight used his influence within the Chinese community to manage it, finding a young woman at the right time, with the right pedigree, under the right circumstances. Joan would have been unmarried when she gave birth to me, and if the father was Caucasian—Pony?—it would have been all the more shameful for her. I was eighteen months old when adopted. Moreover, Dwight had arranged for Joan and her father to become Buddy's caretakers on Lonechap Hill—why not to indulge Joan's attachment to me? That explained her kindness and her sad eyes and the birthday and Christmas cards. It also meant that Dwight must have protected her family from what would have been a damaging scandal. Then why was her father betraying us to the Fowlers, if there was any truth to the sheriff's claim? Were they trying to make a deal? Did Joan decide that she wanted me back? Was there a way she could nullify my adoption? The Fowlers certainly would have supported that. And how could I reconcile that with my hope that Pony was my father? It still wasn't impossible. Pony could have known Joan in the years before I was born. After all, my father was almost certainly a Caucasian. Maybe it was even more likely that Pony and Joan were my parents, I reasoned, because events involving both of them had coincided with my birthday. My mind was tumbling with contradictions, of course, but they clashed with my hopes and so I tried to reconcile them. I would say nothing to anyone about what I had overheard. Or about the Fowler brothers.

12
The Scale of Things

A truck arrived in the afternoon to deliver boxes of fireworks. Pony came back shortly before dinner, brandishing a bill of sale that showed that Bill had come from a bison ranch in Oklahoma. Dwight examined it closely. "Very passable," he said.

"Thanks for the recommendation," said Pony. "He seemed very glad to do a favor for you. I damn sure appreciate it, whatever he owes you. I also picked up something for you, son," he said to me. "I'll show it to you later."

After dinner, we took drinks out to the picnic table and watched the sunset. The clouds looked like spun candy, reddish and fleecy in the half-light that remained of the day. "Those are lovely clouds," said Dwight, "much lovelier because of the emptiness beneath them. This emptiness, this is a great thing to behold, like the soul of the earth at ease."

He was fascinated by Pony's buckskin star chart and studied it closely, nodding and smiling. Using a finger which he covered carefully with a handkerchief, he traced where the Chinese constellations would be on the chart—the mansions and enclosures in the sky. Bill, he said, would have come from the mansion of the ox, in the vicinity of Capricorn. "We see different truths, but we follow the same maps no matter where we think we are going." He looked sideways at Pony, his eyes rolling as if they were independent of each other, and then at me. "We are all displaced from the moment we leave the womb until we reach the grave."

Dwight excused himself and went to use the telephone in the living room. Babe stayed with Pony and me for a walk around the hill. She had pulled her hair back into a pony tail, which emphasized the perfect oval of her stunning face. She wore a simple yellow dress. Her loose skirt danced in the breeze. The sun, as it began to dip behind her, accentuated her figure. At one point, she put her arms around Pony's waist and rested her cheek on his shoulder while I looked away to study the sky. They stood for several moments, holding each other. I couldn't keep another thought from intruding—if Pony was my father and Joan was my mother, where did Babe stand? Did she suspect what I suspected, and would she care if she did? It was far stranger than the double feature.

Babe reminded me of my afternoon in Wendellton. "Tell us about the movies, honey."

"They were okay. Actually, they were stupid. There were no heroes."

"We all need someone who'll look out for us when we can't look out for ourselves," Babe said. "That's Dwight for me. So why don't you and Pony go on and talk about whatever...Phantom Padre or whatever. I've got to visit with Dwight for a while."

She squeezed Pony's hand and kissed me on the cheek and went back to the house.

"I'll show you what I picked up for you," said Pony. "I drove by Harvey's and got it. Remember the Phantom Padre magazine covers he had?"

"Really? Did you get one?"

"I did. Mainly, he just had the covers, framed for the walls. But this one, he had the complete issue." Pony retrieved a zippered document bag from his truck and produced a Frank Leslie's *Illustrated Newspaper*. The cover was ghoulish. A man in a dark suit was in the center, arm outstretched toward the hill behind him. To his left stood a man holding both hands up to a bandaged head. To his right was a weeping woman. On the hill was a cross with a black garment hanging from it and a pistol belt slung over one arm of the cross. The story connected to the illustration was titled "The Death of the Phantom Padre." It was written under the byline of "Your Western Correspondent, S.G. Stanley." We sat on the edge of the porch beneath a light bulb. "Want me to read it to you?" Pony asked. He began before I could answer.

> It was on a blistering hot morning in August at the trading post where he had stopped for sustenance that the Phantom Padre discovered a horrible crime had taken place. A notorious robber we shall call Swineman (not his real name, to protect the innocence of any family members who may read this) had abducted the beautiful barmaid Selenia. Contemplating the terrible fate that awaited her in Swineman's hands, the Padre strapped on his Remington and enlisted the aid of a young Indian tracker he had converted to the faith. The boy was cleverly

disguised with an eye patch and a coolie hat so that Swineman would mistake him for a Chinese laundress instead of the warrior he was, ready to attack. Off they went, along the wagon road that led east from the trading post.

Within a few hours, they came upon Swineman and two members of his crew, driving a wagon of stolen hides. The ravishing Selenia was made to sit next to Swineman. "Hold, Swineman, in the name of God," the Padre cried. He had the drop on the poltroon, but Swineman committed the ultimate sacrilege. He held aloft a jeweled star, a symbol of faith that he carried, hoping the Padre would dare not risk shooting a holy object. When the miscreant swung forward his other arm, it brandished a rifle. The lightning fast Padre had no choice but to draw his Remington and fire. At the same instant, Swineman fired a rifle bullet straight through the heart of the Padre, who was caught by his Indian companion as he fell from his mount.

The Indian lad then threw off his hat, rolled beneath his horse, leaped to his feet, and with his own pistol took out Swineman's two henchmen. Swineman himself had been done for by the Padre in his last brave act. Only one living witness remained at the scene, a henchman of Swineman, badly wounded by the Indian boy, who described the confrontation to all who would listen. He could not say what happened to the wagon or the bodies. At the top of a nearby hill, however, a cross was evident. Soldiers from Fort Griffin who investigated the scene found the bloody cassock of the Phantom Padre hanging over the cross, tied to it with a sash. They removed their hats in silent prayer, then left the hero at his final resting place, buried by which survivors we can only speculate.

Word of all that had happened eventually reached the trading post. The young Indian was never seen again, nor was the beautiful barmaid Selenia. It was said that the boy helped her to the next town, where she was taken in by a widow. Both owed their lives and whatever future happiness they may realize to the great, lamented Servant of God and Mankind, the Phantom Padre.

"If you notice the publication date," Pony said, closing the magazine, "you'll see it's more than a year after the incident. That gave them plenty of time to publish a whole collection of Phantom Padre stories before they killed him off. What do you think?"

"I don't think they killed him. I'm going to listen to what Buddy said on my birthday disks. He wouldn't let the story end there."

Pony's reply was another key to the reason he had come to the hill and, for that matter, a key to my own existence, although I couldn't have known it then. "No story truly ends," he said, as if he were repeating a well-worn axiom. His expression changed, betraying signs of frustration as he continued. "It's somehow connected to another and another and another, often in the least likely ways. And you can't separate yourself from even the strangest and most faraway stories, because it will prove to be part of yours." We heard Babe's voice calling us into the house. Pony crushed a cigar beneath his boot and sighed. "I guess we'll have to continue later."

Babe fed us the rest of my birthday cake, and I promised myself that I would make time the next day to listen to Buddy's newest disks. I told myself I hadn't bothered because I hadn't had the time. The real reason, I now am sure, was that I was enthralled by Pony and Bill and reluctant to return to any vestiges of the lonely and cocooned life I had led, even the unfinished stories that were Buddy's legacy to me.

Early in the morning, when it was dark and silent, I was ready for my new ritual. I kept bunches of carrots in a grocery box on my desk, my own private stash for Bill so I could take some to him and tell him whatever was in my heart while the rest of the world slept. That morning, smoothing out his red blanket, I thanked him for saving me from a beating by the Fowler brothers, or worse. There was no doubt in my mind that Bill's charge down Lonechap Hill was a willful act—that he had sensed my distress from far away and reacted to it as a guardian would. Then, as I stood whispering to him, I heard sounds from below our position. I crawled forward to a small rise and peered over it into the shadows. I had heard the sounds before. They were the tones generated by Pony's metal detector.

Illuminated by a small lantern, Pony was pacing around an area we had visited several times. At one point he set down the detector and used a pickaxe to loosen the soil, striking the hill several times and raking the dirt away from the incision he made.

I held my breath and ducked. Bill was standing so close behind me that I lost my balance and fell backwards. "Hello?" Pony called softly. "Is that you, Bill?" He dropped his pickaxe, picked up the lantern, and walked up the hill. His footsteps barely made a sound.

"Oho," he said when I stood. "What are you doing out at this hour?"

"I come out to talk to Bill," I said.

Pony paused and looked at me for a few uncomfortable seconds. "I'm sure he enjoys the company."

"I heard the metal detector."

"Yeah. Look..." Pony recovered his charm. "With all that's going on, I couldn't sleep. And I've been thinking—remember when Babe said there was something about a drifter who supposedly lived in a dugout here one winter? Well, that's what I think that outcropping might have been. A dugout. I had a hunch, and I couldn't get back to sleep for thinking about it, you know what I mean?"

"I guess."

"Sure you do. Dugouts back then, sometimes they were pretty elaborate—dug way into a hill, supported by poles and sod bricks. And if that was a dugout..." Pony pointed down the hill. "That'd be quite a discovery, wouldn't it? If my hunch is right, it might even surprise you."

"That'd be something."

"You know what? I'd rather do this with you. Might as well wait till the sun's up, anyway." Pony turned a key on his lantern and snuffed out the wick.

"Sure."

"There could be important memories buried here, son."

There it was again. He had called me son a couple of times before, just as Buddy always had. But so had Harvey, for that matter. And so had Wyatt Fowler, which made my skin crawl. I was part Chinese, for God's sake. Everyone called everyone else son in Texas. Still, when Pony said it I wanted to believe it. And I had decided to ask him straight out. But it definitely was not the right time.

Pony patted me on my shoulder. "We can still grab a couple of hours sleep," he said. "Are you up for that? It'll help us make a fresh start, okay?"

"Okay."

"You're a good man." He scratched Bill beneath the eye and patted Bill's red blanket. "Back to sleep, old boy."

Only a few hours later, we began digging together and found what Pony was looking for.

13
Uncovering the Dugout

The dugout was covered by two feet of earth and in a southeastern section of the hill that was blocked from the view of the spook or any other onlooker to the west of us. It extended on a downward slant for about seven feet beneath the top of the outcropping, which was protected by mesquite shrub. Over time, a portion of the hill had collapsed over it. As we dug deeper, Pony's pickaxe struck a leather-hinged wooden door made of wagon planks. The top of the door sank back into the outcropping, but it still protected a small, mostly caved-in living space with a wooden table, a chair, an iron kettle, a water bucket, and a box-shaped cast iron cooking stove. I went to the house to refill our canteens once an hour.

Just before lunch, Babe came down to view the discovery. Dwight had left early that morning, promising to be back in time to set up the fireworks. He didn't say what his business was. Babe put on her heavy garden gloves to help move more dirt from the dugout's living area. We were sweaty, filthy, and sapped by the August heat, but it was impossible to stop.

"Where could he have gotten the wood and the stove around here?" Babe asked.

"Maybe he brought it in a wagon. He used part of a wagon bed for a door. I guess he could have burned buffalo chips and brush, if he had an animal to help him go out and collect it. He might have shared this space with the animal, most likely a mule. So look for signs of that."

"What would he have eaten?"

"Might have traded or bought meat from Indians."

"Why would he choose here, of all places?"

"Maybe we'll find something that tells us."

We ate quickly and returned to the work. In the early afternoon, Pony uncovered the stove and withdrew a large tin box that had been placed inside it. The box was wrapped in two layers of rotting cloth. Gingerly, he carried the box into the open, placed it on a level area, pulled up a latch, and ran a knife beneath the edges of the top. It opened without much resistance. Inside was a thick, black book. Pony lifted it carefully out of the box and blew off the dust.

"My God," said Babe. "What is it?"

"It's a Bible, in Spanish—a *Sagrada Biblia*." He turned back the cover. "It's beautiful. The edges of the pages are gilded, and there's loose pages in the back. They look like they were torn from a diary."

"You read Spanish?" Babe asked. "Mine is passable, but not great—what I learned off the street in San Antonio."

"I can read it, yes. 'May God forgive me for what I have done and save me from what I have seen.' Give me a minute..."

Babe wiped her brow, leaving a streak of dirt from her glove, and watched Pony read. He whispered occasionally in Spanish, then paused, translating silently in his head. I drank from my canteen. There was no breeze on the hill, and we heard only the sound of a faraway train, coming in from the east to pass through Wendellton. Otherwise, nothing broke the stillness—not a bird, not a fly, not the hum of a motor or the lowing of cattle.

Finally, Pony spoke. His throat was tight, and his voice cracked with emotion. Much later, when I thought about it and tried to recreate a picture of that moment, I realized there was something else in his voice and expression—something that had to do with anger or frustration of the type you experience when you finally reach a goal that others have obstructed, and you are reminded of how unnecessarily long it took. "It's mostly a diary. The first entry is dated November 28th. And the last entry is dated December 24th, 1874."

"Christmas Eve," Babe said. "He could have frozen to death here. Didn't he write his name anywhere?"

"He did." Pony held up a page and pointed to the signature at the bottom. "Antonio Peraza."

It did not occur to me then that Pony had found the only thing he came to the hill for—that he had not come for the reasons he gave us, and that he must have had some knowledge of what was buried there. I was too excited to reason things out, because I already had prepared myself so completely to believe that the gods who resided in Lonechap Hill were opening gifts that always had been there to discover, gifts that awaited only the proper circumstances to reveal themselves. Buddy had believed that the Phantom Padre had visited

Lonechap Hill, and now here was the evidence. I was beside myself with joy.

Babe leaned closer to examine the signature. "Antonio Peraza...oh..."

Pony smiled at me. "The Phantom Padre himself."

The living room air conditioner wheezed while Pony leafed carefully through the fragile pages of the diary, laid out on a dictionary table. Babe and I sat on the couch, looking back and forth from him to each other, waiting for him to speak. What had Antonio Peraza written—Antonio Peraza, whose family had discarded him, who studied the stars, who carried out a quest for an ancient gold star studded with priceless jewels, who loved and betrayed his love? The diary must mean that he had lived beyond his fight with Pigeye Lehane. Pony's lips moved silently while he read. He kept one of his sketchbooks next to him and made occasional notes. At one point, Babe and I went into the kitchen for orange juice. Out of the corner of my eye, through the door to the living room, I saw Pony take some folded pages from the Bible and slip them into the notebook, then close the cover.

Babe still couldn't quite believe that the writer of the diary and the mythical imposter-crusader of Buddy's tales were one and the same. She remembered how the director of the Fowler Plains Museum had laughed at Buddy for suggesting an exhibit based on the legends. Finally, after what seemed to be an interminable wait, Pony straightened his back and looked up at us. "It's very sad," he said. "The whole story. Especially his account of what happened to them all after the poker game for the girl's...for Selenia's life."

Pony slowly translated Antonio Peraza's words aloud, and we forgot about lunch. In hindsight, I have no doubt that one of Pony's motives was to dissuade us from learning about other parts of the diary whose contents he wished to conceal and understand for himself. Nevertheless, I remember it as one of the last great moments of that August week on Lonechap Hill, when fact and legend were still indistinguishable, before I had to begin sorting them out as we must then continue to do for the rest of our lives. I felt the joy of hearing a tale told afresh and the risk to my convictions of hearing it unvarnished. The Phantom Padre, Antonio Peraza, was haunted, but thorough in his recollections of the people he met, how they spoke, and how his own motives and deceptions guided him.

14

The Sorrow of the Phantom Padre

May God forgive me for what I have done and save me from what I have seen.

They were the Phantom Padre's words, recited in Pony's quiet voice. It was riveting to hear it not as Buddy told it—which I could follow as a gripping tale from long ago, whose characters somehow were meant to convey a message to me through lives that had been grooved unalterably into acetate and whose consequences were therefore inevitable no matter how many times I listened—but as a first person account, with all the sorrow and self-loathing that accompanied it, as an outcome that could have been changed, when events were still in the hands of fate but were being twisted, slowly, toward a conclusion. In the brief gun battle, Antonio had been wounded in his side by a bullet from Pigeye, but he, in turn, had shot Lehane through the heart. The outlaw dropped from the wagon, dead, and the Star of Andalusia fell with him into the mud. Young Eagle had launched his horse forward and shot down both of Pigeye's confederates. He was unhurt.

Selenia and Young Eagle lifted Antonio into the wagon, raised his head, and placed Pigeye's hat on it so the rain would run off. Young Eagle bound the wound in Antonio's side with a buckskin strip, then cut the shirt from the dead rider, wrapped it around Antonio, and made a sling for his arm. Selenia unstrapped the saddle and bag from Antonio's horse. She dropped the bag into the wagon and quickly searched it for anything that might comfort him. He carried a spare cassock and undergarments, two Bibles, Latin and Spanish, boxes of ammunition, tin eating utensils, some gold Mexican pesos, and a writing pen and inkjar contained in a host box he was given by the priest in Ramosa as he began his journey.

She placed the *Sagrada Biblia* under his left hand and covered him with a length of hide. "You must stay alive," she whispered.

Despite everything she had witnessed, Selenia kept her wits about her. *She was smarter than anyone had bothered to discover,* the Padre wrote. She reasoned that if Pigeye's body weren't found, others would assume that he may have successfully absconded with her, and that her own fate was settled. Her foremost concern was to escape, to disappear, to avoid returning to a life where a man could claim her as he would claim an animal.

Selenia picked up the Star of Andalusia from the mud, but took no time to inspect it. She and Young Eagle hurried to excavate a grave with a pick and shovel from the wagon. They wrapped Pigeye's body in a buffalo hide, placed rocks and branches atop it, and quickly shoveled the muddy earth onto his remains. Young Eagle built a fire over the grave, then tamped the ashes into the dirt. He made a crude cross with branches from a nearby cottonwood. It was Selenia's idea to place the bloody cassock on the cross to further confuse whomever might discover the scene of the killings. People would now contrive their own stories to satisfy the evidence at the scene.

Finally, she carried the Star of Andalusia to the wagon where Antonio lay, and she gasped at its beauty. The Star was embedded at its center with a large ruby. The blood-red gem was surrounded by four smaller, circular rubies. At the ends of the Star's arms, emeralds glistened in settings studded with semicircles of citrine gemstones. Only one of the emeralds that had been set in the Star so long ago was lost. A few of the tiny citrine gemstones also were missing.

Later, she told me she could not comprehend how a man as thoroughly corrupt and brutal as Lehane believed that such a treasure held the key to his survival, even foregoing the wealth he could have realized from it. Perhaps he convinced himself that he had won God's sanction by recovering the star from a heathen Indian. Perhaps he thought its great value also accrued to the man who held it. Perhaps it was the only thing he possessed that contradicted the nature of his life. Whatever reasoning he might have used was beyond her. It had not protected him in the end. She kissed the rubies and placed the Star beneath a buffalo hide next to me. I was too injured to ride a horse, and could barely believe what I beheld. I thought that I had wanted no more than my birthright. And there it was, the Star of Andalusia, symbol of my homeland, my family heritage, my foolhardy dreams. I fainted, whether because of the power of the Star or the severity of my injuries, I do not know...

Despite the danger of leaving tracks that easily could be followed, Selenia and Young Eagle had no choice but to drive the wagon, and the best route would take them into the open country to the south. From there, they could swing west into the unsettled lands, where Young Eagle claimed to know a refuge, a place where they could rest and decide their next move. It was the hill where he had buried his Chenowah father. Selenia remained with Antonio in the wagon. As the rising sun flashed and dodged through the fleeing storm clouds, Young Eagle jumped onto the buckboard, grabbed the reins, whipped the draft horses, and began the journey.

We had not driven an hour when a herd of buffalo came from the east and passed over our path, trampling it into oblivion. Dust swirled and billowed near the center of the multitude, and their bellows drifted like broken chants above the noise of their hoofs. Whatever God sent the doomed herd as a favor to us did so with an obliging sense of timing.

Antonio slept only fitfully as the wagon bounced across the rolling grasslands. They traveled throughout the day and night, stopping only to rest and graze the horses. Selenia gave Antonio water from a large canteen. Finally, he remembered that the vial of laudanum meant for Pigeye was in his pocket, and he drank it. He fell into a deep sleep. He heard breaking and hammering noises as if in a dream. Then he awoke again. Selenia rinsed his forehead with a cold, damp cloth. He was no longer in the wagon. He looked up and saw dark earth above Selenia's face and light beyond her—late afternoon light, supplanted by shadows that crept down a slope.

They were in a dugout. Antonio lay on a pile of blankets. The boxy cast-iron stove that had been in Pigeye's wagon stood against one of the dugout walls.

Selenia smiled. "Take some broth before you speak." She had made the broth from small birds that Young Eagle shot for them. "The Star is here with us. So is everything that was in your saddlebag."

"Lehane?"

"Is buried. He had some money. But he complained when he took me that he had to leave most of it behind. I put what he had in the belt you wore, the one with pouches. It is still a lot, I think."

"My gold belt."

"It is next to you."

"And my guns?"

"They are here, too."

"The Star. May I see it again?"

Selenia pulled the Star from its leather sack. Antonio took it in his hands and raised it above his eyes, wincing from the pain in his side. "It is heavy. And so beautiful." He brought it down to his chest.

"That is what you sought?"

"Yes. I wish I knew what stories it could tell."

"And you will return it to Spain?"

"Some day. When I can do so." He groaned. "If I can do so."

"Let me put it back. It is too heavy."

"Of course." Antonio sighed. "I imagined so many things I would feel if I found it."

"You are injured. That's what you feel now."

"Where are we...?"

"A place that Young Eagle knows. There was already a dugout here. He helped make it in the spring. He cleaned it out and knocked the wagon apart and used some wood to make a door for us. There's jerky from the wagon. Blankets. Tobacco. Even some whiskey."

"Where is he?"

"Gone. He will be back in five or six days." Young Eagle had scattered the draft horses onto the plains as he rode away. He left behind two horses, including Antonio's grullo stallion, so Selenia could ride the hill during the day and check for signs that others might be approaching.

"Gone where?"

"This is where his father was killed. He was the one who made this dugout. He is buried near here beneath some rocks. Young Eagle went to his tribe, to get warriors to take the body back and give his father a proper burial."

"He waited to do this?"

"He waited...until I could escape. Until I was safe."

"Was his father a chief?"

"No. More like a holy man, I think. He was killed by the buffalo hunter named Janssen."

"Ah. I remember you telling me. The one who choked to death."

"Yes."

"Why didn't he kill Young Eagle?"

"Because he thought Young Eagle had a map that showed where Indian gold was buried."

"Ah."

"That's why he let him bury his father. Young Eagle promised to lead him to the gold, but said his father's spirit had to rest, first."

"Where was the map?"

"It was on buckskin. His father carried it in a feathered bag, with other things. I saw the bag on Janssen's belt when he died, and Young Eagle took it back as soon as his hands were free. It wasn't really a gold map."

"What was it?" Antonio propped himself up on his elbows and felt better than he expected. The pain in his side had subsided.

"Easy, Padre." Selenia laughed. "Although you're not a Padre. I don't even know what I should call you now."

"Antonio."

"Antonio."

"I think I'll be all right. Let me try sitting."

"Carefully."

"What did the boy have, if it wasn't a gold map?"

"It is a map of the sky. His father came here every year to read the map for signs of change and add to it. He used to come alone. He brought Young Eagle because he grew blind and needed guidance."

"He was blind and he mapped the sky?"

"He could feel the marks he had made on the buckskin. When he lost his sight, he told Young Eagle he could feel the sting of the stars on his hand."

"He was surely a holy man, then."

"Yes, as I thought. Like a priest." She laughed again. "But not like you."

"Does Young Eagle know that I am not...?"

"I have told no one else."

"Selenia..."

"Yes, Antonio."

"I am sorry. Truly. I had so little courage."

"But you had the courage to come for me, and you freed me."

Antonio tried to sit, but she placed her hand on his forehead. "I had to," he said.

"You came for me and not the Star."

"I had to."

"And now I'll never have to go back."

For the first time, Antonio smiled. Then he slept again.

After nightfall, he awoke and insisted on trying to move from the dugout and into the open. He crawled at first, then rose to his knees, bracing himself against the entrance and struggling into an upright position. Selenia hung onto his arm and refused to let go. After a few seconds, he felt strong enough to stand on his own. He was stunned by the brightness of the Milky Way above them, strung out with a purpose he never before had noticed—dusty, shadowy, formless and yet intelligent and patient, shepherding the stars, extending a brilliant cloak on which to drift across the heavens. Next, he realized that he and Selenia were standing on a hill that rose implausibly from the floor of the plains as if to lift them as near to the stars as they were to the earth below the hill. Fireflies darted around them.

In the morning, she fetched fresh water from a nearby spring and filled two large canteens. Then she rode the perimeter of the hill on the grullo stallion. Not a soul came into sight. When she returned to Antonio, she dressed him in his spare cassock despite his objections. She also opened his Bible to the pages left blank for the notes and names of family members. On two of the pages, she had used a pencil from Antonio's saddlebag to draw small plants, flowers, and animals, including a tiny face of Ah Toy. She had been tempted to try a portrait of Antonio, but did not think it would be appropriate for a holy book.

Young Eagle returned after a week with four warriors and some horses. The Indians were in a bad way. They had been chased by the cavalry across the plains. Their best warriors had been killed and many of their women and children were held captive. What was left of the small tribe to which Young Eagle belonged had come together in Toomis Canyon, and they were preparing to turn themselves in to a reservation in Oklahoma—Indian Territory, then. They had been told that their women and children would not be released until they did.

The night of Young Eagle's return to the hill, he climbed to the top with Antonio and Selenia. The next day, they planned to leave for Toomis Canyon. "We want you to speak for us," he said to Antonio.

"Who do you want me to speak to?"

"Come with us when we give up fighting. You will speak for us. They will believe you. You are a holy man to them."

Antonio did not bother setting Young Eagle straight. He still wore a cassock. "What can I say?"

"Say we are ready to accept their ways. They will give us food and land."

"You're white. They will take you back. They will believe you."

"I am Chenowah."

"Won't the whites want you to return to them?"

"I was shown to a white trader. He came to our camp. I told him I would not go back. I have no white family."

"Because they're dead. They were massacred and you were kidnapped."

"My Chenowah father was killed by whites. I am Chenowah."

"So you have lost two fathers."

Young Eagle remained silent while I considered his sorrows. His eyes betrayed nothing. Whatever atrocities he witnessed as a child were in another life that had perished like the lives of his parents and sisters. Whatever atrocities he had committed were as a son of the culture that had adopted him. He would never see the stars as his ancestors had seen them. He would see in them the eternal truths of another people, the ones who had adopted him. I told him I would be happy to speak for his people if they wished.

Just as if he had seen it from the air, Young Eagle traced into the earth the path they would take from the hill. They would seek the relative safety of the Staked Plains, then turn toward the canyon where the tribe was preparing to follow a river east on its journey of surrender to an Indian agent.

They left early the next morning after covering the entrance to the dugout with sod and shrubs. The decaying body of Young Eagle's father was carried in a travois strapped to a horse. Antonio was well enough to ride, but with frequent rests. The warriors were polite and respectful. Otherwise, they paid little attention to him and Selenia.

They crossed, slowly, a constant and forbidding landscape that had devoured generations of mercenary explorers drawn toward its insatiable horizon. It was a journey that warriors once made at full gallop, barely stopping for food and drink as they rushed home from raids and battles while their pursuers fell farther and farther behind and finally abandoned the chase. On the second day, what Antonio took at first for a mirage proved to be a chain of still, shallow, shimmering lakes.

Red-winged and yellow-headed blackbirds chattered atop cattails, and killdeer flitted to and fro over the mudflats, attending the festivities in the stylish black bands that ringed their breasts, and disrupting the chatter with their shrill calls. Coyotes shadowed the travelers as they moved among the playas. At sundown, the red from the sky spilled into the waters, floated there like spirit fire, then drained into the blackness. When camp was made, Antonio walked with Selenia among the broad, yellow avenues of sunflowers and pink clusters of smartweeds that grew around the playas. Beyond them, a lone bison bull stood in the water as if he were waiting to die. Occasionally, he thrashed his hind legs and bucked without moving forward. Antonio remembered what Wallace the buffalo hunter had told him. He knows the end is near. He's no longer the source of fortunes. Just part of the scrapheap.

Suddenly, the warriors whooped and began running with Young Eagle around the playa and toward the buffalo. The bull's front legs had sunk into the mud beneath the shallow water. Its efforts to gain traction with its hind legs were futile. Young Eagle splashed through the playa, pulled himself atop the buffalo's back, grabbed its horns, and tried to twist the bull's head, talking all the while. The buffalo bellowed loudly and bucked again, but Young Eagle stayed on its hump, hanging dangerously onto the horns. The warriors gathered at the side of the bellowing, kicking animal and pushed. Within a few seconds, the bull began to topple over. Young Eagle jumped off its back, and he and the warriors ran for their lives as the bull landed on its side in the water. Its legs were free. At first, the bull rolled onto its hump as if wallowing. It righted itself with a mighty heave and leaped out of the playa. The bull stopped, bellowed again, and faced the opposite side of the playa where the warriors had sprinted. Finally, it turned and bolted onto the plains, an old and defeated monarch asserting that he wasn't dead yet.

Antonio and Selenia applauded. Young Eagle grinned. "When I became Chenowah," he said, "I got a buffalo calf for play after a hunt. If they come to speak alone with us, it is always with a message. A change. We must keep watch."

"What was his message—the bull you saved?" Antonio asked.

Young Eagle shook his head solemnly and did not reply.

That night, Selenia came to me and we made love. I felt a surge of passion that I did not know was possible. My own pain, from my wound, seemed refreshing and sweet. I also felt desperation. It was not the gloomy or impatient desperation that I had known many times before, but a desperation to remain somehow connected to her, to lose every other thought or care, to forego the identity I had so foolishly pursued. I knew that she could replace everything I had desired. When we lay trembling together, Selenia said she did not want me to leave her. The next morning, as if she were prescient, she borrowed my Sagrada Biblia, and in it, she sketched the face of a child.

They skirted the southern rim of Toomis Canyon and entered it from the west, riding through a narrow passage that sloped sharply downward. Soon, they were surrounded by angular, towering canyon walls, illuminated by the golden light of a late summer afternoon. The canyon widened to form a kind of amphitheater marked by a chimney-like column of rock that rose nearly a hundred feet from the giant foot of its base, kept company by a family of smaller spires to the east. The column rose in sections that were piled crazily together—fractured joints nudged here and there into a precarious balance. A small, shadowy depression opened like a vertical slit in the northern wall behind it. Atop the column was a cap which reminded Antonio of a crown. It appeared much too broad and heavy to sit safely on the formation beneath it. Lizards scurried across a rocky, eroded path lined with yellow-tipped snakeweed. Bison had indented a large and deep wallow into the knee-high grass. The riders passed a grove of mesquite trees bearing bright red seeds, ingredients for breads and sweets made by the Indians who camped there. Behind them, a roadrunner called in mellow, barking noises that were punctuated by a cry of mourning like a dove's. At last, beyond, along a river, lay the tanned buffalo-hide lodges of the Chenowah village.

Not much was left of the band. The fighting men, perhaps thirty of them, were far outnumbered by women, children, and older men.

Many of the survivors were battling ill health or disease. They were preparing for a journey of around 150 miles to the reservation in Indian Territory. Some already knew the life they were headed for, having camped at the reservation in previous winters to obtain supplies of government rations in lieu of starving on the frozen plains. Then, after spring arrived, they grew restless and became nomads again, joining other bands of renegades who convinced themselves they could hold out against the white armies.

Young Eagle rode ahead and was welcomed with affection by a fat, older woman in an elaborately beaded buckskin dress and a worn pair of moccasins. She was the sister of his father. The others who gathered looked away from the shaman's son. He appeared briefly troubled and confused by the reception. Some crowded around Antonio, to touch his cassock. They stared at Selenia with wide eyes.

When Young Eagle's aunt saw her brother's remains, she broke down weeping, then took a knife and began hacking at her hair, arms, and breasts. She was soon joined by dozens of others. The possessions of the shaman were brought from his teepee. His corpse was too badly decomposed to dress, so garments were laid atop it and a bow and quiver placed beside it. A woman made empty motions as if to straighten the limbs of the corpse. Finally, the shaman's body was wrapped in a red blanket. From his teepee, Young Eagle brought a beautiful, round shield made of buffalo hide. Four-pointed stars were painted in red at each of the cardinal directions. At the center was the figure of a bird, with wings spread the width of the shield. The backs of the bird's wings seemed to dissolve into clouds as it sped through the sky. Young Eagle placed the shield on top of the corpse. The women sang a death dirge, a chant unlike anything Antonio had heard, rising in praise, falling in sorrow.

The shaman's body was carried by bearers to a ledge more than halfway up the canyon wall near the crowned column of rock. In a shallow cave behind the ledge, he was buried with his bow and quiver, a clay pipe, a collection of beads and bracelets, and the shield that Young Eagle himself had fashioned under the guidance of his father. Rocks were piled atop the grave.

When night fell, Selenia was invited into the teepee of a warrior's widow. At Antonio's suggestion, she was given a buckskin dress to make her less conspicuous once the group began traveling.

Afterwards, Young Eagle escorted me to the teepee of an old man with a jutting chin, sunken cheeks, and a broad, rigid face, heavily creased but not sagging with age. His white hair, still abundant, was parted in the middle. It lay flat on the sides of his head, then dropped in braids across his chest. His mouth bent downwards at both ends, as if drawn tautly by the weight of his years. He would not speak his name to me. But he hoisted the corners of his mouth into a smile and said, "You may call me old man." He was a keeper of tribal history and legend, a storyteller, and he spoke enough English to communicate with me. He once had acted as liaison between the Chenowah and the reservation agent, but feared he would not be welcomed or believed if he brought his people in again, since they had not stayed before. He said he had foreseen that I would come to take the tribe to its new home.

The canyon grew cold after dark, and the old man built a fire. The smoke rose toward the light of a full moon through a flap at the peak of the teepee.

The old man was curious about Antonio's possessions. He laughed when he saw the *Sagrada Biblia*. "Some warriors take these from whites." He opened the Bible. "We use like this." He lifted his shirt and ran his hand up his chest. "They put in here to catch bullets. Stop arrows. Good medicine." He returned the Bible to Antonio and caught his breath sharply when he saw the Star of Andalusia. Without a word, he extended his hands and Antonio handed the Star to him. The storyteller ran his fingers over the gems and stopped when his finger reached the cavity where an emerald had been set in an arm of the Star. He spoke in Chenowah to Young Eagle. At first, the boy shook his head, but the old man spoke more harshly and Young Eagle opened the buckskin bag he had rescued from his dead father and withdrew a beautiful green stone. The old man took it and placed it in the cavity on the Star. It fit perfectly. He reached for a collection of colored sticks that he kept near the buffalo robes where he slept. He counted through a bundle of notched red sticks. "These are the winters that have passed since we buried a man like you," he said to Antonio. He spoke again in Chenowah.

"He says it was a hundred and many more," Young Eagle said.

The story the old man told was improbable and astounding, but made credible by the emerald that rested in the Star. It was the story of a group of warriors who came upon a brown-robed man riding a mule in a forest. They fired arrows at him to kill him. The man held up a gold star. He said the star flew through the sky to come to them. The arrows of the warriors simply bounced off of it. When his mule was shot out from underneath him, the man laid his star on the animal. Then he fell on his knees and bared his chest to the warriors. Because of his bravery, the leader of the warriors decided not to kill him, but to take him back to their camp, and to keep the star for its magic. They called him Walks-On-His-Knees. He was weakened by the fall from his mule. The warriors told him that if he made them slow, they would leave him. They rode for four days, north across the plains, chased by men in suits of metal. One night, a shower of stars fell from the sky, more plentiful than the warriors ever had seen. They feared it was the end of the world. Walks-On-His-Knees told them it was not the end of the world, but that something wonderful was happening in the heavens and they should not be afraid. He said the star was sent to protect them against death and they would not die.

But at sunrise, he could not ride. The warriors left him and carried the star back to their camp. Walks-On-His-Knees crawled for three moons, following their tracks until he reached the camp on his own. His hands and knees were bloody. His robe was torn. Warriors gathered around him with their bows drawn. Then another shower of stars came from the sky, and they were afraid. Walks-On-His-Knees told them it was a message to them, and that he would tell them what it meant. An old woman took him into her teepee and nursed him back to health. He promised to teach the warriors how to use the star to protect themselves. Before he could do so, the camp was attacked by Comanches who stole the star and then were able to kill Walks-On-His-Knees. They did not want any people to be more powerful than they were. Only a green stone remained on the ground near the body of Walks-On-His-Knees. He was buried in the canyon, but a medicine man kept the stone. The Comanches had many great victories while they held the star, just as Walks-On-His-Knees had said. And now the Star is no longer with the Comanches, the old man noted as he ended his story.

That night, I barely slept, thinking of the Star, listening to all the sounds in the canyon, to the wind and the owls and the wolves and the thud of my own heart. When I did sleep, I had nightmares. I saw ghosts dressed in robes and made up like warriors, stripping me naked while gold stars fell from the sky all around me. I knew that the dream meant that all I had believed in had been the gold. The savages, I told myself, believed in the magic.

The next day saw a grievous turn in their fortunes, beginning with a devastating blow to Young Eagle. He was told in front of a tribal meeting, delayed out of respect for his father, that his destiny had been determined, and it did not lie with the tribe. The Indian agency would give no rations to the Chenowah, nor would the tribe's captives be released, until white captives held by the tribe were surrendered. Young Eagle was the only captive who remained with the Chenowah. He would have to identify himself separately when they reached the reservation. And so the boy who had seen two fathers murdered and crossed from one culture to another could not stay with the Chenowah. He and the tribe would be separated as if death had come between them.

Young Eagle's aunt wept and begged Antonio to find a way of allowing the boy to live as an Indian, but she knew that their fates had been settled by decrees she would never comprehend. It was no consolation that many members of the tribe wanted him to remain with them. Others were ready to give him up to save their own relatives. They suspected him of bringing bad luck. Two or three spiteful warriors threatened to kill him.

Out of shame, he could not bear to stay in the camp where some frowned at him as if he were cursed. Antonio and Selenia walked with him to the rock column near where his father had been buried. The three exiles sat silently for an hour, listening to the echoes of woodpeckers, and watching a breeze jostle patches of goldenrod. A porcupine gnawed at the base of a mesquite tree while a blue jay and cardinal fought among the limbs. Finally, Young Eagle opened the buckskin bag he carried, removed the emerald, and handed it to Antonio.

"It belongs with your star," he said.

"I would very much like to know more about your stars," Antonio said. "The ones that are on your sky map."

Young Eagle hung his head as if thinking for a while, then nodded.

We met again at sunset near the canyon grave. We did not want to call attention to ourselves by building a fire. I brought a buffalo robe to warm Selenia. I had strapped my pistol belt openly around my cassock in case any warriors tried to enforce their threats against Young Eagle. I was prepared to abandon the tribe and escape with Selenia and the boy if danger warranted. I carried the Star of Andalusia in its leather bag. I also wore the gold belt with its supply of coins. As a final precaution, I stuffed my Sagrada Biblia inside my cassock, heeding the story of the old Indian, that the Word of God could also be used to stop arrows and bullets. Young Eagle's aunt had braided Selenia's hair like an Indian's. Attired in buckskin, she looked more beautiful than ever.

They climbed to a large ridge on the canyon wall, under a moon that bathed them in glassy blue light. Gnarled trees rose from the slope beneath them like crippled, grasping fingers. Young Eagle handed Antonio a soft, folded length of buckskin. "I made for my father," he said. "You keep it." It was a duplicate of the oval star chart, with buckskin lacing around its edges, reddish pigment representing the eastern sunrise at one end of the oval, and yellow pigment symbolizing sunset at the other end. It was as wide as the span from Antonio's elbow to his fingertips. The patterns on it were identical to the ones on the chart that Young Eagle spread onto the rock, save for the spatters of blood on the shaman's map that mingled with the tiny, four-pronged stars on its northern edge.

The colors that Young Eagle had added to his map made it easy to align the buckskin by direction, and when Antonio looked from the map to the sky, the stars were in perfect position. Antonio was certain that the map had been plotted at that very time of year. Young Eagle had learned its lessons in anticipation of the day he would replace his father.

Tracing the map with his finger, the boy said the spirits of the Chenowah were blown by a wind from the north end of the sky, through the dust left behind by a racing buffalo, to the bright star at the south end, the place of the dead. A council of chiefs sat together in the northern sky to form and mend alliances. Just below the formation the Greeks called the Great Fish, extending from south to southwest, was a chair-like arrangement of stars that, to Young Eagle, formed a cradle for the child of the Morning and Evening Stars. The cradle rose, resting on the back of the child's aunt as the sky wheeled westward. Geese, on the verge of disappearing from the southern sky, floated away to escape the coming winter. "These are seeds," said Young Eagle, pointing to a cluster of stars. "When it is time to plant, these seeds come into the sky before sunrise. The sun is warm and they will grow. But when they rise after the sun has crossed the sky, they will die if they are planted."

Within what Antonio knew as Auriga, the charioteer, now rising in the east, was the upward curve of a starry bow, an instrument of the hunt given by the gods to humans. Villages were assembled in the eastern and western skies to offer a pattern to life. In the northwest, Ursa Major and Minor contained, not the Big and Little Dippers, but the shapes of travois bearing the sick. The rim and base of each dipper represented the sides of a travois. At each corner was a bearer. The handles of the dippers represented the Chenowah mourners who followed the travois. Together, they traveled around the star that gave wisdom to shamans and balanced the cycles of life and communication among animals and humans. If the South Star ever rose to capture and kill the people on the travois—one young, the other old—that was how the Chenowah would know the world was coming to an end.

The boy's star chart was what all we humans seek—a map of how to live, of relationships between people and nature and the heavens and their gods, the very topic that first got me into trouble during my Jesuit training. The stars are the very source of our vanity. If we could, we would name each star in the heavens, but there are too many. And they are much too staggering a mystery to remain nameless, so we group them together in constellations that tell our own stories. We believe we are their offspring, and we may well be. They rise and fall and chase each other across the sky. They fight and sting and torture each other. In the eastern sky that night was a woman in chains, as Selenia had been. About to rise was a hunter with a belt full of scalps, and he would be done in by a scorpion. The stars are merciless that way, always re-playing ancient history. That is why a river of tears flowed above us. That is why stars have the power to predict. They have seen everything before, and we are even more constant in our behavior than they. We believe that what remains hidden up there will someday be revealed. But what the stars truly tell us is that we do not change, that we will disappear and die at the turn of a wheel.

"My father said, if you question them, they will abandon you," said Young Eagle. "If you boast to them, they will turn against you. If you seek gain from them, they will torture you. We could not live without their teaching."

"But they could exist without us," Antonio replied. "We are nothing but a parody." Antonio stood, looking at the sky and the objects around them. He pulled out his pocketwatch and paused to memorize the positions of the stars in relation to where he stood, near the edge of the cave where Young Eagle's father was buried. The cradle's stars had fully risen on the back of the obliging Aunt who carried it into the sky. Beneath them, a lone star—the hook on the bottom of the cradle—perched like an ember on a spent candlewick at the bottom of a notch where the southern walls of the canyon diverged. And where the Greeks would have found a Centaur in the dust of the Milky Way, what Young Eagle identified as the eye of a bison gleamed like a crowning jewel atop the rock column to the east. Antonio recalled reading as a student the poetry of the *Phenomena*, and the thrill he felt during the last portion of it, when the companies of constellations were reeled out in verse as if for some encyclopedic catalog of all the wants and needs, the punished pride and inexorable sins, the warnings and encouragements, the lessons to heed, the winds that blew foul and fair for humankind, all fixed eternally in the stars.

Selenia interrupted his thoughts. "I have faith that God dwells there. He does not live in our imaginations. We are His children, and I don't think He likes us questioning His gifts. If you have no faith in a creator, how can you believe the stars are worth your study? Or that there is any sense at all in them? If they teach us, they must have a purpose." Selenia smiled. "But I know you are forgiven, Antonio."

They sat quietly again. The air was still, but the grass rustled and bent on the floor of the canyon. Young Eagle's eyes followed the sound. "I like to hear the grass. I had a bison calf in this camp. We stayed together all summer. He followed me everywhere. When winter came and he was killed for food, I dreamed that he spoke to me. He said, 'Wherever you see the grass bend, I am behind you.'"

Despite the cold, they slept on the ridge without returning to the camp.

They were awakened suddenly by a rumbling sound on one side of them, and cries from the camp on the other. They looked down from the ledge in time to see the dark form of a single buffalo, barreling along the canyon floor toward the west. "Quick," said Young Eagle. "We must go." He grabbed Selenia's hand and led her down the slope. They left her robe behind. Antonio presumed that the boy had been driven by superstition on seeing the lone bison. Then he heard gunshots bursting from several directions. Antonio stepped off the ridge and slid down the slope between the gnarled trees. Young Eagle and Selenia were well ahead of him. He could no longer see them.

As Antonio picked himself up, partially concealed by the trees, cavalrymen on horses passed within yards of him, riding east toward the camp. He realized that he had left the Star of Andalusia in its bag on the ridge. He retreated back up the slope toward the cave where Young Eagle's father had been buried. The body was located in the deepest part of the cave, to Antonio's left. To his right was a shallow area, barely high enough to stand in. Antonio quickly removed his gold belt. He pushed it and the leather bag containing the Star as far back into the shallow depression as possible, away from the burial site, beneath a notch in the wall. He covered the notch with rocks. If he were detained and searched, he did not want to be in possession of the Star or the gold.

Finally, he climbed back down the wall, intending to follow the cavalry into the camp and do what he could to stop an attack. It was too late. Abrupt flashes punctured the darkness. Gunshots echoed until they sounded like one long, inexhaustible explosion. Smoke rose to meet the dawn above the canyon walls. The cavalry had attacked just before sunrise. Other soldiers had snuck into positions behind cedars and within ravines on both sides of the canyon. They set up a crossfire into the camp.

The charging cavalry had panicked the buffalo. It had run west, toward the canyon exit. Now, it turned and ran in the opposite direction. Antonio heard the animal behind him, twisted to avoid it, and stumbled into a wallow where he struck his head on a rock.

The next words he heard came from a soldier. "It's either a preacher or a Comanchero dressed like one."

I rose to my knees and drew the attention of a detachment of soldiers who were checking for bodies along the canyon floor. One of them addressed me as Padre and asked if I spoke English. He questioned me about my pistol. I told him I wore it to protect myself from snakes and dangerous animals. Another soldier asked why I was accompanying Comanches. My first instinct was to give a false name...Lopez, I told them. I told them, also, that the Indians were not Comanches. They were going to surrender themselves. The soldiers simply laughed at me and said they had seen no white flags, and that Indians could not be trusted to do what they promised. I replied that the Indians were hospitable and had fed me as I traveled on my mission to find members of the Catholic faith who live on the frontier where there are no cathedrals. I was told that I could resume my search for Catholics because the Indians needed no one but St. Peter to speak for them...

The soldiers took Antonio back into a camp that was smoldering from fires and thick with bodies. Some soldiers ate dried buffalo meat that had been hung from racks by the women of the camp. Others picked through the teepees for buffalo robes and other commodities the Chenowah had obtained from trading at outposts such as Big Fort—army blankets, knives, and cooking kettles among them. After putting aside what they wanted for themselves, the solders set fire to the homes and the possessions that were left within them.

Antonio was introduced to a cavalry lieutenant named Billingham, nicknamed "Hurricane Harry." "That's for the way I like to attack," he told Antonio as he led him through the smoking ruins. Dead women and children were at the center of the camp. The bodies of the warriors lay outside the area, along the river and on canyon trails where some had attempted to retreat. Antonio immediately identified Young Eagle's aunt. He found no sign of Young Eagle or Selenia, nor had the lieutenant been told of any dead warrior who looked like a white captive. "If you saw a white child in this camp, I need to report it," said the lieutenant. "It'd be hard to tell from this. Lots of these bodies are burned black."

"These Indians, I can vouch, they were going to surrender," Antonio said. "You didn't need to fight them."

"You're wrong, Padre," said Billingham. "We tracked two braves here after they split off from a party of renegades that attacked a settler's wagon. I won't bother telling you what they did to them. That was a massacre, too. Our orders are to stop it once and for all. And we will."

Despite Antonio's assertion that the Indians were Chenowah—a tribal name that never had been recorded to the lieutenant's knowledge—Billingham said the army would report a successful attack against a "mixed camp of Comanches and others."

The task that remained for the soldiers was to cut the best horses from the Indian stock, then slaughter the rest so the animals could not be used by survivors or renegades who came to investigate the outcome of the fight.

...but the devastation I saw on that day convinced me that what remained of the people who had called themselves Chenowah—wherever they had come from, whatever alliances they had made, whatever history had defined them—would be forgotten and unrecorded as so many people are, even in the scrupulous journals of war. I declined an offer to ride with a cavalry detachment to the protection of a town. Instead, I accepted a horse, a saddle, and provisions from the lieutenant, and rode out of the canyon alone. For two nights, I camped without a fire on a canyon rim, listening to the shots and screams of horses as the remainder of the herd was destroyed. I spent many idle hours studying the star chart I had been given by Young Eagle. No sooner had the soldiers left than a group of renegade Comanches rode into the burned camp to survey the devastation. Even had it been safe, I did not feel compelled to go back at that time for the Star and the gold. They were well concealed. And I no longer considered that the Star belonged only to my family or to me, not after the events that had occurred. It belonged as much to Selenia and Young Eagle. In addition, I would have to travel alone. I would be safer without the treasure, and the treasure would be safer without me. If I ever find Selenia and the boy, we can easily return to where the Star is hidden...

Antonio first found his way to the Indian Agency, even though he knew Young Eagle would appear there only if he had been captured. To continue his search, he purchased a mule and a cart and traveled through settlements, offering to say mass from the back of the cart and to ask whether anyone had seen travelers fitting the description of Selenia and Young Eagle. They were converts, he said, a brother and sister he had lost track of after meeting them in Indian Territory. No one had seen them. He worried that they had been killed. But he also let himself believe that if they escaped, they would be sharp-witted enough to make themselves over again, into new people.

As I searched, the weather continued to worsen. I was drenched for hours on end by heavy rains, then frozen by the winds that followed. Finally came the sleet and snow and I have returned to this place, the dugout where I once took shelter with Selenia. I have a stockpile of provisions people gave me for saying masses, so for the time being I have plenty of food. I am heated by the small stove.

My mule stays in here with me and pays no attention while I write this apology. Perhaps it is because he understands only English when he chooses to understand at all. I write this in Spanish because it is my first language, the language of my home, and the language of Selenia, my love. I can barely contain my tears on this Christmas Eve when I look at the tiny drawings she made on the blank pages of my Sagrada Biblia, especially the drawing of a baby, smiling, on the final page where one lists a family history. Perhaps, if she is looking for me, she will consider that I might have come to this place to wait and pray for her and to hope that I am forgiven.

Pony closed the book. "And that's where he ends it," he said, although as I discovered later he had omitted some crucial details.

Babe whistled softly. "We'll need to find someone to help preserve it."

"Of course. For...?"

"Not for any museum. For us. And John."

"I'll read this more carefully tonight," said Pony. "You don't mind if I hold onto it, do you?"

"I hope I'm not interrupting." Dwight walked into the living room. "But we have things to do before the afternoon gets away from us. Fireworks, remember?"

15
Fireworks and Betrayals

Dwight needed us all to work setting up the fireworks. Pony packed the Bible into its box and carried the box and his sketchbook out of the room. I had helped lay out the fireworks a couple of times before and would have looked forward to it had it not been for the diary and the newly revealed dugout it came from. "When the fireworks start, no one will notice that they have arrived, not even your occasional spook," Dwight said in an aside to Babe.

"I suppose it's best if I work where I can be out of sight when they come," Pony said.

"Yes. Over on that side," Dwight pointed. "Babe will be between us."

As we began work, Dwight beckoned me. "Tonight we may have to face an unpleasant visit. Some old friends have done us an injury. I need to find out why. You have a right to know what will be happening."

"What old friends?"

"Miss Lee and her father. You remember them, of course."

"Yes." I was convinced that Joan Lee could be my mother, based on the conversation I had overheard after my brush with the Fowler brothers. But why would she, too, seek to injure us?

"Why will it be unpleasant?"

"Well, they are now telling different stories about Buddy's last days. I've sent some friends of mine to pick them up and bring them here when the fireworks start. I don't know, but there may be a confrontation. I hope it won't upset you. In fact, the best thing for you will simply be to enjoy the fireworks. Pony is going to take Bill into the barn and close the door so he won't be bothered. And tomorrow will be a new day."

"I like Joan."

"I know you do. It can't be helped."

If Joan was my mother, I did not want her to be treated badly by anyone, not even Dwight.

Dwight always drew a diagram that showed how the fireworks would be placed. He had studied the plans that Buddy made, and he never had caused a grassfire. He, Babe, and Pony laid out sheets of plywood from the barn over a level area on the east side of the hill, where the wind would blow the sparks away from the house. Then they spent the late afternoon setting up rockets and fountains, mortars with aerial shells, and flying spinners. They stabilized the fireworks with bricks and cinder blocks, cut the fuses, planted rockets in pipes, and set up lanterns to illuminate them. I wasn't much help, as I brooded over Joan Lee.

Dwight beckoned. "Come over and help me set this mortar." I went and stood beside him. "Mind handing me a cinderblock?"

"Sure."

Dwight ruffled my hair and I pulled away. "You asked and I told you. Now behave like the man you are. We are doing everything we can to fix things. You're old enough to understand how and why."

But I did not understand. Not yet.

A few moments after dusk, the phone rang in the house and Dwight went to answer it. He came back out, paced nervously, looked at his watch for ten minutes or so, then signaled to Babe and Pony. "Time to start the fireworks," he said.

As always, Dwight had carefully numbered the mortars. He set off the first one, and Babe and Pony continued the sequence. For the first three breath-taking minutes, the sky flickered with bursts and gushes from a collection of Babe's favorite displays—dazzling fountains from which streamers of pink unfurled into the upper regions, aerial shells that exploded into huge spherical patterns, three-dimensioned balls of white lights that hung like lanterns before they melted harmlessly into the blackness.

A long car, a Lincoln, made its way slowly up the hill, headlights off, illuminated only by spasms of light from the fireworks. During a brief pause in the display, four people got out of the car—two large men and a couple I knew to be Chen Wu Lee and his daughter Joan. I was standing behind the staging area. They passed near me on their way to Dwight. Joan's escort held her arm tightly. She stumbled and caught my eye. "Oh, John, my John," she said—not as a greeting but as a sign of distress. She tried to move toward me but was jerked forward by her escort. When the group was within a few steps of Dwight, he turned his back for a moment and began another sequence of fireworks.

After the first bang of an aerial shell, I heard Dwight say, "You want to see the boy, but you don't want to see me?" Then he began speaking Chinese, in Guangdong dialect, all the while alternating with Babe and Pony in setting off the grand display above us. Addressing Joan directly, he spoke English again. I could barely make out Joan's reply. "If it had not been the truth," she said, "we would never have spoken it. But I cannot lie for the sake of our family. Even if..."

"And you couldn't come to me?" Dwight asked.

"I'm sorry, I'm sorry. They came to us. I told them only the truth. And my father truly did not know what he was signing."

"Exactly what truth? No, stop." Dwight lit a rocket, held up his hand, and began interrogating Joan again, speaking both English and Chinese. Suddenly, Chen dropped to his knees in tears, shaking his head. Dwight turned back to Joan. "Your father cannot think of anything you may have learned that would suit me to let you go on your way. Can you?"

Joan nodded. "I heard them talk..."

A shell leaped from its mortar and into the sky, hurtling sparks over the strange scene, silhouetted by a flash, and I didn't hear her reply. They spoke for a moment longer. Then Dwight gestured for Chen and the two escorts to remain where they were. "You will do this boy a great service if you remember only that much," he said. He took Joan by the arm and led her to me. He was smiling. Joan attempted to smile, but the corners of her mouth trembled and fell. Dwight spoke first. "We are all enjoying the fireworks tonight. You remember Miss Lee?"

Was he threatening her in some way by bringing her to me?

I nodded.

"Miss Lee and her father and I have had a dispute," Dwight said. "They came to work it out with me. Perhaps you heard us speak during the racket?"

"No," I lied.

"It had to be done tonight. They thought they had something to fear from me, but that is ridiculous. I am sorry if it has interrupted your enjoyment, and so is she. Miss Lee?"

Joan smiled at me and ran her fingers gently along my cheek. There were tears in her eyes. "Happy birthday, my love," she said. "I wanted to see how big you have grown. You are becoming a man, a good man like Mr. Buddy, I hope."

"Miss Lee doesn't have much time to stay. Our business is finished."

Joan and Chen Wu Lee both grabbed Dwight's hands as if they were thanking him. Dwight walked away. The escorts took Joan and her father back to the car.

The fireworks intensified. Amid the popping, the pulsating light, the false fading sapphire stars, Dwight gazed alone at the sky while the Lincoln drove off, swallowed by the darkness as it descended Lonechap Hill.

Cleaning up after the fireworks used to be a time for sharing secrets and jokes and wondering what the faraway spectators in Wendellton had thought. That night, after letting Bill out of the barn, we simply loaded the spent trash into old oil drums. We didn't have much to say to each other—not that Dwight didn't try when he took me aside for a moment.

"Did you enjoy the fireworks?"

"Kind of."

"I'm sorry it was necessary to work out our problems on a night like this. I don't blame you for wanting to keep to yourself."

"Thank you. I don't feel that good."

"Go on, then. I'll see you in the morning on a better day. But may I ask you something first?"

"Go ahead."

"I think Babe may be in love. What is your impression?" Dwight's question was unusual in that it was patronizing, as if he sought my opinion to assuage me, not because he wanted or needed it. Dwight was many things, but he was never patronizing.

"I like Pony."

"I'm glad you feel that way. Your judgement has always been sound."

I walked away without saying goodnight. Before I got to the house, Pony stopped me. "That was strange, wasn't it?"

"I don't know."

"Look...we'll get back to the diary tomorrow, okay?"

"Yes, sir." I found it hard to be enthusiastic. Although I heard little of what was said between Dwight and Joan, I had concluded two things, and was now certain of them in my heart. The first was that I was Joan Lee's bastard. The second was that the codicil to Buddy's will was forged. I did not know where or how those conclusions fit into my own story. I couldn't know yet. The deceptions were too thorough and too deep.

The next morning, I could still see Joan Lee's face, tear-streaked, as she wished me a happy birthday. At the breakfast table, Dwight was alert, as always, but Babe, Pony and I were all somewhere else. Pony spoke in half-started, unfinished sentences as if he wanted to tell us something, but couldn't find the right words. Just as Babe excused herself to go to her gardens, we heard the wail of Sheriff Johnston's siren. He had opened our gate and was driving up the hill. The red bubble on top of his car flashed as if he were in pursuit of some criminal. He didn't turn it off until he reached the top of the hill. Dwight came out of the house with us.

The sheriff was accompanied by D.B. Bulland, Fowler's ranch foreman, the man who had tried to castrate Bill. The white Plymouth patrol car dipped to the left, then to the right, as each ponderous man got out, Johnston first. He tugged on his clinging, dark brown trousers and waited for Bulland. Unlike Johnston, Bulland was solidly built and carried an air of menace that discouraged any urge to challenge him. He also wore a badge.

"D.B. is one of my special deputies," Johnston said. "The ranch is good enough to loan him out when I need him. And I need him today. We've been waiting for you. I think you know why."

"I have no idea, Sheriff Johnston," Babe said, walking up to him. However preoccupied she may have been earlier, she was now fully in command.

"Then maybe your boy can tell you."

Babe put her hand on my shoulder. Dwight stepped in front of us. "I represent the family as both a father and an attorney—as you know, Sheriff," he said. "What could this boy possibly have to say to you? Perhaps I can be of help."

Bulland was looking toward where Bill was standing near his wallow west of the barn. Johnston kept his eyes on me. "Well, son?"

I lowered my head, looked at my boots, and swallowed hard. There were tears of exasperation in my eyes. "When I left the movies day before yesterday, I got into a fight with Darryl and Cameron Fowler. I hit Darryl and gave him a bloody nose, then they left."

"Is that all, son?"

"Yes, sir."

"Are you sure?"

I looked away. Babe drew me closer to her. "They followed me all the way home. Darryl said he was going to kill me and he meant it. A policeman saw them when they were following me."

"Mm-hmm. Well, the Fowler boys mentioned the same thing, so we talked to that policeman. He says the three of you were riding together friendly-like, and if anybody was following anybody, you were following Darryl. That sound about right?"

"He cut ahead of me and Cameron stayed behind me. That's how they do things."

Dwight broke in with a bemused look on his broad face. "Sheriff, is that what this is about? A disagreement between these boys?"

"No, Mr. Wong, I was getting to what this is about. Seems this boy dared the Fowlers to follow him over the gate after he hit Darryl. And as soon as the Fowler boys did what he dared..." Johnston pointed to Bill. "That big buffalo bull came charging after them. Might have killed them if they hadn't made it back over the gate with nothing but short seconds to spare. I guess you know we can't have that happening."

"Bill is my...," I began.

Dwight interrupted me. He was smiling. "Whatever the animal did, he is hardly a dangerous beast. He might simply have been on an afternoon jaunt."

Bulland chuckled. Johnston pressed his point. "To my mind, this boy had a duty to stop the attack and did nothing. And there weren't nobody else around to stop it. That's negligence."

"On the part of a twelve year old boy?"

"On the part of whoever. The question is whether a dangerous animal was reasonably secured, and it don't appear to me that he was or is."

"The animal never left the boundaries of this fenced property, did he?"

"Didn't have to. The law don't protect animals that no one has custody over. Like a wild buffalo. Like if he'd-a come onto your property through a hole in your fence, you're saying he'd have protection? Mr. Bulland here, he knows his animals like nobody else and I've asked him to determine whether it's safe to leave that buffalo here, and if not—why, then, we'll have to do something about it."

"I think you both know better, sheriff," said Dwight. "That animal is considered property and is protected like property under Texas law, just like the cattle Mr. Bulland manages."

"I don't see no evidence that he's anyone's property."

"He's mine." Pony finally spoke up.

Bulland walked over to Pony and actually shook his hand. "Congratulations, grifter," he growled. "You know, I must've seen you pulling some other kind of grift aside from racing that buffalo, I just can't remember where. You might get away with it in other places, but we figure people out pretty quick around here. I'll be willing to bet your paperwork has been conveniently misplaced." His eyes narrowed and he smiled. "And I think I *do* know where I seen you. You're a bronco buster, ain't you." It wasn't a question.

Pony laughed. "I'm sure we never met before, Mr. Bulland, because if I'd met you, I would've known to stay away from you the other day. Let's call it even. I'll even buy you the tub of beer you lost. And maybe you can tell me where I can find a good place to get my trailer hitch fixed. Somehow it got broken the day we met."

"This is all meaningless," said Dwight, "if Mr. Antone can prove he is the owner, as he claims to be. I presume you have paperwork, Mr. Antone?"

"I do. First Mr. Bulland is welcome to inspect Bill with me, if he wants to satisfy himself as to Bill's character..."

At that point I let out a frustrated howl. What the hell was everyone doing? The sheriff had completely twisted my story, using the same set of facts. And I couldn't believe that they were discussing Bill as if he were a piece of furniture, arguing over whether he should be destroyed.

Babe pulled me close to her. "It's going to be okay, honey. Why don't you go off and let us take care of this."

I nodded, then ran behind the barn, where no one could see me, and looked at the emptiness to the north. I had never seen a fight to the death on the hill—not between prey and predator or territorial contenders, or because of any mating frenzies—until then, when I watched one male crow kill another in a small arroyo below where I stood. The weaker bird appeared to have injured a wing. It was forced into a tangled growth of scrub by the attacker, who then struck mercilessly with its beak around the neck and exposed breast of its victim.

I looked back toward where the adults were standing. Dwight was having a conversation with the sheriff near the patrol car. Both men seemed relaxed, with their hands in their pockets. It made me even angrier although I knew that was how Dwight operated.

I retreated into the barn. I did not want to hear the sound of their voices. I felt superfluous, even to those events that directly affected me. The sudden, wrenching, alienating curse of adolescence came to life for what it was, a banishment to an uncertain exile, but also a summons to see things through different eyes when conventional authority seems to fail, when responsibility shifts from obeying to initiating. I was angry with everyone, so I finally pulled out Buddy's last five disks and began to listen to them. He never could have had access to the Phantom Padre's diary, but as he finished the stories in disks 21-24, they were—remarkably—nearly identical to the Padre's own account, except that they ended as the Padre began his fruitless search for Selenia and Young Eagle. In Buddy's account, the Padre was left wandering as the winter storms closed in on him. How could Buddy have known that much, with only a few details missing? Who had told him? He never said.

Then I played disk 25, the last one. I was stunned by it—much more so now that I am older, because in his final message, Buddy was both warning me and encouraging me and offering a glimpse of his own regrets, hoping they would not become mine. He was telling me that I couldn't stay on the hill forever. I lifted the disk from the turntable, replaced it in its brown sleeve, and stared at it, head bowed, for several minutes. The wail of the sheriff's siren startled me. My head snapped up and I ran out of the barn to find Dwight, Babe, and Pony huddled together. Dwight's status as a lawyer and Pony's forged papers, showing his ownership of Bill, had managed to help delay whatever the sheriff and Bulland were planning, but not for long.

"What happened? What did they say?" I asked Dwight.

"Oh, you know..."

"Granddad. Please don't say you'll tell me some day when I understand."

"It's okay, Dwight," said Babe. Pony walked away, distracted.

Dwight frowned and nodded. He reached behind his head and rubbed his neck thoughtfully. "You are reasonably upset. And you deserve to know. The sheriff and his friend claim that Bill is a danger to others, most of all you..."

"No..."

"I know, I know. But I suspect they will try to come back in a day, perhaps two. They may have checked to see whether Pony's papers were genuine."

"Come back for Bill?"

"I believe so."

"Why? Why Bill? They hate Babe and me."

"Of course. And that means they will do whatever they can to make life miserable for you both. But let's not talk more about this now. We are going to figure something out."

"I won't let them do anything to Bill."

"I will do my best to find a way to protect him."

Babe snuck up behind me and put her arms around me. "Quit worrying about the sheriff," she said. "I hope you cold-cocked that Fowler boy good. I'm damn proud of what you did. And damn proud of Bill, too."

Pony, a few yards away from us, staring at Bill, called over his shoulder. "Bill's going to be fine, son. Nobody's going to let anything happen to him."

Even then, I suspect that he knew the crisis had, in fact, grown worse. As if in anticipation, the spook cantered up to our fence line and sat motionless on his horse. If the week that had just ended was the best of my life, the night that was about to begin was the worst.

* * *

BUDDY WATKINS [DISK #25]: *Well, son, this is my last recording. And I've been sitting here in my chair on Lonechap Hill, looking north, and sometimes I think I see herds of buffalo out there on the plains, so many that you can look both ways and not see the beginning or the end of them, and I think I'd like to ride out there and join them, run off to the edge of the earth and into the stars.*

The Phantom Padre—*his story is over as far as I know, doomed to wander in a bitter winter, blindly searching. Truly a phantom, he was reminded every day of how incomplete he was. It's easy to hand down stories or hear them again and think of what they may mean to your own life, when you still have time to change, to share your life instead of using it to hoard things that offer only cold comfort. It's hard when the meaning is behind you instead of ahead of you.*

They say getting sick or getting old slows you down, and sure it does, if you're talking about walking up the hill or getting out of chairs. But me, I think it mostly speeds you up. I mean, suddenly you find you've left everything else in the dust and you're looking back and you can't believe you moved so fast that you can barely see what you left behind, the evidence of your life. And, you know, if you left something broke, you've gone too far to run back and fix it. You were in a stampede and didn't even know it. And you're left with the remainders. Tonight, I'm too near a trance to muster more than a gasp of a laugh at my part in that balmy stampede. We feed ourselves on its energy. Stand in awe of it. Feel the rhythm of its thunder vibrating in our thick skulls. And hope till the very end that it leads us to the place where we are meant to be. Good God, how that drives us.

Then we look back, and we're somewhere else.

I've tried never to live with my disappointments, but I've had them. Somehow, people who are so-called civilized can look at the vastness of the universe and pretend there is no room for those unlike them. And look at what they lose by it. They lose the thread of their common stories, the stories that bind us together. When they choose what they wish to hear, they risk being only half told, or less. In the name of claiming what they are, they waste the greatest opportunity of all—the opportunity of being alive—by obsessing on what they are not.

So don't waste time justifying things you never needed and grudges you never should have held and the self-pity you never should have felt. Lonechap Hill, it's been a perfect place for me, where I could sit beneath the stars and think through all the joy and all the sadness and all the contradictions and see them as one and the same. The thing I never had the courage to do, though, was to go back down. So I guess what I want to say to you is—don't be afraid to do it yourself. I know how easy it is to stay here—a place that's given you safety—a place where you could wander on your own and meet yourself on the way back and say how d'you do, nice getting to know you—a place where gardens grow despite the ruins they came from and the lost are welcome to stay a while and enjoy watching the sun go down. But the world is down below. Don't wait for it to sneak up on you here when you least expect it. Because it will. Go and meet it on your own terms. And don't worry. The stars won't come tumbling after you. They'll always be up there, waiting to hear you laugh at what you find. That's it, son. Goodbye from the doorstep to the universe.

16
Pony in a Hurry

Confiding in Bill had become my method of thinking things out, and that's what I planned to do that night.

The light from the living room spilled into the hallway outside my bedroom door when I awoke a little before 1:00 a.m. Babe and Dwight were talking. Pony wasn't with them. I climbed out of my window and onto the hill, where Bill stood alone to the north of the house beneath swollen clouds that looked as if they were rushing, panicked, across the sky. A summer storm was brewing. The breeze carried the scent of it. I was never afraid of storms. I liked them. We didn't even have a tornado cellar on Lonechap Hill because it was Buddy's firm belief that tornados never set down on hills. "They like a nice flat stretch to do their business," he said, "like a big ol' billiard table to knock things about on."

I inhaled the breeze. It was both wholesome and deceptive—crisp and fresh, but foretelling violence.

My eyes stung.

Had I gone straight to Bill, the night and the days that followed might have been different. Instead, I heard sounds coming from the front of the house, and I went around to investigate. Pony was piling his blankets and other gear into the bed of his pickup. Bill's trailer was unhitched. It had never been repaired since it had been tampered with the day of the race. I hid near a corner of the front porch to watch, but the light that leaked through the living room curtains gave me away. Pony saw me move. He stared at me for a moment.

Finally, he spoke in a low voice. "Come on a little closer, John."

I walked to within a few feet of him. It looked as if he had packed everything in his truck. "What are you doing?"

"Being kind of a coward, if you want to know the truth. I have to leave. I don't know for how long. You remember I said I might have an appointment? It's coming up pretty soon."

My heart quickened. "What about Bill?"

"Look—I've got something to say first. I wrote a note for Babe. I didn't know what to say to you, so I guess I thought I could avoid this. But I can't. They're still in the living room. You can talk quiet, can't you?"

"Yes, sir."

"Sir. That's what you called me that first day."

"I guess."

"You don't need to do that."

"Okay. Is Bill going to stay here?"

"He has to till the trailer hitch is fixed. I'm hoping Dwight can get that taken care of as soon as possible."

"But why are you leaving?"

Pony sighed. "Like I said, I wrote Babe a note. I'll leave it in the mailbox by the front gate. I was going to tell you all myself—about this appointment I've got, to finish some family business. But I have to go sooner than I thought. And I might not be able to come back for a while. If you want to know exactly why, I'll tell you. Do you want to?"

"Yes, I do."

"That man that came here with the sheriff, that Bulland, he said he'd seen me and he was right. He can cause trouble for all of us if I stay here. Bill especially. He'll use what he knows against us both."

"Where did he see you before?"

"In a prison rodeo."

"What do you mean? How could he do that?"

"I was riding one of the broncos he brought in from the Fowler ranch. They used to loan out some of their livestock to the prison. It was good publicity, I guess."

"You were there...in prison?"

"I was."

"What for?"

"I killed a man. It was a fair fight. But I did eight years. No parole. I got out eighteen months ago."

"What was the fight over?"

"He tried to steal something from me. Something my family left me. Just an old antique coin. You've probably seen me flipping it, haven't you? It wouldn't be worth a lot if you tried to spend it. But

I carried it with me everywhere and he was just a mean bastard and tried to take it. I fought him and he hit his head on a rock and died. That's what there was to it. You think I'm a bad guy now?"

"I guess not if he tried to steal from you."

"Thank you for that."

"I never thought you was bad."

"But people like Bulland, they'll always believe the reasons that make you look worst, because that's the way they think. That man's got nothing but bad in his heart for you and Babe and me, too. And Bill. If Bulland makes a fuss, or the sheriff does, I might not get there in time...where I'm trying to go."

"Except what about Bill?"

"Son—I love him like you do. He loves me like a father. He loves you like a brother. If you can keep those thoughts, here's what I want to tell you next. I have to leave Bill behind with you. That's the first thing. I could kick myself for not getting the trailer hitch fixed before now, but even if I had, they'd spot me in a minute, hauling Bill. So Bill's your responsibility and I want you to tell me you think you can handle it. You can, can't you?"

"I'm pretty sure. I know I can."

"Then there's something else about Bill. It's a favor I need you to do..."

I interrupted him. "First, can you answer me a question?" It was time.

"Ask it and we'll both know."

"You said your appointment...where you have to go...it's family business."

"That's right."

"But your mom and dad, they're gone. They ain't alive."

"That's right, but...people leave things behind. Is that your question?"

"No. What if this family business..." I stopped and hung my head. For some reason, I couldn't look at him. "What if it...are you my dad?" I had intended to ask boldly, the way you ask when a real answer is what you've earned, what you expect, what you deserve, what you refuse to leave without. But I barely got the words out.

Something changed in Pony's eyes. His voice softened. "What made you think I might be?"

"Well, the way you showed up on my birthday and all. And you taught me how to box. And you drew that boy..."

"That boy on the playas that looks like you. That's the one you mean?"

"That's the one."

"Hmm." His grunt was an acknowledgement. "Those paintings are still in the house. I said you could keep one. You can keep them all."

"And what about the race?"

"I promised you a painting of it, and you'll get it. I just need time."

"And I guess if you was in prison, that would really explain why you never came for me before. And the way you courted Babe, like I thought the two of you and me would stay up here together."

"I'll say one thing. Any man would be proud to have you as a son, and that includes me." Pony paused. "But I'm not going to answer your question tonight. I will some day."

"Well, what day will you tell me?"

"When I can."

"Why won't you tell me now?"

"Because like I said, I'm about to ask a favor of you, and I want you to do it because it's the right thing to do, not because of who you think I am, or who you think I'm not. I want you to make sure Bill gets to the refuge before that sheriff can put him down on some trumped-up charge. It's time for him to go now, anyway, the rut's almost over."

"Why? Why can't he just stay here?"

"You know why. They'll find an excuse to kill him, like they always did for all his kind. Like they always do. Did you learn from him?"

"Yes."

"Just from talking things out."

"Yes."

"So did I. And when you realize that what Bill is, is our future, then you'll have learned all he has to teach. So now it's time to let him go. And it has to be done fast. If you ask Dwight, will he get that hitch fixed soon as possible? Maybe even tomorrow? That's one of the things I put in Babe's note."

"He can get things fixed. He always does."

"And as soon as he does, I'm hoping Babe and Dwight will hitch it up and drive Bill to the buffalo refuge at the west end of Toomis Canyon. The best thing would be if you can do it at night. Sneak him in without attracting notice. That's what I would have done. You can park out of sight and walk a couple of miles along the east fence to a side gate. That's in this note, too. You can do that, because he'll go with you, and you can let him in through the gate." Pony reached into his hip pocket and pulled out a sealed envelope. "No reason I should leave this in the mailbox now that you're here. You give Babe this letter first thing in the morning, will you? And tell her I'm sorry I didn't ask, but I'm going to take something with me. Antonio Peraza's diary. I know you want to know the story. I'll bring it back someday."

"Babe's going to be mad."

"I know."

"I mean, she don't care about the diary, I don't think. She likes you. Maybe loves you."

"I wish I'd..." Pony stopped to think and finally told me what I had begun to suspect. "When I came here, I was looking for something—for the dugout. You guessed that, didn't you? I didn't think I could tell Babe at first because she wouldn't have let me up here. And then I didn't know how to tell her. Or you. Then I wanted to take you to the playas so I'd have time to tell you about that and about this appointment, but the sheriff came to stir things up. Just know that I'll tell you everything when I can. But I have to go now. Have you ever prayed for something?"

"I guess. Not lately."

"How about your talks with Bill? That's not like praying?"

"That would be like asking him for something. Maybe I just want him to hear me."

"With all those stars up there, you don't think there's anything to pray to?"

"I used to. I still got the crap beat out of me at school."

"Well, let me say a prayer for both of us. To the stars." Pony looked up. "Take care of John and Bill and Babe till I can come back and answer all the questions this boy has. And let them get Bill safely back to the refuge. And let them beat the bastards that's trying to kick them off this hill. And don't let me forget that I still owe John the birthday painting I promised."

I waited with my eyes closed until I felt Pony's tap on top of my head. Without another word, he walked away and opened the door to his pickup cab. "Catch," he whispered. He tossed Bill's brush to me. "Make him pretty for the other buffalos. And don't forget his carrots." He paused to look up with a gesture of surrender. "It's not just you, son. We're all a little out of place—as if the world shook instead of spun, and we just tumbled away to somewhere else. Like those falling stars."

Pony leaned forward where the open door was hinged to the cab and pushed until the truck began to roll down the hill. Then he jumped in and pulled the door shut with barely a sound.

He stuck his arm out of the window waved goodbye. He didn't start the engine until he reached the bottom of the hill, and even that noise was covered by a rumble from the sky, the thunder of the approaching storm.

Out of the corner of my eye, I saw something move west of the hill—our spook, galloping away, no doubt to avoid the storm, but also, as I would discover to my dismay a few days later, with information to report on Pony's desertion.

17
A Cosmic Haymaker

My first thought was how to get rid of Pony's note in a way that wouldn't make Babe suspect I knew that he was leaving but didn't alert her. I propped the envelope against one of her basil plants on the front porch. I already had begun to make up excuses for Pony, no matter what he said in the letter. The light remained on in the living room, so I snuck closer to the window to hear what Babe and Dwight were discussing.

Plump drops of rain spattered Babe's irises.

Thunder boomed and Babe cursed.

"We have talked over everything several times," Dwight said. "I know you wish to avoid a decision, but you cannot."

"This god damn storm. I can't think straight in a storm."

"You've been that way since you were young."

"And you've always been patient with me."

"I've tried to do as your father might have done."

"You were as good to me as you could have been, considering how seldom you challenged my mother. You saved our lives. I couldn't forget that, even if mother did."

"Your mother paid her own price."

"As she reminded us every day." Babe laughed briefly, softly. "And you were so helpless when she complained or wanted something..."

"Not exactly helpless. I wish I had that excuse, for your sake."

"Then what?"

"I don't know what. But an ugly man is never deceived by his own reflection, and that reflection has offended my eyes every day of my life. Your mother...shall we say, your mother allowed me to at least look away from it, and in doing so I overcame it."

Another burst of thunder interrupted them. "I hope this is over soon."

"Your father died during a storm."

"As you know. I had to bury the truth to come here. I had to forget it all, even hide it from you so it would die. I keep the truth out there in my garden."

That was my first hint that Babe had secrets she never had told me—the truth about her childhood in Shanghai and, just as disturbing, the truth about her father, who was not Dwight but someone else, someone long buried but never forgotten. As they talked about it, I felt as if I were hearing some drama unfold with characters I didn't know. Babe—like the characters in Buddy's stories—like me, I thought—had been transported from one childhood to another in the blink of an eye. A bomb had fallen by accident on her life in Shanghai, and now, there she was on the opposite side of the earth, on Lonechap Hill, knowing what she had lost and fearing what she could lose by not claiming fiercely the ground on which she stood, as if there could be no question of her rights or her unassailable belief in them. That night, as I listened in the rain, she was as shaken and uncertain as she ever had been. Dwight knew it. He also knew she couldn't stand by idly while the latest threat from the Fowlers unfolded.

"Well?" Dwight asked. "Now that we've gone over it all, do you feel any relief?"

I could not tell from my place near the window, but I thought Babe might be crying. "It's just...it doesn't stop, does it?"

"That is why you must stay ahead of it. Otherwise it will crush you."

"We can't just see how it plays out and make a decision if it goes bad?"

"There's too much risk in that, as I said. Joan and her father cannot be expected to do anything that would endanger their family."

"I didn't realize he gambled."

"With the wrong people. They killed his brother as a warning, and they threatened Joan."

"And the Fowlers have offered him a way out? How did they know?"

"They apparently have had a private eye look into his affairs—and Joan's—several times since the trial."

"Why didn't he come to you for money?"

"I asked him that. He did not believe I would be sympathetic."

215

"Won't they be exposing themselves to perjury charges?"

"It is a risk they're willing to take. They have a large family."

"Can't we show they were bribed by the Fowlers to change their testimony?"

"No money has changed hands yet. And the Fowlers will say they merely conducted an expensive investigation to finally uncover the truth. I suspect a court would agree they had every right to do so."

"Now what?"

"You could just leave here and have it done with, as your mother so often recommended in her undiplomatic way."

"If anybody ever earned a right to be here, I did. My god damn mother knew that better than anyone. If she'd been a real mother, I wouldn't have been here in the first place. And god damn it, Buddy loved me."

"I know he did. I don't dispute anything you say. I take my share of the blame."

"Forget it. You were as good to me as you could have been, and still are."

"And as your guardian, I have to tell you to make a decision about what threatens you now. How Joan Lee and her father were compromised is understandable. What's more sinister is why she was asked for photographs of you and your mother. She claims she gave them nothing. It doesn't mean they'll find nothing."

Babe sounded as if she were choking. "There is the ultimate card, I guess. If we have to go to court."

"The one you said only two hours ago that you would never use. John."

"Because it's dangerous. You can't predict what people will do. Or how it would affect John."

"Then think it through."

What I had heard to that point was bad enough.

What I heard next—what Babe meant by saying I was the ultimate card—shocked and frightened and nauseated me, and instantly robbed me of my equilibrium. I will not write about it now, not until I can make other events clear, except to recall how in so many ways, we are formed by knowledge and circumstances that turn an innocent landscape into a treacherous minefield—parents fighting, colleagues plotting, friends in acts of derision or betrayal.

Expected or not, it doesn't matter. It ruffles your priorities if you are an adult. If you are a child, it lands on you like a cosmic haymaker and alters your location in the universe, displacing you again, leaving you with two slim, alternate hopes—one, that you can somehow reconcile your new position with where you thought you stood before, or two, that you can withstand the brutal knowledge until you control your own fate and are no longer dependent on those you trusted for wisdom and protection. What I overheard had even worse consequences. It made me decide that I had to run for my life.

I felt pain in the palm of my hand, and realized that I had pressed Bill's brush ever more tightly against it while I listened at the window.

I slid off the porch and into the rain. I knew I could not face Babe or Dwight again. I wouldn't know what to say or how to act. In my mind, at that moment, the only logical choice was to run away.

I went back around the house and climbed through the window of my room to gather what I could. Bill stood in the rain only a few yards away from my window. I took it as a sign that I was making the right decision. "I'm not going to leave you, Bill," I said. "I promised to take you back to where you came from, and I'm going to."

I grabbed a stash of candy bars, took the carrots from the grocery box on my desk, and stuffed everything into my back pack, along with Bill's brush. I picked up my jackknife, the Gamble's knife I got for my birthday, and slipped it into my pocket. Then I emptied the six-by-six-inch metal safe where I kept my savings. The safe had a tiny combination lock on the door and a slot on top. When I had money left over from my allowance, I dropped it in. I was impressed to discover that I had saved twelve dollars and change. That—combined with my ten dollar birthday gift and the ten I had won betting on Bill's race—gave me a total of more than 32 dollars, enough to get me started. Finally, I shoved my black cowboy hat onto my head to keep the rain from my eyes.

I had to leave behind the watercolor that Pony had made of Bill during that glorious evening on the hill. I hoped Babe would hang it where she could see it every day—to regret it, because at the time I was so angry at her that I could no longer reason.

A flash of lightning lit the rugged black clouds moving in from the northwest. I climbed out of the window and headed for the barn. Bill followed, but remained outside when I went in. Still dangling near the workbench was the makeshift bridle Pony used when he let me sit atop Bill to brush him. I picked it up and dragged out a crate to stand on.

Nervously, I headed back into the heavy rain. Bill was there, caked in mud, with globs of dirt attached to his hooves. Just behind him was a large section of Babe's front garden that looked as if it had been excavated by a pickaxe. Broken stems dangled from the mane between Bill's horns. A partial stem protruded from his mouth. A box with its lid ajar sat atop a mound of earth, where Bill's romp had exposed it. Inside the box was a round object—a pocket watch.

What finally had possessed Bill to cross the forbidden boundary into Babe's gardens, I did not know. I climbed onto the crate and fitted the bridle around Bill's snout, just as Pony had done. I tied the reins together and pulled them over his head. Then I hoisted myself onto his back, leaning along the lower slope of his hump. I grabbed the reins and as much hair as I could hold, and flattened my cheek against him.

The storm disgorged unbroken sheets of rain. It was as loud and blinding as any I could remember. Some of the shallow breaks in the earth already ran with mud. I could hear the water not only splattering but gurgling, as if the hill were strangling. Waves of thunder pummeled the air and lightning split the sky and the world turned unsparingly wet and dark. As if he could read my mind, Bill headed down the north slope and onto the vast plain that spread before us.

18
A Burnished Sky

We plodded for more than an hour through the despotic storm. When the clouds finally fled and the newly burnished sky appeared, we were engulfed in the midst of a teeming firmament. Now the stars were back above me, secure as ever. Now I was certain of the direction we were taking and confident that because of the storm, we left no evidence of our passing. All four horizons lay flat beyond and behind us, as if the earth had been unfolded and spread like a tablecloth on which to serve a fat full moon. How we would conceal ourselves in the light of day, I had no idea. I hoped to travel east of Wachyerback, then turn northwest into Toomis Canyon, which would provide shelter for us on the way to the buffalo refuge. I knew we could not reach the canyon before daybreak. I estimated that it would take at least one more night to make the journey, and planned to look for abandoned barns or outbuildings on the way north.

What a luxury it would have been just to exist unnoticed, unaffected by the opinions and desires and authority of others. Then we could simply lie unassaulted atop the hill and watch the setting of the sun and wait for the stars. Should I have stayed and assumed that everyone else would act reasonably and not hastily in their judgments? At the age of twelve, I was beginning to understand from Buddy's stories and from experience that authority was not necessarily a rational force. Now I know that it is only when you are, quite literally, reduced again to dust that others will not grasp for a quota of your existence.

The storms blew well to the southeast with the prevailing winds, and we moved forward with seemingly limitless space around and above us. I had no way to judge how fast we were going or how far we had traveled. I fell asleep on Bill's back beneath the star-strewn sky. I have no idea how long I dozed. I was awakened by a snort from Bill. He had stopped cold. I must have been dreaming, I thought, because arrayed on the plains were the silhouettes of animals, large and small. They were all motionless, as if frozen by the same caution that had caused Bill to stop. Directly ahead of us was another bison, larger than Bill. Had we by some miracle, wound up at the refuge? I knew it was much farther than we could have traveled.

Then I heard a chilling noise, as if some great animal were stretching itself and yawning. It was followed by a menacing scream that sent Bill plunging forward, and I saw to my right the form of a wildcat crouched to strike.

19
The Grass Menagerie

When the scream died, the cat seemed to speak.

"You needn't be so jumpy. You were about to wander into my party, that's why I screamed like that cat. Now what do we have here, and who invited you on this night of all nights in particular?"

"That wildcat..."

"That cat can't hurt anyone. She hasn't made a move in ten years or so. But I could hurt you, dear, if you don't identify yourself."

"My name is John, and..."

"And what?"

"I'm taking this buffalo back to his home."

"Who taught you to ride that beast? Buffalos aren't to be ridden. And where might his home be?"

"Up to the refuge west of Toomis Canyon."

"Mmm-hmm. There's a refuge there, that's true. This buffalo just does what you say?"

"We were sent by...by his owner to return him where he belongs."

"Was that owner younger or older than you?"

"He was a lot older. He knew what he was doing."

"Mmm-hmm, I doubt that, if he sent a boy in the middle of the night to ride a buffalo through Toomis Canyon. I doubt he was sane at all, if you're telling the truth."

"I am, ma'am, and he was sane, it just takes a long time to explain."

"We have till dawn, don't we? And I have my own buffalo out there, as you can see. Maybe they'd like to be friends."

"I'm in kind of a hurry..."

"You don't know who I am, do you?"

"No, ma'am."

"Get down off that beast and I'll tell you."

My legs were aching, my butt was sore, and I was drenched, exhausted, and ready for any excuse to return to earth. I swung off of Bill, holding onto the reins, and landed dizzily in the grass. My knees buckled as if they hadn't been used in a year. I bent to regain my balance. My back pack slipped to the side and I fell next to my hat.

"Stand up and straighten up, little man, and put your hat back on. I'm pretty certain you've heard of me," she said, with her hands on her hips. "I'm Old Lady Baker, and those lovely animals out there enjoying their party, I stuffed most of them and I could stuff you and your friend if I had a mind to. It all depends on whether I like you or not." I looked back quickly at Bill. "Don't pretend you can get back on that buffalo. You can barely stand."

I couldn't believe my bad luck. I had intruded on Old Lady Baker—the merciless plains legend who might be 200 years old, according to Harvey Olsen—the fiend who figured in the threats hurled at me by Darryl and Cameron Fowler to kill me and have me stuffed by her. Perhaps it was simply that her passion for taxidermy invited such comparisons, but the old lady herself, in jeans and a denim shirt with its tail hanging out, was built like one of those padded dolls whose fingers, limbs, and torso reveal scant more definition than a sausage. Her small eyes were nearly hidden by the brim of her floppy brown canvas rain hat, which was held firmly on her head by a cord of thick yellow yarn that divided her chin into two lumps. She didn't look 200 years old. She looked about as old as Dwight. Also, she talked like a school teacher, prim and proper, which made her seem even more menacing, considering her reputation. Her voice was smooth and soft—until she made one of her veiled threats, and then it dropped down into a monotone. Her gestures were graceful and expansive. When she smiled, her head tilted downwards and her eyes grew larger, as if to fix me in place like one of her specimens.

Finally, I said the only thing that came to mind, gesturing toward Bill. "That buffalo is dangerous. You'd better stay back away from him."

"He doesn't look so dangerous to me," she said. "He looks wet and filthy, the same as you. And I'll bet he'd like to take off that contraption around his nose. Give me a hand with that." Old Lady Baker seemed to know what she was doing as she helped me take the bridle and reins off of Bill, who remained calm. "See there, he isn't going to run away, is he, dear?" When she called me 'dear,' she made the word sound sinister.

"No, ma'am. I guess not."

"Anyway, I have potions that could paralyze the both of you in a couple of seconds. I use them like bug spray. So don't try to fool me. I'm mad enough already, what with that squall coming on the night I let my menagerie out to have their little party on the plains."

I thought I'd best try to engage her in conversation while I figured out what to do. "Do you let them out every night?"

"Now that would mean I'm crazy, wouldn't it? It takes me four or five hours to get them into the fresh air and arrange them. No, dear, I hold this party once a year, on the anniversary of Old Man Baker's death. You probably heard I stuffed him, too. Well, did you?"

"Yes, ma'am."

"Then come on and follow me, little man, and you'll see what good care I'll take of you and your friend when you join this little party. Don't step on Mister Field Mouse. It took me forever to do him right."

"Ma'am, please don't stuff Bill."

"Let me guess. You mean the buffalo."

"That's his name. He ain't ready to die and he'd be too big."

"Too big? Too big? You don't see Mister Buffalo straight ahead? Nothing's too big to stuff. Nothing and no one, little man. Come with me. And if you've a mind to run, don't think you can get away with it. Don't be a bad boy." She took me by the arm and dragged me toward the silent, soggy menagerie she had assembled. The birds and animals stood on the plains in a bizarre, open-air diorama spread out over an area the size of a football field. Past the crouching cat that had greeted us, the first animal we reached was the bison. Except for the fact that it was frozen in one eternal pose, it looked alive. Its eyes gleamed in the fresh moonlight. "I'd like to claim this stub horn for myself, but I really can't. He's a bookend in my library, you might say. A man named William Hornaday had him stuffed, not even seventy-five years ago. He lived a long time with some bullets in his hump, they say. The buffalo, not Mr. Hornaday. Then he became part of a museum exhibit so people could see what kind of animal they'd displaced and hounded to near extinction. He's been around, all right. I do fix him up when he needs it. And how do you suppose an old lady like me got him out here tonight?"

"You carried him?"

"Carried him? Little man, shame. Why, I suppose if you put that brain of yours on the edge of a razor blade it'd look like a BB rolling down a four-lane highway. Think about it. How could I carry him? I put wheels on his hooves. He roller-skates wherever he goes, don't you see?" She dragged me to the next animal. It had a lustrous, alabaster coat, a brown vest, and a head topped with whorled, curving horns. "Do you know what this is, dear?"

"No, ma'am." I felt as if I were back in school, except the penalty for a wrong answer would be a lot worse than being told to sit in the corner with a paper cone on my head.

"It's a scimitar-horned oryx. From the sub-Sahara, originally. Do you know where that is?"

"It's a desert?"

"Where might it be? Somewhere near Fort Worth, or where?"

"Maybe Africa."

"Well, that saved you, dear. You keep that in mind. Yes, this one was shot right here in Texas, imported by some big game hunters. Now my job, for all of these creatures, is to decide how they stand and what their posture is for their final pose. Whether mister oryx's neck is bent or upright. Things like that. I'll look him up in a book to see what's most flattering and life-like. I may put a friend there with him, like a bird or even an insect, or maybe a brainless boy, if I can find one." She poked me in the ribs with a hard, stubby finger.

Nearby, a black bear stood on its hind legs, holding a silver tray in an upturned paw toward the muzzle of a life-sized longhorn steer with a "Z Bar Z" brand on its rump. "One of my masterpieces," said Old Lady Baker. The longhorn could still have dropped a stack of bull chips, judging by the care applied to the rest of its anatomy. Beyond it was a fully-stuffed wild boar with a six-foot rattlesnake clamped in its mouth. The snake, twisting and baring its fangs, appeared to be aiming a strike at the boar's right eye. Old Lady Baker also had placed a standing prairie dog and a pair of crows— one upright, one bending toward the ground—in the grass around the death struggle. "Do you like Mr. and Mrs. Crow?" she asked. She stopped to cough. There was no telling what her work required her to inhale. "They're not stiff like most of the birds some of my late competitors did. They're still ready for a good time. Something special, eh?"

"Yes, ma'am." I looked around to see if I could spot her husband somewhere in the tableau.

"Lift up that old boar there and take a good look at him if you're not afraid of the snake he's tussling with."

"I wouldn't want to ruin him if I dropped him."

"You won't drop him, little man. He's not that heavy. It's just a mannequin underneath the hide. Molded polyurethane. I got it from Denver. We may call them stuffed, but nobody actually does stuff them, don't you know that?"

"No, ma'am."

"You have a lot to learn. Look into those eyes. They look like they could stare right through you, don't they?"

"Yes, ma'am. Are they real?"

"Of course not. Those glass eyes are from Europe. They're the finest god damned European-imported, custom-colored eyes that anyone or anything ever stared at you with." She bent over to look more closely at me. "And how about your eyes? Are you part Indian?"

"No, ma'am, I'm part Chinese."

"Are you, now? I'll take care with your eyes, then."

I looked away from her. "All these animals—did you shoot them or spray them with your poison?"

"Wouldn't you like to know? Let's just say they met their maker—then Old Lady Baker. If they'd had the chance, I'm sure they all would've said they wanted to look their best, so I obliged them. I could make road kill sing. How about you, little man? You'd like to look your best, I imagine."

"I don't want to be stuffed at all, ma'am."

"Well, then, look here. If you remain ignorant, the way you seem to be, then that's where you'll wind up, joining the party somewhere between Mrs. Bear and Mr. Boar. And your friend back there, he seems perfectly willing to stay near you. Usually the animals know better."

Out on the table land, just before dawn, I had no choice but to follow Old Lady Baker as she capered through her menagerie. She greeted each animal as 'Mr.' or 'Mrs.' and introduced me to them as 'Mr. Little-man.' "I'm still deciding whether Mr. Little-man should join you all in your everlasting party," she said. "What do you think, Mr. Little-man? Look around you. These animals talk to me every day. They say just as much as Old Man Baker used to, and they're a lot prettier. They like to look their best." She wagged a finger in the air. "Old Man Baker never did. I remember what a pleasure it was when I was first learning this strange art—I was just a girl, waiting for a beau who never come back, an Adonis who made it through the Great War then hopped a train to nowhere—what a pleasure it was to study every one of these creatures in detail, as if I was there at the creation when the world was still young, before these plains were ruined by all the—excuse my language—all the crap we call civilized. I could study the fur, the scales, the softness of the feathers, all the things that helped them survive till the grim reaper finally came for them. And I guess I got kind of selfish. I moved out here into the middle of nowhere once I had more than would fit in my house. Can you tell me why, little man? Has your brain drained that hard rain yet?" She trilled her r's. "No? I'll tell you why. I prefer their company to just about any human being I've ever known, Old Man Baker in particular. Do you know what he said to me once? He said if he ever died, I should go to a convent in Amarillo and ask the nuns to take me in. And we weren't even Catholic. 'Oh, it doesn't matter,' he said. 'They'll take you in if you ask. You're nothing but a cleaning lady. You couldn't possibly last a day on your own without me.' That, from a man who never got out of his Barcalounger except to shit and sometimes not even then. Thank God he died. I didn't know which to throw out first, him or the chair."

"You didn't stuff him?"

"Oh, that's right. Well, look around, little man. Do you see anywhere amongst these lovely creatures anything that looks like an old goat? No, the funeral home barely had to waste a powder puff and a short shot of formaldehyde to keep him looking the way he did in life. Why would I bother to stuff him?"

"Everybody says you did."

For the first time, Old Lady Baker laughed. "Now your friend Bill, there, I'd take good care of him. He'd be king of the pasture. I guess I'll just have to wait my turn with him, and if I ever got my turn, you'd recognize him for being the upstanding creature you always knew he was. But, someone of the human persuasion? The only one I can think of who was worthy of my talents was

Valentino." She quit talking for a moment, with a faraway, starstruck look in her eyes. "Now there was a specimen, the kind who comes around only once, and you thank your lucky stars for it. But as for the rest—how could I begin to make an honest example out of any of them? I surely don't know. And that doesn't mean you, little man," she added quickly. "You haven't been hammered into a fully hypocritical human being yet. I'm still making up my mind about you." In the east, the sky was turning. Above the first white and yellow streaks on the horizon were thin clouds, pink and scarlet, with edges tattered like battle pennants. The pre-dawn glow broadened into wide, straight, translucent highways of light that crossed above us, and through which were apparent all of the colors that occur in that mingling of night and day that begins summer mornings in West Texas. "That's why you and your friend Bill will stay as my guests in my barn until night falls again. Then if I decide to let you go, I might just know a way to get you to Toomis Canyon. Can you get Bill Buffalo to come with you?"

"Yes, ma'am."

"I'm watching you, don't forget."

I took a carrot from my backpack, wedged the index and middle fingers of each hand into my mouth as Pony had taught me, and whistled. Bill ambled over to us, took my carrot, and followed us east of the menagerie, past a dilapidated two-wheeled silver trailer with a miniature picket fence set around it, to a large, sturdy barn. East of the barn, angled into the ground, were two metal doors which I took to be the entrance to a storm shelter. She pointed to the shelter doors. "That's the emergency room," she said. Then she pushed open the barn door and switched on a light. "This is the resurrection ward. I assembled them all, every last one of them. And as I said, most of them I did myself, although many are collector's items. Look all you want, dear."

The barn was crowded front to back, top to bottom, with specimens she had preserved—the smallest was a tarantula, the largest was a palomino horse—dogs and foxes, wolves and coyotes, cats big and small, vicious and domestic, owls, an eagle, herons, woodpeckers, hawks, blue jays, mockingbirds, a collection of homing pigeons, hummingbirds, snakes, armadillos, bats, toads, horned lizards, jackrabbits, squirrels, sheep, prairie dogs and prairie chickens, an antelope, coyotes, a saddled mule, pigs, raccoons, possums, and a few exotic species (like the oryx from the Sahara who had absented himself for the party) unknown to Texas. They were placed here and there, on stands and shelves, peering down from a loft, with no particular scheme of organization other than to fill the available space. But there they all were, in the middle of nowhere, frozen in Old Lady Baker's Darwinian tableaus, eyes glazed as if they were waiting to be awakened again.

A large workbench was set against a dividing wall in the back of the barn. Chains hung from a beam above it. A pelt dangled from one of the chains. Behind the wall, Old Lady Baker kept salts, tools, two large chest freezers, a small refrigerator, spools of wire, mounting paraphernalia, and other supplies. The remaining space, at the far northeast section of the barn, contained a floor lamp, a six-foot plaid-upholstered couch, a scarred and bottle-stained coffee table, a pillowed rocking chair, and a large array of standing metal shelves crammed with newspapers, magazines, and catalogs. "I have illustrated papers that go back a century, in case you're interested. Go ahead and make yourself comfortable. It looks as if your friend Bill's not shy about it. I like to keep that fresh hay around just in case these critters need something to munch on when the lights go out."

Bill had followed us in. There was space for him near a haystack just inside the door. He lay down with a wheeze and rested his chin on a clump of hay. Old Lady Baker pushed the barn door shut again, stared at me for a moment, and led me to the small refrigerator. "So when was the last time you ate?"

I didn't answer at first because I didn't want to know what she kept in her freezers. From the refrigerator, she pulled a Coke and a peanut butter sandwich wrapped in wax paper and handed them to me.

"Thanks very much, ma'am, but I'm not really hungry."

"Oh, no? Do you think I put something in these to knock you out so I can get started on you?" She popped the cap off the Coke, ripped the wax paper off the sandwich and took half for herself. "That shows what a scared little boy you are. It's time to grow up if you want to act that way. Take the food. I'll bet you have nothing but candy and carrots in that pack of yours. Sit."

"Thank you." I lifted the Coke bottle to my mouth and drank against my better judgement.

"So there's only one way now for you to keep this going instead of winding up in one of those freezers. And what's that, you ask? Are you paying attention?"

"Yes, ma'am."

"You'd better come clean with me and tell me who the hell you are, dear, and who you ran away from."

"I told you the truth, ma'am."

"You didn't tell me enough truth to fill an ant's pisshole. So it's time for you to talk. To use your memory. You know I have to do something with you, and what it is depends on you. And just in case I'm the last person on earth ever to hear and remember your story, don't you think it ought to be as complete as possible?"

20
Babe is Frantic

For Babe, the morning began with a mystery. A package had been delivered anonymously to the front door, sometime between the time I left and the time she awakened—two silver cans of 16mm film, tightly packed, with adhesive tape around the circumference of the cans. She put them on a chair at the kitchen table without unpacking them, then went to look for me in my bedroom.

When she didn't find me, she went outside to call for me. Stepping off the porch, she discovered that her front garden had been ripped up and flooded—all the memories, past and present, all the future blossoms that she had planted there, destroyed. She picked the pocket watch out of the mud and held it tightly to her breast. It was the watch she had recovered from John Bridges. She cried, convulsing uncontrollably. It was a deliberate act of vandalism, she thought at first, by whomever had left the film cans on the porch. She called for me again. My bicycle was still in the barn. And, of course, I was not there to answer. As she ran around the hill clutching her pocket watch and calling my name, she realized that Bill and Pony were no longer there, either. Bill's broken trailer remained parked near the barn, but Pony's truck was missing.

Dwight walked onto the porch to find her breathless and in a full-fledged dander. "John's gone off somewhere with Pony, and Bill's missing," she called, her voice shaking. "And god damn it, look at how my garden's ruined." She squatted and examined the damage closely, speaking in a nervous cadence that caused her words to run together. "I don't know, maybe it was Bill, the way it's been thrashed around. The storm could've panicked him. It was a god damn bad one. I wish they'd said something if they were going to go off looking for him. But..."

Dwight interrupted her with a raised hand. "I'm sure they didn't feel they had time to spare. They know he'll be shot if others find him first." He leaned against the porch rail. "What's this?"

He removed the envelope I had placed in the hanging basil planter and handed it to Babe. She read it quickly, half-aloud, as if she couldn't believe its contents.

> Babe—I might have lied about a few things, but not about how close I feel to you. I don't know when I'll be back, but I will come back. The reason I came to the hill in the first place was to find something I needed to find. If I had told you at first, maybe you would have sent me away. I didn't know. I was going to tell you, then I couldn't. I'll tell you everything someday.
>
> I've got someplace I have to be in a couple of days. I can't put it off. And I'm afraid the sheriff could interfere with that and make me miss it. I can't go with Bill, but he needs to get to the Toomis Canyon refuge before there's any more trouble from the sheriff. I hope you can count on Dwight to get the trailer fixed, so you and he can drive Bill to the refuge as soon as possible. They'll accept him if you have to ask. But it would be better if you sneak him in, so no one knows that's where he's gone. If you go at night, you can park at a canyon overlook about a mile east of the refuge. He'll follow John. Walk from the overlook till you see the east fence, then walk another couple of miles north along the fence. There's a side gate he can go through. You may have to break a lock. I know it will be hard on John for me to disappear like this. I'll try to make it right. I want everything in the open. I want to love you. I'm sorry for this. Pony.

"My God." Babe shuddered and crumpled the letter. "My God, he didn't take John with him. Or Bill, either. Oh, God, where's John?"

"I suppose there's still the possibility that Bill bolted and John has wandered off on his own to try to find him."

"He would have told us. He would have told us, wouldn't he?"

"With Pony out of the picture, yes, I would think he'd have asked for help."

"Oh, God. What should I do?"

At that moment, they heard Leo Johnston's warning siren and saw his car swerving up the hill on the muddy driveway.

"Maybe the sheriff has found him," said Dwight. "I don't think he'd be visiting this early otherwise."

Babe rushed to the car before the sheriff's door was half-open and saw there was no one else on the seat beside him. "Do you know something about John?" she demanded. "What's happened to John?"

The sheriff appeared confused as he stepped onto the hill carrying a thick manila envelope. "Something about your boy?" he asked. "Did that damn animal get to him?"

"No, no, they're both missing. Pony's gone. Didn't you see him, isn't that why you're here?"

"Well, I...this is..." Johnston stopped before he finished whatever he had planned to say. He tossed the manila envelope onto the driver's seat. "Have you looked all over here for him?"

"We're looking now. Why are *you* here?"

Johnston avoided answering. "I don't want to say I told you so, but I knew that animal was nothing but trouble. Look, we...let's calm down and think about what to do. First thing I'd suggest is to walk the hill, look for signs of them one place or another, see if we can figure out how they left. You with me?"

"Yes. Let's do it fast."

The walk seemed endless. The air was muggy—smothering—and the sun, still low, nevertheless beat down on them unsparingly. Johnston spotted the dugout and walked to the entrance where a wet band of mud had accumulated. "What's this? Did he play in here?"

"It's a dugout. Some...some...old drifter made it decades ago. We just uncovered it again this week. John didn't play in there, he wouldn't, not in a storm in the middle of the night."

"Well, do you mind if I look?"

"Help yourself."

Johnston knelt in the mud and leaned through the opening. "Nope, nobody in there, thank God." He rose and swiped the mud from his knees, leaving his pants wet and darkly stained. "Looked like an old stove, though, and a stool of some kind. What all else did you find in there?"

"It's...god dammit, sheriff, my boy is missing, and you want a list of what was in a god damn dugout? I don't have time. Let's get on with it."

"Calm down, Babe, I hear you."

Occasionally, as they continued around the hill, Johnston bent over to inspect a tuft of grass and shook his head as if he had expected it to tell him something. But because of the storm, by the time they reached the sheriff's car again, they had found no evidence of how Bill and I had left or the direction we took. "Rain washed this hill pretty clean. You know you have my sympathies, Babe. We'll put out an alert and do what we can."

"That's kind of you." As reluctant as she was to accept the sheriff's help, Babe had no other choice.

"Can't believe a boy or a buffalo could get very far without people noticing. You know we'll have to shoot the animal, now."

"Sheriff..." Babe hung her head and clenched her fists. "Okay. Thank you. I'm going to drive around with Dwight and look where I can, so...you can leave and do your own business. Whatever alerts you can spread. Other counties, too, right? I'll call your office when I get back."

"Okay, Babe, but I...well, I got one more thing I have to do. Why I showed up here this early, knowing you're always up with the sun. Now, because of your boy this ain't a good time, I know, but no time's a good time and it might as well be now as later. Just give me a minute, here." Johnston retrieved the manila envelope from the front seat of his car and extended it to Babe. "This is for you. Like I say, better sooner than later for your own sake. With your lawyer here and all. And we'll find your boy, never fear."

As if he were afraid of what Babe might find in the packet, the sheriff hurried into his car and drove away, remembering to secure the gate behind him before he accelerated, tires squealing, onto the county road. In the packet was notice that the Fowlers were suing Babe for 'tortious interference with an inheritance.' She was too drained to go through the papers when she and Dwight took them into the kitchen. She knew they were coming. She went to the cabinet where she had put away her holster and pistol and strapped them back on. "We don't have time for that crap now," she snapped to Dwight. "We need to drive out and look for John."

"Of course."

Babe grabbed the car keys from a wall peg near the refrigerator and Dwight, tucking in the tail of his plaid short-sleeved shirt, followed her out the door. "There's one thing that seems very odd to me."

Babe stopped and wheeled around to face him. "What's that? What's wrong?"

"The sheriff never mentioned Pony, never speculated that John and Bill might have gone with him. We knew they hadn't because of the letter. But did he? I think he would have relished the idea of blaming Pony for John's disappearance. Unless he did when you were walking the hill with him. Or you told him about the letter."

"He didn't. And I didn't tell him." Babe raised her arms into the air and her face to the sky. "God, how stupid am I not to have wondered?"

Dwight gripped her arm and they resumed walking toward the car. "Perhaps not. Perhaps he was the stupid one. It's something to think about later."

"And whatever's in the film cans."

"The film cans?"

"They were at the front door before I realized John was missing. For all I know, the goddam spook left them here—it's no crazier than any of the rest of this business. I put them on a chair in the kitchen. Forgot about them with all this…this shit happening."

"This is too bizarre. And the day has barely started."

Far from the hill, on another day, I would eventually learn what the sheriff had done as soon as he left Babe. He went straight to his office, where D.B. Bulland and Wyatt Fowler awaited him. After a brief conversation, Fowler placed calls to a geologist and an archaeologist at Canyon State University. Bulland returned to the ranch, loaded a rifle and pistol, and saddled his horse, intending to ride immediately to his next destination and search for me and Bill on the way. More than anyone in the county, Bulland knew every inch of the land and was sensitive to the way it changed, to whatever had passed across it. He was always there, always looking, always happiest when he was most suspicious. As he traveled north on horseback that morning, he did something that only D.B. Bulland could have thought of.

He released Killer, Wyatt Fowler's murderous prize bull, from his pasture. Just in case Bill and I had traveled that way, too.

21
Coming Clean

Resolve is easy to break down when someone asks for your story as persuasively as Old Lady Baker did. And a stranger, even a stranger as fearsome and formidable as she, can be the easiest person to tell it to. I drank another Coke. Old Lady Baker started on a six-pack of Shiner and, out of both fear and compulsion, I told her every detail of my life—from my first memories of the hill with Babe and Buddy to my fights with the Fowler brothers to Pony and Bill's arrival and my promise to see Bill back to the refuge. She seemed to pay particular attention to the story of the Phantom Padre's diary. Then I could barely get through an account of the conversation between Babe and Dwight that I had overheard only a few hours before, but I told her as clearly as possible. I was still terrified by what I had learned about myself.

By the time I was through, the morning was done. Old Lady Baker looked at me differently, less disapprovingly, shaking her head slowly as if she had accepted my story as truth. "You certainly can't go out in broad daylight with a buffalo. People will be looking for you—the good ones and the bad ones."

She pressed a thumb against the bulge beneath her chin, pushing it up while she thought. Then she pulled a rumpled, self-rolled cigarette out of the pocket of her short-sleeved yellow-and-brown plaid shirt. An antique lighter hung from a lanyard on her belt. She unscrewed a match-shaped shaft from the body of the lighter and raked it against the side of the case. The case sparked and the metal shaft seemed to catch fire. "World War I vintage," she said, "like the ones Valentino had. That's why I still use one." She inhaled deeply, then exhaled for several seconds, clearing her mind.

"So you have a racing buffalo. That's good. But the diary—that's a prize. I consider myself an expert on those days, although few people ever seemed to care. And the Phantom Padre—if they put a price on the true history of that man, it would sell for a king's ransom."

Old Lady Baker then went off on a tangent, professing to love above all others "those wonderful stories that made you believe you were in another place and time. You could remember them even if you didn't live them." It was a love that began, she said, with her admiration of Valentino. "The man could sell you a story with his eyes alone and send you off to another world." Before she fully retired to the calling through which she created her own world—taxidermy, which she had practiced since late childhood—she worked in the schools of several different towns, starting as a teenager. Her job was to clean toilets, but she was adept at putting library books swiftly back into place, which she did at the end of every shift, wherever she worked, with the blessing of the librarian. She loved tending the shelves of books after finishing her janitorial chores.

She also brought with her small birds and animals whose bodies she had found on the plains—tiny, expired lives to which she paid her respects by exquisitely preserving the corporeal evidence of them with taxidermy. Carefully, gently, she showed them to schoolchildren, explaining what they were, where they had come from, where they fit into the scheme of things, why they should be treated with respect.

She enthralled children with her stories of plains history and legends. But she was fired because of that enthusiasm. Parents who caught her spinning yarns and exhibiting small stuffed animals at the end of a school day were incensed that a cleaning lady was filling their children's heads with strange tales and dead animals and nonsense. What right did she have? What kind of memories would their children have? What would the school board say? All those little minds, needing to be scrubbed clean again. What were their prudently edited textbooks for? She managed to hopscotch into a series of new jobs in towns farther and farther from each other, but eventually her reputation caught up with her and she had to permanently cease and desist her contact with children, confining herself to janitorial duties only. The parents were the ones who started calling her Old Lady Baker, even when she was barely out of her teens. She was really an old witch, they said, in a young woman's body. They frightened their children about her true intentions so the youngsters would never go near her. "And they made fun of the way I spoke, like I can see with my eyes wide open what I'm telling you about," she said.

"I know it's funny. But I stored up a lot of tall stories before they petered out—all of 'em up here." She tapped her head. "Those stories always evaporate when people get too busy to hear them and then they rain down again when you least expect it." She looked at me and sighed. "Oh, hell, why not?" she said. "You know who I'd told those stories to the first time I got fired? It was Buddy Watkins. If I remember, he was about your age when I regaled him with what I knew, and I wasn't much older. He soaked 'em up like a human sponge, he was so dry and empty and lonely. Stuttered all the time, so he couldn't do what he wanted most—to pass them on, tell them to other people, and keep them alive. I guess he solved that problem and left them with you, God rest his soul." Her eyes brightened. "Well...it just so happens that I have something in my collection that I wish I could've shown to Buddy Watkins. Follow me. We'll see how well you learned."

She wended her way through her crowded collection, continuing to talk. "Maybe you heard of the Reverend Phillip Scott Wolf—former hideman and gambler who became a phony preacher and went to help settle Wendellton with his followers. Invited there by Zebulon Fowler himself. Planned to Christianize these parts seeing as how the buffalo were all shot away and martyred and civilization was marching in and he needed a new job. My granddad met him once. Granddad was a buffalo soldier—served at Fort Griffin—thought he'd do some cowboying after he got out. He happened to be passing through Wendellton when the good Reverend and some followers got ahold of him, stripped him down, got a bucket of white paint and scrawled 'Nigger' on his back. Left him naked on the road out of town. He made the mistake of asking whether they couldn't see with their own eyes what he was, so they beat him senseless, too. I got to say, Granddad wound up okay, working with Charles Goodnight in the Palo Duro. And he lasted a lot longer than the Reverend Wolf."

We stopped at a dusty set of shelves with smaller animals arranged on them—cats, mice, rabbits, a couple of terriers, and a group of Gila monsters. An aluminum ladder was propped against the wall. "Get up on the ladder and go to the second shelf from the top. I'll tell you what to hand down from there." She steadied the ladder for me, then pointed as I reached the shelf. "That one right in front of you. Bring her on down, and hold your breath. There'll be dust from the arsenic that preserved her. Recognize her, do you?"

I was pretty certain that I did. "Yes, ma'am."

"Then you may also know that despite his lust for justice, the good Reverend Wolf wound up knifed in the gut one fine day, and that beautiful stuffed tabby you're holding—Ah Toy, her name was—was found, standing on her mahogany mount with her paw raised to strike, just as you see her now, right next to his body. It was like this girlcat had a tenth life, when she got her revenge on the very man who had murdered her one dark night outside the laundry where she lived with her mistress Ping. So, then—if you ask me, the moral is that Ah Toy, our friend here, had another life and another story to tell, even though everything appeared to be over. You never know. You never know. You might not be done in yet, either. Don't forget to look on the bottom of that mahogany."

What I saw when I tilted the board were faint letters, written by a sure and fine hand. They spelled *Fr. Peraza.* "It's just like in Buddy's stories, ma'am. I never thought they...where did you find her?"

"Where I got her was at a shop in Mobeetie. How she got there, I don't know, but she's seen a lot of strange goings on, no doubt. Now she's here looking at you, across all those years. What do you think of that?"

The mottled orange and white cat stared up at me. "She's got pretty eyes."

"Well, you said the right thing again. You're a crafty little man. Are you getting tired?"

"No, ma'am."

"Afraid that if you take a little afternoon nap you'll wake up stuffed? Ah Toy's good company in taxidermyland, I reckon."

"Do you know what you plan to do with me?"

Old Lady Baker laughed. "You are blissfully naive, aren't you? You'd make a specimen, all right, if I had a mind. But I don't stuff anything till after dark, and I'll bet it's a beautiful afternoon outside. Always fresher the day after a storm. So I think I'll take a peek, to see whether it looks safe for you and Bill to have a breath of air. Would you like that?"

"Bill would, I think."

"All right, then. Put Ah Toy back on her shelf while I get the door."

Old Lady Baker slid open the barn door and returned a few seconds later, summoning me with her thick fingers. Bill got up, shook himself, and trotted into the open. I gave him another carrot and he grazed near the barn while Old Lady Baker and I walked among her menagerie and she greeted, with accustomed formality, its impeccably preserved and discreet citizenry. She stopped, brought her feet together, tottered a bit, and bowed. "Good day, Mr. and Mrs. Crow. Rather hot this afternoon, isn't it?" The heat was brutal, wilting—even, I thought, for those who gazed back at us through glass eyes that never winced or turned from the callous glare of the sun. On her animals and birds, the fur and feathers were no longer damp, but were feverish to the touch. I felt on my own skin the kind of heat that seems to accumulate and feed on itself, a rush of it.

Old Lady Baker looked past her tray-wielding butler bear into the obscure distance. Then she turned and nodded toward Bill. "You know, I've got a horse trailer parked over behind the barn. Do you think Bill could ride in it?"

"Yes, ma'am. I know he could."

"Let's go take a look to make sure."

Bill followed us. The trailer looked fine to me. Luckily, we were hidden from view by the barn, because when I started to ask whether Old Lady Baker meant to drive Bill to the refuge—even if she didn't let me go—we heard the gunshot.

She grabbed me by the arm and lunged forward. "You and Bill come with me. Quick."

Old Lady Baker hurried us around the barn to the metal doors of the storm shelter and told us to wait. She darted into the barn. Bill was snorting and unsettled, the languor of his grazing interrupted. I scratched him under the eye. In less than a minute, Old Lady Baker returned with a .357 Magnum Colt Python revolver tucked into the back of her jeans. "We need to keep you out of sight," she said. "If that was some range cowboy shooting at my party, I'll kick his ass. But it might be someone looking for you."

It was.

22
Babe Summons Her Enemy

Babe couldn't hide her exhaustion, although it was only a few minutes past 4:00 p.m. She and Dwight sat at the kitchen table. "They've had planes and riders out," she said. "We've driven all the back roads around here. I've even phoned Harvey Olsen. What next?" Her eyes were too tired to maintain steady contact, drifting downward or sideways as she spoke. "I can't think anymore, Dwight. How could we miss a boy and a buffalo?"

Dwight called the sheriff's office and reached a deputy who reported no progress. "Interpret it as a good sign," he said to Babe.

"A sign of what?"

"They are still alive and moving." Dwight was taking notes and already shifting through the papers having to do with her legal battles with the Fowlers. The unopened cans of film sat next to him. "I shouldn't ignore these papers, but you should try to get some rest, Babe."

"God damn it." Babe swept the papers off the table. "That's what started all of this. Christ."

For almost all of Buddy Watkins' life, his will had specified that the hill and all his lands would go to his lawful heirs, the Fowlers, through the corporate entity that represented their consolidated interests. The codicil, as filed, clearly stated a different disposition.

> ...All the rest, residue and remainder of my estate to my wife, if I am married at the time of my death and she survives me, or, if my wife predeceases me, to my children, natural or adopted. If no wife or child survives me, to my lawful heirs.

The problem was, Buddy had grown too feeble to sign the document by the time he asked Dwight to draw it up. Joan Lee was in the room when Dwight read the codicil to him and Buddy nodded weakly. "If he simply drags a pen across this," Dwight said to Babe, "it will be questioned, surely. Questioned for his ability to understand. Questioned even more for his ability to resist." Four days later, copies of the will, fully signed, were placed before Joan Lee and her father. Buddy had died the day before. "I regret to inconvenience you both with details," Dwight told them. "Joan, you saw that Buddy agreed to this, but at the time he was unable to sign it. The proper way to mourn him is to secure the future of his wife and son. You must both agree that you witnessed this signature of his, which is dated on the day of his consent—the consent you did indeed witness, Joan. You may be challenged in court, but you must stand by this claim, knowing that you are standing by his last wishes."

The night of the fireworks, Joan had promised Dwight all he could reasonably hope for, considering the dilemma in which she and her father had been placed by the Fowlers. The Lees already had recanted their claims of having witnessed Buddy's signature. That might be all that was necessary to invalidate the codicil. But Dwight had questioned her severely, as a lawyer might in court, about whether she believed the signature had been forged. He had not threatened her, although a threat was no doubt implied. She swore as he cross-examined her that she never had considered whether the signature was forged. "Nor," Dwight asked, "did you think Babe or I might have done such a thing?"

"No."

Dwight spoke again in Chinese. That was when Chen Wu Lee dropped to his knees in tears, shaking his head. No, he would not think such a thing of Dwight or Babe. Both he and Joan were trembling.

Patiently, Dwight picked up the papers from the kitchen floor and paused for a moment, thinking through the conversation again. Babe held her head in her hands. "I can extend this whole process, if you wish," Dwight said. "As far as I can determine, courts in Texas haven't previously addressed the issues of what exactly constitutes a cause of action for tortious interference with an inheritance. So the court will survey the law in other jurisdictions. That will take time. As the executor of the will, I can take responsibility for any misunderstandings that may have occurred over what the Lees thought they were signing. We are still within the statute of limitations for fraud, but whatever the decision is, they cannot prove malice against you. But the hill—I would think the Fowlers will have this hill at the end of it." He looked at the film cans on the chair next to him. "And I suppose I should see how these are somehow connected to this day of coincidence. Go on, Babe. We'll form a strategy later."

"I can't sleep, Dwight, don't treat me like a baby."

"As you say." Dwight removed the tape from the cans of film. Each can contained a 1,200-foot 16mm reel. When he lifted out the first reel, intending to hold a length of film up to the light to see if he could recognize an image, he found a newspaper photo beneath it. It was a picture of Babe, taken after a San Antonio Battle of Flowers parade. Her mother had refused to pose with her on that day, but could clearly be seen in the background. Bei Lian's face was circled. A note was paper-clipped to the photo. "A visit by a Shanghai movie star and her Chinese daughter?" the note read.

"I think we should look at this now," said Dwight. "I'll get Buddy's projector."

"It's in the hall closet." Babe spoke with a heavy sigh, certain that the film would make a bad day even worse.

Dwight placed the old projector on the kitchen table, threaded a reel of film, and aimed the machine at a blank space on the wall. What they saw left Babe shaking and in tears. The reels contained a grainy print of a movie made by Bei Lian in 1930. It was a silent Magic Spirit film, *The Girl Bandit-Avenger*, one of the predecessors of all martial arts movies. Bei Lian played a *nüxia* warrior, a female knight-errant. In the story, she was taught the magic of flying by a Daoist master. Her task was to avenge the death of the only male heir in her family, a village guardian who was murdered by corrupt forces. As an actress, she was the definition of grace, beauty, and power, but the ground-breaking roles in which she excelled would soon be forgotten, smothered by history along with her career. It was the first time Babe had seen one of her mother's films. She cried throughout, in awe of her mother, and in anger and fear. Someone had gone to the trouble to locate the film to hurt Babe. It made her life in San Antonio a lie. It would invalidate her adoption of me. She was an illegal visitor with none of the rights she had claimed.

Babe ran her thumb along the handle of her pistol. "They don't even need to go to court. Not with this." She wiped a tear from her cheek and cleared her throat. "I'm done crying, Dwight. I'm ready to kill someone."

"You've always had the same rigorous spirit as your mother. They must have paid a lot of money to investigate every aspect of your life." Dwight rubbed his eyes as the film rewound on the projector. "And to think I searched for years, believing that something like this might have been brought over to San Francisco or New York. There was nothing. No evidence of who she had been or what she had done. And she could never tell anyone. It would have meant disaster..."

"It does mean disaster. Between the papers and the film they'll have the choice of putting me in jail or throwing me out of the country. And John. The adoption..."

"Well..."

"I know what I've got to do, Dwight," she interrupted, "and so do you. This has gotten out of hand. I don't even know whether my boy is still alive. If we find him, I can't have him come back to this."

"What is it you want to do?"

"You know how to get in touch with Wyatt Fowler."

"I know someone who can, of course."

"He has to know how bad this can hurt him. I can't let it go on. Do it now. Let's meet first thing tomorrow. And God help John."

23
The Cannibal Bugs

Old Lady Baker grabbed the tongue of a long, flat wagon with rusty wheels next to the barn. She pointed to the storm cellar doors. "You and Bill're going to wait there till I know what this is about. Can he stand staying down there?"

"He's stayed in barns and trailers..."

"Then let's go." Another shot rang out from the distance. "Hurry." Old Lady Baker dragged the wagon behind us.

With the strength of a Titan, she pulled open one six-foot door, then the next. The doors spread apart like giant wings, revealing a packed dirt ramp that led into the ground. "Lucky for you and Bill I need that ramp to get my creatures in and out," she said. "Otherwise there'd be no place for him to hide lest he's good on a ladder." I hesitated. "Well, get in there quick."

Bill followed the carrot in my hand halfway down the ramp. Then he bucked, jumped onto the floor, and backed up quickly, disoriented and snorting. I had seen him leap many times on Lonechap Hill, soaring from one place to the next, and I worried that he might hurt himself in the shadowy space that confined us. "This is no time for Bill to get temperamental," said Old Lady Baker. "Calm him down."

I could see only what was illuminated by the daylight streaming through the doors. Bill tried to turn back toward the ramp. I held out the carrot, waving it. He followed my hand, paused, snatched the carrot and ate it. Then he turned to Old Lady Baker and licked her bare forearm with his giant, abrasive tongue. She started backwards, but it was too late. "What the hell was that?" she asked, rubbing her swelling arm. "This is no time for affection. You may not have anything to be grateful for."

Old Lady Baker stepped quickly ahead of us, farther into the cellar. In the middle of the floor was a table with a large, rectangular glass object next to a post. "Sorry to put you down here with the arsenic and borax. There's a light switch on this post." Old Lady Baker flicked the switch. The room was lit by a single, naked bulb that exposed networks of silky spider webs undulating above us in the currents of air. When I saw clearly what was on the table, I nearly retched. I turned away from it with a moan and walked back toward the ramp.

The glass object was an aquarium containing a skull, still covered with shreds of raw flesh. The skull was teeming with beetles. A ravenous mob of them writhed in the circle of an empty eye socket. Another cluster swarmed at the base of the skull. "Oh, hell, turn back around and look," Old Lady Baker said. "The dermestid beetles are just cleaning off that bobcat head so I can make it pretty again. That's the way nature works. If you have a problem with it, then you've got a problem with Mother Nature." She picked up a large silver flashlight that was next to the aquarium. "Behind that ramp is a space where you and Bill can park yourselves. You'd best try to get him to stay there with you. It's going to get very dark. Can you handle it?"

"I guess so."

She slapped her palm with the flashlight. "So come on around here."

Bill's hooves clattered on the concrete floor.

The shelter was large for its type—about sixteen feet by twenty feet, lined with shelves containing God-knows-what in rows of jars. The shelves also were stacked with moisture-proof containers of books, candles, and matches. Foldaway lawn furniture leaned against the wall opposite the ramp. On the inside of the ramp was a large empty space behind a line of posts that supported the back of the ramp. That's where Old Lady Baker led us. She handed me a lawn chair. "Take this flashlight. If you hear me step on those cellar doors, switch it off and don't make a sound unless I give you the all clear."

She turned off the overhead light bulb and propelled herself up the ramp toward the daylight, taking long, wide strides with her stocky legs. "I have to run that wagon over your tracks." The doors shut with a loud thud. I have never known such darkness before or since. I was sure I felt beetles crawling up my legs. Bill flicked his tail and caught me on the back of my arm. I turned on the flashlight, dropped the lawn chair, and spent the next couple of minutes scratching and squeezing and pushing on my pants, shining the light everywhere, feeling for flesh-eating attackers.

245

Bill stood in the gloom the way he had stood with me so many times on Lonechap Hill. I listened to his breathing, a slow churn, a low hum. There was one other sound, like a sinister whisper, barely audible, the sound of the beetles at work, consuming dead flesh. The odor of Bill's coat was pungent and earthy. He shifted toward the wall. I wanted to keep him calm. I got his brush out of my backpack and ran it along his side, occasionally pulling out tufts of hair as I'd seen Pony do. After a few minutes, I tugged on his beard—also something I'd seen Pony do when he took Bill onto the hill with his blanket—and Bill dropped to his knees and lay down with a snort on a thin, worn, moldy length of carpet. Then his breathing grew easy again.

How little time I'd had to believe that my life had taken a turn for the better. Only a week or so. Now, facing a different world from the bright one I had envisioned, I did not know what I believed. I felt stripped of any ability to express even my anger and confusion, like the skull whose vestiges of identity and self-expression were stripped by beetles in the blackness where I waited.

I did know that I loved Bill. I had shared with him my deepest emotions and my darkest confessions, and even depended on him to defend me. And as I sat in the cellar with him, I believed that if he ever was going to communicate with me, it would be there, when I was at my most desperate. But there was no ringing in my brain, no call to me—nothing. My thoughts flew here and there, aimlessly. After a few more minutes, I shook my head and calmed down and thought how foolish I must have sounded to Bill if he was indeed paying attention. He was like some mythical beast, taking the form he took for reasons I didn't understand, a crossover that would never come again, who was there to teach a lesson I needed to grasp.

The disturbance that Old Lady Baker left to investigate was the threat I had feared. She was outraged, as she told me later, when she went onto the plains where she had arranged her menagerie and found that someone had fired two bullets into the muzzle of her stuffed bison. One round had struck the forehead. The other knocked the nose askew. A man rode toward her with a hunting rifle held in an upright position. She stood in front of the bison until the rider was within a few yards of her.

"What the hell is this about?" she yelled. "Who the hell are you?"

"D.B. Bulland," said the man with the rifle. "What are these, stuffed animals? Are you crazy, lady?"

"Just crazy enough to sue your sorry ass, dearie. Look what you did to my antique buffalo. God damn it, he already had two bullets in his hump for a hundred years. Where were you when you fired that shot, anyway?"

Bulland pointed west. "Way back there. I was off my horse, having a smoke. I saw the silhouette and couldn't tell what the hell he was standing near."

"So?"

"So I fired once from my shoulder and nothing happened. Then I got down on the ground to steady myself, took careful aim and fired again. That damn thing was still standing..."

"Well, congratulations on your marksmanship. You're just as dead-eyed as that poor departed beast you shot."

"God damn it, I had good reason to do what I did. There's a damn dangerous buffalo some fool let loose yesterday. Attacked some school children down by Wendellton. There's lots of people out looking for him. You'd best put these here back in your barn or wherever they came from."

"I was airing them out, if it's any of your business."

Bulland scanned the ground and dismounted. "You're Old Lady Baker, ain't you," he said as he walked through the grass with his eyes down.

"What's it to you?"

Bulland shrugged. "Not a thing. You could try to send a bill to Mr. Fowler if you want to fix that thing up."

"I'd rather sue your ass."

"Watch how you talk uppity to me, like you was somebody. I'm asking you a question. You ain't seen that buffalo, have you? Or a boy might of been with him?"

"You didn't mention a boy. I thought your buffalo stomped all over children."

"This boy's a runaway."

"I haven't seen anything."

"We lost the animal's tracks cause of the storm, otherwise we'd have him by now." Bulland brushed back some grass with his boot, then looked toward the barn. "You been in there lately? That'd be a place a boy could hide, maybe you wouldn't even notice."

"Of course I've been in there. I can assure you, there's no boy hiding in there. No buffalo, either."

"Mind if I take a look? This is serious business."

Old Lady Baker reached behind her back and pulled out her Colt Python. "So is this."

"I'm trying to help you, woman. You don't want the law on your head over this."

"I'm not saying you can't have a look. Just put your rifle down in the grass and I'll escort you wherever you want to go. You might've forgotten that there's people besides your boss who own some of this land. You're trespassing."

Bulland did as he was told. Old Lady Baker rolled open the doors and led him into the barn. He walked through quickly, said nothing, and left with Old Lady Baker at his back. "Mind if I look on the other side?" he asked.

"Go ahead."

"That a storm cellar behind here?"

"It is. I wouldn't recommend you look there."

"Why not?"

"Not at this time, I wouldn't recommend it."

"There's tracks I'd like to check."

"You mean those? Those wagon tracks?"

"Those're fresh wagon tracks. And others, maybe."

"Did you see those animals of mine out in the field? How do you think they get from here to there? They may not have a heartbeat any more, but they still make tracks."

"I can send the sheriff back here. You talk to him like you been talkin' to me, you'll have to find space for all them beasts with you in a jail cell."

"Suit yourself." Old Lady Baker picked another of the flashlights from a box by the storm cellar doors. She stepped heavily onto the doors, then backed away. "You open the doors. I'll go in first. Don't you forget, dear, I have a gun in one hand and a flashlight in the other."

Bulland pulled the creaking doors open. "A storm cellar with a ramp? That, I've never seen."

"When you've got cartloads of stuff to move, there's nothing like it." Old Lady Baker's voice echoed as she stepped forward.

"So you think there may be some runaway in here? I guarantee you, there's nothing alive. This is where I keep my chemicals and my cannibal bugs." The beam from her flashlight arced back and forth as she stepped down the ramp. "You stop right here, just before the floor levels out," she told Bulland. "Now, look there. I'm afraid that's all you'll find."

"What the hell is that?"

"My cannibal bugs. They live down here, and they strip down my skulls and carcasses before I stuff them. The problem is, I had a little accident. Those little cannibals are all over the place, now." She ran the beam of her flashlight over the back wall of the cellar. "If there's a runaway in here, he isn't even skin and bone by now. Just bone. The same for a buffalo. And isn't that one on your pants?"

I heard a slap. "I seen maggots and things before," Bulland said. "Is this some kind of voodoo?"

"Well, that's one way we like to use them. Oh, but these aren't like maggots, Mr. Bulland. These are more like piranhas. They get in your skin and multiply. You see how this arm of mine is swelling up? That was from just one of them, leaped onto me out of nowhere. I had to cut him out."

I heard another slap. "Hell, woman—"

"Hell was booked full when these creatures were made, so they just crawled up among us, I reckon. Voodoo, you know."

"What do you do when you want to go down there?"

"I keep them in that glass box. Every so often they get out of it. Now I have to fumigate the place and get a new bunch before I can come down here again. It happens. You missed one on your boot."

Slap. "I seen enough."

"Are you sure?"

"This is messed up."

"Then get back up there. And know that I don't take responsibility for whatever you picked up down there."

"You got bug spray in the barn?"

"That's for me."

The cellar doors shut again.

24
Showdown at Toomis Canyon

Old Lady Baker hustled us from the shelter after Bulland rode out of sight. Bill sprinted onto the grass and dropped for a wallow. "You're thinking he got some of those dermestids on him," she chuckled. "Unfortunately, not a chance."

"I thought you said..."

"There's none outside of their box and if there were some, they couldn't care less about you and me and Bill. You have to be dead and putrefied to get their attention. Then they put on one hell of a show. Do you know the man who was looking for you? That Bulland? The son of a bitch shot my antique buffalo. Thought I was some kind of voodoo queen, I might add."

"Yes, ma'am."

"Up to no good, is he?"

"He'd kill Bill. Maybe me, too."

"Well, then, what can we do about it?"

"I promised to get Bill to the refuge."

"Well, as soon as it gets dark, I'll drive you there. It's just past Toomis Canyon. And you're sure Bill can ride my trailer, can he?"

"Yes, ma'am. I'm sure."

"So we'll take him there, you and me, then we'll figure what to do about you."

"I can't go back home."

"I didn't say anything about that. But there are advantages to being chosen, you know. I don't know your mama, but it sounds to me as if she had plenty of choices about you, and she and Buddy did everything in their power to pick you and keep you and see that you lived at the very top of the hill. You'd pick her, too, I have a feeling. And that makes a pretty good match."

"But..."

"I know. She didn't tell all to you. So what? You fought for her anyway and there was a reason for that, better than even you knew. Why do you think Buddy wanted you to hear those stories, and spread 'em out for you like he did? So you'd learn something about people in that empty little head of yours." Old Lady Baker pointed to her plains menagerie. "I'm used to living with my stuffed friends, there. They can be whatever I want them to be. But you need to decide about your life. Any time you start a war with yourself between the present and the past, you're going to foul up the future. Then somebody will find your dugout in a hundred years and they'll wonder what your story was."

I wasn't sure I needed the lecture. "You're not who they say you are either."

"Is that a compliment? I will accept it as such. No, I'm not. But don't take me as an example. I let myself play the role that others were all too willing to assign to me. Like the Padre did. Like you've done. Even when it hurt me to do so. And I ran away and created my own world, where I can say anything I want to those beasts and make myself believe they're happy to hear it. Do you even know I have a first name? No one has called me by it since I can remember. And yes, I liked giving you a scare. Once, in the days of Valentino, I had better sense. But if you've figured out that I'm not going to poison and stuff you and Bill, well, good for you. So before I take you on your way tonight, I don't think I want to leave my menagerie in the field alone. If you'll help me get them back into our barn, we can have another sandwich and plan Bill's freedom ride." She stopped and put her hands on her hips. "Voodoo lady. Been called a witch, but that's a new one. I'll have those animals dancing on the plains under a full moon."

The field outside Old Lady Baker's barn was clean and barren again when we walked through it one last time before leaving. Bill had rubbed himself several times on the corner of the barn, and he and I jogged through the grass while Old Lady Baker watched the vacant horizon. Before long, the moon hung above us, bright and heedful, minding a growing brood of stars. She packed sandwiches and a thermos of coffee to bring with us on the drive. She was impressed with the way Bill walked coolly into her trailer. It was already hooked to an immense black 1948 Packard touring sedan parked north of the barn. "They called this baby the pregnant elephant," she said as the ignition wheezed. "That's why I love her."

A long, narrow dirt road led off her property to the east and intersected with a north-south county road that was barely wide enough to hold the car. She drove north until she hit the two-lane blacktop that took us west again.

We never saw headlights, nor did we see even hazy spores of light straining against the darkness from the two small towns we passed. For the most part, bumping and rattling along, we might as well have been the only three creatures beneath the avalanche of stars that tumbled through the universe, and the feeling of peace was deceptive. "To think a hundred years ago, Bill could've been out there in the moonlit grass," said Old Lady Baker. "Out there in a herd you couldn't see the end of. Now they're extinct."

"But they're not. They were rescued."

"Not extinct in kind, but, for all intents and purposes extinct in his true place, I mean. Certainly he can't return out there on the plains. These plains, they have serenity in the moonlight—just look at them, how beautiful—but to me it's the serenity of a battlefield dedicated to posterity following the burial of its dead. Something has been taken from him, as it is from all of us when we're lined up and handed the dog tags we'll wear for the rest of our lives. You're doing the best for him, despite everything. He may not need to know it, but you need to."

The short grasses gave way in stretches to taller grass—little bluestem and a bluish-green sideoats grama, sturdy, easy to graze, and delicious to the bison that once roamed there. Shrubs and junipers sprang up out of the shadows on the land ahead of us. "We're near the canyon, now," Old Lady Baker said. "The earth suddenly seems to fall away when you see it. It should be right beyond that sign." She pulled the Packard onto a dirt turnoff with a historical marker and stopped. "Let's take a look before we go on to the refuge. And I want to see Bill where he should be seen, one last time."

She opened the trailer gate and Bill stepped out. We waited for a while as he grazed, then we took a short walk. At first we saw no break in the flat landscape, but we didn't go far before we skirted what appeared to be a severe erosion in the ground. In an instant, we found ourselves looking down into a dark breach in the earth—Toomis Canyon, twisting its way toward the northwest, with walls rising as high as 600 feet. "Damn," said Old Lady Baker. "What a layout." We must have stood there, held motionless by the sight of the moonlit canyon for five minutes or so. Finally, I felt her hand on my shoulder. "We have to move on," she said.

We turned back toward the field where Bill had been grazing across the road. He had wandered farther south, away from the canyon. I rubbed my eyes because I thought I saw another figure in the field. Old Lady Baker gasped. We hurried across the narrow road toward Bill. "This is my fault, for stopping. You stay here and let me see what this is about."

I already knew. A large animal was stalking Bill, moving forward, feinting, and moving forward again. It was Wyatt Fowler's prize bull, Killer, released on an impulse by D.B. Bulland for the very reason I feared most—to remove Bill if he came across him—to end Bill's existence as a nuisance, a trespasser, the troublesome outlier he had become. Bill trotted back toward us and stopped cold, looking completely unprepared for a challenge, as he had in the corral when Killer had threatened him once before. Then, Pony had broken up what could have been a fatal encounter. There, under a throng of stars, the two animals stood, less than a hundred yards from us, with nothing between them, nothing to hold them back.

I whistled, but Bill didn't respond. Old Lady Baker was hustling toward the animals as if she were Mother Nature preparing to reprimand two of her wayward children. She even cried, "Stop that." She moved clumsily but quickly with her thick and aging body, and I followed immediately behind her. Bill was my responsibility. Before I could overtake her, she stepped into a break in the ground and tumbled forward onto her face. "God damn it," she mumbled. I bent over her as she tried to push herself back into a standing position, but she collapsed again. "It's my damn ankle." She looked toward Killer and Bill. "And it's too late." She slumped in the grass, helpless. Killer bellowed and lowered his head. As futile as I knew my attempts would be, I decided to run toward the confrontation, to try to divert the bull. My mind was full of the promise I had made, full of the memory of Bill chasing the Fowler brothers and carrying me through the storm. Old Lady Baker knew what I was thinking, too. She grabbed me by the ankle and I fell to my knees. "No you don't, young man," she said. "It's too late, truly." Her grip was surprisingly strong. I couldn't pull out of it. "I'm an old lady and can do what I want. You're still learning."

"Let me go."

"Shhh."

It was as if the world held its breath—silent and stifled and ready to burst. My mouth went bone dry. I couldn't swallow. The sky seemed to darken, although there were no clouds. Bill was standing broadside to Killer, as he had when the two animals first met in the corral in Wachyerback and I was ashamed that he appeared so unwilling to fight.

Killer charged. I could not avert my eyes. Then, at the last second, Bill pivoted out of his broadside position. He lowered his head and lunged forward just as Killer arrived. The collision sounded like the crack of a tree splitting in a windstorm.

The bull dropped to his knees, stunned.

Bill backed away.

Killer was not done. He rose again slowly, and shook himself. With an enraged roar, he charged again.

Again, Bill met him unbowed and head-on, and the sound of that collision rang across the plains, louder than the first and more definitive, a sound that must have reached all the way to the dust in the stars.

Killer did not get up. He lay on his side in the grass, stunned or dead, I could not tell which. Bill remained perfectly still, as if regarding his domain. His silhouette dominated the landscape alone. The plains, for that moment, had been returned to him.

"I thought he didn't know how..." I whispered.

"Well, he did, dear. Because there he is, and I'll never forget the sight he's given us. He stood as he did—broadside—do you know why? It was to show the bull his size before the fight. The bull should have heeded the warning. Whatever Bill is to you, he's a glory unto himself. Magnificent. But you know...we can't leave him there. He's also a fish out of water. Kind of like you."

I called Bill's name. He walked slowly toward us.

"I need to get up," said Old Lady Baker. She released my ankle and I helped her stand. I could barely support her weight. "We've got to get him back in the trailer. But I don't think that bull's going to try to stop us." She limped back to the road, leaning on me. "Whistle him over here, why don't you?" I tried to whistle, but my mouth was still too dry. Nothing came out. "That's not much of a whistle," she said. She placed her fingers in her mouth. "This is what you mean to do."

Her whistle sliced through the night and flew as well into the fathomless dark of the canyon beyond us. The sound of it quickly reached the walls of the opposite side, where it accumulated into a chorus of vibrations, flocks of echoes rising, multiplying here and there in the blackness, summoning and summoning again.

Suddenly, Bill broke into a run and bolted past us toward the prolonged, rolling echoes, each one calling him, inviting him to race. "Whoaa, Bill," I shouted, but he continued onto a trail that led past clusters of junipers and descended along the canyon walls. Old Lady Baker pushed away from me and hopped toward her car. "What a stupid old lady I am," she said. She struck the roof of her car in frustration. "Well, go get him. I'll take care of myself. And if..." She stopped and shifted her weight. "You know if you follow that canyon northwest it'll lead you right where you want to go. To the refuge. Go on, young man. Otherwise, strike your pose and join my menagerie. I'll try to make you look pretty, even though you're slower than a lame old lady."

"Thank you," was all I could think to say. I ran to the edge of the canyon and stumbled down the trail as fast as I could, with my pack bumping against my shoulders. Old Lady Baker called after me one last time. "And I think I would like it...if you need to speak of me...dear...please have the courtesy to use my first name."

"What is it?" I cried. But I couldn't understand her response.

I thought I heard Bill's hoofbeats and imagined him running his race again toward nothing, nothing but echoes. The trail hugged the south wall of the canyon and was somewhat shielded by trees. Then, thicker vegetation—yucca plants and small, evergreen mountain mahogany trees with lopsided, brain-shaped crowns, mats of buffalo grass and purple coneflowers whose long petals swooned in the moonlight—began to cascade down the terraced slopes toward the narrow, summer-shallow Toomis River, lined with cottonwoods. I followed the broadening canyon terraces toward the river and looked into a deep, protected recess in the wall, but Bill had not stopped there.

Far across the canyon near its northwest flank, I saw a pinnacle beneath the stars with what looked to be a spiral lane running up the sides of the rock, as if the hands of nature had wrung it from both ends. Along the canyon walls, large, shadowy shapes crouched forward, ready to pounce. In fact, the shapes were rocks, balancing precariously atop eroded columns of mudstone called hoodoos.

Moving on, I reached gentler, more open slopes that led to the river. I stood to gather my bearings, thinking I would follow the river to look for Bill. I thought I could hear water rushing. It grew louder and louder, like the rush of blood pounding in my ears from my quickening heart. Out of breath, companionless, unprotected, I could not help but fear the worst, that I would still be alone when daylight broke. I edged carefully through a dark stand of cedars. Hoping for a better view, I stepped onto a large overhang—a spur of barren rock covered with a slick film of calcite. I ran my tongue around my mouth to wet it, feeling I had no alternative but to try to whistle again. Then I thrust my fingers between my lips, pushed back the tip of my tongue, and let loose with a blast that surprised even me. I lurched sideways without thinking, slipped on the calcite, and heard myself yell. The back of my head cracked against the rock and before I lost consciousness I was vaguely aware that I was sliding off the overhang and into a void.

I have no idea how long I was knocked out, but when I awoke again a man was bending over me, tying my hands behind my back. He had removed my backpack and placed it beside me. His horse grazed nearby. "You're just who everybody's been looking for," he said. He finished tying my hands and flipped me over. His face, jowls sagging as he leaned closer, came into focus. It was D.B. Bulland. "Heard your whistle and knew you must've been somewhere out here with your buffalo. Figured you must be calling him, like the grifter did for the race. Took me a while to find you, but you've always been troublesome." He grinned. "I'm right, ain't I." It wasn't a question. I didn't respond.

"You don't have to talk. I don't care whether you do or not, but it's better for you if you do," Bulland said. "Up you go, son." He lifted me roughly onto his saddle, then shifted me forward with one arm as he mounted the horse and settled himself in the saddle. He hoisted me into a seated position in front of him and placed my backpack between us. "But I'll promise you two things, right now. I'm going to see you go back where you belong. And I'm going to track down your buffalo. Should be easy to find now that you're both out of wherever you hid. Where was that, anyway?"

Bulland guided his horse slowly, heading east toward the sunrise along the south wall of the canyon, a direction opposite the way to the refuge, although at that point, for Bill's safety, it made no difference. There was no truly safe haven for Bill even in the open spaces, vast as they were, that sprawled and rolled around us. I kept my silence and clenched my eyelids so he would not see the tears. I had lost Bill. He would meander, I thought, grazing, drinking at the river, alone where millions of his kind used to wander, until someone unknown, Bulland or one of his agents, rode up and put a bullet in him.

After fifteen or twenty minutes, we stopped just outside a campsite with several tents pitched nearby and the sound of generators beyond. Bulland dismounted, then tossed down my backpack and lowered me onto the ground, where I sat not far from the dying embers of a fire in a ring of stones. "Don't go anywhere," he said, chuckling. "I'll be right back."

I turned onto my side to struggle against my bonds, but I couldn't loosen them and so I lay quietly, facing away from the tents and the sun. I heard footsteps approaching. They stopped. Hot liquid splattered over my eyes and cheeks. I leaned back and looked up. The stream of Darryl Fowler's urine arced over my head and splattered onto the ground a few inches from my face while his brother stood behind him, laughing. "We're gonna piss on your fucking buffalo, too," Darryl said.

25
Captured

"All right, boys, you've had your fun." Stepping around the puddle of piss, Bulland rolled me away from it, lifted me by the crook of my arm, set me on a large rock, and placed my backpack beneath my feet. My boots dangled a few inches off the ground. I kicked the rock nervously with my heels. He regarded me, shaking his head like a disappointed teacher. "Don't you know there's people looking for you? You wantta tell me how you got here?"

"No."

Darryl broke in. "He almost had us killed once for no reason. He's crazy."

"Okay, Darryl. Everybody be patient."

I tried to reckon where I was and why Bulland and the Fowler brothers were also there. I could see a small party of men climbing above the tent lines as they examined the looming canyon wall. The sky was bleached blue-white by the rising sun. Painted in slashes of burnt reds and gold, the canyon walls seemed to pulsate with colors when struck by the intensifying sunlight or touched by the shadow of a passing cloud. A tall column of rock rose near the work party, not far from the base of the wall. All in all, it was a perfect late summer morning had it not been for its stifling air of menace. I not only felt threatened, but very close to a position in which my life might be in danger because of who I was and what I knew. In any event, my plan of escape—of saving Bill at the very least then worrying about myself—seemed hopelessly stupid as I sat on a rock at the mercy of my erstwhile tormentors. Even worse, I had failed Bill.

Bulland's jaws moved as if he was chewing on something sinewy, then he spat. "You must've rode something to get this far. You steal a horse?"

"No."

Bulland raised his eyebrows and snorted. "Well, whatever you done, now that we've found you, I expect we'll find that buffalo soon."

Darryl leaned into my face. "We'll blow his ass off and I'll take his hide for a blanket."

I looked at Bulland. It was better to say something, I decided, rather than subject myself to more harassment by Darryl and Cameron. Nor did I want Bulland to suspect Old Lady Baker. I told him that Bill and I had stayed in a deserted barn after the storm. The next morning, I said, Bill took off on his own and I followed him for what seemed like hours, with no sign of people, until he finally ran off in the evening. "He could be out of the state by now."

Bulland scratched himself on the leg. "You expect me to believe that, son?"

"You can believe anything you want."

"Well, then, how did you come to be in this canyon here?"

"Your bull. That was why Bill ran off. Your bull was out there last night."

"Was he, now?" Bulland's eyes narrowed and glinted with satisfaction. A positive sign—they hadn't found Killer yet.

"Maybe you know he was."

Bulland's cheek twitched and he raised the corners of his mouth into a crooked grin. "Why didn't you just say so in the first place?"

"Because I didn't want to make Bill seem a coward." The story that Bulland wanted to hear rolled out easily once I began. "First, that bull chased Bill. Bill took off that way, like I said, fast as he could go. Then the bull turned toward me and I started running. Hoped I was close to Wachyerback and could make it there. Instead, the ground just opened up and I went down a slope. I was scared. I hoped Bill would hear—but I guess he was too far away. Then I walked out onto a rock to see where I was. That's when I whistled. I wanted to climb out if I could but I slipped off the rock and fell again. That's how you found me."

Bulland chuckled. "Buffalos are stupid, all right. Except when it comes to running away. They panic like chickens, you know. That's a fact. And you think Killer chased him toward Oklahoma, you say."

"I saw it all. As much as I could before I had to run."

Darryl and Cameron snorted together. "You ain't so brave by yourself, are you?" Darryl said.

"We always knew that," Cameron added.

"Well, one thing you can be sure of, son." Bulland raised his hat and ran a hand through his greasy scalp. "You were lucky to get away. And wherever he is, the buffalo's too damn big and too damn stupid to hide hisself. He'll be found soon enough."

Cameron raised his arms to his shoulder as if he were sighting a rifle. "Pow. Pow. Pow. Buffalo down."

"Not if Pony finds him first," I mumbled. "Pony'll know how to look for him."

Bulland croaked a laugh. "You figure that grifter for some kind of hero, do you? Well, then I got news for you. He ain't about to look for a buffalo or come for you. You should of heard him yesterday morning. He gave up the lot of you."

The small hopes that remained to me were shattered when I heard Bulland's account of what happened to Pony in the hours after he coasted down Lonechap Hill and I saw the spook galloping away, apparently to report what he saw. Because as the storm broke on his way past Wendellton, Pony was stopped by deputies, taken to the sheriff's office, tossed in a jail cell, and informed that he was suspected of theft—of stealing Bill when he was a calf. At 6 a.m. when Sheriff Johnston arrived, Pony seemed addled and anxious to work out some kind of deal. He insisted that the sheriff call D.B. Bulland, who arrived at the jail within the hour.

"It was a smart move on his part, maybe the only smart thing he done," said Bulland. "Your man had been in prison for manslaughter, did you know that? First thing he admitted he knew I was onto him—I'd seen him ride bulls in the prison rodeo—and he says he didn't want more trouble because of his grifting, so right there in the sheriff's office, he throwed in the towel for his freedom and a finder's fee." Bulland paused a moment. "Do you want to know what he gave up?"

"I guess."

"He gave up the treasure we're here to dig out, son."

For a change, Darryl and Cameron said nothing, knowing what punishment it would be for me to hear Bulland's account of Pony's sellout. But the expressions on their faces changed frequently, from feigned surprise to open-mouthed silent laughter.

With the *Sagrada Biblia*, the buckskin star chart, and other papers he had recovered from the dugout, Pony laid out a convincing case for having discovered the location of the Star of Andalusia and the bag of gold coins that had been buried with it. As additional evidence, he produced an emerald which, he said, belonged on the Star. "Call Wyatt Fowler," he challenged. "See if he doesn't think these are real."

When Fowler arrived, he inspected the emerald and the papers, including a scale drawing of the Star. Then Pony spread out the buckskin chart. It was the key, he said, to the location of the treasure. And he had solved it.

"Now your man is ready to make his deal," Bulland said. "And he's willing to let us in on it for a cut and a free pass out of jail."

It was a shameless betrayal that Bulland described. From the beginning, Pony told them, he had intended to sell the information about the treasure because he didn't have the resources or equipment to uncover it himself. What he wanted was a finder's fee of $10,000 and an additional $5,000 for the emerald. First, he said, he would use the key on the buckskin chart to draw a map to the Star of Andalusia. After the Star was found and he was paid, he would then draw the map to the gold.

Capable and educated as he was, Wyatt Fowler was not immune to the same windfall fevers that infected lesser men. Unlike them, he had nothing to lose and the chance to acquire a priceless, timeless object. He sent Sheriff Johnston to Lonechap Hill to confirm that a dugout was where Pony said it was, and, as an additional blow, to serve Babe with the papers that would force her off the hill. After receiving confirmation from the sheriff, Fowler called in experts, including a geologist and an archaeologist, to put together an exploration party based on the map Pony drew.

"Anyway, Mr. Fowler's due here by the early afternoon. And your man won't be far behind him." Bulland had ridden to the site on horseback. The men and equipment—and the Fowler brothers—had come to the canyon in two jeeps and a pickup. "They're doing the survey now," Bulland added, "then they'll string ropes to section off the wall and start the excavation when Mr. Fowler says. And if the star's where your hero says it is, I guarantee one thing. You'll never see him again. He knows how to disappear, no doubt."

I was flushed with embarrassment and anger. How could Pony have been so ready to violate our trust, to corrupt the hill and the lives we enjoyed? "Whatever he got off the hill, that's not his. It's Babe's."

"You're thinking the hill is hers and maybe yours someday," Bulland grinned, "but it ain't. It's going back to Mr. Fowler sooner rather than later."

Finally, Cameron couldn't resist an outburst. "You got no right to be on our land. You don't belong. You cost my dad money. That's a sin. You live with a whore. And you piss us off. You're no different from that dumb animal."

I felt beaten. Why bother to respond? Maybe the Fowler brothers were right in wanting to rid themselves of me and—if they'd only known—of a useless uncle.

"Hold on." Bulland had spotted something. A man was coming toward us through a stand of cedars to the west. He carried a rifle, barrel upright. When he was within a hundred yards of us, something shiny on his body caught the sun for an instant and threw it back into our eyes.

"I'm coming on in, okay?" the man called.

Bulland drew the sidearm from his holster and cocked it.

26
The Truth in an Alias

That same morning, beneath a glorious sunrise that fanned across the sky in blades of light, a rider approached the western fence line at the boundary of Lonechap Hill. "Here comes the head spook," Babe said as she watched. The horseman opened a gate and rode up the hill. Babe and Dwight stood in front of the house to meet Wyatt Fowler as he dismounted from the magnificent sorrel stallion he had ridden in his race with Bill. He carried a satchel, possibly with legal paperwork in it. At first, he was relaxed, smiling, and cordial. "I'm glad we can work it out this way," he said to Babe. "This was never personal. And thank you for making it early. I have other plans today that you'll learn about soon enough." He took a deep breath, expanded his chest, and exhaled slowly as he surveyed the eastern sky. "And I can't believe how beautiful the sunrise is from up here. Spectacular. I'll enjoy it many times in the future, I'm sure."

Babe took off her holster and set it on the picnic table. "This isn't personal either," she said. "I just don't want you inside my house. If you don't mind, we'll sit at the picnic table and you can watch the sun rise from here for the first and last time. Coffee?"

"I'd love some." Babe was clearly prickly and Fowler couldn't resist the challenge. "And just so you know, I've got my people out looking for your boy, too."

"Mm-hmm."

"How're you holding up?"

"Just fine."

"He'll turn up, don't worry. You should take some time to relax. Take in a movie, something like that." Fowler raised his eyes to Babe. "Seen any good movies lately?"

"I'll be back in a moment."

Wyatt and Dwight exchanged brief nods, but neither man spoke. Dwight's briefcase rested next to him in the grass. Babe brought a tray with a coffee pot, styrofoam cups, and a bottle of Wild Turkey. She poured coffee for the two men and bourbon for herself.

"Well," said Fowler, lifting his cup to the table. "Cheers, then. I presume you want a way to work this out as quickly as possible..." He took a sip for dramatic effect. "...and without anyone getting hurt."

"Oh," said Babe, downing a shot of bourbon, "someone's going to get hurt."

Babe began slowly, without looking directly at Wyatt Fowler. Occasionally, she glanced at Dwight, who remained impassive. "My mother had ambitions for me. They were the same that her mother had for her. To get a wealthy man as a protector. Insurance against the future.

"She and Dwight argued about it. But Dwight didn't...he couldn't oppose her. She'd dedicated her life to him." Babe put her hand over Dwight's. "He'd made her a promise to care for us. As soon as I hit my teens, when America got into the war, I volunteered for all kinds of events. War relief fund-raisers. I rode a float in the Battle of Flowers parade. But mother had other ideas for me. She took me to museums where rich people were, not just in San Antonio, but in Houston and Dallas. When I was barely seventeen, a very rich man from a very prominent family in Houston was infatuated with me. He pursued me through my mom. He didn't tell his family—there would have been hell to pay—but he married me. The only way he could have done it was with my mother and Dwight's permission. They gave it. And he went through with it. He was that weak and that crazy. But he was rich. Our marriage—it was worse than a sick nightmare."

Babe paused, lifted her hand from Dwight's, and took another drink. Fowler appeared restless. "You don't need to tell me all this," he said. "It's water under the bridge. Look, as I said, I've actually got somewhere else to be—joining my kids on a campout, if you want to know. They're already there..."

"Yes, I do have to tell you all this. Your kids can wait. It isn't water under the bridge. The marriage lasted all of two months. When mother learned what was happening, even she was shocked and mortified. She and Dwight—they got pictures of what he was doing. I helped them, even though I was afraid he would kill me. That night, he tied me up and used a whip on me, a braided quirt. Blonde leather. There were blood spatters on it. Mother took the pictures to the family. She took the quirt to prove the blood on it was mine. And that ended it, as she knew it would. They gave us a quarter of a million dollars. The marriage was annulled. If you're wondering whether I hated my mother for getting me into it, the answer is yes. I went back to school—a private school, this time—and graduated with the rest of the kids my age as if nothing had happened."

Fowler shrugged. "So you had a diploma and money. Sounds like everyone knew what they were doing."

Babe ignored him. "Mother used a lot of the settlement money for jewels she wanted me to have, as if they would prove she was trying to do what was right for me. She believed in them more than anything else. They're currency for hard times, she said. You can always spend them, no matter what. If the stock market crashes, if the government topples, if the store burns down, if you are held prisoner by the spirits of terror and darkness, jewels will buy freedom and escape. And when times are good, they are like friendly spirits you receive from the goddesses of the Earth. They share the secret dreams you had when you chose them..." Babe laughed. "I saw your mother decked out in jewels once, Wyatt, and I thought of how much alike those two women probably were, my mother and yours, even though they would've been sworn enemies if they'd known each other."

Fowler rolled his eyes and flexed the muscles that accented his square chin. "Babe...I'm only here because my lawyer thinks we can settle and I'm willing not to embarrass you if that's why you're telling me this. What you're saying—that's an embarrassment in itself."

"The agreement," Dwight said, "was that this conversation is confidential."

Fowler gave a short laugh. "I'm not submitting it to *True Confessions* magazine if you're not. Is there more coffee, then?" Babe poured. "Okay, so you're spilling your guts to me because Buddy knew all this and felt sorry for you? Is that where you're going?"

"Buddy didn't know everything. He knew enough. He knew about the affair my mother arranged for me afterwards with still another man. Another rich man, naturally. A new conquest that she was certain would be right for me. This new millionaire, he'd seen me with my crazy husband at a few parties. When the marriage was over, he tracked us down and asked about me, even before I graduated high school. That's the reason why...things are the way they are today."

"As long as I only have to listen to it once. But go ahead."

"This man, he was the opposite of my ex-husband at first. He seemed kind and concerned. All mother told me was that his name was George Stanley and he was richer than my ex-husband had been, and that he could see to it that our future—my future, was the way she put it—was secure. The summer I graduated, we went to Dallas and he gave me a private tour of the museum of art, just him and us and a guide. I loved it. George was the one who arranged for me to go to college and study art. He paid my tuition. I started that fall at Trinity University, and then at the end of the first semester—to celebrate—he flew mother and me to New York for a Christmas party at a big gallery. They knew George as a collector, but they didn't know anything else about him—only that he showed up once or twice a year, spent a lot of money, and had an agent pick up the art for him. Anyway, everyone was there—the mayor, some Hollywood people, singers, dancers, writers, fashion designers. No photographers, just the elite. We were part of a big entrance, just behind the mayor. George squeezed my hand, and then he swept me through the doors, and the first thing I noticed, because my head was spinning, was how the music swelled once we were inside that magnificent gallery, with chamber musicians playing Christmas carols in a corner of the room near the bar.

"And the people we were with—they were so charming, every last one of them. They seemed to own the place. Mother was stunning in a gown that George had bought for her, and you could spot her from almost anywhere in a crowd. She appeared surrounded by surplus space, as if it were her birthright. She winked at me, and that's when I made up my mind about George. I was going to marry him, which I suppose is what mother intended.

"Well, the gallery had a private room in back, and George took me there to look at his latest purchases. Some were hanging on the wall and some—the sketchbooks—were laid out on a table. George was mad for art because it made him feel like, owning it, he was the master of their souls—the artists and their subjects. It was a beautiful room. The walls were lit by the glow of a snowy winter night from a skylight above us. I was already a little drunk on champagne. The snowflakes were dancing, pirouetting in the wind. And it was so quiet in there. We were alone, and George set down the two extra glasses of champagne he was carrying and locked the door. He picked up a small frame from the table. He said he'd bought everything in the room, the sketchbooks, the illustrations, and all. But the frame, it was his favorite thing. A portrait of a nun. I didn't get it. I thought it was a little cartoonish. I asked if there was something humorous about it. Not exactly, he said. Then he pulled the portrait out of its frame and turned it over. It was a portrait of the same woman, nude, leering, looking straight out toward the viewer. George laughed and said it was once owned by a respectable businessman who had kept it on his desk at home, with the nun in the frame, of course. And nobody suspected that the woman was his mistress but he loved her enough to always keep her near and he took out the bare tits portrait every night to stare at it. George said the artist was a Charles St. George..."

Wyatt's head turned perceptibly before he regained his composure.

"...Stanley," Babe continued, "and that he'd done all the work in the room—an unknown and underappreciated western artist and illustrator. George planned to corner the market on his works and then make him famous. The sketchbooks were full of nudes, and we looked at them together. Then George made eye contact in a way that boiled my heart. He handed me a champagne glass and picked up the other for himself. 'The least we can do is toast the artist,' he said.

Babe raised her cup toward Fowler and swallowed still another bourbon. But she never slurred her words. They were sharp as the bladed sunrise. "I didn't even think it ironic that his name was so similar to the artist's. And to make a long story short, there was an antique box in a corner of the room, and that was the first place we made love, right then, and I was desperately trying to sort out my feelings while I was screwing him. I was stupid enough to be glad I did it at the time. When we left the room, there was mother standing alone near the door, watching it. She smiled at me, then slipped away while George and I were straightening ourselves to go back to the party. And he was so charming for the rest of the evening. You have the same kind of charm, Wyatt, when you want to use it. And I know why you haven't interrupted me again. You know who George Stanley was, don't you? And you know where that art collection is now—in your museum, where your father built a special private room for it. I'll bet you saw the nun on his desk, didn't you?"

Fowler looked at Babe in disgust and slammed his hand on the table. "You're saying George Stanley was actually my father. And you were his mistress? That's impossible. It's low even for you, Babe."

Babe shrugged. "He traveled under assumed names all the time. Everyone knew that."

"You know..." Fowler was flustered. He swung his legs over the bench and stood. "To hell with you. This is over."

"Don't you want to know how we can prove it? Sit down and finish your coffee, Wyatt. Dwight, show him the papers."

Dwight opened his briefcase and withdrew copies of checks from Lloyd Fowler to Trinity University. "So what?" Fowler sat again and shoved the papers aside. "He gave money to lots of universities."

"That money corresponded to Babe's tuition costs for each semester she was enrolled," Dwight said.

"I had George's—Lloyd's—baby between semesters. Lloyd knew. Dwight found Joan Lee to look after the baby secretly in case there was any danger..."

"Even lowlife shake-down artists like you should know that's weak. Show me the birth certificate with his name on it."

"His name's not on the birth certificate..."

"And you—you adopted your own son?"

"My boy deserved a chance to be brought up with dignity, with his own history—not as Lloyd Fowler's unwanted bastard. I'd been used enough. For me, it was a chance to wipe the past clean—to say to my son and the world that I had *chosen* him. But as for the legal process, technically, when it happened, it was Buddy who was the adoptive parent..." Babe stopped, clenching her fist, squeezing her eyes shut.

Dwight continued calmly. "...Of a child whose mother he married and whose father was listed as unknown. But these papers are blood tests." Dwight lifted another sheaf from his briefcase. "They could be used to establish the likelihood of Lloyd Fowler's paternity in the case of a baby born in August of 1948..."

"Bullshit. He would never have given blood for a paternity test."

"He didn't. The blood was taken when he was admitted to a hospital in 1948. I had it tested. I know a doctor who will confirm that it was Lloyd's. You may remember. He fell and struck his head during a trip to San Antonio. You may not know that it was Babe's mother and I who took him to the hospital. You and your mother made a trip there to bring him back. You were fresh out of college."

"You chickenshit. How do you explain bribing a fucking doctor? You could have forged the blood test..."

"I'm not a forger."

"So you're saying you took all these elaborate measures for the sake of some worthless little bastard of Babe's? And you couldn't have my father, Babe, so you seduced that idiot Buddy instead?"

"Buddy couldn't have been seduced by anyone—and nobody tried harder than your own goddam family. He loved me. And I loved Buddy. We would never have married unless we both felt that way."

"You expect people to believe that after this bullshit story? I'm going to have you both sent to jail."

"You're welcome to try," said Dwight, "if you wish to expose your father as well."

"And what happens if I expose Babe's past? And her mother's?"

"Perhaps it won't be necessary. In any case..."

"You think I wouldn't? Your so-called evidence is all circumstantial. In any case, what?"

Dwight produced a thick, heavy 16-inch disk in a brown paper sleeve. "This is the final item. Did you ever know that Buddy once had a stammer?"

"Everybody knew it." Fowler smiled sarcastically. "They used to j-j-j-joke about it when I was a kid. But they say he got rid of it somehow. So what?"

"Do you know how he got rid of it?"

"No, and I don't care."

"He bought a machine during the Depression. It made what they called electrical transcriptions onto disks like records. It's how radio stations archived programs and distributed commercials. Buddy used his machine to record himself. When he spoke into the microphone, he no longer stammered. After a few weeks of practice, he quit stammering altogether."

"What a goddam miracle."

"This is the last disk Buddy made before the fire that burned his house down—the only disk from his early collection that wasn't destroyed, because he kept it away from the others. Here's a transcript of what's on it. And here's a tape recording made from the disk. You can play the tape in the privacy of your home. You may also keep the copies of this paperwork. Babe used to think the disk was just something Buddy had a sentimental attachment to, maybe one of the first recordings he made for himself when he was learning to control his stammer. But he didn't want her to hear it, and the reason was, it's a conversation between him and your father, recorded in Buddy's living room shortly after he and Babe became engaged during the Christmas holidays in 1949."

Fowler took the reel of magnetic tape and examined it. "And this tape is a supposed copy?"

"Yes. Not supposed. A true copy."

"And I suppose it's a weeping admission of all this bullshit you've just laid out."

"As a matter of fact, yes. Your father was sitting not far from the machine and saw Buddy start it. He'd never seen a phonograph that made recordings. He asks what it is. Buddy tells him it's a record-making machine, that he's getting it ready to record children that might come by to sing Christmas carols. Lloyd grunts. Apparently, he has no idea that it's recording *them*, with the needle cutting nice little threads of acetate that curl off the surface of the disk, because he then proceeds into a frank and angry conversation. He berates Buddy for his engagement to Babe. Buddy replies in the politest possible way that, first of all, he's in love with her, and, second, that it's barely an amends for the way Lloyd had used Babe since she was in high school. 'It was her mother who used her,' Lloyd says. 'She brought her to me. She was standing outside the door when I screwed the girl for the first time in New York.'

"There's a long silence. Lloyd is impatient. He asks Buddy if he can't stop that damn thing, meaning the machine, and do whatever he has to do with it later, because the smell from the lathe digging into the disk is giving him one of his headaches. Buddy says, no, once it's started he has to wait till the project is finished—about fifteen minutes. And then Buddy asks if Lloyd plans to do anything about the baby boy. 'Why should I?' Lloyd says. 'No one can prove he's mine.' 'Certainly, your name's not on the birth certificate,' Buddy says. 'So I won't have to ask your permission for my plan to adopt him after Babe and I are married. And for everyone's good, we'll say that Babe was part of the adoption, too, that we did it together. It'll all be taken care of by our lawyer, who knows the whole story. The woman who's been caring for him as his mother knew the day would come.'

"Lloyd's not finished. 'Your own family's fought and worked for the freedom to live their lives here where they choose. To work their own land. To associate with their own people. You're willing to give up our rights, our freedom?' 'The problem, Lloyd,' Buddy says, 'is that your definition of freedom spans the universe between the hip pocket where your wallet is and the end of your nose.'

"That's when Lloyd explodes into threats I won't repeat here— he doesn't want the child within a million miles of the Fowlers— and he makes clear there are lives at stake, and if Buddy doesn't believe him he can think about what happened to his own father, Peter, who was killed in Lubbock. After another silence, Buddy answers very slowly. He says that he and Babe want to make a clean start...that Lloyd was the one who came to *him* to complain, and that as far as he's concerned the worst thing that could happen would be to expose what Lloyd did and how Babe suffered because of it."

Dwight thumbed through the pages of the transcript to read from it. "'Life isn't meant to be lived like a broken record,' Buddy says. 'I just want to make sure she'll be left alone. You can take your secrets to the grave with you. What's more, I mean to raise John like a good father.' At that point, Lloyd laughs and says, 'What the hell can someone like you teach him? He did come from my loins.' 'I don't know,' says Buddy, 'but I'll figure it out. And excuse me a minute, I think my machine is done.' That's where the recording stops, after fourteen-and-a-half minutes. Maybe Lloyd never suspected anything, and maybe it was just an accident...or maybe Lloyd started thinking about what had happened and asked some questions...but Buddy's house burned down not long after that. So it was fortunate that Buddy had put this disk in a safe place before the fire. And that's all we have to say."

Fowler put the papers into his satchel and stood up. He jerked his head toward Dwight and spat. "That's all you have to say," he repeated.

"Except I don't see any reason to continue this nonsense about the hill. Especially since the will was upheld once."

"And you want me to believe that was Buddy's doing, too. The family idiot."

Babe bristled, but spoke calmly. "Since the truth has been laid about as bare as it can get—no, it wasn't his doing until the very end. At first—despite everything, he couldn't bring himself to go back on his word when he promised to return this hill to your family. He only started having second thoughts in his last days. But he knew before he died what would happen—the codicil—because I told him. He smiled. He felt John deserved to be taken care of. He knew your family wouldn't do it. And neither of us wanted the complications that would have occurred if John was known as anyone other than the son we both adopted and loved."

"So the will—the will *was* forged. I was right all along about the goddam forgery."

Dwight shrugged. "And John Watkins is your half brother. Your own father brags that John came from his loins. But we're the only three people who know it, aside from the doctor, and he'd have to have his memory prompted in court, I'm sure. Even Joan Lee, who took him in after Babe gave birth doesn't know who the father was."

Wyatt began to sputter. "I could have you thrown out of the country, Babe...prosecuted. You're as illegal as they come."

Dwight raised his hands and spread them in the air. "But not John. He was born here. Read the Fourteenth Amendment. He is as much a Texan and an heir as you are."

"God damn you both."

"And that entertaining movie we received—we have no idea why—we are thankful for it. The resemblance between the actress and Babe's mother was uncanny. But it has nothing to do with us."

"You are lower than vultures."

"I'll never tell John," Babe said as Fowler headed toward his horse and the sky flooded with light. "It would be impossible for him to live with it if everyone knew. He'd be wondering who the hell he was and what he was going to turn into and whether he'd live long enough to figure it out." Babe drew her pistol from the holster on the picnic table and fired it into the air. "Now get the hell off my land. And you can tell that spook there's nothing to see here anymore."

27
Odee's Depot

"Come on in, then," Bulland called, "but keep your rifle in the air and walk slow."

When the stranger got closer, we could see that he was wearing a brown leather Sam Browne belt and that the object flashing in the sun was a silver star—a badge—affixed to the belt's diagonal strap. "Deputy George Cabús," he said. "I saw the activity here and wondered whether you might have seen a strange boy and a buffalo since you been here."

"Deputy from where?" Bulland asked, stepping in front of me. "You're Mexican, ain't you?"

"Well, to answer your first question, Armstrong County." The deputy's watery eyes glistened brightly as he smiled to respond and seemed troubled when he paused, rubbing a closely-trimmed white beard, to continue. "To answer the second, well, sir, I'm American as they come, fought in the big war—War Number One—for Uncle Sam, but I do get sent on wild goose chases a lot, sir. You know, them shit details that no one else wants. That's why I'm out looking for a boy and a buffalo that some other sheriff put out an alert for. And that's about it, sir. Jeep's up on the canyon rim and I'd just as soon get back to it if you ain't seen neither."

Bulland looked away, cleared his throat, spat, and seemed to be thinking of a response. I worried that he would want to keep me there, especially since I had heard the plans for excavating the site. For once, I was grateful that Darryl was constitutionally unable to contain himself. "That's the boy right there," he said, ducking behind Bulland and gesturing toward me with both hands as if he were unveiling the missing body in a magic trick. "We captured him this morning. The buffalo's run off to Oklahoma or somewheres, but we'll get him, too."

"Hmm. I see," said the deputy. "Mind if I ask a question, then, sir? Mister...?"

"Bulland. Go on, if you want."

Bulland stepped aside and the deputy planted himself in front of me. "You the runaway?"

"Yes, sir." If I was to be hauled away, better with someone who didn't know me.

"You kind of a bad boy, then, ain't you? Caused a lot of trouble, you know."

"He's always been a troublemaker," Cameron chimed in. "He tried to have us killed once."

"Well..." The deputy took a deep breath and turned to Bulland. "I guess I'd better take him off your hands."

"Not necessary. We know where he belongs," Bulland said. "We can..."

"Look kind of bad if I was to report the boy found and just left him there," the deputy interrupted. "I'm sure you know how those things go, sir. I'll get him back where he belongs. And what might be going on over there, with them other men?"

"It's...a kind of survey, never been done," Bulland said.

"That's the old massacre site, ain't it? Cavalry whipped the Indians back to the reservation. During the Red River Wars, I believe."

"Yeah, they're surveying for the Fowler museum, the one at Big Fort. Also looking for some artifacts, some kind of a religious star and a bag of coins. These other two boys are with me, here to learn something. They're the sons of Mr. Wyatt Fowler. You might of heard of him."

"Yes, sir, I might've, like everyone else." The deputy winked at Bulland. "Well, surveys mean nothing to me, sir, no offense, so I'll probably have forgot about it by the time I get this boy where he's supposed to be. Don't care much about religious stars neither, whatever they are. Ain't my business to look for permits and such."

Bulland's problem, of course, wasn't a lack of permits. Fowler could arrange for whatever was needed, including backdated papers. The problem was that I could reveal the value of the treasure as soon as I was away from them. "All I can say is, you're bound to hear a lot of lies before you get him there."

"What kind of lies might they be?"

"Boy's got it in his mind, it's all part of some buried treasure."

The deputy threw back his head and laughed. "Only treasure around here is the bones of the dead and the bullets that killed 'em.

That much, I know. Son," he said to me, shaking a finger, "if you try any of that made-up shit on me, it's gonna be a rough few hours ride. Best thing you can hope for, we'll put you up in our jail, call the people that's looking for you, get you transferred sometime tomorrow. Before that happens, I expect you to shut up and behave. You understand?"

I nodded, but said nothing.

"His hands're already tied, you can see," Bulland said.

"Then they can stay that way for a while," said the deputy. "I thank you for your cooperation, sir, and you can be sure this boy ain't gonna put one over on me. I heard it all before. This badge is the best lie detector there is. And say...if you happen to see the buffalo..."

Bulland waved a hand as if to dismiss the thought. "That buffalo won't live much longer, not when we catch up to him. He's a dangerous animal, like we've known for a long time."

"Well, then, thank you for all of us in law enforcement, Mr. Bulland." The deputy glanced in the direction he came from. "We got a walk and a climb to make, son, up to my jeep. So get yourself ready." I slid off the rock and he pulled me in front of him, then picked up my backpack and slung the straps over his shoulder. "And I hope you have good luck finding what you want, Mr. Bulland. Putting together details of the battle, I guess, like they done for Custer."

"That's right."

"Well...you don't have to worry about this one no more. We'll be on our way."

The deputy marched me back along the path that Bulland had used to bring me to the site, through the cedars and onto a rocky trail. We walked in silence for more than ten minutes, then reached another trail that led, not up, but wound through a gap in some mesquite trees. The rock I had fallen from was still farther west of us. "That way," he said. He stopped and looked behind us, then took out a knife and cut the ropes that bound my hands. "That feel better?"

"Yes, sir."

"I had to make sure no one followed us. Didn't want an escort. You rub your wrists as long as you want and we'll be out of here in not too long." He handed my backpack to me. "You can put that on again." He took off his Sam Browne belt, then pulled the tails of his khaki shirt out of the waist of his jeans. "That was all a little tight for me," he said. "Haven't worn that belt in years. Brought it back from the Big War, rescued it from a German who took it from a Brit, hoped to wear it like a hero back home, but that's not how things go." He adjusted the boots that came up well over his calves. "Let's get out of here, son." He folded the belt, wrapped it over his rifle, and pointed to the trees.

"Don't you have a car?"

He stopped me with a laugh. His voice now was lilting, almost musical, and the bristles of his thick, white moustache seemed to expand and contract on his upper lip when he talked. "You still think I'm some kind of deputy? You're supposed to be smarter than that. Did you bother to look at this badge? Carried it since I was six, when my mama made it for me out of tin cans. And my name ain't Cabús, either, 'cause I'm the engineer."

I stepped away from him, prepared to run. "What are you going to do? What's going to happen to me?"

"Slow down. One thing at a time."

"Look, mister, you need to tell someone. Back there, what they were looking for was more like a treasure. Bulland lied to you."

"Well, that's no surprise. But they won't find no treasure there."

"How do you know?"

"I just do. Why do they think it's there?"

My words spilled out fast and bitter. "I had a friend, stole a real treasure map from a dugout where I lived, then he sold it. That's why they think it's there." I told him about Pony and the betrayals that Bulland had attributed to him. It infuriated me that Pony might be joining Wyatt Fowler and Bulland later that day at the excavation site. Whatever Pony's reasons for trying to save himself—even if the story of how he had killed another man was true—selling what he had taken from Lonechap Hill was proof, I thought, of a cold and calculated larceny beyond anything I could have imagined.

The deputy shook his head slowly. "Well, some lessons come too early and some too late. Yours was both, wasn't it? But you can believe what I said. There ain't no treasure where they're looking. Now we've wasted enough time..."

"But..."

"You ever rode the back of a motorbike? A simple answer'll do."

"No, sir."

"Well, here's the thing. I don't have no jeep. I got a handmade bike—handmade by me. It's hidden in them trees, good for running over rough country and such. Stashed it in freight cars when I worked for the T&P, used it for side trips. It's rough, but if you hold on tight, we'll get where we're going. It's a little noisy, too, and if I told you what the deal is you wouldn't hear me for the racket. I'll tell you when we get there and we need to get going now, son. So you better follow me and hop on for your own good and mine, too. Runaways like you can't be too picky. And I ain't the Phantom Padre, but my real name is Odee Valentino." Odee slid his rifle into a sheath on the side of the motorbike. "And I'm trying to be your friend, son. Let's go."

The Phantom Padre. If Odee Valentino saw fit to invoke him, I was willing to ride along. "You know about the Phantom Padre?" I asked.

"Not *about* him, son. I knew him for real. But now we gotta go."

We bounced and swerved and twisted and skidded through the canyon on Odee's small custom trail bike, but he guided it expertly. Never once did we topple. He was right about the noise. As the exhaust pipes rumbled and the engine struggled, propelling us rapidly then gingerly through the changing environment, I wouldn't have heard a word he spoke. Finally, we saw cottonwoods in the distance where the river ran. Odee sped without pausing across the widening canyon floor, dodging clusters of sagebrush. Occasionally a bump would send us vaulting into the air and onto a rough landing that caused him to shout with joy.

I saw that we were headed for the back of some kind of cinderblock structure, something like a garage. It looked old. Once it had been painted dark green, but the paint was worn and faded, and tall grasses and a few mesquite trees grew around the edges of the structure. Odee drove up to the rear door and hopped off the bike, keeping it steady for me. "My depot's on the other side," he grinned. He saw how rubbery my legs were when I tried to stand on my own. "Take a moment. Get your land legs back."

I managed to work out the wobble in a few steps. "I'm okay."

"All right, then." He opened the door, walked the bike into the darkness, and lowered the kickstand. I followed him. I could see a shaft of sunlight where two large double doors came together at the other end of the structure. The place smelled of oil and leather and tools and sweat. Also something foul, like sewage. "Watch my crib there," Odee cautioned as we passed a cot next to a table with a lamp, barely visible in the shadows on the other side of a large tool bench. I heard a loud grunt, then a clatter on the cement floor, and suddenly something rough and spongy raked across my arm. As Odee flicked on his lamp, I landed on my ass and watched Bill hopping back and forth in his trademark stiff-legged dance.

"Woke me up with a bellow, maybe four a.m.," Odee said. "Don't know why, unless he was looking for something. Or asking for something. Lucky I had some carrots. He followed me right in here. Good a place as any to hide." He extended a hand to me. "Get on up. You got nothing to say?"

I broke down crying. It was one of those moments that defy any words as insufficient, any gestures as melodramatic, any exclamations as gratuitous. All my effort went into breathing through my sobs. Otherwise, I was numb, from my brain to the scrape on my arm that Bill had left with his tongue.

"I'll let you two catch up while I do something about that business he made. Whew!"

Odee slid open the double doors and gestured for us to follow him outside. I reached into my backpack and drew out a carrot for Bill. He followed me through the doors and into the grass and snatched it away. It didn't occur to me to wonder how Odee already knew that Bill liked carrots.

"Thank you...thank you, mister..." I didn't know what else to add at that point.

"Odee Valentino, like I said. Be right back. We ain't done yet."

Bill and I stood together while Odee hosed down the garage and I drank in the sights around us. There, in the midst of the canyon wilderness, a small locomotive with two open-air cars sat parked at a concrete platform beneath an overhang. Adjacent to the garage was a small, charming adobe depot, freshly painted a pale yellow, with a ticket window and souvenir shop. A track extended away from it, toward the northwest; and on the south side of the garage where Bill and I stood, the track returned as if it had made a long, circular journey. A late morning sky, blue and cloudless, spread above us. I had learned to read the sky from the top of Lonechap Hill, where it unfurled over all of creation, an endless, expansive sky. But at the bottom of Toomis Canyon, I first was aware of the walls behind and beyond me, first felt the depth of the place, and only then looked into the blue, which now seemed more like a lid over the natural world, a finite sky. I gazed at it, then stared again at Bill. Thinking back on how I felt then, I am aware that my mind, instead of racing with the dozens of questions it would have been logical to ask, was tranquil, almost blank, all the pain and guilt and desperation having been erased from it before it had a chance to refill with exhilaration and curiosity and doubts.

I kicked a tall clump of grass and, almost simultaneously, Bill dropped into a wallow. Odee whistled appreciatively as Bill twisted and twirled on his back. "The hairy tornado," he cried.

"He'd like some water from the hose," I said.

"Why, sure he would. You go ahead." Odee handed me the hose and I sprayed Bill and the dirt where he wallowed, relishing every second. Finally, Odee shut off the water and rolled up the hose. "I'll bet you want to know where you are, now that the introductions are over," he said.

"Yes, sir."

"Well, first off, how 'bout you and Bill take a look at my pride and joy, see if it suits your purposes." Odee clapped me on the shoulder and gestured toward the train.

Odee's locomotive was amusement park-sized but built to scale. A fire-engine-red smokestack rose from the front of the black, cylindrical body of the engine. A cowcatcher, tapering like a broad, precision-crafted blade to a point at its middle, was poised over the track. The cowcatcher and the spokes of the three sets of driving wheels were painted the same bright red as the smokestack. An arched roof covered the engineer's cab, barely spacious enough even for a small man like Odee Valentino. A silver whistle, activated by a tug on its cord, was mounted on the front of the cab. Between the engine and the two dark blue tourist cars, a black tender, like every other component, looked so new as to be virtually untouched. "She was all rust when I found her." Odee tapped the engine with a fist. "Hadn't been run since the war. I mean War Number One. My war. Before Two, before Korea. Well, times are good again and families are coming back to see the frontiers that God has set out for them to behold. Them tourists, you know, they got time to do things. So I took my T&P railroad retirement and my savings. Got the sovereign state of Texas to sell me this abandoned franchise. You know what this is?"

"No, sir."

"This is the once-famous Royal Hoodoo Railroad, named for that big rock spire way off to the west of us there. Almost eight stories high and shaped like a totem pole. You see it? Some people call em fairy chimneys. The proper name is hoodoo. That one's called the Royal Hoodoo because why? Because the rock that sits atop it looks like a crown. This ole railroad was built to take folks around the floor of this canyon, on by the hoodoo for a good look. Then back here for the round trip. But it fell on hard times and got abandoned. Had to fix it up all by myself, starting with this steam engine. Took me more than a year." He walked toward the passenger cars, running his hand along the side of the train, caressing it. "Fixed up them open-air cars, too, and the tracks besides. Hoped to be finished before summer began, 'cause I'll only run her on weekends once school starts. Then I shut her down again for winter. Didn't quite make that schedule, though, because I wanted to do her just right. What do you think, boy?"

"I think it's beautiful."

"She. Not 'it.' She's beautiful. Name of Minny." Odee stood lost in reverie for a moment, then turned back toward me. His eyes had changed from bright to troubled. He smacked his lips and crossed his arms. "I'm not going to play tricks on you. I know a bit about you, young John, as you might've guessed by now."

"How..." My question died in my throat.

He held up his hands as if to calm me. "Part Chinese, though you could pass for lots of half-breeds. As for Bill, he loves his carrots, don't he? He's a racer, too. And you two are on the run together. You don't need to be nervous of me. Nor does Bill. But you want to hear how I know, don't you?"

"Yes, sir."

"Here's the deal. It seems we have a mutual acquaintance. Told me your folks was looking for you and Bill and so was the law. Thought I should keep an eye out."

"If it was the sheriff, he's a liar, too..."

Odee threw back his head and laughed till his throat squeaked. "Not that we ain't had bootlegging, good-for-nothing sheriffs. But

Harvey Olsen weren't one of them. Also told me to watch my money in case I seen you. You do know Harvey, don't you?"

"Yes, sir...I spent my birthday..."

"At his saloon. He told me all about it. He rode an old broke down horse through here yesterday evening lookin' for you or Bill or both of you. Your mom called him, you know. I guess you forgot to tell her where you was going. Is that what it was?"

"Yes, sir. Sort of." I couldn't look him in the eye. "Did he say anything about Pony? They were friends."

"Told me a bit about him. Didn't seem to think he was a bad sort. But that's the kind that always sneaks up on you, ain't it? Anyway, it's thanks to Harvey I pulled out my tin badge and impersonated one of our fine Texas lawmen and went out to look for you on my motorbike. Saw a fresh trail and decided to sneak in to where them men was working. So here you are."

"Are you gonna try to take me back home?"

"I figure that's your business, son, not mine. I seen my share of runaways before I retired from the T&P, even one or two as young as you. Even my own self. I know what it's like to live off of lies, I learned 'em like they was sacred prayers, the kind that save your skin. I know what it's like to need friends. Once when I ran away I took my raggedy-ass dog along. He tried to go back soon as he got hungry." Odee chuckled. "But you did me one better. You ran away with a buffalo, it seems. That's a first in my book. What you need to decide now is what you want to happen next."

"I promised to get Bill to the refuge. That's why we ran."

"So the refuge...that'll keep him away from his enemies, like that Mr. Bulland. He was a bruiser, that man, and not in a good way. I ran into plenty like him on the T&P."

"Yes, sir. That's why I can't stop now."

"Well, then, you arrived at the proper place. First off, you can't claim to be much of a runaway unless you've hopped a train to make it official." Odee stretched and slowly swiveled his creaking body to the right and left, scanning the canyon with his rheumy eyes. He rubbed his beard and turned back to me. "So I reckon my train can take you and Bill close to that refuge—it's another two or three miles or so beyond where the tracks turn back past the Royal Hoodoo—but I wouldn't recommend we do it in the daylight. Any riders still looking for you, you and him would be a hell of a sight in one of them cars. If we see anybody today, you two can hide out in the garage. That okay?"

"Yes, sir. Thank you."

"Better for him to be behind fences. I guess you can't argue with that. Where else could he go to enjoy life? As a buffalo, he ain't exactly free to go where he pleases no more."

"I was hoping he could stay with me."

"But you saw it weren't possible for other people to let you and him be, didn't you?"

"Yes, sir."

"At least Bill had his taste of freedom," Odee said. "That's why you got to run away once or twice. Give yourself a good story to tell, to fool yourself as much as other people. Life is what it is. A good story is what you make it. Freedom—all too often it's something you once had. And my Mama said nothing happens till you remember it, anyways. So you might as well pick and choose what to remember. They can't take that away from you. And while it's on my mind...I am curious about one thing, could make you the king of the runaways. Where the hell was you hidin' in all that empty space between there and here? Did Bill and you manage to disappear somehow?"

"You won't tell?"

"If I come onto a secret that good, so as to make yourself invisible in plain sight, I ain't gonna share it with no one else. I can tell you that."

"Bill and me hid out with Old Lady Baker."

Odee squinted at me, pursed his lips, and rubbed his moustache. "Old Lady Baker, you say?"

"Yes, sir, then she drove me to the canyon last night. She's kind of famous."

"So I heard. She live alone, or what?"

"Yes, sir, she had a place, kind of in the middle of nowhere. A barn and a trailer. She keeps stuffed animals. She likes their company better than people. Her husband's gone and passed away, but she didn't stuff him like they say. And she is old."

Odee cocked his head with a rueful grin. "Why don't you pin that down a bit. Old like me or older?"

"Old like you."

"Does she still wear a bonnet? Holds it on with a length of yellow yarn tied just below her chin?"

"I think so. It was some kind of hat."

The water drained from Odee's eyes and ran down his cheeks. "God dammit, I always knew she was out there, but I was afraid to see for myself, especially after what people made her out to be. What a god damn fool I am." He crossed himself. "And was she the most beautiful woman you ever saw?"

"Not exactly."

"Once she was."

"Maybe, I guess." Odee seemed to be getting emotional and I didn't want to disagree with him.

"You can take my word for it. She don't deserve that other name. People been calling her that since she was still a young woman, tried to scare their kids away from her. World's fit for war but not for peace, not when folks can't even respect a proper name. Minny is her name." Odee leaned against the rim of one of the locomotive wheels and rubbed it with his hand. "Look at this train. Remember what I call her?"

"Minny."

"That's right. She's why. And her last name wasn't Baker. Baker was the no-good she married. Her name was Jones when I met her."

"You were friends with Old...with Mrs...?"

"Minny. Say it and don't forget it. We was more than friends." Odee spoke in short bursts, breaking up his sentences with pauses, sometimes for thought, sometimes for emphasis. "First time we saw each other, I don't know how to put it—we was still teenagers, but we both kind of lost our breath, like we'd known each other forever. She was working at a school and I was delivering books and stuff. Neither one of us knew that many people. But we couldn't exactly meet like we was sweet on each other. I mean, look at my skin. Look at hers. Just a few shades apart, like dusk and darkness, but enough to be against the law. Still is. Having a dance together, that would've got us strung up some moonless night, no doubt. So we used to meet at a rail station, sit on a bench, holding books like we was waiting for a train, and tell each other stories. The ones she liked best were the Phantom Padre stories I told her.

"Well, then we had something called the Great War and I ran off to it. Maybe things would be different for us when I got back, I thought. I told her we wouldn't just have to meet at the railroad station like third-class travelers, I'd take her on a journey on the finest train with the finest food, and we'd ride right off into the future. She waited for me during that war, but something was blasted right out of me. I couldn't stop running away when the war wound up. First over there, walking the poisoned earth. Waiting for the grass to grow back over the bodies. Then here, when I realized nothing had changed, not as far as my dreams was concerned, so I started looking for my lost self by working on the railroads. Couldn't face no one, least of all her. She was the beginning of my story, but I couldn't...I couldn't make it to the end. So we never put ourselves together and it was my fault. My regret. Minny. Hard to say Baker after that beautiful name. Minny Jones, she was. Should've been Valentino. Minny Valentino. Been mad at me and the rest of the world for more'n forty years, but I'm glad she took to you."

For a while, we said nothing. Odee seemed far away, as if he'd forgotten I was there. I figured it was up to me to break the silence. "The Phantom Padre. Did you really know him, like you said?"

"Indeed I did, son." Odee placed the tips of his fingers together and flexed his hands several times. "You say your fair-weather fellow, I mean the artist and convict, he found the Padre's actual diary?"

"Yes, sir. I saw it myself."

"Well, even that diary, that wouldn't tell you the whole story, because he wrote it when he still had years and years to live, way more'n thirty. When I was a boy as young as you, *amigo*, that's when I knew the Phantom Padre really and truly, right up to the end. I knew him personal. If you want to know how the end came, it won't take long to tell you. Then when it gets dark we can put you and Bill on the train. You game for it?"

"Yes, sir, I'm game."

"Come in the depot and have a seat, then." Odee led me to the small adobe depot with the ticket window and souvenir store. "We'll keep an eye out for any riders."

28
The Weatherman

I sat on a stool behind the ticket window. Odee leaned back in a folding chair and put his feet up onto a metal desk. "You heard of Presidio? Straight south of here all the way to the Mexican border. It's where I grew up. My dad was a migrant worker. It was him told me my first Phantom Padre story, about the Padre getting the drop on three outlaws tryin' to murder everybody in a camp of buffalo hunters. Then I found my own stories, where the drugstore owner had a stack of old Frank Leslie's papers that he'd kept for years. Helped me learn how to read and write. Phantom Padre Saves the Orphans. Phantom Padre and the Widow's Homestead. Phantom Padre and the Laundry Cat. Phantom Padre Reaches for the Stars. Phantom Padre and the Religion of Poker. That's when he bests a villain at his own game and rescues a beautiful girl. There was even one where the Padre was captured by Indians and saved by the chief's daughter who sees the Virgin Mary. That one beat all. But the Padre was an all-around hero. Loved animals and children and anyone in trouble. Hated injustice and tyranny. So I ran around pretending to be the Phantom Padre. Fighting the devil and the bad guys at the same time.

"My Mama, they called her the burro woman because she went up and down the road with a burro, looking for things people threw away. She'd pick them up, change them into good luck charms, and sell them. She made crosses out of bullet shells. Candle holders and planters out of cans and bottles. Dolls out of wood and cloth. Rosaries out of foil. Made my badge out of tin cans, like I said. My Mama could make anything. And she could make anybody believe it would bring them good luck.

"She didn't like me pretending to be the Phantom Padre when my dad was gone, because I'd run off all kinds of places to hide out. And she couldn't find me. So when dad went off she got me a kind of job with a man named Lopez. He was old, I dunno, older than you think I am now by a good ten or fifteen years. And he was the weatherman for Presidio. Said he could read the weather in the stars, and people believed him. That's how good of a weatherman he was at first. But his eyesight failed him eventually. The stars got dim and he could hardly read the thermometer he'd put in his garden. So I'd go there every day, look at the thermometer, and record the temperature. Then I'd check the rain gauge. Which it was almost always dry. I wrote the figures down and gave the paper to Lopez. He'd sign it with his initials. Then I'd take it to the telegraph office and they'd send the information on to El Paso for the newspapers and such. They were proud in Presidio about how it could be hotter than anywhere else. The fact that Lopez couldn't see the stars no more like he used to, they let that go.

"Well, one day I did my job and got my toy gun and headed out to see if I could find a place like the one where the Phantom Padre gunned down those outlaws. Fact is, it could've been maybe hundreds of miles away, but I didn't know any better, so I started walking north of town, about a mile west of the highway. I didn't know nothing about how far things were then. I guess you could call it my first runaway. So I just kept walking and pretending to shoot at anything that moved. And don't you know, I got lost. But the coyotes found me. It got to be late, and I heard the coyotes howl closer and closer. Like they knew I was fresh meat. Then I heard a bang and a yip and Mama came out of nowhere, leading her burro. Riding on that burro was Lopez the weatherman. He had a pistol in his hand, and he'd fired the shot that grazed the coyote. I ran to him and thanked him. Then I asked him how he could see the beast, considering he was near blind. 'Sometimes your ears tell you just as much,' he said.

"Mama didn't say nothing to me. She just grabbed me by the ear and walked me home, leading the burro with Lopez the weatherman on it. I wanted to ask him all kinds of questions, but Mama'd had enough of me. And she was hurting bad from her limp. But she got up the next morning and gave me a bullet-shell cross, one of her good luck charms. Told me to take it to Lopez the weatherman. He could make a wish on it, she said, and it would come true. She told me to go apologize to him and not take a cent from him for a month—he paid me three cents a day to read his thermometer. Then she went to work with the burro, like she always did.

"Well, I did as she said, and he looked at the charm and rolled it around in his hand. Said thanks, but there was only one thing he could think of to wish for and it wasn't possible no more. So I read his thermometer for him and checked the rain gauge. And being a kid, I was kind of mad about not making money for a month. I ran around his garden, hiding behind trees, coming out of nowhere, or so I thought, and yelling 'Bang, bang, I got you.' You know, just to see if Lopez could place me like he placed that coyote. He seemed to follow me pretty good, and he laughed like it was no bother. Finally, he asked, 'Who do you think you are, shooting up my garden like that?' And I said, 'I am the Phantom Padre. A great hero.' He seemed kind of taken by surprise that I was pretending to be the Padre and he asked me to tell him stories about this gunslinger who dressed like a priest. So I told him the one my daddy told, and some others I'd heard from old men in town or read in Frank Leslie. And he shook his head at them all and said I shouldn't believe everything I heard. I got mad again and asked him if he didn't think the Phantom Padre was any kind of hero. He thought for a minute like he wanted to say 'No.' Then he put his hand on my shoulder and said, 'As long as you swear to do good like what you believe your heroes did, it ain't a man's place to tell you otherwise about them.'

"Well, the summer went on and I did my job for nothing. But then after a month, Lopez give me a dollar. He said I was good to keep my bargain and do as my Mama said. But she didn't say nothing about whether I could earn it as back pay, so there it was, with an extra ten cents thrown in. And he hoped I'd do even more good by passing it on to her for whatever we needed.

"It was when the summer ended that he told me who he really was. Why he picked me to tell—that's part of the story, too. What's the last you know about him?"

"Well, he left the treasure here in Toomis Canyon and he went off to look for Young Eagle and Selenia. But he never found them."

"Mm-hmm. That treasure, as you know, was the Star of Andalusia and a beltful of gold coins. Hid 'em in this canyon, all right, that much is true, then he went off like you said, hoping he would somehow find Selenia, the girl he loved, and Young Eagle, too. When the winter closed in on him, he feared they might've been killed. But he also let himself think that if they escaped, they would be savvy enough to say they was someone other than who they were, like he had done. Last thing they'd want is for someone to notice who they really were, right?"

"Yes, sir. It would be fine with me if nobody ever noticed me."

"But that won't happen, now, will it?"

"No, sir."

"Not that the Padre didn't hope the same thing, too. But when they didn't turn up, he headed back to the dugout with enough provisions to last him a few weeks. Ran a stovepipe up through the earth, shared the space with his mule while he wrote his diary. Left notes about where the treasure was, too, thinking that only Selenia or Young Eagle could figure them out. He also made a drawing of the stars he'd seen on that last night they spent together, and the time he'd seen them, and which ones they were on the buckskin star maps that Young Eagle and his Indian daddy had made. And that's about the end of what you know, ain't it?"

"Yes, sir."

"Well, the Padre traveled a bit more afterwards. The plains was a lot safer when the Red River Wars was done. Went as far west as Santa Fe in case Selenia had gone that way somehow. All the while, he still pretended he was a priest. Used the name Lopez because he thought his real name was too dangerous. Stayed for a while at a monastery outside of Santa Fe.

"Finally, he went south again toward the Rio Grande. And the funniest thing stopped him there in Presidio, where I come from. There's a mountain, Santa Cruz, other side of the border. Locals say that's where the Devil took up residence. The night the Padre arrived, there was a storm bad as all get-out. Lightning come from everywhere. Destroyed a little chapel the people had built on that mountain to drive the devil off. The Padre, he figured he'd gone far enough without coming face-to-face with Beelzebub. He took off his cassock and became just plain Lopez. Worked the fields, did odd jobs. Knew a lot about the stars, especially what they told you about life. Things like when to plant and whatnot. When the winds would change. So they made him the weatherman. And that's how I met him. I was a boy, almost twelve, in case I didn't say. That's about how old you are now, am I right?"

"Yes, sir. For less than two weeks."

"Well, as it happened, there was a good reason that he decided to reveal his true identity to me after hiding it for so long. That time when he rescued me from coyotes, my mother thanked him in the only way she could. I told you, she made and sold all kinds of things from the junk she collected along the road. People believed that the charms she made had the power to bring good luck. And remember, to show her appreciation for what the weatherman had done, she fashioned a cross for him from the bullet casings she had collected. He was grateful when I give it to him, but he told me it was way too late for the only wish he would make on it. Well, he was wrong about that.

"One morning not long after, I went to his garden to read his thermometer and he looked like he'd seen a ghost though he was near blind. The day before, a man that claimed to be a healer arrived in town, set up a tent, promised to cure people of whatever. He had a buffalo calf traveled with him. I asked Lopez if something was wrong and he asked if I'd heard about the healer. I told him yes. He had my Mama's bullet cross in his hand, and he kissed it. He said he had an appointment with the healer that evening and he asked me to lead him there, just south of town. He said I wouldn't have to wait for him because he might not come back. I told him I'd do whatever he wanted, and he patted me on the shoulder. Then he said something I never can forget. He said, 'Before we go, I must make a confession to you, boy. My name's not Lopez. I am Antonio Peraza. I was once the Phantom Padre you heard of, even though the stories you hear are lies.'

"I'm ashamed I didn't believe him at first. Then he told me how to find his guns in a wood box beneath a floorboard in the shack. One was an old Remington pistol in a holster. Another was a kind of derringer. There was also a metal box next to the wood one. The metal box had a priest's clothes in it. And a piece of buckskin with stars painted on it. There was also a couple of gold coins, a pretty green stone, and a silver dollar."

"Well, then and there he told me his whole story. The way he told it, I could barely move while I listened. When he was done, he asked if I believed him. I did, and I said so. Then he asked if I'd do a favor for him, but not because he was the Phantom Padre. I said I would've done it anyways, whoever he was. He was always fair to me. He said, 'Then bring me that metal box, if you would.' I did, and he took out the stone and the silver dollar and give me the gold coins. Those coins fed me and my Mama and Papa for a long time after. And nobody questioned where they come from, cause Mama was the burro woman and she knew about good luck. 'Put the coins in your pocket,' he said, 'and come back after sundown to do me my favor.'

"It still gives me the shivers to think about what I saw when I went back that evening. There he stood, waiting for me, dressed in his cassock with his gun strapped around his waist. He was so thin he used some rope as suspenders to hold up his gun belt. The moonlight made his white hair kind of spooky. But he was a handsome fella, did I tell you that? Even in his old age. Still had a strong jaw. Wide forehead. Cheeks high on both sides. Nose like an aristocrat. I guess he *was* one if you think about it. Only thing was his eyes didn't have much life left in them. He was turning his silver dollar in his hand.

"I led him in the dark to where the healer was camped. There was a buffalo calf staked near the tent. Man came out to greet us, looked to be forty or so, hard to tell. Straight as an arrow. I heard the Padre ask, 'How did you know where to find me?'

"'Never stopped looking,' says the man. 'Heard about a weatherman relied on the stars to do his predicting.'

"'I can't see them no more,' the Padre says.

"The man takes his hand. 'They're still up there,' he says. He squeezes the Padre's hand with both of his. 'She stood before you last night in your garden to make sure, but you couldn't see her. And now she's waiting for you.'

"The Padre starts to ask a question. 'Is there...?' Then he stops.

"'There was a boy, only lived for two years. She's never stopped crying for him,' says the healer.

"The Padre seems to tremble. He asks if there might be others, and the healer says there's two, ages 19 and 17. Boy and a girl. The Padre takes the buckskin with the stars on it out of his pocket and lays the green stone and the silver dollar on top of it. 'I kept these just in case,' he says. 'And I wrote my story out on the hill where I stayed with her. It's there to find if anyone wants to.'"

Odee paused for several seconds, plumbing his memory, before he finished his story.

"Last I saw, the figure of a woman appeared like a ghost out of the darkness, walking toward them. The healer turns to me. 'You can go, boy,' he says. 'Give him his last moments with her. Go.'

"I went back the next morning to see if the Padre needed help, but the tent was taken up and the healer was gone. It wasn't till I went to check the thermometer in the Padre's garden that I saw him sitting in his chair. Head tilted back toward the stars. What little life had been left in his eyes had disappeared. In the garden, where the wind blew it after it fell from his hand, was a pencil sketch. Beautiful face. A boy around two years old."

29
Odee in Exile

"Now, I'll bet you want to know if I ever looked for that treasure. I know this much—it was hid in a cave near a hoodoo. Might have been the very one this railroad is named for. But without the diary the Padre left behind, it'd be a crapshoot trying to dig for it. Not that I didn't think about it. But can you guess why I never followed up?" Odee didn't wait for my answer. "Wouldn't be mine to claim. That sound stupid to you? Most other people would think so. They'd want to know why shouldn't I look for it? But they didn't have the dream I had. There I was, thinking I might put two and two together to find where the star was hid. Then this creature come to me in a dream. Dressed like a priest and had wings like a Mexican free-tailed bat. What it said was, 'Whenever you thought you were lost, you really weren't, because your Mama found you and the Padre saved you. The very same Phantom Padre as was your hero. Now is your time to show them you were worth finding. That treasure wasn't hid for you. You'll be cursed if you steal it. If you don't, then what else happens in your life is up to you. That's the best I can do for you.' Turned its back, spread its wings and flew away straight up to the moon. It was only years later, after I buried Mama, that I understood why that message came from a bat. But I believed what it said, dream or no dream. And my life has been pretty much up to my own self, the good and the bad. Well, look out there, now. It's near dark. About time to eat and get you and Bill ready for your train ride."

Odee made peanut butter and grape jelly sandwiches for both of us. He gave me a 7-Up and a bag of Fritos from the vending machines in the souvenir store. While we ate, he filled a giant mug with two Shiner beers that lapped onto his moustache. Finally, he wiped his mouth and we were ready to travel.

"Yeah, I did one or two test runs at night already. Just to introduce myself to all the lost souls who ain't seen a train for awhile or heard it's rumble. Everyone from conquistadores to treasure hunters, Indian tribes and priests. They're all out there.

And the Padre, too. They came here and disappeared and left their ghosts. Well, now they can ride my train, too. Take a load off if they want. I even hear the buffalo out there, stampeding along the tracks. There's one in particular—a legend of a lone buffalo that raced and bellowed through an Indian camp in this canyon. Woke up the warriors and their families just before an attack. He saved many lives before he turned and ran back into the sunrise. Some say he dissolved into dust that rose like a tornado into the sky. Yes, sir."

As he talked, Odee removed the seats from the train's forward tourist car. He left only the flat bed of the car, the low siding that protected passengers from falling out, and the canopy that shielded them from the sun. I climbed onto the car, and Bill got on with me.

"He's not going to break your train, is he?" I asked.

Odee shook his head. "Weighs no more than the eighteen fat passengers it'll hold. He knows how to ride, I hope."

"He does. He had his own trailer."

"Fancy him. Well, then, hold on, boys." As he took his seat, Odee waved to us and put on a striped denim hat with a high crown and wide visor. "Enjoy the ride."

From the steam whistle came two short toots, then the engine lurched and the car swayed around a curve in the track as we rolled out of the station. After that, the ride was smooth. "Modeled after a Prairie 2-6-2, this engine is," Odee announced. "You'll forgive me if I keep the front lantern off. Gonna take it a little slow, about twelve or fifteen miles an hour." It was six miles to the Royal Hoodoo.

I put my hand on Bill's shoulder and gave him another carrot, then I brushed him. I had one carrot left after that. I planned to offer it to him when we said goodbye. With Bill riding calmly next to me past the ghosts of great herds, the train chugged steadily and in perfect rhythm through the darkening canyon whose features assumed the fearsome qualities of a mythology come to life—stone during the day, but transformed by the mind's eye into quivering flesh and blood at night. During our ride, Odee tested the speaker system he had installed to communicate with his riders. "Can you hear me back there?" I assured him with a signal that everything was loud and clear, and then he began a non-stop rehearsal of the tourist mini-lectures he planned as we passed by various landmarks. "Back in 1541 the famous explorer Coronado and his con-KEES-Stadors..." He paused for breath. "...rode into these parts seeking the FAB-ulous seven cities of GOLD." He looked back and grinned at Bill and me. "Why, I don't suppose things have changed much, do you think?" A large shadow undulated across the moonlit landscape as if it were following us. Odee pointed upwards, waving a finger in circles. "If you look way above you," he droned in tour-guide mode, "that black river you see rushing across the moon right now is a colony of Mexican free-tailed bats. They fly forty to sixty miles an hour on their way to feast on whatever insects they can find. Like some good, tender moths. Their colonies are the largest congregations of mammals on this entire earth. Yes, sir, in just one cave here in Texas, they say there's twenty million of them. But that makes no difference to the mama bats. When that mama goes back to the nursery cave where millions of baby bats are waiting to be fed, do you think she gets confused? No sir, she goes straight to her own baby bat. Cause she remembers where she left it and how it sounds when it cries for food. Not one little baby bat gets lost or goes hungry. Those are Mexican free-tailed bats. Admire them while you can. They honor my own Mama. Yours, too, son. Never forget that. Now look at them rock spires we're passing. They're telling you to please direct your attention to the right as we approach the Royal Hoodoo."

The life of a hoodoo far surpasses the time that is allowed to those of us who live and breathe—but measured by geologic eras, it will barely survive infancy before it tumbles. The idiosyncratic rock balances atop a much softer pedestal—a column of mudstone that has melted through erosion from beneath the rock, then slopes forward to the canyon floor. Despite its relative daintiness by epochal standards, the Royal Hoodoo, resembling nothing more than a giant, disorderly totem pole, did continue to stand atop a pedestal that looked like the wrinkled hoof of some colossal beast—perhaps the playful, clumsy, monster who assembled it as a distraction.

The hoodoo soared into the sky at the peak of a ridge that grew in elevation as the ridge extended from east to west and formed the back wall of the canyon. There was a sheer drop away from the hoodoo on its west side. Odee had diverted his railroad tracks to take the train behind a cluster of large boulders and offer an unobstructed view of the spire. Along the pedestal on which the hoodoo sat was a natural ramp forming a steep, switchback trail up the side of the wall. "Royal Hoodoo coming up," he called cheerfully.

Odee brought the train to a halt. The tracks curved to our left beyond the stopping point. They crossed to the other side of the canyon, then turned east, back toward the depot where the tourists' ride began and ended. Bill and I stepped down from the car. Odee shook my hand. "So here you go, boy. You can do what you got to do. If I didn't think you could, I wouldn't of brought you here. You gave your word like a man. Best you finish it like a man. On your own. Now you'll find out what it means. You and Bill keep going west beyond the hoodoo. The canyon floor rises, but it ain't so steep as to slow you down. Should take you less than two hours to walk it out, then just a bit beyond is the back fence on the east side of the buffalo refuge. One more thing." He handed the crowbar to me. "That fence has a gate. You should be able to bust off a lock and chain with this to let Bill in. You won't see any riders long as it's dark. When you're done, follow the fence south and you'll reach a parking lot with an office building. Got a pay phone in the parking lot. Here." He gave me a handful of coins. "You're an official runaway. Hopped a train. Did yourself proud. Nobody can take that away from you. No shame if you feel like making a call. Like I never did."

He shuffled his feet and looked over his shoulder. "I hope you remember me as no better or worse than I am, boy. It was my own damn foolishness, not to finish those stories for Minny. And, don't you know, all the times I thought about giving her that train ride? Hell, I own the train now. What a sight that would be, her and me, riding by and telling the world to mind its own business. I could've done that. But..." He made a sweeping gesture toward the railroad tracks. "...here I am, built myself a circle, always winds up back in the same place." He tipped his striped cap. "Well, boy, you and Bill done me an honor—my first live customers. I thank you for that."

Odee turned his back with a wave and climbed into the engine cab. A few seconds later, I heard two short blasts from the locomotive's steam whistle. "Let's go, Minny," he coaxed in his lilting voice, releasing the brakes and easing open the throttle. "You know," he added, now speaking only to himself, "maybe it's time I tried to look her up."

I stood with Bill as the train steamed across the canyon and vanished. We were on our own. The night was clear and the stars sparkled brilliantly, but the hoodoo loomed over us like a living thing questioning our presence. "C'mon, Bill," I urged, suddenly on edge.

I thought I saw a shadow move. Then I was certain I heard footsteps. I was determined not to freeze, so I continued to walk straight ahead past the hoodoo. Bill snorted and turned as if to run the other direction. An instant later, someone clamped a hand over my mouth and lifted me off my feet.

30
Pony Tells His Story

"Calm down, god dammit. Keep quiet and I'll let you go."

It was Pony. I stopped struggling and he lowered me to the ground and released me. His straw hat fell off. When he bent to pick it up, Bill nudged him with his massive head and nearly sent him sprawling. "Hey, Bill. How the hell...?" Bill trotted around in a circle, then broke into his stiff-legged dance. Pony looked back at me.

I lunged toward him with my fists swinging. "You goddam sonofabitch, I'd kill you if I could."

Pony grabbed my wrists, my hat tipped over my eyes, and I lost my balance and fell to the ground. He continued to pin me down, repeating "You're going to hurt yourself," until I stopped struggling. Then he pushed himself free. "What the hell is your problem? Jesus! Put your hat back on and try to make some sense."

"You sold us out, you sonofabitch." I shoved my hat onto my head and pulled down the front brim. "You sold the Star. You stole from Babe. You left us all behind..."

"Where did you get that idea? Shut the hell up for a minute and I'll tell you what happened. Can you be quiet and listen? Otherwise I'll gag you and make you listen. Are you going to shut up?"

I nodded reluctantly. "Yeah."

"You promise?"

"I keep my promises. Not like you."

"Well, for the time being I'll just ignore the question of why you and Bill are here all alone..." Pony paused, then seemed to grin. "Hell of a sight, you two riding that tourist train run by some crazy old man instead of having Babe and Dwight drive you like I asked." His grin sank into a frown. "That's the god damndest thing. Decided to hitchhike, the both of you, did you? But I'll wait to hear how you kept that promise. Now you sit there and listen to me and pay attention. What the hell did you hear, anyway?"

"I ran away with Bill..."

"I don't want to hear about that yet. I want to know what you heard about me."

I brushed myself off and sat on the ground a few yards away from Pony, out of his reach, where I could pour out a bitter account of his betrayal. When he laughed, I gripped a rock and nearly heaved it at his head, but then he repeated what Odee had told me. "They won't find anything there. Once they'd pulled me in, I had to come up with something so they wouldn't try to hold me and then go for Bill—so I could be right where I am tonight. I did some hocus-pocus with the star chart and the Padre's papers, drew them a map that was...well, basically it was upside down. Sent them to the south canyon. I had to get them off my back. Because this is my business. Family business. Now you listen to me." He paused to stretch his legs and his voice became softer. "Why do you think I'm here instead of at the other end of the canyon? That appointment I told you about? It's tonight. Tonight I'm the one who's going to find the Star of Andalusia. I know exactly how to do it." He reached into his pocket and pulled out a stone. "The part about the emerald I showed them—that was true. This is it. Take a look. It's real."

I took the stone and rotated it in my fingers, feeling its smooth facets and the sharp defining edges. "Where did you get it? Was it in the dugout? Did you steal it?"

"No. For Chrissake. Don't you believe me so far?"

"I don't know. Everybody lies, nobody is who they say they are." I handed the stone back to him.

"Fair enough. You don't have to believe me, then. Not till I keep my appointment. It's only a couple of hours from now and you can be there with me. Okay?"

"I guess."

"Now it's your turn."

"To do what?"

"To quit being a little shit. You can start with how you and Bill got here."

Something about being with Pony, maybe the fear, maybe the fact that I desperately wanted to believe him—wanted to believe someone, anyone—made me decide to open up. "Okay, you really want to know? Or maybe you don't. Well, then..." I breathed heavily. "Babe is a whore, like they said."

Pony walked over to me, leaned down, lifted the brim of my hat, and tried to look me in the eyes. I averted my head. "You don't mean that, son."

"And the hill ain't ours. The hill ain't ours. Babe and Dwight, they made a phony will."

Pony loosened his grip. "Jesus, kid, how much shit have you heard since I saw you last? It sounds like your whole goddam world has fallen apart."

"And my real father...he's dead now, god damn him."

"Who?"

"It's Wyatt Fowler's father. He's my father, too."

Pony's face contorted into an expression that was quizzical and dismissive. "What?" Then he laughed. "Bullshit. How do you know that?"

"The night you went, that's what I heard Babe and Dwight talking about when I left your note on the porch and the storm came. That's why I had to run away."

"Does Fowler know this?"

"No, but if they found out his boys would kill me—if he didn't. They want to kill me, anyway. They damn near got the chance this morning. I thought Bill and me were both goners."

Pony leaned back and exhaled slowly. "How did Babe get mixed up with that man—with Wyatt's father? Do you know?"

"He used to visit Babe all the time in San Antonio. He bought her from my grandmother or something."

"Bought her? Bought Babe?"

"Even though she hated him." I had to add something in her defense.

"So she's not your adopted mother. She's the mother you were born to."

"Why wouldn't she tell me that?"

Pony shook his head. "There's things you don't know about why people do what they do."

"And someday I'll understand. That's what you're supposed to tell me?"

"Not if you don't want to hear it."

"And the hill ain't ours. I can't live up there like I used to. The only thing I could do was run away. To save my own skin. And Bill's."

"Is that what you think?"

"I know so. And the phony will, that's the only use I was to her. No more than..." I looked over at Bill. He was looking back at me with a fixed eye, the way he did when I talked to him on the hill. He lowered his head and wrenched a tuft of grass from the ground.

"Calm down, okay?"

Pony sat in the dirt in front of me and waited for me to say something. After a long minute, I did. "Why wouldn't she just tell me? Why would she pretend she wasn't my mother? I can't go back there, now. Don't you see why? Everything is lies. It's not even my life any more."

"I see why you believe that. But let me tell you something. You don't make headway in life when everything you believe is proved to be true. It's when it turns out to be otherwise. That's when you move on. So catch your breath. I've got something to eat and coffee over there. We're not here for a long stay. I just came in a few hours ago."

As Odee's train had approached, Pony had doused a small campfire he built behind a boulder, but the coffee was still warm and he had a bag of jerky and candy bars. He had parked on an overlook and walked into the canyon just before dark, pulling a small wheelbarrow to carry his tools. While we talked, I gave Pony as full an account as I could of the past couple of days. When I told him how Bill had left Killer in the dust, his arm went limp and the coffee spilled out of his tin cup and he asked me to go over the battle again and again until he finally fell silent and refilled his cup. Bill did something I never had seen him do before. He lay down next to us and rested his giant head on Pony's leg. His eyes appeared to be staring into the distance, as if he were in a trance. Maybe he was, because bison have poor eyesight. Maybe he already knew what was going to happen.

Pony took a final sip of coffee, then tossed the rest into the dirt. "Okay, here we come to the end game," he said. Careful not to move Bill's head, he gently turned his leg, pulled the silver dollar out of his pocket and held it up. "I showed you this before. You know what it is, don't you?"

"It's your silver dollar."

"That's right. It's what I killed a man for in a fight, when he tried to take it from me out of meanness, because he could see it meant something to me, and to him it was worthless. It's what gives me the right to be here. I've never told anyone about it, because what would have happened if I had? Everyone would have been on my tail. I was looking for the dugout when I went to the hill, true enough. But I also wanted to do right by your mom and you. I just didn't know how to make it all work out. And this..." He flicked the silver dollar. "Does this tell you something else about me?"

"I guess so."

"I won't make you guess. Selenia was my grandmother. The last time they met, the Padre gave this back to her, along with the emerald that Young Eagle had given him. The child he fathered with her had died. He said if she didn't want to claim the treasure herself, she could give this to one of her living children, along with this piece of buckskin." Pony reached into a pack and pulled out the buckskin star chart he had showed me on his first night on Lonechap Hill, a chart I now knew had been made by Young Eagle and his father to understand what the stars could tell them. It was also the chart that Pony had used to deceive Bulland and Wyatt Fowler. "The Padre had written out instructions on how to use the chart to locate the treasure, and he'd left them in the dugout. Selenia—my grandmother—she did have kids, of course, but they were from her marriage to Young Eagle. His family name before the Indians took him was Steffan. Josiah Steffan. But he knew he could never go back to being that person any more than he could stay an Indian. He wanted to change his last name to stand on his own. The Phantom Padre's true name, you know, was Antonio. So Young Eagle—Josiah—made his last name Antone, for both him and Selenia. And that's how he passed himself off, as Josiah Antone.

"The painting that Babe thought looked like you, that was meant to be my grandpa Josiah. Young Eagle. I tried to show both sides of him, even though he had no Indian blood. The quote beneath it came from him. 'When I lie down at night my history is in my heart, and when I rise in the morning it is still there.' He knew not to listen to what other people told him he was." Pony lit one of his crooked cigars and gestured with it toward me.

He puffed impatiently and blew the smoke toward the sky. "After Josiah and my grandmother escaped from here, they worked their way north, all the way to Canada. He had a knack for healing people and animals, both—taught by his Indian father. He made a living from that. Grandma did domestic work while she raised their kids. Out of the blue one spring, Josiah discovered an abandoned buffalo calf, all alone, hiding in some tall grass. He blew into its nose and raised it for a year, and it reminded him of the old days like nothing else had. Carefree but wild, it was. Then he made sure it got to one of the few herds that was left before it grew too big. After that, every year he'd travel to where a bison herd was—people started raising them on ranches—and he'd buy a calf and keep it with him while he and Grandma and the kids traveled from place to place. He got to be known for that, and people believed it had something to do with his powers of healing.

"When I was growing up, we couldn't afford much of a vacation, but my Dad—Selenia and Josiah's son—he used to take me to the refuge at the end of this canyon just to watch the animals. Before Josiah died, it was the last place he left one of his calves. Bill might be a relative. I like to think so. That's why I went there looking for a calf after I got out of prison, and that's why Bill has to go back there." He rubbed Bill's head. Bill continued to snooze.

"My grandma kept this silver dollar to remember the Padre by—and the emerald, too—but she and Josiah never wanted to go back to look for the treasure. She never told either my Dad or my aunt about it. My aunt married a shit heel—that might have been one reason why—and my Dad, he was a good and simple man. I don't think Grandma could have imagined him chasing after gold. There'd been too much pain connected with it, besides. This silver dollar—that was enough of a fortune for her.

"When the Depression was at its worst, after Josiah died, she did go back one last time on her own to look at the site and saw the hoodoo was there, but the walls had changed. Some parts had collapsed. She could never have found where that little cave used to be if she'd wanted to.

"And this silver dollar and the emerald—I didn't know about them until the year I got out of the Army. My parents had been killed in a car wreck and I was cleaning out the house where we'd lived. On a top shelf in the closet of the room where Grandma stayed was her old watercolor kit. And underneath a tray in that kit was this silver dollar and the buckskin star chart with the emerald wrapped in it and some blue composition books—the kind we used to write essays in school—held together by rubber bands. That's how she'd set down her story bit by bit over the years. It wasn't like the Padre's story, full of regret for what he'd done. It was the other side of the same coin, the struggle and the fear and not knowing what the next day would bring but never losing faith. Never. You could tell by the way her handwriting changed and how she might end in the middle of a sentence—it was hard for her to go on with it, to re-live the things that had happened. But she did. That's how I learned the stories. From her blue books. And she left an envelope with my name on it and a note in it, as if she knew I'd find that watercolor kit someday and the story inside it. You can read the note if you want to. I brought it with me so a part of her would be here on this night."

Pony reached into the pocket of his shirt and handed me a folded piece of paper. He gave me his flashlight so I could read the letter. It was dated on the same day in August that, for us, was now well past nightfall.

Dear Pony,

My grandson, you have been the joy of my life. I loved getting to do all I ever wanted to do as a girl, and do it with someone as special as you. I never got to be much of a painter. You are. I wanted someone to share it with so bad, because when I was drawing or painting I was happy, no matter what else was going on. And it made me feel good to know that you would have something to make you happy because life doesn't always agree. You'll be a man if you ever find this, so you'll know what I mean by then.

I ask myself whether I want you to find this, and then I say to myself it's not up to me, so here is what I am telling you. This is a map of the stars that your Grandpa made and gave to a man we knew. That man, named Antonio, was sometimes called the Phantom Padre. I loved him before I loved your Grandpa. When he returned the map to us, he left instructions with it on how to find a hill where we stayed once, a hill where I was happy. On that hill, we lived for a week—just a week—in a little dugout. That's where Antonio left his Bible and where it still may be. In the back of the Bible, he wrote how to find a treasure. He told me when I last saw him that it must be done on the day he hid it so long ago. That is why I thought of it today. This is the anniversary of the day everything happened and we were separated until the last day of Antonio's life. Once I went to look at where I knew the treasure was buried. It was after your Grandpa Josiah died that I went there, just to see. Time had changed everything. But then was when I knew again that I never wanted the treasure, anyway. Neither did your grandpa. It is a gold star with bright jewels, very beautiful, from Spain. People died for it. The emerald you will find here came from it. There are also gold coins. They came from card games and maybe a robbery.

You are the last to know about this, now that we are gone. I never told your Pa or your Aunt. If you want to know all of the story, I have tried my best to put it in my blue books, even when my hands began to shake and refused to write any more. I know whatever you do about the treasure will be right. I know that if you never find it, you will still look at what is beautiful and paint your pictures. I know you will be happy when you do.

This silver dollar, I once gave as payment to Antonio for a favor. The Saint of Liberty is on it. It had to do with a sad woman who lost her best friend, a cat, so I hope I turned it from bad to good. I never knew. The night he returned the map, Antonio gave this back to me, too. It was the fortune we shared. I love you, grandson, and will tell you something Josiah used to say. "Whenever you see the grass bend, I am behind you." Listen for my footstep.

Your Loving Grandma

"I had a lot of time in prison to think about what she said before I decided to find this place," Pony said when I handed the letter back to him. "I wasn't sure what I'd do when I got here, but I know now. What the Phantom Padre wrote down in the diary he left in the dugout on your hill, that was his confession to Grandma and Grandpa and his legacy—he wanted them to know the key to how to use the stars.

"So you and me—all our secrets are out, now, huh? And the star chart—this is the time of year it matches the sky, and that's how the Padre said it should be, to coincide with his own observations. That's why I showed up at your place with Bill when I did. Now it won't be long before Bulland and Fowler realize they've been had and Bulland gets back to tracking all three of us—you, me, and Bill. The outlaw buffalo. Before this goes any further, I intend to find what's hidden up there. I know what Grandma said, and I respect it. But to me, it's unfinished business. It's the story of my family." He glanced behind the hoodoo. "Young Eagle's Chenowah father was buried in a cave somewhere along that wall. Everything else has tumbled and changed, but the hoodoo and the stars are the same. If you want to know the truth, I probably could calculate this on another day, even another hour. But I wanted it to be this day, this hour. I want to see exactly what they saw in the stars, the way they saw it."

"What about afterwards?"

"What about it?"

"I can't go home again. I'll go with you. I won't cause trouble, and you can leave me wherever you want."

"That doesn't sound too wise to me."

"I don't care."

Pony shrugged. "Whatever you say, kid. You're not the first to run away from something he couldn't handle. As for me—I'll have to head out of state for a while, at least till things cool off. Then sneak back in."

"And what about Bill?"

"Bill's not going anywhere. He's stayed with us both when he could've taken off a million times on his own." Pony rested his hand on Bill's head. "He and I have seen where everything happened, made pictures of it, walked through the playas, smelled the flowers. Went to the top of the hill. We drank it all in. It's right that he should be here, now. We can still get him to the refuge by not long after sunrise. Time to get up, Bill. We've got an appointment to keep."

31
Using the Star Chart

As if on cue, Bill rose clumsily, lurching and snorting, while Pony made his preparations. First, Pony held his flashlight on the buckskin chart. Then he produced two thin pieces of paper with figures inked onto them. "These were in the dugout," he said, "part of what I found folded into the Bible. A key that goes with the star chart. This is what I used to mislead Bulland and Fowler—like it was a ground map, but it's not. It's a map of what's up there." Laid end to end, the papers formed an overlay on the bottom half of the chart, where it was apparent that the inked figures were meant to outline stars representing the shapes of two constellations—not the Western constellations the Padre had studied, but the ones the Indians had assigned to the heavens. "This one..." Pony tapped on the larger figure. "This one is the bison. The circle the Padre drew is over the bison's eye. And what he sketched just beneath the eye—that's this hoodoo we're sitting near, to the southwest of us. The bison's eye is one of the stars that will line up, when it wheels down from the sky to the top of the hoodoo."

He moved his finger across the chart and placed it on the other inked figure. "These stars formed what the Indians believed was a child's cradle, the kind a mother wore to carry a baby. The cradle has a hook on the end of it. That's the other star we'll look for. Here's how it should happen. When the bison's eye reaches the crown of the hoodoo, this cradlehook star will be visible, for just a few minutes, in a 'v' shaped notch in the canyon wall." With his eyes still on the chart, Pony raised a hand and pointed toward the other side of the canyon. "The 'v' represents that cleft you can see in the wall, directly south of us. Do you see what I'm talking about?" He jabbed his finger in the direction of the cleft.

"Yes, sir. I see it."

"Okay. If we're standing where we can see both stars in those positions—the bison's eye on top of the hoodoo, and the cradlehook star in the cleft of the wall—then we're standing somewhere near where the Padre stood, at the point where the lines from the stars would intersect. We know he was here on this date. We know the time it's supposed to happen—1:47 a.m., according to his notes. A little more than an hour from now. So the next thing to do is climb up the trail past those trees. Then we'll have time to pace around and watch the stars come into position. The bison's eye tells us how high we have to be on the trail. That's the first point. The cradlehook star tells us how far east or west of that point we have to be to locate where the cave was." Pony folded the chart and its overlay and put them back in his pack. "Are you game?"

I nodded and laughed weakly. "This the appointment you talked about."

"It is. And I'll owe you one, if you want to know the truth. This'll be a lot easier with two of us than it would have been for me alone."

Pony pulled his pick and shovel from the wheelbarrow and handed me the metal detector.

Bill followed us for a while. Nicked by the sharp and brittle branches of stunted trees, we took a path that wound up along the canyon wall. Far above us, the upper layers of rock were exposed like broad, horizontal stripes, dull but apparent even in the moonlight, along a sheer cliff. I slipped repeatedly on the rocks that covered the trail, and steadied myself by using the metal detector as a brace. Pony made his way deliberately and carefully, flicking his flashlight on and off, looking back to keep Bill and me in his sights. Bill had no trouble following us and keeping his balance, despite his oversized head and his puny rump. He already had demonstrated his agility on Lonechap Hill.

Somewhere near, eighty-six years before, Antonio, Selenia, and Young Eagle had gathered for their last evening together—until the end in Presidio. The ridge where they sat no longer existed as it was then, and I understood, while making the climb, why it would be difficult to locate the spot without some kind of guidance. The area was rocky, treacherous in places, and broad.

Pony stopped occasionally to keep track of the bison's eye until he was satisfied, after fifteen minutes or so, that we had climbed high enough to approximate the viewpoint from where the star would seem to shine atop the center of the hoodoo's crown at 1:47 a.m. We stood looking west-southwest toward the hoodoo's spire and the stars beyond. We could see the bison on its path, rotating downwards from a position where its head was angled toward earth, its eye still above and to the left of the hoodoo. "Just a little while longer. Then we'll make our appointment with the stars," Pony said. He took off his hat and raised his eyes. "God, what a sight."

I stared upwards until the stars seemed to wobble and dance. The illusion made me dizzy, and I squeezed my eyes shut for a few seconds.

Pony looked at his watch again and reckoned we were too high on the trail to see the star touch the crown at 1:47 a.m., so we climbed a few steps lower and waited. Then he paced horizontally, noting the Indian cradle's position in the heavens and making a guess as to where the companion star, the cradlehook star, would appear in the crook on the south wall. "Why don't you stand here," he said when he stopped, "and tell me what you see when I call the time." He walked back to his first position, a good two hundred yards west of me, and stood tapping his foot restlessly. Bill had not followed us all the way up the trail. He rested, still upright, below us, in a wide, flat area where we had stopped to catch our breath. His head and upper body were outlined by the moonlight, and he stood proudly, as he had on the hill and on the plains, after he won the battle for his life. The howl of a coyote broke the silence. It was answered by another and another, the voices blending and echoing over the rocks, sorrowful and fading as they approached the desolate moon.

A couple of minutes before 1:47, Pony alerted me to watch for my star. I saw nothing, not a glimmer. I moved farther west, back toward Pony, thinking of how the star moved in connection with the child's cradle. Other, dim stars were in the region, but none were in the position of alignment. "I think I have the bison's eye," Pony called. He had guessed well. He was on a level only a short distance below where I stood.

"I don't see anything," I said.

"I don't see the other star, either. Move down, if you can, and walk the other way." Pony began to walk gingerly in my direction as he spoke, looking back constantly at the star over the hoodoo. I climbed down another one or two feet. I don't know how far east I walked—maybe as far as fifty yards. Then, it appeared—a star whose brightness was like the dying ember on a candlewick, slightly to the left of the crook in the opposite wall, but clearly coming into view as it transited, unaccompanied by any companions that might confuse the issue.

"I see it," I cried.

Pony dropped his pick and shovel and hurried toward me. "Just like the Padre said it would," he said. The cradlehook star came into position. I stared at it, unbelieving. Before I thought to look back for the star on the hoodoo, Pony slipped and slid down the trail, feet first. "Don't move," he grunted while he slid.

And for that moment, I stood alone, looking at the alignment. The bison's eye seemed to have rotated to its place, a ceremonial diamond nestled onto the crown of the hoodoo. In that blazing sky, where shooting stars sprinted out of their hiding places and tumbled across the blackness, where the Milky Way's dusty racepath lay within reach of the bison, where messages were written and left for future civilizations to discover, two stars had fixed me in the place where I stood. They conveyed, more than any ancient artifact could have, a sense of timelessness and the immediacy—the only appropriate word I can think of—the immediacy of the past.

Pony was fine. He looked up and waved. Finally, he scrambled back up the trail and retrieved his pick and shovel. His cheek was badly scraped, but he was smiling. He joined me in time to enjoy the last few moments of the alignment before the bison dipped away toward its extinction beneath the horizon, the diamantine eye toppled from its crown, and the cradle followed its own path, arcing toward the western sky.

"I'll poke around," Pony said. "The place'll be back a bit toward the hoodoo."

Using his shovel, Pony discovered a soft spot in the wall just beneath a ledge of thinly-layered rock, almost exactly where he had calculated the recess would be. He reached toward me without speaking, and I handed him the metal detector. As he swept it back and forth, it produced a tone which rose over the soft spot and fell on either side. He held the detector over the area where the tone was most insistent, then gave the instrument back to me and plunged his shovel into the wall.

32
Finding Treasure

The signal from the metal detector grew stronger as Pony dug. The earth was loose above the hole, but firmer near the base. In less than half an hour, we saw the outline of an arch-shaped indentation over the ledge where we stood. "I think this is it," Pony said. Over the years, through winds and rains, water had seeped through the porous sides of the small cave and caused its floor to sink near the back wall, where the gold belt and the Star of Andalusia would have been wedged by the Padre before he fled after Selenia and Young Eagle. For every two feet Pony dug, another foot of earth crumbled from the roof of the depression. But by three a.m. Pony had cleared an entrance large enough—roughly the size of a barrel—to slide into. He no longer needed to use the metal detector. There was no doubt that something was behind the growing indentation, and that we were close to it.

Pony tossed his hat aside and worked his way about two or three feet into the opening. He sat and leaned forward until his head nearly reached his knees. He slid the shovel into the hole, extending his arms as far as they would go and chopping at any resistance. The shovel's handle angled downward where the floor sagged. Finally, he struck something solid. His flashlight revealed a stack of rocks and what looked like the ragged corner of a piece of canvas behind the rocks. He turned back to me. "You're small enough to get in. How would you like to see if you can grab hold of that?"

With a rope from Pony's pack looped tightly around my waist, I lay on my belly and crawled backwards, feet first. The opening extended about eight feet into the wall, including the downward slope. When my feet touched the other end, I kicked aside the rocks as best I could. Then I bent my knees and reached down with my right hand, grasping for anything that felt like canvas or leather. I got a grip on the corner of a wide belt and pulled. At first, it wouldn't budge, but as I tugged on it repeatedly with all my strength, the earth around it began to loosen. The rocks shifted. And the belt moved free. I was able to turn onto my side and grip it with both hands. Neither Pony nor I had spoken a word until then. "Hang on to what you've got, and I'll pull you out," Pony said.

A few seconds later, we were looking at a belt in remarkably good shape whose eight pouches were secured by strings of rawhide wrapped around metal buttons. Half of the pouches were empty, but three contained twenty-dollar gold pieces and a fourth was crammed with wads of currency. Pony didn't count the coins then, but he estimated that the belt weighed around six pounds. "Maybe fifty gold coins," he said. "I wonder how many there would have been if Lehane hadn't had to leave his winnings behind when he kidnapped my grandma."

Without further scrutiny, Pony set the belt down—he seemed strangely disinterested, I thought—and placed his flashlight back into a groove he had scooped out at the entrance of the cave. "The bag should be near it or just behind where you found it. I don't know how I thought I'd do this alone." He looked at me and smiled. "We need to work fast, before more dirt comes down."

Above the cave, where another shelf of rock extended, debris was falling in small bunches of pebbles. Some of it landed on the back of my head when, secured by Pony's rope, I slid back into the opening. "I'm going to pull you out if that gets any worse," Pony said. I crouched again when I reached the wall and managed to touch the edge of a leather bag with the tips of my fingers. It was much more difficult to grasp than the canvas belt. Bits of debris continued to fall towards me, but my heart beat rapidly at the prospect of finding the object that would complete the story. With a grunt and a shove, I was able to grab the leather and yank the bag up towards me. I wrapped my arms around it.

"I've got it."

Pony began to pull me out of the hole. He was a few seconds too late. I saw a large chunk of rock fall to my right, and, after it, the writhing form of a snake landed only inches from me. Its thick, scaled body whipped into a coil. Its menacing rattle fractured the silence. The serpent's flat, triangular head was aimed towards the light, towards Pony—its curved fangs, venomous needles, rotating out of its jaw for a strike. "Shit!" I heard Pony cry. The snake drew its head back then sprang forward, and the cave suddenly went dark.

33
Goodbye, Bill

I slid back down the slope of the floor. Pony had let go of the rope when he dropped his flashlight.

I heard him cursing loudly and slamming his shovel repeatedly into the earth.

Then the beam from the flashlight shined into the cave again, and Pony pulled me out.

I hadn't let go of the leather bag.

Pony paid no attention to it when I emerged. "Are you okay?"

"I think so...did it get you?"

"The damn thing did get me, barely, when I sidestepped—right on the calf, through my jeans. Shit. It was a whole family. Tucked into their rock hideout."

A dead rattler, cut in half by the shovel, was next to Pony. Two other snakes that had fallen forward out of their rocky nest also lay dead.

"There was one that got away, down the wall," Pony said. "He won't come back for us, don't worry."

"Are you...what will the poison do to you?"

"Depends on how much venom he had. Sometimes if they're surprised, they don't inject as much when they bite. If I'm lucky, it was a dry bite. I suppose I'll know soon enough."

"Let's go. Please."

"I need to finish this, first. Somewhere deeper in there, over to the left, my grandpa's Indian father is buried. I don't want to leave an open hole."

"Can't you come back?"

"Maybe." Pony sighed and slumped into a sitting position. "No. I can't. Of course I can't. I'll be getting the hell out of here. I need to rest a moment and think straight."

"Should you cut where the bite is? I'd suck the poison out."

He shook his head. "It's my right leg, but forget it. That never works. Toss me my hat, will you?" I did, and Pony fanned himself with the straw hat. "How's Bill doing?"

At first, I didn't spot Bill and felt a surge of panic. Then I saw that he had descended to the floor of the canyon and traveled to the bank of the river, where he was partially concealed by a canebreak. "I think he's getting a drink. He's pretty far away."

Pony laughed. "He's fine. He's just thirsty. The rest of us, we're way too unhinged compared to him. You still got that fine new birthday jackknife of yours?"

"Yep." I handed it to Pony. "I thought I might need it along the way..."

"Well, let me break it in for you." Pony cut open the jeans on his lower right leg. If there was a mark from the bite, it was barely visible. He cut two strips from his shirttail and tied them loosely on either side of the wound. Afterwards, he took a deep breath, closed the knife, and tossed it back to me. "Now pass me the bag. Let's see if we got what we came for."

Pony opened the leather bag.

Out of it, he lifted the Star of Andalusia.

It was smaller than I had imagined it, and thicker, but there at its center was the ruby encircled by four smaller ones, and there on its arms were the emeralds, except for the one that was missing. As I examined it, I was still recovering from the shock of facing death. That may have had something to do with why I felt relief, but no real sense of excitement upon looking at the 500-year-old treasure. I wondered if Pony felt the same. He extended his arm to its full length, holding the star above his head as if he wished to measure it against the firmament.

"What do you think?" I asked finally.

"It's what I came for." Pony lowered his arm. The star rested in his palm. "What do you think?"

"How old it is."

"You're not jumping up and down."

"No, not after the snakes."

"I don't mean that," Pony laughed. "I mean that when people go looking for treasure, they can feel like they own it if they find it. I know I don't own this. I know that money over there was left over from a stash that was used to buy my grandma."

"What are you going to do with it?"

"I've got something in mind. I think she'd approve. I just couldn't let it lie."

"What am I supposed to do if you die from that snake bite?"

"I got a plan for that, too. So let me take a couple more breaths, and we'll get us and Bill out of here."

"You're going to take me with you, aren't you?"

"Did I say I would?"

"I mean, to Mexico or somewhere. Wherever you're going."

Pony smiled and shuddered, absently rubbing his shoulder. After a few moments, he rose, bracing himself on his unbitten leg. He began to shovel dirt back into the cave. I collected some weeds and brush and piled them over the dirt. Pony looked around briefly and found a large, flat stone, which he placed on the entrance before throwing more dirt and brush onto it. "I'm done," he said finally. "If there's chiefs up there in the stars, they'll make it rain. Seal it up even better."

On our way down, I took the metal detector and the bag with the cross. Pony slung the gold belt over his shoulder and balanced the pick and shovel under his arm. When we reached the canyon floor, we put everything into the wheelbarrow. The handles extended well beyond the tub, so Pony was able to pull the wheelbarrow behind him as we walked. We headed west, with Bill beside us.

We barely talked. I didn't want to put extra strain on Pony, although he did tell me not to worry about him. "I'll still have time to get treatment. I'm not feeling too bad, really. There's no burning pain, that's a good sign."

"How do you know?"

"I've been bit before. Took some anti-venom serum to get me through."

"Do you have some?"

He laughed. "Not on me. I know where to find some, though. Come on, let's just concentrate on getting out of here."

Bill trotted in front of us and, occasionally, circled around us. He stopped to rub himself on a cedar tree with a huge burl on its trunk. Afterwards, he stepped away, paused, lowered his head, and sniffed the air. Then he ambled ahead, less frisky. I tried not to think about where we were going. But the floor was rising, and we had walked out of the canyon and onto the plains by the time the rim of the sun appeared in the east and threw our long, distorted, weary shadows over the grass ahead of us. Bill was in no hurry. He stopped to eat and, once, to wallow.

Pony knew exactly where the gate was. There was a cattle guard beneath it, covering a drainage area. Bill stood with us, as if waiting for our next move. Pony lifted the padlock on the chained gate. "The train man—Odee—he gave you a crowbar, right?"

I pulled the crowbar out of my backpack and Pony broke the lock.

The moment always comes, regardless of how well you pretend that it won't or distract yourself by cherishing every second before it does. The fence looked endless, stretching and leaning into the grassy, featureless distance toward a large, low, cloud that hovered between the earth and the fading stars. Pony began to unwrap the chain from the gate post. The sound of it rang in my ears.

Bill walked to my side and grazed. I listened to him pulling up the grass by its roots. Pony's eyes glistened. He tested the gate, which swung out toward us. Then he took off his hat and leaned against the fence, thin and exhausted. I worried that the poison was taking effect and that hospital care in Amarillo was much too far away. Pony ran his hand through his hair. He shoved his hat back onto his head and opened the gate wide enough for Bill to pass through. "I wonder where the rest of them are," he said.

No members of the herd were in the vicinity.

"I have a carrot. My last one."

"Sure. Why don't you step inside the gate and give it to him? I'll go with you."

"I don't want to go in there."

"It's a good time to do it. Nobody's around, men or animals."

With my head down, I walked to the other side of the gate. Pony came with me. I pulled the last carrot from my backpack. Bill jumped over the cattle guard and into the refuge. He swallowed the carrot quickly. Pony looked back toward the sun. "You still got his brush?"

"Yes."

"Let's do it together."

Pony pulled out a few tufts of hair and brushed Bill along his hump and back. Then he handed the brush to me. Bill took a quick step forward as if I'd tickled him. Otherwise, he stood perfectly still. I knew I couldn't go on forever. After three or four minutes, I gave up. That was when Bill lowered his head and caught his horn in my belt. Slowly, he lifted his head again, and me with it. I hung suspended above the ground on Bill's horn and we looked at each other, eye to eye, as if he had intended it to be that way. Just as carefully, he returned me to my feet.

"We have to go." Pony touched me on the shoulder. "Can I see that jackknife again?" I handed it to him without a question. "Stand back a little." When I moved aside, Pony grabbed Bill by the tousled mat on his forehead and cut off a lock of hair. He returned the knife to me, gave me half of the lock, and put the rest into his front shirt pocket. He patted Bill on the shoulder. "Good luck, Bill," he whispered.

I turned and walked away with Pony. He closed the gate, wrapped the chain around the posts, and ran the hook of the broken padlock through the chain. Bill continued to watch us. It was dark beyond him, where the sunlight had not reached.

"He's going to be fine," Pony said. "It's best for him if we walk away now."

Pony pulled his wheelbarrow and I walked beside him toward the sun. I looked back once, after we had gone two or three hundred yards. Bill stood watching us. He was alone for the first time since Pony took him from the refuge as a motherless calf. I wondered how he must have felt, to have been abandoned so surgically and quietly, behind a fence which was the best he could hope for in a life that would be fraught with danger if he were not confined. Suddenly, I was afraid that I might forget what he looked like running free. I was off balance, uncomfortable, and faintly ill.

Although I could not have articulated it then, I felt a sense of kinship with that great, powerful, lumbering and obsolete beast. At its simplest, we loved, we played, we feared death, we felt joy and pain. But, by extension, we also existed at the pleasure of those who cajole us, terrorize us, experiment on us, and control us, often at our own strange behest. They drive us toward extinction; then they protect us when we are diminished. If we succeed in our protected states—the great, galloping middle runners, striving to make headway; tolerated until we cross an invisible line and make ourselves fair game again—they await the opportunity to drive us back to oblivion, or at least to use us for sport. It is our common history and our common fate, to be the source and the scrapheap of fortunes.

34
Return to Wachyerback

We walked for nearly three miles along the southern rim of the canyon, to where Pony had parked his truck at an overlook. We put the tools and the wheelbarrow in the bed of the pickup, and Pony shoved the gold belt and the leather bag behind the driver's seat.

"Are we going to the hospital first?" I asked.

"No need to," said Pony. "I have a friend who can take care of a snake bite. You know him, too."

Within twenty minutes, by eight a.m., we were entering Wachyerback.

It was much too early for Harvey Olsen. Pony banged for at least a couple of minutes on the back door of Harvey's saloon. Finally, Harvey himself appeared, with heavy stubble on his face and eyes still swollen from drink and sleep. He carried his shotgun under one arm. "I oughtta blow your goddam hand off," he called through the swarm of flies around his screen, "so you'll never knock on my door again, whoever you are."

"Open your eyes, old man," said Pony. "It's me."

"And what gives you the almighty right to disturb a old man in his sleep?"

"The boy's with me, too. John. You remember."

"'Course I do. That boy had me ridin' an old borrowed nag around the canyon, lookin' for him and Bill before the law caught up with 'em. His ma was damned worried, otherwise she'd never have called a good-for-nothing like me. Where's Bill?"

"He's in the refuge."

"Home safe. Not a chance they'll be able to pick him outta that herd, either, no sir. So that leaves you and this troublesome lad..."

"For starters," said Pony, "he's still running away and I'm helping."

"That so?" Harvey opened the door with a grin. "Well, Merry Christmas, son. You got enough whiskey for your little odyssey? Come on in and have a drink to put some hair on your chest. Now that you're a free man, that's what you do, else some lawman might think you belong in school."

"There's more, Harvey. I need some help," said Pony. "I've been bit by a rattler."

"Well, I bet you finally got to see a snake spit, then. How long ago?"

"A little more than four hours."

"You figured to cut it close, did you?"

We wound our way through the kitchen and into the saloon. Above the cardboard longhorn, the Louisville Slugger that Babe used against Wyatt Fowler's cowboys had been replaced in its case, but the glass was still missing. Next to it was the door that read 'In case of rattlesnake bite.' Harvey opened it and took out a syringe. "Last one I got," he said. "You'd be surprised how often I have to stick them fatassed city people when they bring their scopes and rifles to clear the damn wildlife out of that canyon. They always miss the rattlers."

We went back to the kitchen, where he retrieved a bottle of antivenom from his refrigerator. "Fellow that uses this pays for the next fellow," Harvey said, squinting at Pony. "You good for it?"

I thought I saw Pony wink at Harvey. "What do you think?"

"I ain't gonna let you pay me with no painting of the snake that bit you. I got to put the order in this morning. I need more of these butt-stickers, too."

"How much?"

"Twenty dollar."

"I'm good for it. You take it in coin?"

"However you got it, son. You gettin' dizzy yet?"

"John, do me a favor. Go get Harvey his money. You know where from. Make sure it's still hidden when you've got the money. You'll need these." He tossed his keys to me.

"Better skedaddle, son. Ole Pony's startin' to turn white on us."

I couldn't believe that Harvey really was insisting on payment in advance before he saved Pony's life, but I rushed out through the kitchen to where the truck was parked. Beyond me was the field where Bill won his race on my birthday, less than two weeks before. I had held my feelings in check when I walked away from Bill. I didn't want Pony to think he'd be taking a crybaby wherever it was he planned to go. But when I saw the juniper tree and the sunlight spreading over the haycolored grass, I choked up for the first time. I stood shaking, releasing my breath in spasms, until I could calm myself. Then I unlocked the truck door and pulled the gold belt out from behind the seat. Carefully, I unwound the rawhide that held one of the pouch flaps in place, and removed a twenty-dollar gold piece. I tied the flap down again and replaced the belt behind the seat. I stopped to wipe my face and nose before I locked the truck again.

Harvey met me in the kitchen. Pony wasn't there. "I done stuck him already, since I figured you was good for it if he wasn't. My cot has a few fleas that like to think it's theirs, too, so we put two tables together in the saloon and he's lyin' down out there now. Rolled up a apron for his pillow. Hold your nose, 'cause I had to take his boots off, his shirt's tore, and his jeans look kind of tattered."

Harvey didn't ask for the money, so I held it out to him. He whistled, took the gold coin in his fingers and bit it, then flipped it in the air, caught it, and shoved it into a pocket. "I ain't gonna ask who you two robbed for a 1868 Liberty Double Eagle, but if anybody does, you better tell 'em you found it in a draw in the canyon after a rainstorm. Send 'em on a treasure hunt."

"It *was* a treasure we found."

"Uh-huh. Just remember to stick with that. You know, one of those could finance your runaway habit for a good long time. Don't tell me no more. I prefer to make up my own lies."

Pony lay on his back atop vinyl red-and-white checkered tablecloths that had been spread over two tables. His hands were folded over his stomach. Harvey had switched on the electric train that ran on tracks over his bar, and Pony's head was turned toward it. Pony smiled at me, but looked as if something was bothering him. "I'm gonna be fine," he said. "Barely broke the skin. Harvey thinks it could have been a dry bite, not much venom or none at all." He didn't look me in the eye. His eyes were following the train.

"You can lay there two hours 'fore I open," said Harvey. "Or maybe I could charge admission to see the latest fool got bit when he should've backed off. And since John here is a gamblin' man, maybe he could sit for a few hands of poker to kill some time. What do you say, son?"

We sat next to the picture frame with Frank Leslie's *Illustrated Newspaper* cover, headlined 'The Phantom Padre and the Religion of Poker.' I asked Harvey where he got it. "Gift from a old ladyfriend," he said. "You ever hear of the Phantom Padre?"

"Not exactly." I wanted to hear Harvey's version.

It was short. "Some ole boy went around robbin' the rich and preachin' to the poor, kind of like a holy Zorro, comin' out of nowhere when you least expect him. Had his own hoard of gold, too. You pull out another one of them coins and someone asks you where you got it, you tell 'em it was from the Phantom Padre's treasure. You wantta deal, or should I?"

We played for toothpicks for more than an hour-and-a-half, with a break for coffee and eggs. Pony ate, too. When Harvey dealt, the cards flew off the deck and I got a lot of high pairs. He was letting me win. "It's another Merry Christmas," he declared each time I showed a winning hand.

"How come it's always Christmas in here?" I asked during one of Harvey's endless shuffles.

"'Fraid I can't tell you that, son. Some stories ain't meant to be told. They like to be kept hid and there ain't no coaxin' 'em out."

We had just finished a hand—I won with jacks over fours—when the pay phone rang on the wall of the saloon. Harvey got up to answer it without a comment. He listened for a moment, then hung up. "Might've been that damn pay phone near the gas pump," he said. "Sometimes the wires get crossed. Let's go see."

He unlocked the front door, and he and I walked into the sunlight. There, standing next to the pay phone at the corner of the building, was Babe. Harvey gripped my shoulder. "Well, fancy that you should be here, too, on this fine morning, Mrs. Watkins," he said. "I bet you come to say you're sorry for whatever made this boy think he'd leave home and become a gambler. Not that he couldn't."

Babe held out her arms, came towards me, then knelt and embraced me, sobbing. Harvey removed his hand from my shoulder. "Maybe I should leave you two alone for now."

Babe ran her fingers through my hair. "You had us scared to death. Whyever you left, honey, I'm going to make it right."

I was surprised, but not confused. I knew immediately that Pony must have called Babe when I went to the truck for the gold coin. I was happy to see Babe, but I was equally furious that I had been betrayed. "I don't think you can."

"We'll talk it out, whatever it is. And I have some good news for you."

"I don't want to hear it."

"I promise, honey, I promise it's the best news." Babe's eyes strayed past me. "Hi, Pony."

Pony stood behind us, leaning against the open door of the saloon. "Hi, Babe."

"I hope your leg falls off," I said, refusing to look back.

"I don't blame you, son."

"Don't call me son."

"Babe, if you don't mind, I'd like to talk privately with John for a moment. Just for a moment."

"Is that okay with you, honey?"

"No."

"You wanted to act like a man, then you can face me like one," said Pony, mustering enough energy to make it sound like a command. "I don't blame you for being mad."

Babe stood and I turned to face Pony. He gestured to me and walked away from the saloon toward an emory oak. I followed him. "You're a liar just like I always knew," I said. Tears stung my eyes.

"Maybe so."

"Why didn't you want to take me with you?"

"Because you're twelve years old. You need to make your own life."

"What if I tell people about the treasure?"

"Tell who? Bulland? Wyatt Fowler? You won't. You're going to leave that place in peace and me in peace, because you're a good man. Because that's not what your fight is. Right now you can make up any story you want. Tell 'em you ran away from Odee—you don't want to get him in trouble either, do you? For impersonating a law officer? He'd probably go to jail and lose his railroad. Tell 'em you looked some more for Bill but couldn't find him. You know they want to kill him. Hell, tell any story you want to. And when you do, maybe you'll understand the choices that I've made. And your mom, too."

"Yeah, and I won't forget to make up the worst one. That's the one they'll believe. So you say."

"I hope you'll quit being mad someday."

"You double-crossed me."

"That's the way you see it. I did what I thought was best."

"Did you double-cross Bill that way?"

"God dammit, Bill needed to go to his own place. It was time. And he couldn't have if it hadn't been for you. You should be proud of that. He's in his place. Now you need to go back to your place on the hill. And try to live the kind of life that...that isn't like mine."

"I don't care whether I do. And what are you going to do, anyway?"

"Well, I'm not going to die of a snake bite, so I'll have to work out what I do next. Where I'm going to go. When you quit being mad, maybe I'll let you know someday."

"You just wanted to be rich."

"No, I didn't. And I don't."

"What about the Phantom Padre's star?"

"That's enough. Go back to your mom and work things out with her."

"I even thought you were my dad once," I sputtered. Then I held my tongue.

"I wish I was." That was the last thing Pony said to me that day.

He nodded to Babe. She came and took my hand. They gazed at each other for a moment, but didn't speak. Pony disappeared into the saloon. I didn't look back when we drove away.

I told Babe on the ride to Lonechap Hill that I knew what she had done and who my father was, and that I left because I was afraid my life would be in danger when the story came out. Besides, I had promised that I would see Bill to a safe place. She had to pull off the road and cry. I didn't want to hear her side of the story, but I let her tell it, anyway. And as mad as I was, I understood. "Most of all," she said, "the one thing I wanted most for you was not to be a Fowler bastard. I was willing to do anything so that you wouldn't know and no one else would know. Both Buddy and I thought it was the only chance you had of growing up to be your own man. And sweetheart...you're not in danger. But I know why you thought you were. And I'm...God, I'm sorry for it."

She told me how the fight over the hill was finished—that Wyatt Fowler had given up and would soon sign papers acknowledging

Babe's ownership. It gave neither of us the satisfaction we would have felt only a couple of weeks before.

Dwight seemed delighted to see me. He also realized that I was tired and didn't want to talk. He brought me a Dr. Pepper while I stood in front of Bill's trailer. "I'm not going to make you listen to a lecture," he said. "But I can't help but think about my mother. You never knew her, of course. People called her Ping. Because of the life she'd lived, she believed it was good luck when things got worse and bad luck when they got better. She also hoped I'd have better sense than to believe the same thing."

Reluctantly, I admitted to myself that I hoped I would see Pony's crappy truck driving up to the gate so I could make amends. It's funny about mentors. You think you have them all to yourself, that they recognize your gifts as a fully-formed human being and are dedicated to helping you use them. They're surrogate parents without the baggage that parents carry. When they step across that line and send you back to the home you're trying to run away from, it's a painful reminder of all the things you're not yet ready for, even though you see them in the stars.

The front garden was a mess. Babe had done nothing to the flowerbed that Bill dug up during the thunderstorm. "I guess I'll be up early to deal with that," she said. "Back to my usual routine. First, this is for you." She gave me the pocketwatch that had belonged to my grandfather, John Bridges.

That night, in my own bed, with the narcotic breeze from the rotating fan sweeping over me, I still couldn't unwind. After midnight, I climbed out of my window and sat for a while in the grass, looking at the Milky Way. Clutching the lock of Bill's mane in my hand, I walked to his trailer, wadded up his red blanket, smelled the unsalvageable past, lay down, and went to sleep.

35
Epilogue

I walked along the eastern fence of the refuge, carrying a crowbar in my backpack, hoping to remain unseen. I had practiced my whistle for a couple of days. It had been ten years since I last saw Bill, when Pony and I left him behind the fences that were the best we could offer creatures like him, no longer the most valuable commodity on the plains, no longer a source of fortunes, discarded but preserved as long as they did not tread past the boundaries that were set for them. The sun was lowering, injecting the sky with dense streaks of orange, but I didn't want to wait until night fell because if Bill was there, if he had survived, I wanted to see him clearly, and I wanted to know whether he remembered.

I had just been discharged from the army after spending two years with people who looked vaguely like me fighting people who looked vaguely like me. I had no college deferment at the time. So I got drafted. I carried John Bridges' watch with me and kept it in the pocket of my jungle fatigue shirt. Its story finally ended when it saved my life. It took a bullet for me.

Earlier that day, in August of 1970, before stealing along the refuge fence, I went back to the hill for the first time since we had vacated it shortly after the Christmas holidays of my 12th year. Babe sold the hill to a rich wildcatter because I begged her to, even though the Fowler brothers seemed less eager to bully me. The thought that they were my secret nephews was too much to take. Besides, we had won the right to claim the hill and we did not descend it in defeat. The stars didn't tumble from the sky. Childhood ended, that was all. I never again laid eyes on my half-brother, Wyatt Fowler, nor did I want to. He was none the worse for suppressing the secret. The Fowler empire grew and prospered. Babe and I moved to a nice spread north of San Antonio and Babe threw herself into gardening again. It took me a while to make my peace with her after we left the hill, but I did. She had placed herself in a no-win situation. She could have given into the Fowlers by returning the land to them. The only other course she saw was the one she took—to commit fraud, protecting me and following Buddy's wishes, but having to live with the possibility that some day it would unravel. I can't stop thinking of her as a dispossessed princess. She died of lung cancer the year I was drafted. Her last words were, "I still owe you one for the bullfight."

The house on Lonechap Hill had been razed and parts of the hill had been graded to create lots for a subdivision. A front gate, tall and imposing, with a guard house next to it, already had been constructed. Above it was a sign that read 'Longview Hill Estates.' It would have been foolish to try to climb the hill. I already had decided not to, no matter what was there. It would have robbed me of something I didn't want to lose. And I would have dreaded coming down.

Pony did come back to us after we moved to San Antonio, although he and Babe never married. He showed up from time to time, and they were happy together for as long as it lasted. He always said the right things about her gardens and helped her with the dirty work when she asked. Each time he left again, it was to paint. Babe made him take a bag of her basil with him for good luck. He became fairly well known as a western artist, and Babe kept clippings of articles about him. He published a book, *Paintings of the Playas*, that included watercolors and poems like the ones he had left for me. He dedicated the book to me. But we never talked about my twelfth birthday, or Bill, or any of the promises that may have been made that August. Neither of us mentioned the treasure, either. But I knew what he had done with part of it. I saw an article in the San Antonio *Express* about a small church in Mexico where a miracle had occurred. One morning, before mass, a priest had discovered on the altar an antique gold star, exquisitely designed and jeweled, and described by one appraiser as "priceless." When word of the "miracle" spread worldwide, an aristocratic Spanish family claimed the star as its own. A public relations spokesman for the family produced the original 15th Century drawings used in its design, as well as the billing the family received and a long history of the search that had been made for the star after it was carried to the New World. The family, which owned one of the oldest soap-and-perfume manufacturing businesses in Europe, demanded the return of the star and promised to finance a playground for the church in return. The *Express* article was written when a judge ruled in favor of the family.

I don't know what happened to Pony after Babe's death. I called his publisher and some galleries where I knew he sold paintings, but no one knew how to contact him. Then I got drafted, and I guess when he found out about Babe, he didn't know how to contact me.

I did stop and take a photo of the hill. I had a new Pentax Spotmatic. The army sent me to its pictorial school after I returned from Vietnam, and I received an offer to break in as a newsreel cameraman at a station in Tulsa. I got the job thanks to a former army friend who had fought with me on Hamburger Hill and who worked at the station. The condition I agreed to was that I would also enroll in Tulsa Community College to study journalism at night. It seemed right for me to become a journalist because, as Pony once said, no story truly ends, and I liked following where the paths led. For Buddy's sake, too.

On my way to the refuge, I couldn't resist driving through Wachyerback. Not much of what I remembered was left there, either. It had been re-developed as a resort area for tourists and hunters visiting Toomis Canyon. The Royal Hoodoo Railroad had been abandoned. Now it was just a ghost line, joining the other phantoms in the canyon. But there in the middle of town, looking like it was about to collapse, Harvey Olsen's saloon and gas station still stood, so I stopped to see if he had survived. He had. He didn't recognize me at first, but as soon as I told him my name he threw his arms around me and slapped me on the back of the neck several times before leaning away and taking a good look.

"I'll be good god damned," he said. "If you'd of come a week later, we'd of never seen each other cause this old place is about to go under a dozer. Your friend Wyatt's decided it's time to make it upscale, have some tourists and some bidness retreats and some good ole boys diddling their way-from-home girlfriends afore they go hunting down to the canyon."

"Well, congratulations on being the last one to go," I said.

"Yeah, I guess. Have a beer on me, old son. Don't mind the boxes."

Harvey's Christmas lights dangled from a cardboard box on the bar. The cars from his train set were packed in another. Harvey poured a Shiner for each of us and we sat beneath where the track once ran. "Here's to them two rascals Pony and Bill." For an old man with a trembling throat, Harvey could swallow a lot of beer.

"You knew Pony's father, right?"

"I did indeed." As if he were toasting a memory, Harvey wiped his mouth and raised his glass toward a shaft of light that came through a boarded-up window. "His daddy was a hard worker, honest as the day is long, never caught a break but never backed down from a fight. His granddaddy was what they called a buffalo shaman. Magic man, went around, let people pray to his damn buffalo, made some money." Harvey winked. "They also say he raced the sonofabitch now and then. Pony had a lot of both men in him and he had his own ways. He was a wild one sometimes, like all them artist types. You knew that, right?"

"Sort of."

"But you was with him when ole Bill got cut loose back to the refuge, wasn't you? When Pony faked a snakebite?"

That was a new one. "He faked getting bit?"

"So he'd have a chance to call your mom when you wasn't looking. You never knew that?"

"No." I shook my head slowly. "I guess I should have, though."

"It don't matter. Pony laid low for a while in Mexico and you and Bill both got home again."

"Yep."

"Ever see ole Bill again after that? Go visit? Take him a tub of beer?"

"No." I stared into the thinning coat of foam that floated like spittle in my glass. I didn't want to tell Harvey where I was headed because I felt it was a private matter, one I did not want to answer to because I did not know how I would feel.

"Well, there's probably some stud bull running around there with his blood right now. You ever seen a buffalo make love?"

"No."

"Damndest thing. Lasts about ten seconds. Hell, I bet Bill could go twice as long as that. He was a hell of a animal."

"Yeah. More than we knew."

"Yeah, man. Well, hell I don't want to bore you. You must of come here for what Pony left you."

"Pony? He didn't leave me anything."

"Then son, you got a sorry damn memory. You forgot all about that race Bill won, did you?"

"Come on. How could I forget that? That was the best day of my life."

"Well, hey, sure it was. Cause you was connected, son, to the whole race, from the dust to the finish line. Lucky for you it came early, when you was still spry enough to jump for joy and you don't have to wait and wonder your whole life long whether it's ever gonna happen. A day like that, you know you ain't just wasting time here, even when you have to move on to the next day. 'Cause at least one promise was kept like it should of been."

"I never thought of it like that..."

"You never did? Well, allow me to refresh your memory all the way, then. Come on back to my office, see if you don't remember what you was promised. Been sitting back there a almighty while, since the last time I saw that grifter myself."

Harvey removed a rolled up foot-long canvas and handed it to me. I unrolled it. And there it was, the painting Pony had promised me on my twelfth birthday—Bill winning the race in Wachyerback.

"Well, what do you think?" Harvey asked.

"It brings back a lot of memories." I was a bit stunned, and unprepared to say more. I rolled up the canvas again and put it in a loop of my backpack, where it fit securely. "Thank you, Harvey," I said, "for everything."

"Better than a photo, like I said. You remember I said that, do you?"

"I remember. You were right."

"Better than a photo every time. Cause, you know what? We're all born liars and bullshitters, every last one of us. So let's just hope you always lie in the cause of truth. You know what I mean?"

Harvey's logic seemed unassailable. "I guess I do."

"You know, people made up the wildest stories about me and them twinkle lights and that train and what must have happened to me when I was just a boy some long ago Christmas, and I was fine with it. It kept folks talking stead of fighting. Made me a tad famous. When the deal always was—once I put them lights up, I was just too fuckin' lazy to take 'em down again."

"Well, Merry Christmas, Harvey."

"You, too, old son. And you take care."

"I will."

When I reached the east gate, I took out the crowbar, broke the lock, and walked onto the refuge. In the distance, I saw what appeared to be a portion of a herd. I told myself I was being stupid not to have a better plan, but I continued with the one I had. I jogged through the grass for a half-mile or so, until I was certain I was nearing a cluster of animals. Then I stopped, caught my breath, shoved my fingers into my mouth, and whistled. I turned to my left and right, and whistled several more times. The sound of it bit through the air, rising like a bird flushed out of hiding and falling somewhere beyond the horizon. A group of bison seemed to stir restlessly, but no animal emerged.

I decided to stand and wait.

I waited too long.

A rider galloped toward me from the south, where the public entrance to the refuge was. Rather than run like a fugitive, I stayed in position. I was wearing the pants from my Vietnam jungle fatigues, as well as my sand-colored boots, and I hoped that being a veteran would buy me some kind of credit.

I held up my hand to indicate I saw the rider. He stopped a few yards away from me. "What the hell do you think you're doing here? You're trespassing, and one of those animals could squash you like a bug."

"I just got back from 'Nam. A friend of mine used to work here, and he said I should come see it."

"Then come to the front, where they got a fence you can stand behind and watch. You better not have a gun."

"I don't."

"How'd you get in?"

"Through the gate back there. The lock was broken."

"That was your whistle?"

"Yes."

"What for?"

"I wanted to see..." I didn't finish my sentence. From the northwest, a lone buffalo ran, breaking the horizon with his giant silhouette, moving swiftly but awkwardly, relentlessly, as if driven by some secret memory.

"Shit. You come over here by me. Slowly."

The bison came to a halt and snorted. The wrangler charged the bull on his horse, hoping to frighten him. Instead, the animal dodged and stopped again. I walked toward him. "I'm okay," I said to the wrangler.

"You better hope so, buddy. If I try to spook him again, he's close enough to gore you. There's nothing I can do for you now."

The buffalo had grown to an extraordinary size. I wanted it to be Bill, but I wasn't positive that it was. I was willing to risk a nasty scene to find out. He was six-and-a-half feet high at his shoulder, eight inches taller than I. A zany, tangled mass of hair fell over his forehead like a two-foot-long clutch of black moss hanging from a horned rock. His horns were at least a yard apart on his enormous noggin. It was summer, so his coat looked old, worn, mottled, and uneven, as if large tufts had been pulled from it. His legs were bedecked with hairy pantaloons. He weighed a ton, probably more. No doubt he had survived and won his share of fights, and earned the right to be a loner.

He snorted again. I don't know how long we stared at each other, standing only a few yards apart, neither of us moving a muscle. If it was Bill, I thought, we had become different beings. Our old selves were out of reach, and if we could have communicated—did I still expect it to be possible?—the years that had passed would have left us with nothing to say. What I expected from him, I don't know. Maybe his presence, as he stood there regarding me, was enough. I sensed his power and was moved by it, and by his restraint of it. But what seemed possible, necessary, even eternal, a spirit that was born of yearning, framed by stars, protected in some high place from fear, memories that will sustain you through your darkest hours and give you the first, all-important measure of yourself—all of that, I finally understood, had to be placed elsewhere in my heart. Those things for which we are most grateful are the ones that are irrecoverable. Whether or not Bill had become the magnificent animal who stood facing me, I had seen what I needed to see.

The moon was rising in the last patch of blue in the sky. "I'm going to leave the way I came in," I said to the wrangler.

"Back up and turn around slow. I'll follow behind you."

"I understand."

I looked at the bison again and began to back away.

He snorted and seemed to hop, doing what passed for a clumsy but stiff-legged dance in the grass.

I retrieved the carrots I had brought in my backpack and left them where I stood.

"I don't know what that was about," the wrangler said as we walked toward the fence, "and I don't suppose you'd care to tell me. I never seen a buffalo whisperer. No such thing."

"I was lucky," I said.

"Animal seemed to know you."

"It's a long story. I'm sorry to have caused you trouble."

The bison had disappeared by the time we reached the fence.

"I never saw you, soldier, in case you're wondering," said the wrangler. "You know where you're going from here?"

"I do, thanks. I'm parked at an overlook on the canyon rim."

"Sorry I don't have time to hear it."

"What?"

"The long story."

I pulled Pony's painting from the loop in my backpack, unrolled it, and held it up toward the dying western light.

Bill and I were the only ones in it. No one else was there—no cowboys, no horse, no Wyatt, no Babe. Bill dominated it, left of center, trotting toward me. On the other side of the painting, much farther away and smaller, was a juniper tree. And I was running toward him from the lower right, with my arms in the air and an absolute look of innocence and delight on my face. Just me and Bill. In the distance was a conspicuous rise, Lonechap Hill. Above us, on a darkening sky, was a trail of dust in the stars.

ACKNOWLEDGEMENTS

First, I want to acknowledge the help and inspiration of my wife, Nancy, who is as indispensable as she is brilliant and beautiful.

My son and musical genius, Kevin, has given me a sense of joy so profound that I can borrow happily on it whenever needed.

My brother Gene offered invaluable criticism; my brother Don supplied humor.

Historian Marc Abrams, author of *Sioux War Dispatches: Reports from the Field, 1876-1877* (Westholme Publishing, 2012), helped track down important details and writings ("Crying for Scalps") of the Flashmanesque artist and adventurer Charles St. George Stanley, who did, in fact, exist, but about whom little is known. St. George Stanley's writings in two instances contributed directly to his dialog. Abrams also made valuable suggestions for changes in the manuscript. In addition, Abrams' extraordinary, 16-volume compilation of letters, reports, and journalism chronicling the U.S.-Indian wars is as eye-opening as it is informative.

The book *The Captured: A True Story of Abduction by Indians on the Texas Frontier* by Scott Zesch (St. Martin's Griffin, 2005) contains compelling and little-known accounts of the 'Indianization' of several captive children.

Dr. Michael Shara of the American Museum of Natural History, head of the astrophysics research fund to support the research of graduate students and postdoctoral fellows, supplied information about how the alignments of stars can be used to pinpoint locations such as caves in canyon walls.

The story of an authentic Indian star chart is told in the book *When Stars Came Down to Earth*, by Von Del Chamberlain (Ballena Press/Center for Archaeoastronomy Cooperative, 1982), and the chart itself can be found in Chicago's Field Museum.

James Mcfarlane, of the American Watercolor Society, educated me on the watercolor techniques used by Pony to paint Bill against a dying sunset.

Peggy Wennerlind of Midland, Texas, gave me a thorough education in the trials, tribulations and rewards of gardening in West Texas, and any faults in my descriptions are my own.

ACKNOWLEDGEMENTS

I am indebted to Zhang Zhen, Associate Professor of Cinema at New York University's Tisch School of the Arts, who, over a delightful lunch, offered fascinating insights into Shanghai's cinema in the 1920's and 30's, and the personalities of its stars. She is author of *An Amorous History of the Silver Screen: Shanghai Cinema 1896-1937* (University of Chicago Press, 2005).

The Angel Island Conservancy provided help on how Bei Lian and Babe could have entered the U.S. in 1937 with help from Dwight, given the state of the terrible exclusion laws.

More valuable insight and information came from Bryan Burrough's *The Big Rich: The Rise and Fall of the Greatest Texas Oil Fortunes* (New York: The Penguin Press, 2009).

I must also acknowledge Julie Lemish, who arranged details of an extensive visit to China which included several days with the unforgettable Uttara Sarkar Crees; and Mel Brown, whom I did not meet, but who wrote an engrossing history of the Chinese community in San Antonio, Texas, *Chinese Heart of Texas* (Lily on the Water Publishing, 2005). Any characterizations to which he might object are mine alone. Prof. Anna Fahy of El Paso Community College helped to direct my inquiries.

I will always appreciate the contributions of the WFAA-TV cameramen who roamed the length and breadth of Texas with me in the 1970's, from McGarrity's Saloon to the Waxahachie Courthouse to a weatherman's garden in Presidio; from Hipp's Bubble Room to the now defunct Sad Monkey Railroad to the remarkable studio of the artist Randy Steffan. They were the first to see the hill.

I am likewise grateful for help from mining engineer Jack Burgess, Joe Mussey, and others who do God's work at the Chihuahuan Desert Research Institute in Fort Davis, Texas.

Les Turner was an amusing and valuable source of information on antique taxidermy.

Chris Gardner, author (with Quincy Troupe) and subject of *The Pursuit of Happyness*, is an irresistible force whose encouragement, with that of Lynn Redmond, has been of key importance.

Late as it is for me in life, I also have many people to thank for a career in broadcasting that lasted fifty years, and if this is my only opportunity to do so in print, I don't want to bypass it, beginning with my thanks to Keith Bretz, Jim Hartz, and Dick Schmitz.

ACKNOWLEDGEMENTS

Clayton Vaughn has been a friend, critic, and teacher since the 1960's, and was once willing to indulge one of my first experiments in long-form storytelling, a twelve-minute television piece on molasses.

Executive Producer Av Westin guided me through the good and bad of writing and story structure during my first years as a correspondent at ABC and with the magazine show *20/20*. No one is better. I will forever be grateful for the support of a true gentleman and role model, Hugh Downs; the indefatigable and gracious Barbara Walters, whose notes I still treasure; Peter Jennings; Michael Clemente; the ebullient James Walker; Meredith White, a rare muse in an industry that often neglects to invoke its better spirits; and Lynn Sherr, a supremely talented writer and cubicle mate.

Betsy Osha and the late Ashbel Green, whom I did not wish to disappoint, offered their counsel and insights. If there is an Earth Mother, it is Betsy.

Rob Wallace, invaluable as a friend and producer, panicked through a spin-out with me in a rental car on an ice-slick road in West Texas, during which we might have been saved from worse by the ballast provided by a case of beer in the trunk.

Nola Safro has reduced the standard six degrees of separation to no more than three (at the very least, you know someone who knows someone who knows her and whose life is richer for it).

Nancy Pfifferling proved with her life that teachers are our true stars.

Terry and Donna Morrison taught me to see, and always wrote my first lines with their film images.

Bud Proctor multiplied whatever was good by his editing, which can make even the mundane beautifully polished. Ruth Iwano, another talented editor, kept me writing by never letting me forget what I had left unfinished. Brad LaRosa arranged the impossible on request. Trish Arico and Joan LeFosse saved me from embarrassment with their impeccable research and support.

Dr. Robert Goldstein offered early morning rides to a writing place. Barbara Kalmanash is a supportive spirit whose motto, should she choose to adopt one, could be summed up in one word: "Onward."

Producer Joe Pfifferling added a grace and focus to my stories that I could never have achieved alone. I could not ask for a better friend.

And finally, I want to thank my first mentor, the late Milton E. Haynes, whose symphonic joy in writing and storytelling was, I believe, unequaled.

AUTHOR

Robert Brown spent a 50-year career in broadcasting, including 33 years (1977-2010) as a correspondent for ABC News and the magazine show 20/20. Among other honors, he is the recipient of six Emmy awards; an Alfred I. duPont award; National Headliner and Investigative Reporters awards; and a Bronze Wrangler Award for Television Documentary Writing from the National Cowboy Hall of Fame.

Films based on stories he reported include the children's classic *Fly Away Home*; the Emmy-winning TV movie *Door-to-Door*; and *The Pursuit of Happyness*.

His early career was spent in Tulsa, Houston and Dallas, from where he traveled throughout Texas to originate a series that retraced the state's legends and mysteries.

Made in the USA
Lexington, KY
04 November 2016